River

Of

Stones

by

Seymour Hamilton

Library and Archives Canada Cataloguing in Publication

Hamilton, Seymour

River of Stones

ISBN: 978-0-9949499-6-7

Published by Seymour Hamilton "Colophon" / Old Salt Press

Also by Seymour Hamilton

The Astreya Trilogy (Fireship/Cortero Press, 2011)

Book I: The Voyage South

Book II: The Men of the Sea

Book III: The Wanderer's Curse.

The Laughing Princess (Açedrex, 2014),

illustrated by Shirley MacKenzie

The Hippies Who Meant It (Colophon/Scribl 2015)

All are available in ebook and audio read by Seymour Hamilton,

through Amazon and Scribl.

Author's Website: SeymourHamilton.com

Acknowledgements

The Old Salt Press

Many thanks to the accomplished authors Alaric Bond, Linda Collison, Joan Druett, Christopher Durbin; EV Ulett, Antoine Vanner; and especially Rick Spillman, the founder of the Old Salt Press. By welcoming me into this international group of people who write about the days of sail, they gave me the confidence to bring *River of Stones* to publication.

The team that took my draft manuscript to the status of a paperback and ebook were: Jessica Knauss, editor; who once again corrected my many inconsistencies, Mary Montague, who indefatigably prepared the text; Shirley Mackenzie who drew the in-text drawings, *www.shirleymackenzie.com,* and Ed Whiting, photographer *www.fromtheblue.co.uk,* who took the schooner photo on the cover.

None of this would have happened without Katherine, who makes it possible for me to write.

Contents

Who's Who in River of Stones

In order of when and where they first appear

§ Those who wear the clasp stone of a Navigator

* Those who wear a ring stone

Aboard *Cygnus*

Mairi	§	Daughter of Astreya and Lindey, Mate, *Cygnus*
Betel	*	Mate, Cygnus. Oldest man aboard.
Marley		Recently brought aboard *Cygnus* by Astreya
Cam	*	Mate, *Cygnus*
Astreya	§	Master, *Cygnus*, Father of Mairi and Trogen
Lindey	§	Navigator, *Cygnus*, Mother of Mairi and Trogen

Aboard Elusive

Dabih	§	Master, *Elusive*, Father of Seren, Ellie, Maia
Damon	*	Mate, *Elusive*

At the Home

Catriona "Cat"		Healer, Mother of Dabih
Walt	*	Mate, *Elusive*,
Becky		Mother of Seren, Ellie, Maia, Lena
Seren	§	Carpenter, Healer, *Elusive* Daughter of Dabih and Becky
Ellie	§	Cadet, *Cygnus*, Daughter of Dabih and Becky
Maia		Daughter of Dabih and Becky
Drew		Shipwright
Ellen		Mistress of the Home
Janice		Self-appointed critic at the Home
Jeb		Representative of the farmers

Aboard Cygnet

Mairi	§	Mistress
Trogen	§	Navigator
Cam	*	Mate
Marley		Steersman
Seren	§	Mate
Neil	*	Cadet, late of *Elusive*
Peter	*	Cadet, late of *Cygnus*
Alan		Sailor, seconded from *Elusive*

In the Sunny Isles

Lady Orinda	Mother of Marley, Chad
Maximilian	Big Man of the Island, Father of Chad
Chad	Son of Maximilian and Lady Orinda

Aboard the ketch

Moke	Sailor of unusual size
Cookie	Sailor with a high voice
Jake	Sailor
Fred	Inventor

At Cottontown

Keef	Innkeeper
Mirak	Survivor, mate of *Cygnus* 20 years earlier.

At the Village

Scarm	Old blind sailor, mentor to Astreya and Cam
Mollie	Widow, caring for Scarm
Red Ian	Senior Skipper
Jack	Young lad of the Village

Book One

Sailing Home

1. In which Cygnus suffers an unprovoked attack

The three-masted schooner *Cygnus* slipped her hawser from the buoy, her mainsail creaked aloft to catch a light wind, and the steersman spun the wheel to port. Helped by an ebbing tide, the vessel headed down the long narrow bay. Sailors hauled on the throat and peak halyards at the mizzen and foremasts, the two sails filling with a soft flap. The staysail and jib caught the evening breeze and the great ship gathered way, her soft-filled canvass providing just enough steerage way to avoid the clutter of small boats anchored in the harbour. Gathering speed on the port tack, she slid majestically past lighters, barges, coasters and fishing boats, her mast-heads higher than the crests of the steep-sided granite shoreline.

Mairi, first mate and daughter of Grand Master Astreya, stood beside the binnacle, watching the sails belly out as the wind freshened. Strands of her neck-length blonde hair escaped its tight braiding and blew across her face.

"Breezing up," she said to the old sailing master who stood beside her.

"Enough to flutter the tell-tales," said Betel, cocking his head to one side so that he could use his good eye.

Mairi knew that Betel was no longer able to see the threads of wool that waved from the shrouds to help the steersman, but the old man could tell the set of the sails from the wind on his cheek.

After a long lifetime aboard, Betel was almost a part of *Cygnus*. Mairi understood the relationship between ship and man better than most, since she, too, was sea-born aboard the great ship. Betel was one of the last of the Men of the Sea who had kept the great ships sailing for more than a century. She was part of a new generation, most of whom were land-born, but in that she and her twin brother, Trogen, had started their lives afloat, she shared a bond with the old man. Betel's birth had been at least eighty years ago, whereas her nineteenth birthday was less than a week away, but all three were sea-born, and that made the ship their home and the sea their country.

Mairi took six steps to the port rail and looked along the length of the ship. Astern of the mainmast, the other second mate was tugging a tarpaulin over the main cargo hatch. Cam was a small, agile man in his late thirties. Mouse-coloured hair topped a clean-shaven face that wore an almost perpetual grin. As Mairi watched, a tall sailor came up the aft companionway, stopped beside Cam and knuckled his forehead. Ropes of hair that framed his stern black face were swept back and tied behind his neck. His impassive expression was that of a man who had been disciplined by disappointment.

"Seaman Marley, sir. Lookin' for the mate of the starboard watch."

Cam glanced up from his work, his hands still busy, then looked again. His eyes skimmed over a new shirt and breeks, standard *Cygnus* issue for all aboard, and then scanned a second time, noticing how well the man filled out what for most people was a comfortably loose uniform. He looked up into the man's face, and raised his eyebrows a fraction: the new sailor was the first black man to serve aboard the big schooner.

"That's me. Secure the other corner of this tarp. We'll stretch it over and wedge it down. What 'cha doin' wi' your hand?"

"I was saluting t'show respect, an' that I'm followin' your order, sir."

"Well, stop it. I don't care what you did on your last ship, but aboard *Cygnus*, I just want to hear you say, 'aye' or 'right' and get on with it. 'Streya told me to expect a new man an' that's you, I'm thinkin'. I'm to show you the ropes. But since you've served on a schooner before, you know them all already, right?"

"No two ships belay their halliards the same place, sir."

"The name's Cam. Save the formalities for the mucky-mucks. That was a good answer, by the way. Now let's get this cargo hatch covered. 'Streya wants all secure afore we get to open sea. He's standing lookout at the foremast shrouds, and any moment now he'll be on his way to the quarterdeck. He'll be walkin' where you're standin' doing nothing, if you catch my drift."

"The master's standin' lookout?"

"We're light on crew, there's small craft milling about, and he likes to see for himself. He's on the port side, Navigator's got the lee. First mate's astern with the steersman. T'other mate is on the quarterdeck, doin' somethin' important. You'll know the navigator when you see her. Lindey looks a bit like her daughter Mairi, the mate what's watchin' us not workin'. Here, pull that strop over the coaming, and I'll drive in a wedge to keep it there."

The schooner gathered speed as she approached the buoy that marked a shoal at the harbour mouth. She heeled to starboard a few degrees as her sails caught a northwest sea wind. Astreya glanced at Lindey, mother of their twins Mairi and Trogen, who was crouched to look under the foresail boom. The wind off the sail blew her earlobe-length blonde hair back from her face. She raised an arm to point toward a little skipjack, idling under only one sail just beyond *Cygnus* wind shadow. Astreya nodded, and they both started for the quarterdeck. They were dressed alike in blue officers' shirts and breeks, but in all else, they were a contrast. Astreya's hair and beard were black, his skin dark tanned, and his green eyes were set amid lines drawn by staring into wind and weather. Lindey matched his stride beside him, though the crown of her head barely topped his shoulder. Different as they appeared, when they glanced at each other, understanding flowed between them.

At the aft cargo hatch, Cam drove in the last wedge. He cocked his head sideways to look up into the tall man's eyes.

"Good job, Marley. But yer looking puzzled. What's wrong?"

"I'm not used to working alongside a mate."

"The job takes two. The rest of the watch is securing the other hatches."

"Me last ship's mate would've been tellin' me what to do and watchin' t' make sure I did it the way he wanted. The ship before that, the bugger would have given me a clip over the ear to get me started."

"That ain't my style. Or the way this ship works. But don't expect me to take your turn cleaning the heads or hold your hand when we're thrashing around in a nor'easter. Look alive, 'Streya's coming aft, an' we'll have sails to trim in a jiffy. Me an' you have the main."

Since a course change was imminent, Mairi headed for the companionway to the navigation space, traditionally called the Forbidden Room. She saw a seaman nod to Lindey as he passed her on his way towards the bow.

Nobody saw the skipjack hoist her jib and change course to cut across the big schooner's bows, because the little boat was concealed by the big schooner's foresail and jib. The lookout's shout came as the boat's mast fouled *Cygnus'* bowsprit. The schooner barely slowed as she first dismasted and then crushed the skipjack, which disappeared under the port bow. Astreya leaned over the rail to see what had happened.

The skipjack exploded.

Cygnus' bowsprit shattered into shards of wood. Jibs and foresails bellied out of shape, no longer sustained by the mainstay. Debris rained into the sea and onto the deck where Astreya lay sprawled on his back. The ship's side gaped, the bow festooned with the remains of the bowsprit and dolphin striker. Above, the severed end of the mainstay flailed as all three masts sagged sternward, robbed of support.

Mairi barely paused when she heard the first thud of impact with the little boat, thinking it perhaps caused by a random piece of flotsam that had escaped the lookout's notice. She put her hand on the metal door and focused her mind to use the power of her clasp. Then came the explosion. Her hands flew up to her ears as the big vessel reverberated like a beaten drum. When the deafening moment passed, she heard shouts, the sound of running feet overhead, and a deep groaning like a huge animal in pain. Mairi turned and ran up the companionway. Betel, the most experienced man aboard, stood with his head thrown back, peering up at the masthead.

"What's happening?" Mairi demanded.

Betel pointed to the three masts sagging sternwards. The mainstay hung slack from the head of the foremast, swinging uselessly. Again, Mairi heard groaning above the noise of wind and water. She felt vibration under her feet and realized that the masts were swaying, rubbing against the decks, and grinding in their steps on the keel. She ran to the port rail. Ahead, the bowsprit was a splintered stump. She struggled with a dilemma. The obvious response to trouble aloft was to turn head-to-wind. But if they luffed up under full sail with a broken mainstay, even a light wind could collapse all three masts.

"Turn downwind. Relieve the masts," said the steersman quietly. She swung around, recognizing Marley, the new man.

"You're right," she murmured, and then raised her voice in command. "Stand by to jibe! Brail up and strike sail! Haul them down!"

Sailors ran to obey her order.

"Jibe!" she shouted.

Marley nodded and spun the wheel. Betel's mouth hung open in disbelief. To his mind, Mairi's maneuver was the exact opposite of the tried-and-true response, which was to head upwind and then locate, confine, and deal with whatever had gone wrong. Ignoring his distress, Mairi encouraged men and women who were struggling to strike wind-filled, flapping canvass that resisted their efforts and threatened to toss them into the sea.

"Good call, Mairi." Cam's voice at her elbow calmed her.

"Cam! What's going on? What's happened?"

"Damn great 'splosion. Holed the bow. 'Streya's down. Lindey lookin' after him. Gotta go help her."

During their exchange, confusion began to resolve into order. Men and women at the halyards, brails, and sheets collaborated to collapse and lower the sails until they could be manhandled into folds around the booms. Sailors loosed halyards and topping lifts and brought spars and booms amidships, tugged the foresails inboard and bundled them. With the sails no longer blocking her view, Mairi saw that the mainstay was looping from mast to mast to mast to the free-swinging length of heavy, tarred rope, that was no longer connected to the missing bowsprit.

What she saw still threatened disaster, but the masts no longer groaned. *Cygnus* was stable under bare poles, wind-driven south-east, out to sea.

"Steersman, hold her on this course."

"Mairi!"

It was her mother's voice, uncharacteristically shrill. Mairi looked along the deck and saw Astreya being carried astern, his head supported by Lindey, his body cradled in the linked arms of two sailors. Something wooden stuck out of a bloody smear on his right hip. Mairi stood, torn between love and duty. As the human stretcher carried her father towards the companionway, Lindey bent over Astreya, her face invisible behind her hair. She spoke without raising her head.

"Mairi, you're in command."

2. In which Astreya is transferred to Elusive

"Right," said Mairi with a confidence she did not feel. She resolutely put aside what she had just seen. Her responsibility was now solely for the ship.

"Steersman, hold your course. Betel, choose a team to jury-rig the mainstay. I'm going forward to assess damage."

She picked her way among sailors bringing order to hastily-bundled sails. As she passed the middle mast, her foot slipped, and she looked down at a dark, smeared pool that a part of her mind identified as her father's blood. Pausing for only an instant, she tapped a sailor on the shoulder.

"Swab the deck before someone slips and falls."

Without waiting to see if her order was obeyed, she scuffed her shoe sole clean and continued on to the port bow, where the knee-high rail ended in splintered wood. She peered cautiously over the edge, wrinkling her nose at an unfamiliar acrid smell. Quick footfalls sounded behind her.

"We're holed at the waterline," said Cam. "I got help on the way wi' canvass for a patch. I'm goin' over the side."

She swung around and saw him settle a bight of rope under his thighs, the other end of which was held by two burly sailors.

"Is she taking on water?"

"Could be worse. Chain locker must be about knee-deep. But we're pumpin' and she's holding her own."

He nodded to the sailors and eased himself carefully over the side. Mairi was aware of expectant faces staring at her. For an instant, she stood, feeling the burden of command like a physical weight. She could see that the patch would keep out spray, but every time the ship heeled to port on the starboard tack the hole would be partly underwater, and if the wind piped up and the bow plunged into the waves, the patch would not survive.

She hesitated, considering turning back to the harbour they had just left. The steep-sided anchorage offered temporary safety, but none of the resources necessary to repair a ship the size of *Cygnus*. A heartbeat later, she decided that *Cygnus* must continue northwards to her home port where there was a shipyard able to set her to rights.

"Right. We have to get her bow up, so we'll weigh her stern down. First, secure the deadlights on all stern scuttles. Then move both anchors astern, along with the chain. Then carry whatever we can as far aft as possible. Heaviest objects first. Deck cargo, boats and spare spars onto the quarterdeck. Move as much cargo, gear, tools, and provisions as you can into the aft cabins. Leading seamen, organize teams port and starboard. Then pass the small stuff hand-to-hand. Let's get to it."

Heads nodded. Faces that had been blank with expectation now wore purposeful expressions. They understood. They were following her orders. Shortly after she returned to the command position, the ship's carpenter sent word that the jury-rigged mainstay was taking the strain. Bit by bit, the ship was reorganized. Gradually, the stern squatted lower in the water and the bow rose. Eventually, Cam came aft, dripping wet and shivering, tar on his hands and shirt.

"What happened?" Mairi asked.

"That confounded little scow must'a been carryin' 'splosives. What made him decide to cut across our bows we'll never know, 'cause most likely he blew hisself up along with his boat."

"There's no chance of anything being still aboard that could..."

"Blow up? Nah. But I got two down below lookin' to check the patch for leaks, an' to make sure there ain't goin' to be no more sudden ructions. She ain't fixed, but she'll do."

A little while later, Mairi stood on the quarterdeck, feeling unexpectedly confident. A part of her mind worried about what might be waiting in the next minute, next hour, next watch, next day. But for now, the situation was under control. Cautiously, she brought the ship back towards her original course, adding sails gradually, trying not to wince at each slap of a wave against the ship's side. *Cygnus* headed north under double-reefed main and mizzen with a storm foresail and air where her jibs and staysail should have been.

Every time Mairi thought about her father, anxiety gnawed at her self-confidence. When no word came from below, she reasoned that so long as Lindey was with him, Astreya must still be alive. The long day passed, the minutes counted by the rhythm of the waves, the hours by the slow crawl of shadows across the decks. The watch changed, but Mairi waved away Betel's reminder that it was her turn below.

When evening came, Lindey appeared on deck. At Mairi's questioning look, her hands made a calming gesture. She did not speak until she was close.

"He's asleep and breathing steadily. The bleeding has stopped. We've done all we can until we can get him back to the Home where Catriona can work her magic. Who's that on the wheel?"

"The new man, Marley. It was he who saw we needed to jibe. He whispered to me and I gave the order."

"Good for both of you. Where is Betel?"

"Below. He's not able to…"

"He's getting old. I've messaged *Elusive*. She's only hours away."

Mairi nodded. She had felt the stone on her arm tingle a few hours earlier.

"You need to eat something, Mairi."

"You too, Mother."

The day's steady breeze continued to blow from the land, just out of sight to port. As the night watch prepared to reduce sail even further, Mairi leaned against the rail on the port quarter, the waterline disturbingly close below her feet. Once more, she methodically scanned along the length of the repaired mainstay, seeing again that *Cygnus* was loose in stays, her stump of a bow cocked up, her stern low in the water.

"Beggin' your attention mistress, I got a mug o' hot soup and ship's biscuit here for yer."

"Is that you, Marley?"

"T'is, mistress."

"Call me Mairi, Marley," she said and surprised herself by laughing at the close-sounding names.

"I ain't quite used to yer ways yet, miss ... Mairi. It ain't that I don't like it, but..."

"It's our way. My father's way."

"I never saw a man so quiet that could command respect like he does."

"You've talked with him ... of course. He brought you aboard."

"He did that, right enough."

"Thanks for the soup. And thanks for the tip that let me give the right order. You may well have saved us from losing all three sticks."

"I spoke without thinkin'. You'd'a thought of it yourself soon enough."

"I hope so, but we'll never know."

"Good night ... Mairi."

Revived by hot food, Mairi settled into an intense version of routine watch-keeping in which she continually checked and re-checked the set of the sails, the state of the rigging, and the integrity of the patch. Before the long night was over she had to struggle to keep her eyelids from drooping, even as she constantly paced the length of the ship, forward on the starboard side, port on the way back. High cloud moved in from the west in the small hours, then cleared away again for the false dawn. The sky lightened; the sea remained dark. When her mother came on deck, the rim of the sun pushed over the edge of the horizon and light spilled across the sea. Moments later, they both saw the upper staysails of their sister ship *Elusive* and joined the lookout in a chorus of "Sail ho!" At first, the three-masted schooner appeared to be moving slowly, but as she drew closer, her speed became apparent. Mairi took a long look at *Cygnus'* dismal state and slow, ungainly progress and shook her head. Her mother saw the gesture and sympathized.

"Good work, Mairi. You've got us sailing," said Lindey.

"Not very well," said Mairi.

"Well enough to get us home, slow but reasonably sure. It's up to *Elusive* to get Astreya there faster. We'll swing him across. I'll get him ready. Just keep *Cygnus* going as she is, and Dabih can come alongside in our lee."

Mairi nodded, watched her mother go back down the companionway, and returned to her position at the port quarter. A short time later, she startled, wondering how long she had been inattentive.

"Lass, you need sleep."

"Cam."

"Listen, the wind's steady from the northwest, we're on the port tack with the patch clear out of the water. You got me an ' Betel—along wi' that right some handy black fellow what saved us from what could'a been a real nasty lash-up. Gives me the willies t' think o' how it could'a happened. Great snarled-up tangle o' sails and spars and masts across the decks an' into the salt-chuck."

"I'll stay on deck until Father is aboard *Elusive*."

"An' that'll be soon. Dabih's cracked on all the canvass she'll carry."

They both stared eastward to where the big schooner loomed out of the sunrise against a mackerel-back sky. *Elusive's* many staysails flickered, one moment gleaming and close in sunlit patches, then dull and distant as clouds darkened the sea around her.

"Cam, ready the jack-stay, heaving lines, fenders," said Mairi.

"On me way," Cam answered.

Mairi watched *Elusive* alter course to approach *Cygnus* from astern, her sailors striking topsails and spilling wind as the schooner matched speed with her crippled sister ship. Mairi moved to the starboard quarter to see past the detail who were rigging the tackle for an open-ocean transfer.

"Harden her in, please, Betel. We don't want our boom to foul their rigging. Prepare to brail up the main if we have to. Steersman, don't pinch her. Keep her sailing well short of luffing."

Elusive was closing fast. Sailors were dowsing upper staysails and easing the mainsail. Mairi heard the big schooner's bow-wave hiss into the sea. The schooner entered the wind-shadow from *Cygnus'* sails.

"Spill wind from the main!" Mairi shouted.

Cygnus slowed, and the ships' speed matched. Heaving lines arced into the confused air between them, some falling back into the sea. Cam's was caught by a man in *Elusive's* waist, who immediately began hauling. The transfer line from *Cygnus* splashed down, and moments later broke surface in the choppy waves between the ships to be hauled aboard *Elusive*. A snatch-block rose to the head of a jackstay and the transfer lines between the two ships looped into the air.

Mairi's uncle Dabih waved at Mairi from *Elusive's* quarterdeck.

"Hold your course and speed!" he shouted.

"Ready!" she yelled back.

Lindey and the stretcher-bearers maneuvered Astreya into position. Cam secured the traveller to the slings of the stretcher-cradle. Lindey bent over Astreya's head for an instant and then stepped back. The transfer-rope dipped as it took the weight, then recovered as sailors on both ships hauled it taut again. The stretcher bobbed and swung above the narrow strip of choppy water between the schooners. The ships came a little closer, and the rope sagged. Waves splashed the underside of the cradle. Then as crews on both ships hauled again, the stretcher swung over *Elusive's* rail, where it was grabbed by many hands.

Dabih raised both arms over his head, hands clasped, then flung them apart. Sailors on his ship released their end of the transfer line. As it splashed into the sea and streamed astern of *Cygnus*, *Elusive* turned aside and her crew began raising the sails they had lowered only moments earlier.

Mairi indistinctly heard Dabih giving orders to make all the sail *Elusive* could carry. She watched spray from the schooner's bow-wave rise against the black hull as she gathered speed and pulled away.

Lindey joined Mairi at the rail, and the two of them stood side by side staring as their sister ship diminished into the distance. Silent and dry-eyed, they shared the unspoken fear that Astreya might be dying. Then they both went about sailing *Cygnus* home with her bow canted up, her stern almost awash, her sail-area diminished, and her masts only an unexpected gust away from being snapped or sprung.

3. In which Astreya returns, wounded

It was Trogen's nineteenth birthday, but nobody seemed to have noticed.

He looked older than his years, partly because of his height and well-developed shoulders, partly because of his close-trimmed black beard. He stood on the wharf and stared at the distant harbour mouth. Morning sun dazzled on little wind-blown ripples. He shielded his eyes with a hand scarred across the palm.

The long sea bay was smooth as a lake. The hills that almost surrounded the shining water were broken only by the narrow passage between the headlands called the Two Feet. Behind him, a steep earth redoubt more than four times his height hid the stronghold like a wall. As the morning dew evaporated in the sun, the green slope gave off a subtle scent of growing grasses. Inside the steep slope was the Home, where women were going about their daily tasks. A stone's throw from the wharf, a stream met the saltwater. Out of sight, further up the little river, farmers were already several hours into their day. From the shipyard to his left came the thud of hammers, axes, and adzes, and the keening of saws.

Men and women, many of them roughly Trogen's age, were working at the shipyard, or on the farms, or at sea – where he should have been had he not burned his hands. Four months of enforced idleness were over, and except for some scarring he had recovered, but as the one idler in a community where everyone contributed to the general welfare in some way or another, sympathy had not lasted beyond the first few bandaged days. The shipbuilders were tolerant if he joined them for a beer at the end of their day's work, but he wasn't one of them. They lived and worked ashore: his life was at sea.

Trogen let his gaze linger on the smooth curves of a little two-masted schooner, soon to be launched. The new schooner was still unblemished by use; she still belonged to the shipwrights, who anticipated her naming and first voyage like parents about to say farewell to their child. For a little while longer, the ship on which they worked was theirs; soon, she would be at her skipper's command.

Trogen devoured the schooner with his eyes, longing to be her master. His gaze stroked her pine planking, gleaming from many coats of varnish. He admired her unusually tall masts, imagining himself taking command, giving orders, sailing her down the wide, almost land-locked bay, tacking between the Two Feet, and then heading out into the open ocean, setting a course for adventure.

The bracelet on his left arm tingled and then began to pulse. Trogen stood, concentrating as he translated the sequence into words.

Cygnus damaged

He immediately recognized his cousin Dabih's painfully slow messaging style. As the message was arriving, Trogen began to ask questions, unaware that he was speaking out loud.

"Where? What kind of damage? How much?"

Astreya aboard

"Of course, Astreya's aboard. Where else would he be? Clarify! Aboard *Cygnus* or *Elusive*?"

Badly hurt

"Who? Must be Astreya. Badly? How bad? Details, Skipper. Details!"

Alert Cat

"It would help if you told me why..."

Elusive

" That's you, Dabih. You're done? That's it? No position? No estimated time of arrival? And if it's Astreya who's hurt, why isn't Mother signalling?"

Still muttering, Trogen climbed the zig-zag path up the earth redoubt until the water's edge was more than a mast's height below him. At the top, he turned to look over his shoulder, half expecting to see his uncle's three-masted schooner between the headlands. He turned away from the sea and started down worn stone steps into the fortified enclosure that was large enough to hold barns, cottages, sheds, stables and the white stone building known simply as the Home. Once through the nail-studded black pass-door set into the arched main entrance, Trogen walked past the schoolrooms where more than a dozen women taught three times as many children. He strode down a stone-floored corridor between whitewashed walls to the infirmary, where the chief healer of Matris, his aunt Catriona, better known as Cat, was sorting bunches of dried herbs that perfumed the room with a mixture of astringent scents. She posed the question he had been asking himself.

"What's wrong?"

He repeated the curt message.

"Astreya hurt? That's all you know? What's happened?"

"I have no idea, Aunt Cat. I don't even know where *Elusive* is. No fix. Nothing but six words from Dabih ... uh, the master of *Elusive*."

"You don't have to be formal. He's my son and your cousin. We're not on his quarterdeck."

"It's a habit. He's been my skipper for five years. Until Father..."

"Where is he?

"Judging by the strength of his signal, *Elusive's* very close, just beyond the headlands, I'd guess."

"Nothing from either Astreya or Lindey?"

He shook his head.

"Your mother and father..."

"The Grand Master and Chief Navigator who beached me..."

"Trogen, don't be petulant. You needed to heal ashore. What good would you be aboard ship if you couldn't use your hands?"

Trogen clamped his teeth together, stung by her reproof and annoyed with himself for allowing his resentment to show. She stepped quickly towards him, took both his hands, examined his palms, and nodded.

"You're still tender. Sail if you wish. Wear gloves. Don't row. You need to build up some callouses first. Let's be on our way."

Her feet invisible below her blue skirt, Catriona led the way swiftly out of the building. Trogen lengthened his stride. Instead of climbing the steps Trogen had descended, they headed east through a gate in the ramparts, then down a lane to the shipyard, where the new schooner stood on the ways between the boatbuilding barn and the water. As they walked to the end of the shipyard's wharf, the wind freshened, flapping Catriona's skirt. She swept her dark hair out of her eyes with a thumb, Trogen shaded his eyes with one scarred hand, and together they scanned the sea-lake.

A white foresail caught the morning sun between the headlands, then one by one, three masts of a staysail schooner appeared in the gap. The sails shook and refilled as the ship turned to run down-wind towards her moorings.

"We'll go to meet them. Trogen, ask Drew for a longboat."

Trogen left Catriona waiting on the wharf and ran to find the shipwright and harbourmaster. Soon, four of the younger shipbuilders ran a rowing boat down the hard and brought it alongside at their feet. Trogen stepped into the stern sheets and moments later, Catriona climbed into the bow. Tiller in one hand, Trogen waited for the two girls and two boys to shove off and ship their oars.

"Ready.... Give way!"

With the smooth efficiency of people to whom rowing was as natural as walking, the four reached towards the stern, their oars creaking in leather-lined oarlocks. The blades dug into the water at the same instant, then left swirling eddies in the boat's wake as the rowers leaned back on their oars. Four pairs of hands dipped to recover and return. In three strong pulls, they took the launch to cruising speed and then settled into longer, slower strokes. With nothing to do but steer, Trogen looked over their swaying heads, three fair, one dark, and on towards the big schooner, which was already heading for her moorings in a wide, smooth turn. The morning wind astern, she slid through the water, her black sides high, her masts vertical.

"Steady," said Trogen quietly.

The boat's oars dripped into the water as the rowers held them level. The launch moved silently forward on its momentum as they all watched the great ship *Elusive* draw nearer, running free. The ship laid a curved wake astern as she turned to take the wind on her starboard side. Sailors sheeted in the mainsail, then as she completed her turn into the wind, the curve of her staysails fell slack. The main boom swung inboard until it was amidships. High above the deck, canvass shivered. The halyards squeaked, the main boom dropped into its head-high crutch, and sailors bundled the sail. Then one by one, the staysails shook and then collapsed downwards. Finally, two sailors dowsed the jib and *Elusive* headed up-wind under bare poles, leaving barely a ripple under her forefoot as she neared the heavy wooden buoy that waited for her return. A figure standing on the bobstay stooped, ran a braided hawser through the becket atop the buoy and passed the end back up the hawsehole to be belayed. The schooner over-rode her buoy, checked, held her position for a few heartbeats and then slid back as the wind on her bare masts pushed her astern until she rested on her moorings.

Trogen nodded, admiring the seemingly casual seamanship by the ship on which he had served for years, before manoeuvring the launch alongside the schooner. He looked up at the deck, where the crew was bundling sails and bracing halyards into harbour trim. A scrambling net unrolled down the ship's side, deployed by unseen hands above him. A young woman leaned over the rail. Gleaming copper curls escaped from under a white wool watch-cap above blue eyes, wide with concern.

"Grandmother! Come aboard. You need to check Master Astreya before we sway him down to the boat. Wait! We'll rig a bosun's chair for you!"

"Don't bother, Seren. I can manage."

Catriona kilted her skirts and leaped out of the boat onto the scrambling net, her medical kit over one shoulder. Trogen looked up to see Dabih, Master of *Elusive,* his captain since he had been a cadet. His cousin's face was a blurred version of his father, Astreya's, which in turn was an echo of their shared great grandfather.

"Trogen? Good. Soon as mother ... when Healer Catriona gives the word, we'll have Master Astreya down to you on a stretcher."

"At your command, Master Dabih."

Trogen acknowledged the order formally, the past four months ashore forgotten.

Dabih nodded and disappeared. As Trogen stared upward, a tall dark-haired man looked over the rail at him. White teeth flashed in a warm smile, the ends of a splendid moustache rose, and the lines around his brown eyes creased.

"Hello there, Trogen. How're your hands?"

"Damon! What's happening?"

"There was an explosion aboard *Cygnus*. Astreya was hurt, so we took him aboard to get him back home ahead of *Cygnus*, which has a hole in her bow and is limping home under Lindey's command. Cat's checking Astreya out. He can't stand. Lost a lot of blood. Seren did her best, but she didn't want to move him until..."

"Seren's a carpenter, not a surgeon, and she's only seventeen, even if she's taller than most of the crew. What does she know about...?"

Invisible above him, Catriona's voice reproved him.

"Enough, Trogen. Seren's done a commendable job. Now get ready to receive a wounded man."

Damon gave orders, a stretcher swung outboard into the air above the boat and descended slowly. Trogen stood, the tiller between his knees. He reached up to steady the end of the stretcher as it was eased down to the level of his head, then his chest, his waist, and finally arrived with only a gentle bump along the centreline of the boat. He looked up at Damon and waved.

"He's aboard. We've got him."

"Hello, Trogen. Good to see you, son."

Trogen nearly lost his balance. He stared down into his father's lean, green-eyed face, disconcertingly upside down and below him. Astreya's brow was furrowed and his cheeks hollow.

Catriona came down the scrambling net and swung herself aboard as if she did so every day.

"Out of my way, Trogen. I need to be at his head. Squeeze over, you rowers, and don't poke him or me with the loom of your oars."

Trogen gave orders, the launch pulled away from the schooner and he steered for the wharf, painfully aware that his father, the Master of *Cygnus* and Grand Master of the fleet, was lying injured within his arm's reach.

Astreya's voice came up to him softly, gently, almost a whisper.

"Take me to the shipyard slip, Trogen. It's a bit further, but it'll avoid a steep climb up the defences. You can put me onto a cart and shove me up the hill, through the gate and on into the Home."

Trogen masked his discomposure with the formal response.

"At your command, Master."

"Trogen," Astreya whispered, "Despite all this, try to enjoy your birthday."

"Right," said Catriona briskly. "No more talking. Rest easy, Astreya."

Trogen opened his mouth and shut it again. Astreya's words shocked him. His father's soft-spoken politeness to his officers and men was legendary, but the whispered wish made Trogen feel as if he were still a little boy. He concentrated on his seamanship all the way to the shipyard and then helped with the slow uphill carry on the track around the grassy berm to the gates through the earthworks into the grounds and the Home at their centre.

His private mind was revisiting his childhood, in the days before he became a sailor, when he and Mairi, his twin, lived aboard the great ship where they had been born. The face that had looked up at him from the stretcher was the lean, impersonal, green-eyed mask that had watched him over the years as he progressed from sailor to cadet to junior officer. Astreya's piercing eyes were half-closed, the usually chilling expression softened, the lips no longer firm. For the first time, Trogen saw grey in the beard and black, curly hair, and deep lines at the corners of the mouth and eyes. As he helped carry Astreya through the door of the Home and on into the infirmary, Trogen was convinced his father was dying.

He turned to the men and women who had rowed and then carried Astreya, but the thanks he expressed was formal, the product of training. Before he could complete the stilted phrases, Catrona took charge of transferring Astreya's inert body onto a bed.

"Right, off you go, all of you. Thanks for your help, but now he's my patient, and I need to be left to do my work. You too, Trogen."

"Is he...?"

"He's going to be fine. Well, not immediately fine, but certainly alive. Seren brought him through the worst part, stopped the bleeding, kept him from making himself worse by moving."

"Aunt Cat, he hasn't spoken since ... since the boat."

"After what I gave him aboard *Elusive*, I'm surprised he said anything at all. And now while he still isn't feeling too much pain, I will tidy him up and get him on the way back to being himself."

"But..."

"Just go, Trogen."

Trogen walked out from the whitewashed walls of the infirmary, through the doors, up the earthworks that surrounded the Home, and stood on their crest. He focussed on the narrow gap in the cliffs that led to the open sea. As he watched, a fog bank rolled between the Two Feet and spread quickly across the long bay, propelled by a freshening wind. Somewhere beyond the encircling hills was his father's disabled ship, now under his mother's command.

Uncomfortable though it had been before, Trogen's life was now worse. The father he rebelled against was suddenly at risk. Everyone's future was now uncertain. Trogen could be returned to his rank and role as second mate of *Elusive*, but if *Cygnus* was to be laid up for long, he feared he could effectively be demoted. Earlier, for one enraptured moment he had imagined himself commanding the little schooner he had watched a-building. Now he despaired at the thought of again being left behind in Matris, beached.

4. In which Cygnus returns

For a long week, *Cygnus* made her slow, careful way north, with mother and daughter standing watch-and-watch, hyper-alert for the least change in the ship, the wind or the sea. They had no time to chat nor the inclination to try, lest they lose the calm essential for doing their job. From time to time, they exchanged brittle reassurances.

"You all right, Mairi?"

"Yes, Mother. You?"

"I can manage."

"Good, then."

And so it went, day and night until they raised the Two Feet through a light fog, ahead of where the bowsprit should have been pointing. Cam was the first to yell "Land ho!" Moments later, the clasp on Mairi's arm tingled as Lindey messaged the shore.

Cygnus passing the Two Feet

Clear passage to shipyard

As Lindey came up from the Forbidden Room, she was the last on deck. The entire crew was ready for what they all knew was going to be a series of difficult maneuvers with *Cygnus* under-sailed and unresponsive. Lindey spoke to them in a quiet, measured voice.

"It's not been easy, but there's more to do. We're going to ground *Cygnus* on the mudbank beside the shipyard. Stay alert, stay safe. Marley, you have the wheel."

As they cleared the passage between the headlands, *Cygnus* came out of a light sea mist into sunlight on the wide, almost landlocked bay which was her home port. A gentle breeze barely ruffled the water. Ahead, Mairi could see their sister ship *Elusive* at her buoy, and closer to the wharf, another smaller schooner.

"Right," said Lindey. "We're bringing *Cygnus* in goose-winged on main and mizzen. Bring her around gently. Leave *Elusive* to starboard."

Mairi watched Marley swing the wheel. Beside her, she heard Betel muttering.

"Unhandy... stern deep... steer with sails... not much wind."

If Lindey heard the old man, she did not show it.

"Ease the main, jibe the mizzen! We'll beach her on the mud to port of the shipyard."

With the wind astern, the sagging mainstay went taut. The masts groaned in their steps. Every head tipped back, watching the spars rock forward into their true position.

Cygnus glided over water muddy from the little river, her crew tense. Cordage creaked, and the wake burbled under the stern.

"I can't see..." Marley began.

"Mairi, we'll con her in together. You take the port side."

Lindey moved swiftly along the starboard side until she could see past the main boom, Mairi hurried forward along the port side where the deck was gouged by debris from the explosion. She stood beside the broken rail where her father had fallen and stared at the shipyard ahead.

To starboard alongside the wharf, lay the new schooner that had been a keel and ribs in the barn when *Cygnus* had left months earlier. Freshly varnished wood glinted in the sunlight. Ignoring what a part of her mind told her was a truly pretty sight, she focussed on the muddy shore ahead.

"I think she needs a touch to port. Mairi, do you agree?" Lindey's voice reached Mairi as she was about to ask her mother the same question.

"Agreed."

Lindey gave the order, and Mairi watched the shoreline as the ragged stump of the bowsprit swung to point at the mudbank.

"Enough! Hold her there!"

The mangled bow steadied on their target.

"Nearing fast, now, Mother. Do you think...?

"Agreed. Brail the main! Dowse the mizzen!"

The deck drummed to the sound of running feet, the mizzen sail collapsed downwards in a rush. The mainsail's brails folded the middle of the sail towards the mast, the boom rose and was hauled amidships, and the sail furled. The wind no longer filling the sails, the damaged bow yawed. Astern at the wheel, Marley brought her back on course.

"Everybody aft!" Lindey shouted, and hurried to the quarterdeck, Mairi only a few steps behind.

The crew clustered astern of the mainmast until Lindey shooed them to stand as far astern as possible among the boats and gear that cluttered the quarterdeck. The older and more experienced men and women cast glances aloft. Mairi knew what they were thinking. When *Cygnus* stuck in the mud, the masts could whiplash and snap the splice that had held the mainstay together since the explosion. If that were to happen, masts could shatter and fall in pieces to the deck below.

The ship slid closer to shore under bare poles, her sea-stained hull moving slowly through the water. As the distance between ship and shore diminished, Mairi grimaced, concerned that *Cygnus* might lose way, go dead in the water, and be pushed back by the outflow of the river at the head of the bay. Then as she watched, it seemed as if the big schooner picked up dangerous speed.

The gap between ship and shore diminished. Mairi could see ripples pulsing along the muddy beach. She tried to estimate when the ship would touch bottom, knowing as she did so that there was nothing more that anyone could do. At a shouted order ashore, men and women ran a six-oared cutter down hard into the water. The carpenters and riggers clustered at the shipyard, ready to deal with what might be a catastrophic arrival.

In an eerie silence, Mairi heard old Betel muttering.

"Gently ... gently ... She'll snap her sticks if she hits too hard."

The schooner's bow neared the tide line, rose up and over the ripples along the shore, and slid onto the mud. _Cygnus_ stuck. Mairi saw dry land under the broken stump of the bowsprit. The mastheads dipped and swayed, but the jury-rigged mainstay held.

Cygnus lay half in and half out of the water, stern deck almost awash. The masts leaned a few degrees to starboard as her keel settled. Mairi flinched when she felt the ship sink lower by a hand's breadth. Sailors jumped into the mud and slogged knee-deep towards dry land with hawsers over their shoulders, meeting workers from the shipyard with lines of their own. Their slow, muddy efforts would continue until _Cygnus_ was braced on both sides.

Lindey leaned over the rail on the quarterdeck and looked down towards the rudder where a curling brown trail of mud was sinking to the bottom. Mairi came to her side.

"We're safe, Mother. You brought _Cygnus_ home."

"We did, Mairi. It wouldn't have happened without you."

"We all did, Mother."

Mairi saw something more than tiredness in her mother's eyes.

"We're home, Mairi, but we're still a long way from safe." She turned abruptly and headed for the companionway. "Call the launch over to the stern so we won't have to wade through the mud. Shore leave for everyone when she's fully secured. Come with me. Tell Betel he's coming, too."

5. In which Astreya returns to Elusive

Astreya awoke, expecting to find himself aboard the schooner. Instead, he recognized the white-washed walls of the Home infirmary, exactly where he had lain more than two decades earlier when he was seventeen. His moment of confusion faded as he looked up at a small, heart-shaped face bending over him. He smiled up at Catriona, the Home's healer.

"Cat," said Astreya. "You patched me up. Again. Thank you."

"Once every twenty years, or so."

"I seem to remember landing on my back, looking up at the mizzenmast, wondering how I got there. Then Lindey told me *Cygnus* had been holed in the bow, and then she put me aboard *Elusive*, and then Trogen was carrying me into the Home, and then …"

"And then, as you said, we patched you up. A splinter from the bowsprit went into your hip. We only got the last of it out last night. Up to then, you were pretty much in your own world."

"Hallucinating?"

Catriona nodded.

"Listen, Cat. I can't just lie here. There's a lot to be decided and acted upon. I need to talk with Lindey, Dabih, Walt, …"

"You can talk to Walt very soon. He's cadging a late breakfast from Ellen. He was sitting here beside your bed most of the nights, watching over you like a mother hen. Dabih's in the harbour aboard *Elusive*. Lindey's got *Cygnus* moving under reduced sail, and she's due soon. Right now, you have to do what I say. Start by having something to eat and drink."

Recognizing Catriona's good sense, Astreya obeyed. Then as he lay back, mug in hand, there was a knock at his door, and an unusually short, astonishingly broad, black-haired man stood in the doorway. Teeth gleamed in a wide grin below deep-set eyes under bushy brows.

"Yer awake. Capital. Mind if I join yer? I brung me own coffee."

"Walt!

"Large as life an' twice as ugly. How're yer doin'?"

"A whole lot better than when I was aboard *Elusive*."

"I'll say. You had us worried. I never knew you so quiet. 'Cept for the occasional groan, I'd'a thought you was a goner."

"Walt, how long is it since...?"

"Since a rotten little skiff blew a thumpin' big hole in *Cygnus'* port bow? Goin' on fer eight days."

"I couldn't believe he'd try to cut ahead of us. What happened to him?"

"Dunno. When Lindey sent for us, *Elusive* was the best part of a day and a half away. When we caught up to *Cygnus*, she was limpin' along with her bow cocked up in the air, her stern near awash, missin' everything that should be ahead o' the foremast."

"Lindey?"

"She was coping, like the tough-minded lady she is. Her and Cam and old Betel had shifted everything that the crew could pick up and move astern so's to lift the patch on the bow above the waterline. When we left her to bring you to the Home, *Cygnus* was crabbin' an' crank, but she was makin' way, right enough."

"I don't suppose you know how long it'll take to make repairs."

Walt shook his head.

"I've had a chat wi' Drew down at the yard, and he's gettin' things ready, but until he has a good look fer hisself, there's no knowin 'what has to be done, or how to do it. So while he's been waiting fer Lindey to bring *Cygnus* back, he's been concentratin' on puttin' the finishin' touches on the little schooner he's been buildin'."

"A little two-masted schooner can't do duty for *Cygnus*."

"You got that right. Still, perhaps we can limp along with a ship and a half until 'Drew can work a miracle or two. Then we'll have a fleet o' almost three. An' then, we'll need to sort out who's in charge o 'what."

"Drew has never done major repairs to one of the great ships. Nobody alive has. We don't know how they cooked up the heavy woad for the hulls of *Cygnus* and *Elusive* – as well as the rest of the great fleet that's so long gone, now. It's way over a century since the last of them was built."

"There's a lot they did *Before* that we can't do now, an' don't want to. Like sailin' on forever, led by that crafty old bugger Oron what tried to control everything in the fleet."

"People are learning, Walt. In the twenty years we've been sailing the circuit we've seen a lot of changes. It's coming back."

"Yer right, 'Streya. But it ain't all good, not by a long haul. I mean, that new glass in our scuttles an' skylights is right nice, an' I got no complaints with the winches they're forgin' today, but you can't tell me you like havin' yer ship near to blown up wi' 'splosives by some brainless sculpin."

Astreya nodded.

"It could be that someone's been experimenting, trying to reinvent some of the explosives from *Before*, and maybe he was shipping it somewhere, and by chance ... "

"That's a lot o' chances. More likely, it were deliberate. You done anyone any serious wrong recently?"

Astreya shook his head.

"Even if I had, surely there are rational, reasonable solutions for inadvertent wrongdoing that don't necessitate resorting to violence."

"Yeah. Now yer talkin' like Lindey. But she knows folk can be perverse, and I'd like to remind you that she never goes ashore without her stick. She's not afraid to use it, neither."

There was a silence as they both contemplated Lindey's pre-emptive approach to threats.

"Y'know, 'Streya, this means there's got to be decisions. Like, who gets which ship an' what they're s'posed to do with it."

Walt's gaze slid down to the sheet that covered his injuries. Astreya ignored the yearning note in Walt's voice.

"We will decide at a meeting of masters and navigators, as we always have."

Astreya's right hand cupped over the bracelet on his left arm, and Walt shook his left hand as if the ring on his little finger had burned him.

"What's up? I can't tell like you can."

"Lindey must be inside the headlands. Walt, I have to go aboard *Elusive*."

Astreya started to swing his legs out of bed. His grunt of pain coincided with Catriona coming back into the room.

"Where do you think you're going, Astreya? I told you ..."

"Lindey's back, Cat. I have to go."

"You have to wait until Lindey has *Cygnus* on her moorings, climbs the ramparts and ..."

"No, Cat. She wants me aboard *Elusive* along with ..."

"You're rubbing your arm with the bracelet, Astreya. It was a message, wasn't it?"

Astreya nodded. His mouth hardened into a thin line as he levered himself over the edge of the bed. As his feet touched the floor, he clenched his teeth. Catriona frowned.

"We've not had long enough to see if you're healing properly. You've been taking powerful pain relievers. When they wear off, you'll... You're not listening, are you? All right. I'll let you go, but I'm doing this under protest, and I'm coming with you. You'll need clothes. Help me with him, Walt."

A little while later, Astreya left the infirmary supported by two much shorter figures, one tiny, slim and quick, the other squat, wide and powerful. None of them said anything on a painful journey out of the Home, across the wide enclosed field of close-cropped grass, up the worn stone steps on one side of the encircling earthworks and down the zig-zag path on the other.

Even with his teeth clamped together, Astreya could not restrain occasional grunts at the pain that stabbed up his body at each step he took. When they arrived at the dock, his face was grey, and standing was all he could do.

"Hang in there, 'Streya. Here's Drew wi' the shipyard launch. Lindey's with 'im."

Astreya looked down on the boat as it drew alongside the dock, wondering how he was going to get aboard. Then he felt himself lifted by the armpits and lowered into the boat by Walt's two big hands. For a moment, he was suspended, facing Lindey, only a handspan from him, her blue eyes bright with concern. Then she was helping him sit in the stern, and all his concentration was on refusing to be engulfed by the purple cloud he saw whenever he shut his eyes. He did not notice Mairi in the bow.

6. In which Mairi and Trogen are shut out

The short trip to the schooner was silent save for the regular plash as oars bit into the water. When the boat was alongside *Elusive,* and Astreya hoisted aboard in a bosun's chair, Mairi followed Lindey up the scrambling net that hung down the schooner's salt-streaked black hull. As her head came above the ship's rail, she saw Lindey and Drew heading for the stern companionway. She was climbing aboard, intending to follow them, when she saw her brother, Trogen, standing by the rail. They took a step towards each other, then stopped short. Mairi's voice was restrained and formal, even though her words were a private tradition from their childhood.

"Trogen! It's a bit late, but happy birthday to us."

"Happy birthday to us, Mairi."

They shared the same shy smile. Though they were twins, their features were only similar. Trogen had inherited his father's high cheekbones, black hair, and short, curly beard, whereas Mairi's face more resembled her mother's. Trogen was almost as tall as his father so that Mairi had to lift her chin to see into his eyes. They both blinked quickly, her eyes blue, his soft green. She wanted to hug him, but they were on the quarterdeck of one of the two great ships on which they were both second mates.

Their shared moment was interrupted by Walt, who came stamping across the deck until he was between them. The squat, black-haired man was their second cousin, older than their father. Although shorter than Mairi, he was fiercely intimidating, especially now he was aboard the ship in which he was first mate.

"Right, you two second mates. You ain't part of nothin' goin' on here. Just wait on the quarterdeck."

Trogen and Mairi looked at each other, dumbfounded, and spoke at the same moment.

"He wanted me aboard..."

"Mother told me to come ..."

Walt ignored their objections and shooed them astern. Trogen glowered down at him but was restrained by Mairi's hand on his arm.

"Mother will straighten things out," said Mairi.

"Not a chance," said Trogen. "We're excluded. As usual."

He turned his back on her and strode to the stern rail, on which he leaned his elbows, stared toward the shore and spoke as if to himself.

"So, Father gets his way. Again."

Mairi glanced around to reassure herself that they could not be heard.

"What's Father doing aboard? Shouldn't he be ashore in Cat's sickbay?"

Trogen shrugged.

"Cat's aboard as well. She's looking after him."

"Why did she let him out of her infirmary?"

"He does what he wants, Mairi, you know that."

"How is he?"

Trogen chose his words with care.

"When he arrived five days ago, Astreya, Grand Master of the Fleet, our respected, admired and greatly revered father, with his ship holed in the bow and a slice of the bowsprit stuck in his hip, looked up at me from his stretcher and wished the son he'd beached a happy birthday."

Mairi blinked at him.

"Wow. Next, you'll be telling me he gave you a great big hug."

"It was almost as if he was heading that way."

"What got him out of bed and here aboard *Elusive*?"

"Mother's signal. You must have felt it, you were aboard *Cygnus*."

"All it said was that we'd made it to the Two Feet, and…"

"You didn't hear the rest?"

"What rest?"

"The secret part, about a meeting here, afloat."

Mairi looked at Trogen, wondering what she had missed in their mother's signal.

"It can't be about the accident, because everyone ashore will know all about it by now. Mother gave *Cygnus'* crew shore leave, and you know how news travels…"

Trogen cut her off angrily.

"Mairi, there's something being shared by everyone but us, and it's going on right now in the cabin under our feet."

"There must be some other explanation. Mother's exhausted. The attack, Father injured, the ship holed, a difficult passage home under jury rig, Father not with her …"

"Don't try to excuse them. I know what I heard. As usual, it's all because the great Astreya has to show he's in charge, even though he's barely able to walk and has to get Walt to do his dirty work. And Mother's part of it, even if she brought *Cygnus* back without him."

"Trogen, all I meant to say was that she did well, as our father would say, and is probably saying to her right now. He always says 'well done' to anyone who's done a good job."

"Except to me. I am never good enough. That's why he beached me."

"He left you at the Home because you burned both your hands so badly you couldn't hold a pen, much less an oar or a rope. Mother agreed that it was necessary."

"It's both of them. And they don't have the right."

Hearing her brother's irritation at Astreya and Lindey, Mairi tried another approach.

"Trogen, it's because they're not just our parents. They're the heart and leadership of the company that's brought prosperity to the Home, and is bringing ..."

"...you and me nothing. Less than nothing. Just work and no part in deciding anything."

"That's not the way it is, Trogen."

"It certainly is. What do you care? Go ashore and visit Becky. Admire her brood. Go talk to the women at the Home. I'm sure they're dying to hear the latest news. Oh, I forgot. We don't have the latest news. Walt and Betel do. Even Drew and Cat do. We don't."

Trogen strode to the other side of the quarterdeck.

A rowing skiff bumped the side of the ship. Betel climbed carefully over the rail of the quarterdeck. Cam followed him, grumbling.

"Hot damn, she left us aboard *Cygnus*. Come on, Betel. Where is everybody? Ahoy, Damon!"

A tall brown-haired man in an officer's blue jacket waved from the quarterdeck and walked swiftly toward Cam. The two slapped hands, Cam grinning up at his friend, who was more than a head taller.

"Damon, you an' me and Betel better get below an' find out what's happenin'."

"It's my watch," said Damon.

"The ship's made fast to her buoy in homeport, for goo'ness sake. Yer not needed on deck, Damon, an' y'know it. Yer crew all know what to do." As he headed towards the companionway, Cam noticed Mairi and Trogen. "Why are you two standin 'about, hangin 'onto the slack? Why ain'tcha below wi 'the mucky-mucks?"

"Not wanted," Trogen spat the words, and stalked back to the stern rail.

"We'll see about that," said Cam, as he led Betel and Damon below.

Mairi went to stand next to Trogen, but he turned away from her and started pacing. After several turns, Mairi again attempted calming words.

"Father must have a good reason..." she began.

"Listen, little sister. Our parents aren't all sweetness and light. They turned the tools of navigation into weapons. They blew up evil old Mufrid. Took him down with the power of the stones. Everyone knows that they did it, but nobody knows how, and nobody talks about it. You ever think of that?"

"*Big* sister, little brother. I'm three minutes older than you. That's all history now. He's our father, Trogen. He cares for us."

"I thought for a moment back then when I landed him on a stretcher that he might be human, but it was just a way of saying that I'm a disappointment to him."

"When you burned your hands, he had to leave you ashore. You weren't able to do anything aboard. Not even navigation."

"I could have..."

Mairi had had enough. She contradicted Trogen as she would a delinquent cadet.

"No, you couldn't, Trogen. You were lucky that Cat saved you from having no hands at all. You grabbed a red-hot knife blade, remember?"

"Not likely I'll forget. Or being beached."

"Trogen! Why are you being so ... so perverse?"

"Because I'm not anything. Not flesh, not fish, not even a herring. The crew thinks, 'He's Astreya's son, that's how he got promoted.' And Astreya thinks I'm not worthy to be included among the officers. So I'm nowhere."

Walt's heavy footfalls came up the companionway and then aft towards them. They both turned aside, rather than let him see they had been arguing.

"Well now, Trog an' Mairi. I see yer can't think of nothin' to do. So I'll tell yer. *Cygnus* has to be unloaded, an' you, Mairi, are goin' to do the inventory of what's in her, notin' where it all was supposed to be goin', if the ... ah... accident hadn't happened. Sooner you get it done, sooner we'll know what to restow aboard '*Sieve* so's we can get her on her way to do the work of two ships. There's more for you Trog, m'boy. You're goin' t'be aboard *Cygnus*, t'make copies of her charts and rutters. An' you, Mairi, lass, you also got the job o' preparin' that little schooner for sea. Cam will be joinin' you to help out, soon as he's been told what her cargo's goin' t'be. So get about it."

"At your command, Mr. Mate," said Trogen, stiffening into a full, formal salute, then turned on his heel and stamped off to where the launch waited at the ship's side.

"What's up wi' him, Mairi?"

"He's upset about Father," said Mairi.

"So are we all, lass. So are we all. Away you go."

A little later, Mairi sat in the shipyard's launch. Walt was at the tiller, taking them ashore. Beside her, Trogen fumed with barely suppressed rage, which she tried to ignore. The tide had receded since Mairi and Lindey had left *Cygnus*, and as Walt maneuvered the launch until its stern was beside the big schooner's counter, the sternmost pair of oars dug their blades into the mud.

"Right, you two. We're here. Have fun."

They climbed aboard the mud-bound ship and the launch pulled away.

7. In which Lindey is dismayed

For three days, Astreya stayed aboard *Elusive* in the care of Lindey and Catriona. During that time, lighters and rowboats plied back and forth between the shipyard and the schooners, loaded with outgoing and incoming cargo. On the afternoon of the fourth day, Catriona pronounced Astreya ready to move, and Lindey helped him aboard a launch which took them to the shipyard, where a pair of huge horses stood waiting hitched to a lumber cart on which was a large and comfortable chair. The horses nickered to Lindey when she greeted them by name. They drove up the hill to their on-shore home in the big house they shared with Dabih's family during the winter months.

There, with Mairi as her messenger, Lindey took charge of coordinating *Cygnus'* repair and refit. At first, people came looking for the Grand Master to solve their problems, but when she was adamant that Astreya was not to be troubled, they had to be content with her judgment. At the end of each day, she gave Astreya an edited version of difficulties sorted, schedules updated, and conflicts resolved.

The sailors and shipwrights knew their work and got on with it. However, when Lindey sent Mairi to assess inventories and needs at the Home, she had to deal with a more contentious situation. Mairi left the big house and walked to the Home. Inside the age-blackened oak door, she paused to look around the big kitchen where the women of the Home made meals for all those living and working in the big building.

Ellen, the plump, sweet-faced chief cook and acknowledged mainstay of the Home, welcomed Mairi with a smile that brought dimples to her cheeks. Eager to know how Astreya was faring, she sat Mairi down at the white-scrubbed kitchen table, poured fragrant cups of tea, and produced a handful of lists from the pocket in her apron, laid them to one side and settled herself to gossip. Before Mairi could begin to satisfy Ellen's curiosity, Janice, a thin, sharp-nosed, grey-haired woman, bustled in, her long black skirt flapping at her boot-heels.

Seeing Mairi, she stopped, crossed her arms over her thin chest, pursed her lips and assumed her favourite role as the self-appointed custodian of decency and good behaviour. Before Ellen could invite her to sit down and talk over tea and scones, Janice was in full moralistic flight.

"I don't see why our entire world should come to a halt just because Astreya has hurt himself. We're fast running out of coffee and spices, the storeroom is chock full of trade goods from weaving to maple syrup, and a visitor from Charton told me that they'll have to start throwing salt fish away if the ships don't come soon."

"Janice," Mairi began, "I'm here to take inventory of goods and needs so that..."

"About time. Goodness knows you've been hanging around for long enough, doing nothing. You haven't even bothered to change out of those repellent sailor clothes. Breeks like a man. Disgusting. And why can't you make yourself useful by rowing out to Dabih's big boat and reminding him of his responsibilities to us on shore? He's just having a good old time drinking and talking about all the fun they'll be having when next they're in one of those depraved regions to the south."

"Where your coffee and sugar come from. Not to mention glass and metal and ..."

Janice talked down Mairi's interruption.

"It's bad enough that whenever the boats are tied up here, the men loll around, telling each other stories about their squalid little adventures among foreigners with no more morals than a cat. I don't understand how it is that your mother can countenance, no, *encourage* the shameful behaviour that must go on between the young men and women all crammed together in those boats, undoubtedly getting up to all kinds of immoral and disgusting ...

interactions of a sensual nature. And it's Lindey who's behind it all. She started it, selfishly breaking the rules. You know that, don't you?"

Before Mairi could decide which of the accusations to answer, Ellen intervened.

"Oh, for goodness' sake, Janice, you know they're all busy patching up *Cygnus* and re-stocking *Elusive*."

"Indolent, irresponsible men with no thought for..."

Mairi straightened her spine and glared.

"Janice, you know perfectly well that Astreya, Dabih, and their ships have made Matris safe and prosperous. And that's not the way it was *Before*, when we all lived in fear of the next time the Home would be attacked and children kidnapped. Thanks to the great ships and the men and women in them, you're safe, and Matris is the envy of every port of call from Charton to the Sunny Isles."

She could have saved her breath. Janice had her own version of history.

"I tell you that Matris was envied long before all this gadabout sailing ship nonsense. I won't stand for it. There must be an end to this secret male society, living in those big boats, ruining the lives of the young women they have impressed into their service."

While Janice ranted on, Mairi and Ellen exchanged glances. Ellen gave Mairi the lists of needs and supplies and squeezed her hands in farewell.

"*Cygnus* and *Elusive* are not boats," said Mairi over her shoulder as she left the kitchen. "They're ships."

As she crossed the flagstone steps to the door, Janice's voice shrilled on.

"There you go, running away from responsibility, just the way all the men do. You can't bear the truth, so you leave us behind, tearing off to sea, where you'll go on with your wicked, abusive..."

Mairi closed the door behind her, resisting the urge to slam it shut. Janice's voice reduced to a muffled whine, Mairi climbed the steps of the seaward rampart and took the steep path down to the wharf. Ripples whispered along the shore and tiny clopping sounds came from around the pilings. Sea wind waved the topmost branches of the pines on the little island that guarded the approach to Matris, but even though it was less than an hour since breakfast, the sun had already warmed their boughs enough for the air to be fragrant. *Elusive* lay at anchor, wind-rode in slack water at tide turn, her bow pointed west.

Mairi's gaze turned to the little schooner moored in the bay. Golden fresh-varnished planking glowed above the waterline, spars and masts gleamed as sunlight slid along them, reflected off the water and rippled under the overhang of her stern. When two of the shipyard people test-hoisted the mainsail, the little schooner tugged at her moorings as if anxious to challenge the sea.

Mairi turned and saw her three youngest cousins coming down the zig-zag path towards her. They were led by green-eyed Ellie, the second of Becky's daughters, who at thirteen was the youngest girl to serve on the great ships. No taller than Mairi's shoulder, she walked proudly with her long, straight black hair streaming over a white blouse down to her sailor's brown breeks. Her freckle-faced sister, Lena, saw Mairi and ran ahead, pursued by the littlest sister, Maia, whose short, plump legs could not keep up.

"Mairi! Lindey 'n' 'Streya's looking for you!" shouted Lena. Her blonde hair flying, her overalls flapping on her fat little legs, she ran down the steep path and flung herself into Mairi's arms.

"Baby Lena!"

"I'm not a baby. I'm five. Maia's the baby."

Mairi hugged the little girl, who struggled free, took her hand and started to drag her back towards the Home.

"I've just come from there, Lena."

"Doesn't matter. We all have to go to the Home along with well, *everybody!*"

"'Streya's called a meeting," said Ellie, as she scooped up Maia onto her slim hip. "So we get to spend time with the Home girls in the big kitchen. They're going to make doughnuts. I'm not."

Lena took Mairi's hand and they headed back towards the Home. Mairi thought for a moment that she should be carrying Maia, but Ellie shot her a green-eyed glance that Mairi knew better than to challenge.

When they reached the Home, Seren was waiting for them. Taller than almost all the men both ashore and afloat, she wore seagoing clothes. Her hair gleamed like polished copper in the sunlight as she coped with a direct assault from Maia, who had wrestled out of Ellie's grasp to climb her eldest sister hand over hand.

Ellie rolled her green eyes and stubbornly raised her pointed chin. She obeyed Seren without argument, but Mairi knew she would extort reparations later. The three youngest headed for the Home kitchen, while Mairi and Seren joined a stream of adults walking towards the great hall at the other end of the big stone building. When they reached the doors, Seren gave Mairi a deferential little nod and joined the other sailors from her ship. Mairi accepted Seren's acknowledgment but wished that their difference in rank did not come between them. Mairi stood outside the door, where she was joined by Trogen. They exchanged glances and stood in an awkward silence neither wanted to break.

~⌃~

Lindey and Astreya walked slowly towards the gate in the earthworks. Astreya walked with a stick; Lindey was beside him, ready should he stumble. Despite their closeness, there was an unusual tension between them. Pain kept him shuttered and impassive, as he had been with Becky and Dabih less than an hour before. Dabih had shaken his head, and Becky's eyes had overflowed with silent tears. Instead of their twenty years' habit of talking towards consensus, Astreya had announced his decision at the outset. Dabih's agreement was never in doubt. Becky had wept but eventually nodded.

"Are you at ease with what we have decided, Lindey?"

"Of course not, Astreya. But you're in no shape to head north to look for more stones, so we have to protect the ones we have."

"If we hadn't given them to the children ..."

"If we hadn't given them to the children, we wouldn't have two first-rate skippers in waiting, and one little girl who quite possibly has more talent than any of us. Even you."

"I've made all of them into targets. Any of them could be kidnapped and enslaved the way Dabih was used by Mufrid."

"That's why we have to send them away, Astreya. It was your idea, and it's the only practical thing to do—unless you count the unacceptable option of beaching them all here at Matris with no explanation and nothing to do."

"Eventually, Dabih and Becky appeared to be comfortable with the outcome. But are you at ease with the decision?"

"You don't have to soften your words for me, Astreya. Nobody is 'at ease' or 'comfortable' with your plan. It's a hard choice to separate parents from their children. And it's not just about our families, it's the expectations of everyone afloat and ashore."

Astreya and Lindey walked the path to the oaken doors of the big building where sailors, shipwrights, farmers and the women of the Home were already gathered. Astreya drew Lindey closer to him, and for a brief instant, they looked into each other's eyes. When they looked away, they saw Mairi and Trogen waiting at the door, absorbed in their own thoughts.

Trogen fidgeted from one foot to the other, tense with anticipation. Mairi watched her parents' moment of mutual reassurance and for an instant, she felt a sliver of the jealousy that possessed her brother. They silently followed their parents inside, knowing from experience the futility of asking questions.

The men and women who filled the great hall clustered in distinct groups. The sailors, who stood almost shoulder to shoulder, wore loose, brown shirts and calf-length breeks, their officers in blue jackets. Many were bearded, tattoos showed on wrists and necks even of the women among them, who like the men wore their hair blunt cut at the earlobe. The group varied in size, physique, complexion, and all shades of white skin. Marley, the one black man, stood out both for his colour and height.

The farmers and their wives formed a loose group on the north side. The men and their sons were generally lean and work-hardened, most of them fair or red-haired. Their wives and daughters wore smocked blouses and full, calf-length homespun skirts, their hair tied, braided, or coiled to be both practical and to express their varied looks and personalities. Women and the older girls of the Home, who held themselves apart on the south side of the hall, wore grey, long-sleeved, ankle-length dresses, all of the same severe cut. Most of the girls were slim and willowy; they wore their hair loose, simply tied to fall down their backs. Where the individuality of the sailors and farmers was easy to see, most of the girls and women seemed to be striving for anonymity. The faces of both young and old were all pale, in contrast to the sailors and farmers, whose skin was weathered from their outdoor lives.

The sound of many conversations blended into background noise that rose up and was lost among the dark beams of the ceiling two stories above their heads. Halfway up the back wall was a narrow balcony where some of the older children watched covertly, only their heads showing over its carved wooden railing. Mairi glanced upwards and saw Ellie, her green eyes wide with concentration on Astreya and Lindey as they made their way through the crowd to the raised platform at one end of the hall. Their pace was slow, acknowledging as they went the looks and nods of the women and men who served in the fleet or ashore. Most people were silent, but as Trogen and Mairi followed a few paces behind their parents, they heard scraps of conversation among the sailors making way for the Grand Master.

"... the Old Man can't a'been hurt too bad..."

"... back on his feet, anyway..."

"... wi' a stiffener o' poteen, t' keep him goin'."

"... See his stick? An 'Lindey's makin' sure he don't stagger. 'E's hurt bad, he is."

"What's Walt doin' up there wi' the mucky-mucks?"

"Whatcher think about 'im for master o' the little schooner?"

"All he's got is a ring. Same as Cam, Damon, an' old Betel. He can't work them stones."

"Then that leaves the family, same's usual."

"... odds on Lindey takes over *Cygnus,* an' 'Streya swallows the killick.*"

"'Streya beached? No way."

"... maybe Betel gets the rank, and one of the twins does the work."

"That happens, an' you'll get to wear one o' them bracelets, an' I'll be the next Gran' Master..."

"Yeah. Right. Gran' Master of a pair of dories."

Lindey held Astreya's arm as they climbed two shallow steps and turned to face the solid mass of people. She stepped aside, he steadied himself on his stick, and they stood separately. Mairi and Trogen looked up at them from among the sailors. Astreya began quietly, speaking over a dwindling murmur of voices.

"With your agreement..."

A short, square figure thrust to the front of the dais.

"Belay!"

Walt's bellow produced instant silence. Astreya pressed his lips together, then nodded to the black-haired, squat figure and addressed the hall, his voice soft, but pitched loud enough to be heard by all.

"I'd like to thank all of you for coming at such short notice, especially Ellen, who as Mistress of the Home has graciously allowed us all the use of the hall. Ellen, would you please join us? Healer Catriona, and Janice, too, of course. Drew, our shipwright, you should come forward, and Jeb for the farmers, too, if you please."

Two bearded men stepped forward. Jeb the farmer was a lean, middle-aged man with hands like tree-roots and a face tanned to the colour of old leather; Drew was a heavy-set young man with a fiery red beard that reached down to below his collar and up to blend with curly ginger hair above a snub nose and two vividly blue eyes.

Astreya remained standing, and when the elders were seated, he continued to speak.

"If I may, I will give you a short account of what has happened, and what we propose to do about it. There's been quite a lot of speculation, but the facts are that _Cygnus_ was in an accident involving a small boat that we believe was loaded with some kind of explosive, which blew up, causing considerable damage. _Cygnus_ has a hole in her hull and will need extensive work on her top hamper and bowsprit. That's the sails, masts, and also the pointy thing that sticks out the front of the boat."

A smothered guffaw came from a few of the sailors and shipyard workers; some of the farmers and their wives looked puzzled. Janice glanced at the tight group of white-haired, black-clad older women, who followed her lead in looking prim and patronized.

"Thanks to the good work of all aboard, *Cygnus* came home on her own. Drew tells me that he hopes to have my ship back in service in three months, perhaps less. To help accomplish this, some of *Cygnus'* crew will be working with and for him."

Some sailors nodded, a few looked dubious. Drew glared at the hall, nodding his fiery red-haired head as if challenging anyone to argue. Astreya continued evenly.

"I won't go into all the details, but we believe that there should not be any permanent alterations to how we conduct our trade. We will continue to make good on all our promises to the people with whom we do business, starting with Matris and Charton. We're going to use the new two-masted schooner, which Drew assures me will make up in speed what she lacks in cargo space. She'll sail in cooperation with *Elusive* until *Cygnus* is repaired."

Astreya paused for the murmur that followed, but before people could become too involved in discussion, he raised one hand and spoke into near-silence.

"I know you all have work that this meeting has interrupted, but before you go, I want to invite everyone to celebrate the naming of the new schooner, tomorrow evening. Listen for bells ringing afloat and ashore. There should be a good view from the ramparts, and some of you who have small craft may want to watch from the water. When a short ceremony is over, *Cygnus* and *Elusive* will host a celebration at the shipyard in honour of all those who worked to build the addition to the fleet. The new schooner will be named by Mairi, who will take command. Trogen will be navigator. The rest of the crew will be notified as and when they are chosen. Thank you all for coming."

8. In which Mairi receives her sailing orders

Mairi stood dumbfounded. She stared up at her father, her mouth half-open. There was complete silence for several heartbeats, and then the people who had surrounded her drew back. Her hearing became unusually acute, and she heard what seemed to her an inventory of her own misgivings.

"... a girl!..."

"... be a dry day on the ocean floor when I serve under a woman."

"... take a look at Walt. He ain't happy..."

"... expectin' he would get the nod, wi' Trogen fer navigator..."

"... it's that Lindey, pulling strings..."

"... can't see any way that was by vote..."

"... sure it was. Like, 'Streya decided an' they all voted to agree."

Mairi did not see Walt scowling at Astreya's back as he and Lindey left the hall by a side door, nor did she notice Trogen standing while the hall emptied around him. She felt someone pluck her sleeve and looked down Catriona's heart-shaped face.

"Mairi, congratulations. Now you're to come with us."

Mairi blinked, frowned, and followed the diminutive, dark-haired figure who seemed to glide across the floor, her feet invisible under her long blue dress. Mairi heard the side door close behind her, shutting off the sounds of people who were still leaving the hall by the main entrance. Ahead of her, she saw Lindey put her arm around Astreya's waist. Now that they were almost alone, he transferred his stick to his other hand and accepted her help. Mairi hesitated, wondering if she should go to Astreya's other side, but before she could move, Catriona darted past her to put a hand under Astreya's elbow, and the three led the way toward the Home's guest cottage, only a stone's throw from the hall. For a moment, Mairi felt excluded, until she heard Dabih's voice behind her.

"We'll talk among ourselves. Just the family. Easier on 'Streya."

Mairi blinked. Dabih, Master of *Elusive* and son of Catriona, who had always seemed distant and withdrawn, had just spoken to her as if she were his equal. He shepherded her towards a single chair arranged to face four others. Directly opposite her, Astreya sighed as he sank into the largest, and allowed Catriona to position a stool under his feet.

"You know, the last time I was in this cottage..." he began.

"We were all still finding out how we were connected," said Catriona as she sat beside Dabih.

And now, Mairi continued in her mind, *Catriona is looking after Astreya, whose adventures two decades ago reunited her with her son.*

Mairi looked around the familiar faces. As their next generation, she was outside their bond, knowing only the history of events through which they had lived.

"Sit, Mairi, we've got a lot to tell you," said Lindey.

Mairi sat, her back to the window, and looked at the half-circle of her relatives, who stared back at her.

"And I'm sorry to say that there'll be much you have to find out for yourself," said Astreya.

"Will you stop terrifying her, both of you," said Catriona. "It's really quite simple. You've got a promotion, a ship, and a crew."

"There's also the matter of specific objectives..." Lindey began.

"... in the context of the general principles that guide our enterprise, which are..." Astreya cut in, and then paused expectantly in mid-sentence.

With four pairs of eyes on her, Mairi responded mechanically with words she had learned as a child.

"Trade fairly, encourage knowledge, and avoid entanglements."

"Exactly," said Lindey.

"Buy and sell goods, tools, and books; but don't mess with the way the lubbers live," added Dabih.

"And?" Catriona asked.

Mairi looked at her, puzzled.

"Never reveal the secrets of the stones," Catriona prompted.

"She knows that, Cat," said Lindey. "She didn't mention it, because she knows you're the only one here who hasn't got one."

"By my choice," said Catriona.

"You're the only person without one who fully understands their history and significance," said Astreya.

Mairi frowned.

"What about Walt, Cam, Damon?"

"Ring stones," said Dabih.

"You've given clasps to Trogen, Seren and even Ellie, as well as me," said Mairi.

"They're not yet ready for a full understanding," said Astreya.

"You are," said Lindey.

"To know what?" Mairi demanded, surprising herself with her own vehemence. "And why me?" she added.

Catriona's thumb tucked a strand of her long black hair into place behind one ear. It was an unconscious gesture that was her prelude to speech, and it was both familiar and heartening to Mairi.

"You're ready because you can stand up to the four of us and ask sensible questions when we're waffling about trying to find a way of telling you what's what. The fact is, Mairi, there are only three shipstones and seven clasps left."

"There were more," said Lindey. "Cam had a bag of them..."

"Cam? Then why...?"

"Some of them were duds," said Dabih. "Even 'Streya couldn't light them."

"And we wasted one finding out how to waterproof them all," said Catriona.

"Then why give the last one to Ellie?" Mari asked.

"We didn't," said Astreya. "We were about to give her one of the ring-stones when she lit up the last clasp herself."

"We'd given ourselves headaches trying," said Lindey, "but we only raised the smallest flicker. Just enough to stop us from flinging the thing over the side. Then in came your daughter, Dabih, and we all looked like fools when she made it light up brighter than a shipstone, and then asked whether there were any more."

"Then she knows, too," said Mairi.

"Yes," said Astreya. "We had to tell her."

"Then why isn't she here today?"

"Because she isn't in command of a ship, and you are," said Lindey.

"And because of Mirak," said Dabih.

"Who's Mirak?"

"First mate of *Cygnus* when I was aboard," said Astreya, pressing his lips together lest he say more.

"Nasty, duplicitous, double-dealing scoundrel," said Lindey. "I should have hit him harder."

"We all thought he was dead," said Dabih. "But now he ..."

"... or someone he's talked to..." Lindey inserted.

" ... is after our stones. It's the only explanation we can find for the attack on *Cygnus*," said Dabih.

"But we're not entirely certain," Astreya added softly.

"It's our working assumption," said Lindey. "Along with the uncomfortable fact that he knows the stones can be used by people who aren't of Zubin's line."

"Such as you, Mother," said Mairi. Lindey nodded.

"And that's why we're sending you and the little schooner to where we think he isn't likely to look for people with clasps. People he might try to control," said Catriona.

"And more particularly we're entrusting you with the last shipstone," Dabih added.

Mairi nodded, speechless. To be mistress of her own ship was breathtaking, but to have charge of a shipstone was to be responsible for one of the three invaluable stones of power. Her little *Cygnet* would be able to communicate with the great ships *Elusive* and *Cygnus* and like them, navigate where compasses failed.

Astreya produced a leather-covered book and handed it to her. She opened to the first page and saw words written in Astreya's distinctive hand.

"Read it out loud," said Lindey.

"Log of the Schooner—the name is left blank—Mistress: Mairi, daughter of Lindey and Astreya."

"I thought it should be 'master'," said Catriona. But Astreya insisted that his great-aunt Meissa always corrected people when they called her 'master'. And since your shipstone is the very one she worked when she was mas... mistress of *Silver Swan,* it seemed appropriate."

Mairi turned the page. She frowned at a list of names. "What's wrong, Mairi?" Lindey asked.

"It's usual ... I would have expected ..."

"To choose your own crew," supplied Astreya. He paused, pressing his lips together, and then continued deliberately. "You're right. But your crew is part of the reason for your command."

Mairi turned three pages quickly and spoke without thinking.

"As nursemaid to Ellie, Neil, and the lad Peter from Charton? They're all underage."

"As both you and Trogen were when you became crew members aboard *Cygnus* and *Elusive*," said Lindey.

"More importantly, they are all capable of wielding shipstones, if we had any more. Read on, Mairi," said Astreya.

When Mairi read Trogen's name she knew she would have to deal with his resentment and possibly hostility. She turned the page, and surprise replaced concern.

"Why Marley?" she asked. "He's an experienced seaman, and I'm glad to have him aboard, but ..."

"I promised him passage to the Sunny Isles, where you'll make your first port of call," said Astreya.

"We're to head south? I thought the new schooner would complement *Elusive*—visit the lesser ports, handle the low-weight, high-value cargo, rendezvous and off-load when..."

Mairi's voice trailed off.

"We're overdue to visit Three Mountain Island," said Astreya. "Besides, an open-ocean voyage makes for a good shakedown for a new crew."

"A test?" Mairi asked.

"A confirmation," said Catriona.

Mairi looked up in time to catch subtle expressions of agreement. She looked back down at a page she had turned too quickly, and her mood brightened.

"Seren! That's good. I'd have picked her. And Cam, too! How did he take to being shipped out under the command of the girl who used to sit on his knee?"

"He said he'd scuttle the little schooner unless he was aboard. 'There ain't no way yer lettin' Mairi go off on her own wi'out someone to keep the boys in line an' the girls from gigglin'.'"

Lindey's imitation of Cam's outspoken style drew smiles.

"Right at this moment, he's probably informing your crew about their good fortune," said Catriona.

Mairi looked from face to face.

They're waiting for me to say something.

She stood up.

"I accept the command and the responsibilities it involves."

There was a moment when her formal words seemed to hang in the air. Then Mairi was blinking back tears of amazement as Catriona clapped her hands, Lindey's arms were around her, Astreya was levering himself to his feet, one hand reaching for hers, and Dabih was patting her back. They all laughed, and as suddenly as they had embraced her, they disengaged, stepped back and stood smiling. Curiously, though they were distanced from her by their varied experience, as well as age, position, and tradition, Mairi felt part of them as never before.

Then Lindey spoke as if nothing of consequence had been said or done.

"Becky knows as well, so when you're ready, we'll all go and see what she has cooked up for supper."

9. In which Trogen, Damon, and Cam drink beer

Trogen stood in the hall, staring at nothing, unaware of the people who walked around him, talking in pairs or groups about what they had heard. When he realized that he was almost alone, Trogen shook his head, strode out of the Home, climbed up and over the rampart, and down to the water's edge. After looking gloomily at the little schooner moored near the shipyard, he walked along the pebble beach, stopping every few steps to throw stones into the sea.

He skipped a stone so hard that he felt his shoulder twinge, looked up from counting the splashes, and saw the two mates in a rowing skiff, on their way back to *Elusive*. Though he could not hear their words, Trogen knew that Cam was heckling Damon, as he did whenever they were together. This happened rarely because Cam had the starboard watch on *Cygnus*, and Damon the port on *Elusive*. The two were like uncles to Trogen, even though, and perhaps because, they were not related either to him or to anyone else at Matris. Trogen waved at them.

Damon held water, both blades invisible below the ripples. They bent their heads together and spoke too softly for Trogen to hear. He was about to turn and walk away, when they beckoned, and turned their little rowboat towards the shipyard. He jogged along the waterline to the road that led around the mudbanks and on to the shipyard, meeting them as they pulled their boat beyond the tideline. When they had turned it over and stowed the oars underneath, Damon looked down at Trogen, and Cam looked up at him, and they both grinned.

"Beer," said Damon.

"Finest kind," said Cam. "Me private stock. Even Walt says it's right some good."

They walked up the shore road to Cam's ramshackle house. An old sailor who made the tent-like building had lived in it until he was well past a century old. When he died, Cam took it over for himself and a constantly changing crew of boys—and some girls—who had become fed up with their parents, or the farm where they had been brought up, or the school at the Home. In the winter months, Cam prepared them for life afloat, teaching them about wind, stars, knots, and generally how to look after themselves at sea. He also took them rowing or sailing in the bay in all kinds of weather, got them soaking wet and cold, showed them how to sort themselves out afterward, and somehow transformed the experience into the greatest game imaginable.

Cam led the way into the kitchen, where he poured mugs of beer, and then shooed them out the back door onto a hillock from which they could look down onto the little lake just west of the Home. They sat around a fire pit in chairs made by the boys and girls who had survived CHAOS—Cam's Hero Academy of Seamanship. Trogen sat in the one he had constructed out of barrel-staves and discarded ends of hawser-weight rope.

When they had taken a couple of swigs to make sure that it was indeed from the best barrel, Cam looked at Damon and nodded, Damon looked back at him and stroked his moustache. Then they both looked at Trogen. Cam began.

"Right, Trogen, listen, and then belt up, 'cause we never told you nothin'. Got that?"

Trogen nodded. Cam paused to swig, and Damon took over.

"Now that you know that the only thing the three of us talked about today was the excellence of Cam's beer, let me inform you of what little we know. Firstly, in temporal terms, comes the..."

"Great smoking rope-ends, Damon. We all know yer an eddy-cated man, but give it a rest, will yer? The lad needs to know stuff today, an' before the sun sets."

Damon preened his moustache, unabashed.

"Trogen, we are going to enlighten you about the meeting aboard *Elusive* during which you were pacing the deck above us."

"The one Walt stopped me and Mairi from attending."

"The one Damon an' me almost didn't get to," said Cam. "When I saw the launch takin' 'Streya, Lindey, and all the rest of you to *Elusive*, I wasn't goin' t'be left out, so I grabbed a skiff, loaded old Betel aboard, rowed out to the ship, collected Damon, an' then bust in on the weirdest fam'ly gatherin' I've ever been at. Dabih was there, an' so was Cat so's she could look after 'Streya, who was lookin' like death leanin' on a broken oar. Lindey was all calm on the outside but nigh on knackered from bringin' *Cygnus* home jury-rigged and leakin'. An' then there was Walt, all of a sudden so full of hisself and the need to take charge o' everyone, whether they asked for it, wanted it, or needed it. Behavin' like a mother hen, he was."

"Like Lindey and the others, he was exhibiting a totally understandable concern for Astreya," said Damon.

"Exhibitin' a roarin' great determination to have his own way, no matter what, an' doin' it by somehow makin' everyone sound like they was back in the bad old days of the Men of the Sea when nobody dared say boo to a mate, let alone a master. An' Walt was gettin' away wi' it 'cause 'Streya was so busy keepin' himself from lettin' out heart-rendin' groans that he never noticed. So I up an' told 'im what I was thinkin'."

"Trogen, as you have probably noticed over the years, Cam is not what you might call a master of diplomacy and protocol."

"Too right," said Trogen into his beer mug.

Cam ignored the interruption.

"So I said, 'Lindey, did'ja think you could leave us behind? Me an' Betel had to row all by ourselves.' Then I think I said summat to Dabih about it bein' nice to be aboard his ship. I was mostly polite, 'cause I was some upset at how serious bad Astreya was lookin'."

"And then old Betel weighed in with a formal report," said Damon. "It was as if Cam hadn't said a word. You'd think he was deaf as well as half-blind. Sonorous and laconic. Let me demonstrate."

Damon cupped his hands around his mouth and spoke as low as he could.

"Grand Master, *Cygnus* is secure as is possible. Pumped dry, resting on an even keel, her mainstay rough-spliced, bearing the strain."

Cam endorsed the performance with a grin and continued his account.

"So then, Lindey, all wound up tighter than cable on a capstan, made a little formal speech about how she'd never have been able to bring *Cygnus* home wi'out old Betel, like Mairi hadn't been there, doin' just about everyone's job as well as her own."

"At which point, Cam, who as you may have noticed, is somewhat more forward with his opinions than most, really stuck his oar in."

"All I did was ask, real polite, 'What is it with you people? It's not like the whole crew was sittin' in on this here meetin'. Yer callin' each other Master this, an' Navigator that, like we ain't been livin' an' workin' together fer long enough that some of you has children what are all grown up an' older than we was when we all first went adventurin' t'gether. An' then I asked, by the bye, where was those young ones, meanin' you an' Mairi."

"And then Astreya gave him that green-eyed stare of his," said Damon.

"You know the look, Trogen, when he presses his lips together like he was concentratin' on stopping himself from chewing you up and spittin' out the bits"

Trogen nodded, and Cam pressed on.

"So then I said, 'Don't look at me like that, 'Streya. It's 'cause they're yours, ain't it? Yer thinkin,' 'not in front of the children,' ain'tcha?' And then 'Streya said, 'That's enough, Cam.' But I don't think his heart was in it. Or maybe it was just that he could barely listen without pitchin' face down on the table. So I said, 'No it ain't, 'Streya.' And then I kind'a ran on a bit about how I remember when him an' me was growin' up in the Village, cuttin' bait an' rackin' cod t' dry, an' all of it a very long time afore he got to be Grand Master."

"Cam rattled on until Astreya laughed, coughed, and then looked as if someone had stabbed him. We all were wondering why Cat or Lindey didn't stop the meeting. That's when Walt confessed."

"S'right. He said he was the one what told you and Mairi you wasn't wanted."

"That's when I asked Walt why in the flamin' blazes he did that, an' he said he had a feelin' you two shouldn't hear what Lindey, Betel, an' Damon had to say."

"For goodness' sake! What was it, then?" Trogen demanded.

"All in good time, Trog. There's stuff you gotta hear first," said Cam.

"So then Lindey gave a clear, concise, and seamanlike account of the explosion and the voyage back to Matris," said Damon.

Trogen fidgeted in his chair.

"More beer, Trogen?"

Trogen nodded, and while Cam was fetching another jug, Damon recounted what he had heard about how *Cygnus* had been holed and Astreya harpooned by a splinter from the bowsprit.

Cam started talking as he came back with the beer.

"Now then, let me tell you what I said when Lindey was done wi' her strictly-the-unvarnished-facts story. My piece wasn't so much about what happened, but some of the how and why. It was like this. When I went over the side to inspect the damage and clear away anything that might a' been left hangin' under our forefoot, I was wonderin' how one small single-masted skipjack could have done that much damage. Until I smelled somethin' what reminded me o' black powder but wasn't. Right then I knew. We wasn't just collided with. We was blown up. An' it weren't no accident."

"Do you know what your mother said, Trogen?" Damon added. "'Irrational. Unreasonable.' And then she asked why anyone would do such a thing."

"An' then Damon here explained the bleeding obvious about the envy and jealousy some folks have for what we do. He spoke his piece right nice, not at all the way I'd have done it. The words came out of him like you could write them down in ink an' never have to cross anything out."

"Yes, well, before I could become too smug and self-satisfied with my penetrating analysis of the historical record, Walt asked Betel to speak."

"An' that were some disturbin', let me tell you. So now, Damon, do your imitation of Betel again."

Damon caught not only Betel's deep voice, but also the hesitant, staccato way the old sailor talked, like a man plucking out a tune in single notes on an aged fiddle.

"I'll try. Here goes: 'Twas in Glassport. Last visit. Heard his voice. Drinking in a tavern. Near to dark. Candles on tables. Single lantern overhead. Doubt he saw me. 'Twas Mirak.'"

"So then 'Streya an' Lindey both said, 'He's dead.' But then Damon an' me remembered we'd never seen Mirak's body, although it were what Damon here would call a 'reasonable supposition' that one man on a skimmer way up north wouldn't make it very far before he was feedin' the fishes."

"Mirak," said Trogen. "Mate of *Elusive* under Mufrid?"

"Nah. Don't cha know yer own fam'ly history? Mirak was— maybe is—the two-faced, double-crossing, traitorous spawn of a dogfish that near to killed 'Streya more'n once, back when your da was learnin' how to work the stones from his grand-da Oron aboard *Cygnus*. Get it straight in your mind: we're talking Mirak, now. Not yer not-so-distant relative Mufrid, who was the pirate yer ma and da ... um ... well ... permanently discharged from duty."

"That would be the Mufrid whose head my fa... Astreya blew up."

"That's the one. An' it weren't exactly blown up. But when they all did whatever it is they do with their stones, he was just ... well ..."

"Dead," said Damon.

"'Streya had help from Lindey an' Dabih, an' there were two shipstones aboard, an'..."

"I've heard a ... a more colourful version," said Trogen. "So you think Mirak blew up *Cygnus*. Why?"

"Jealousy."

"It's a whole lot more'n that, Damon. That man's more twisted than a braided four-strand hawser. He's after power. He's seen a lot of it, back when he was executioner for Oron..."

"Executioner?

"They didn't tell you that part, did they, Trogen? Mirak was the one what tied men's hands and pushed them over the stern. Liked to watch them drown, I'm told. If he'd taken a scunner to someone in the crew, he'd make a case against him, Oron would condemn him, and then Mirak would do him in."

"The man is a definition of ruthlessness."

"You got that right, Damon. He used people. And he had the trick of makin' it seem like he was righteous. He used 'Dramin 'til wicked old Mufrid cut his finger off and left him to bleed to death. Mirak saw him drippin' blood onto the deck an' walked away. It was Walt what saved 'Dramin to die another day and way that still ain't all that clear."

"Leaving that on one side, the point is, Trogen, that Mirak wants what we have. He's after the stones. And our ships. The fleet. The power that comes with trading among the ports we visit. And he especially wants Astreya to suffer."

"Why?"

"'Cause Astreya let him go."

"I'd have thought that ..."

"Yeah, Trogen," said Cam. "If Mirak was a decent man, he'd 'a been grateful. But because he's a devious, treacherous, schemin' bottom-feeder, he hates it that Astreya didn't hate him back."

"One of the very few times I have ever disagreed with Astreya," said Damon. "Mirak should have been killed."

"So, Cam, what is Father ... the master ... Astreya ... going to do about it ... um ... him?"

"Dunno. 'Cause in the meetin' just before we were goin' to get into that part, 'Streya kinda' swayed, an' then Lindey caught him from one side, an' Cat from the other, an' the two of them said 'Later' in the kind of way that nobody could argue with, not even me."

All three were silent, each pursuing his own thoughts.

"*Elusive* alone cannot accomplish everything that she and *Cygnus* did together," said Damon.

"We got the new two-masted schooner near ready to go," said Cam.

Trogen took a deep breath to rant about the unfairness of Mairi getting command, but fearing lest he be pitied, he refocussed his mind on practicalities.

"There are several ways to keep the enterprise going. Changing the order and timing of when we visit our ports of call; having *Elusive* make the southern run and then off-load lighter, more compact cargo onto the little schooner, and then..."

"Right you are, Trogen, but that's simple compared to knowing who does what if 'Streya's in no shape to continue as Grand Master."

All three silently considered what might happen to the chain of command if Astreya was no longer leading the ships and the enterprise he and Lindey had created. Even if his condition was only temporary, they knew that friendships would be strained, traditions broken, family ties wrenched. But none of them could voice their shared thought that Astreya's wound might be fatal.

"Well now, Trogen," said Cam. "History lesson's over. More beer?"

Trogen tipped his mug back and swallowed repeatedly, then held it out for more.

"Easy, Trogen. We got summat else to say. Mebbe Walt told yer, but if so, here it is again. 'Streya says you're to be sure that you get or make copies of the rutters and charts of the coast, 'specially all the way south to the Sunny Isles, an' t' keep yer trap shut about it. So don't tie one so bad that you're cross-eyed tomorrow."

Trogen groaned. Cam and Damon glanced at each other and made commiserative noise.

10. In which Cygnet undergoes sea trials

Mairi stood on the stern deck of the new two-masted schooner, feeling the pride and anxiety of her first command. Two days before, she had been invited to stand between Astreya and Dabih to be proclaimed master, and then to give the schooner the name she had chosen: *Cygnet*. The celebration had been well fuelled with food and beer. Someone from *Elusive* had soon nicknamed her ship *Baby Duck*, and her crew was ruefully accepting their inevitable fate of being called the Cygnets.

There was a condescending quality to the looks and comments from the other sailors, a sense that at less than half the length of the great ships, *Cygnet* was a children's plaything, sleek and pretty, but not a serious addition to the fleet. Mairi had heard dismissive remarks about her little ship's seaworthyness in anything more than light airs, glum predictions that the cockpit would ship more water than its drains could handle, and disparaging contrasts between the expansive topside spaces of the great ships and *Cygnet's* sleek, trim decks. Clearly, they all believed that *Cygnet* was not an adequate replacement for *Cygnus*.

When Astreya left the dockyard, exhausted by having to stand for so long, the crowd soon thinned down to the serious drinkers. Lanterns on the wharf edge gleamed on *Cygnet's* new varnish and threw long wiggling lines of light on the water. Finally, Drew's shipbuilders extinguished all but the lamp above the last barrel of ale where Trogen stood, leaned and sat with the last of the drinkers, all of them determined to see it empty.

One by one, *Cygnet's* crew climbed aboard, settled into their new quarters and rolled into their bunks. Astern, in the little schooner's tiny version of a master's cabin, Mairi felt her ship bob and sway as Trogen climbed unsteadily down the companionway. She heard him swear as he bumped into something in the dark, a muttered complaint from Cam, and then soft snoring. Inhaling the faint scent of new varnish and lulled almost imperceptible sounds of ripples lapping against the ship's hull only a handspan from her pillow, Mairi slept.

She woke early, mindful that she faced sea trials that would evaluate the performance of both the schooner and her ability to command. She had walked, climbed, and crawled in and over her ship, studied Drew's plans, felt the quality of her new sails, rigging and cordage, overseen the placement of goods in the forward hold, assigned berths in the cabin, done everything she could imagine short of taking her ship out to sea. Now that it was time for *Cygnet's* maiden voyage, Mairi was poised between childish delight at a new toy, and trepidation lest she break it.

When she reached the deck, the morning wind was strengthening. The sun had risen above a distant bank of sea mist and was lighting the undersides of little white cloudlets rolling out of the west. A halyard tapped against the mainmast, and then two more rattled at the foremast. *Cygnet* moved subtly, nudging her fenders against the dock. Mairi put one hand on the wheel as if feeling the schooner's pulse.

The night had seemed too short for everyone, but when Cam had roused the crew and put mugs of coffee in their hands, they climbed up the companionway, awake and eager for their first sail together. All of them had been kitted out with new shore-going clothes that they had worn the night before, but this morning they wore their seagoing gear of loose-fitting shirts and breeks, ready for work.

Seven expectant faces stared at Mairi. She deliberately put aside the fact that she had known all but one of them for years, and instead tried to think of them as a shipmaster. Marley: tall, taciturn, enigmatic but undeniably strong and skilled. Cam, small, wiry, an all-around seaman ever since he was old enough to climb into a dory. Neil, nearly seventeen, trying to get his mouse-coloured hair to grow into a beard, fit and able from six years of seagoing aboard *Elusive*. Peter, barely sixteen but already hard-handed from years of fishing with his father. Green-eyed Ellie, as determined as she was delicate. Seren, Ellie's blue-eyed eldest sister, taller than everyone save Marley. Finally, Trogen, standing apart from the others beside the port stays, scowling. During the ship-naming party, he had stuck close to the beer kegs and had helped drink to the bottom of all of them. Today, he was paying the price.

Cam looked up at her.

"Skipper, we've all got a feelin' we'd like to thank you for yesterday."

"Nice of you, Cam, but the whole show was laid on for us by *Cygnus*, *Elusive*, and the shipyard.

"And Matris. Good eats. That was a mighty fine cake Ellen made. Big, too. But that ain't it. Las' night the party were too busy fer us to be together-like. So there's just one thing to do afore we set off. Most of us know the tradition, but fer Marley an' Peter an' Neil, an' to remind the rest of us, we did aught to confirm yer position as master ... um ... mistress. So, to show we're all willin' to be under Mairi's command, let's all give the traditional salute an' say the words. 'At yer command'."

Without an instant's hesitation, Cam, Seren, and Ellie brought their right fists to below their chins, and after a quick glance at them, so did Peter, Neil, and Marley. Their voices blended as they spoke the words at different speeds and pitches. Trogen's arm came up slowest, his face expressionless, with his the last word falling into silence.

"So there y' are, mistress Mairi. Now you know we're pleased to be Aboard *Cygnet*—nice name that—an' glad t' be under your command."

"Thank you," said Mairi. Feeling a blush start up her neck, she focused on the day to come. "It's a lovely day for a first sail. Favourable wind, good visibility. We'll have the mains'l, fores'l, stays'l and working jib up, and head down the bay on the starboard tack. Marley, I'd like you on the wheel. Cam, will you and Ellie hoist the jib and stays'l, then stand by to slip? Peter, retrieve the fenders. Let go the springs first ..."

Trogen cut her off.

"Peter, get the stoppers off the main. Neil, join Seren on the winch. Look alive."

Ellie's small, sleek, black-haired head tilted to stare up at Trogen. Mairi saw her glance at her sister and roll her eyes.

Mairi sharpened her tone without raising her voice. "Trogen, will you hoist the foresail? Cam ..."

"I don't need help, Mairi.

Trogen ran up the foresail up, belayed the halyards, stepped casually back onto the rail and stood, one arm hooked around the starboard stays, watching the others at work.

"Not like that, Pete, you carrot-haired lubber," said Trogen. "Belay the halyards neat so's they don't tangle. You're not on a sloppy little fish-boat now. Neil, do it for him."

Neil swiftly coiled the slack, passed a bight through the coil, and then hung a neat bundle on the belaying pin. Peter blushed to the roots of his red hair. Trogen continued to hector the crew.

"Now get yourself to the mast and swig on the downhaul. Neil and Seren can't do all the work. Hop to it!"

Red, black and copper-coloured heads rose and fell as Peter, Neil and Seren hauled the throat and peak halyards together.

"Pete! Strain the halyard out from the mast, let Seren catch what you gain, then ... I suppose I'll have to show you. Out of my way, lubber."

Mairi watched, her lips pursed, shocked at Trogen's behaviour. Before she could decide to intervene, Marley spoke beside her.

"An' what'll the course be, Master ... um ... Mistress ... Skipper?"

"See if you can get her heading for the Two Feet. That's the two lumpy headlands on either side of the gap."

"Aye, sir. Um ... Ma'am."

"Mairi, please, Marley. Or if you must, Skipper. There are only eight of us."

"Aye, then ... Skipper."

The mainsail reached the masthead. Ahead, the jib flapped. Mairi coordinated the maneuver.

"Cam! Harden in the jib to port. Ellie, let slip as she draws away from the dock."

"Slip!" Trogen shouted.

"Thank you, Trogen. I think she heard me. Would you sheet in the main as it fills?"

Ignoring Mairi, Trogen left Seren to handle the mainsheet and stood aloof on the rail, leaning on the stays. As her sails began to draw, *Cygnet* came alive. Ripples chuckled under her forefoot, new rigging creaked, the mainsail filled with one soft flap, and the schooner heeled gently to port in the freshening wind.

"May I have you all together astern?"

"Right! Get aft for further orders!" Trogen shouted.

From her position just ahead of Marley, Mairi watched her crew assemble. They clustered in the cockpit ahead of the binnacle and wheel, glancing now at the sails, now at the bubbling wake, now at each other. Seren moved with the competence of experience, as Mairi had expected. Neil was eager to have his expertise noticed. Peter was breathlessly expectant, trying too hard. Ellie's green eyes lingered on Trogen, one slim eyebrow raised. Mairi took a calming breath and ignored her brother. She glanced at Cam, who wore his usual cheerful grin. Heartened, she spoke with what she hoped was confidence.

"Drew and his shipwrights built *Cygnet* for us, so we're going to spend the day making sure everything works the way it should and everybody knows what they're doing. In a little while, we'll be out of the bay and at sea, where there's going to be a bit more wind, and we'll see how she goes. How's she heading, Marley?"

"Should make it through the gap on this tack, Skipper."

"Best check that, Mairi," said Trogen. "The steersman's pinching her. There's no way we'll do it in one tack with this wind."

Mairi saw one of Marley's hands momentarily leave the spokes of the wheel, and quickly grip the wheel again. She frowned, puzzled, and then looked upward. Narrowing her eyes against the bright new sails in the sunshine, she focussed on the tell-tale scraps of wool on the stays. She nodded to Marley, to confirm that *Cygnet* was sailing efficiently—indeed, better than she had anticipated.

"I think you'll find that Marley is right, Trogen," she said evenly. "Viewed from amidships, it's clear we're heading for the gap, full and by."

Instead of joining the crew, Trogen stepped outboard of the foremast shrouds and hung from one hand looking down at the schooner's starboard side, where the red of her anti-fouling paint was now well out of the water.

"Peter ... no, someone who knows what he's doing, Seren, go lookout on the port bow. We're about to run the gap. I've got the starboard side covered. Steady as she goes, steersman. Expect dead air as we go through."

Mairi again pursed her lips. Trogen was abrogating her authority. His orders were unnecessary, his tone arrogant and his glances at her condescending. She bit back hot words she knew would only worsen the situation.

The schooner's sails darkened as she sailed into the shadow cast by headlands that rose twice the height of her masthead. Wet black rock gleamed at the cliff-foot on either side, less than the ship's length away. The schooner slid through the water, her sails shadowed and slack, her hull soundless. Gulls plunged into the air from their nests in the cliff face and wove in circles in the sunlight, high above them. The schooner's bow dipped and rose as it met the long swells of the open sea and lost way against a rising tide. *Cygnet* wallowed, her sails slatting. For anxious moments, Mairi checked and rechecked their speed against the cliff sides. Then the sun backlit first the jib, then the staysail, foresail and the main, and they were no longer in the dark tunnel-like gap.

As they cleared the rocky cliffs, Mairi glanced upwards at a flock of clouds sweeping westward. Upwind, where the wind ruffled the water, she saw a dark patch only just in time to warn her crew.

"Cygnets, hang on!"

The squall hit *Cygnet* while she was still moving slowly. It slapped her down, rolling her port rail under. The tip of the main boom scraped the side of a wave, and water poured over the lip of the cockpit. Her shout had given the crew enough time to hang on to whatever was closest, but Seren and Cam lost their footing, shin-deep in water, and had to grab at the cabin. Neil thrashed about, clutching a handhold on lashings that secured the ship's boat to the foredeck. Mairi saw Trogen twirl in a complete circle, one arm hooked around the starboard shrouds. He almost recovered, but missed his handhold and crossed the precipitous deck in a staggering run. Mairi caught sight of him through the gap between the mainmast and foresail, sliding down the deck, arms and legs flailing. Before she could react, *Cygnet* righted herself. Water sluiced off her decks as she began to convert wind into speed.

"Ellie! Peter!" Mairi screamed.

Two faces appeared over the cabin top. Peter's red curls were plastered to his scalp; Ellie's fine black hair blew free. They were both wide-eyed with shock.

"Here! We're still here!" shrilled Ellie. "But Trogen's overboard!"

She pointed over the port quarter. Before anyone else could react, Cam had thrown an emergency float astern.

"Jibe!" shouted Mairi. "Ellie, hold fast. Just keep pointing at him!"

Ellie instantly became a statue, her whole body a living signpost. The last of the water was still running off *Cygnet's* lee deck and out of the scuppers as Marley twirled the wheel. Neil let fly the jib and shortened the mizzen sheet, Cam and Seren hauled frantically on the mainsheet, recovering enough slack that when the stern passed through the wind's eye, the main boom snapped across a short, safe distance. Ahead, the mizzen jerked from port to starboard with a thud. *Cygnet* scudded towards the cliff walls, her wake foaming. Ellie pivoted like a dancer to keep her arm pointing where she had last seen Trogen. Her concentration drew eyes to her, and on into the water where a dark head appeared momentarily among the waves.

"Where is he, Ellie?"

"There! There!"

Two voices yelled, and Seren's outstretched arm joined Ellie's.

"I see him," said Mairi. "Marley, drop downwind a bit and be ready to luff up beside him. Seren, get ready to pass a line to Trogen; Neil, hang on to Seren's feet."

Seren prepared to slide out of the cockpit to lie on the narrow, wet deck between the low gunwale and the cabin. Cam tied a bowline in a heaving line and handed it to her. Neil crouched in the cockpit, ready to hold her ankles.

"Ready!" Seren shouted.

"Luff!" Mairi ordered, and then added softly, "Don't run him down!"

The mainsail flapped as Marley turned into the wind, forcing *Cygnet* into irons. Sails a-shake, jib streaming to leeward, her bowsprit plunging, *Cygnet* lurched into the wind's eye, losing speed. Mairi glimpsed Trogen, one arm over the float, the other splashing as he turned to face them.

"Now!" Mairi shouted.

Marley swung the wheel, changing *Cygnet's* course just enough to put Trogen fine on the starboard bow. Seren swung her arm and dropped a bight of rope over Trogen's upraised arm. Instantly, he was slung against the ship's side, his legs streaming behind him, unable to haul himself up to the deck. Marley twitched the wheel again, and *Cygnet* leaned into the wind, her scuppers filling with water, drenching Seren to her waist. For a wave and spray-filled moment, the crew of *Cygnet* wondered where Trogen was. Mairi glanced over her shoulder at the nearing cliff face, seeing that another jibing circle would put the little schooner on the rocks.

"We got him! He's inboard!"

Hearing Cam's voice, Mairi did not hesitate.

"Sheet her in!"

Peter hauled the jib-sheet, Marley swung the wheel, and *Cygnet* broke out of irons onto the starboard tack, her sails filling.

Three dripping figures stood in the cockpit. Seren and Neil were flushed with their achievement. Trogen's eyes were downcast.

"Course to steer, Skipper?"

Marley's deep voice held a tone of respect that went beyond deference to rank. Impressed by how smoothly the rescue had been accomplished, his eyes flickered past Trogen, soaked and shamefaced, to Seren standing beside him almost as wet, to Neil, who was entranced by the way Seren's clothes clung to her body. Marley blinked and re-focussed on his steering.

"She'll do nicely on this heading, Marley. Cam, when we're trimmed, would you check to see that nothing came adrift in all the excitement?"

Mairi rolled her left sleeve back so that she could see the green stone on her bracelet, glanced astern at the Two Feet for a bearing, and then shrugged.

"We'll keep her on a reach until we're sure everything and everybody is all of a piece. Trogen, Seren, go below and get into dry gear."

As Cam went forward. Ellie came back into the cockpit, where she consulted her stone as Mairi had done.

"What you did was just the thing, Miz Ellie," said Marley softly.

"S'what Mairi told me t' do," said Ellie.

"An' you did it real fine. Kept us all knowin' where he was. Saved him, likely."

"'Oh, I'm sure Mairi and you knew all along. She had it all planned, didn't she?"

Marley looked steadily at her. Ellie raised one eyebrow. Marley swivelled one hand at the wrist. They nodded at each other and grinned.

A short while later, Trogen and Seren reappeared on deck. Mairi climbed out of the cockpit onto the stern deck where she could look down on her crew.

"Right, Cygnets. I was planning to do a surprise man overboard routine. Thank you, Trogen, for your ... um ... realistic timing. Now we're all dried off and squared away, we have the rest of our sea trials to attend to."

Neil slid into the cockpit below Mairi and held up a dripping arm.

"Skipper, can I shift into dry clothes, too, or will you be wanting me to jump overside so's we can do it all over again?"

Ellie giggled, Peter guffawed, Cam gave a snort of suppressed laughter. Trogen's face coloured; Seren frowned. Ellie looked up at her sister, her green eyes wide. "What a silly man Trogen is!" she whispered.

"Away you go, Neil," said Mairi, keeping her face and voice neutral. "Marley, we'll be sailing in sight of land and by the wind today. The compass is unreliable until we're a couple of days sailing to the south."

As the day progressed, Mairi began to feel wickedly grateful for the frantic activity of Trogen's rescue. Her suggestion that the event had been planned ahead deceived no one, but at a deep level of awareness, all seven of her crew had been taught a lesson. They now knew that they were interdependent aboard their little ship, with *Cygnet* an almost living partner in all they did. Her crew was beginning to work together as a team. The weight of an unknowable future lifted somewhat, allowing Mairi to enjoy the moment-to-moment pleasure of sailing her own command.

Late in the afternoon, after testing the little schooner on all points of sail, with and without topsails and flying jib, they turned homeward. As they approached the coastline, they sighted *Elusive,* her sails lit by the slanting rays of the westering sun as she slid out from between the Two Feet, laden to her marks with goods to be sold, bartered and exchanged. The two ships quickly drew closer on opposite tacks, *Elusive* having the right of way. Mairi gave the order to steer to the big schooner's lee, and then to luff the jib in salute. *Elusive's* jib spilled wind in the expected acknowledgment, but as the two ships passed each other, Mairi heard voices raised in a cheer and was surprised to see the big ship's crew along the lee rail, waving. *Cygnet's* crew stood, waved and cheered in return, none with more enthusiasm than Peter. When he discovered that the others had all returned to whatever they were doing, he blushed furiously.

"Nice to be noticed," said Cam. "That don't happen every day." After a bewildered moment, Peter grinned back, sharing his satisfaction.

When *Cygnet* was back in the long bay, easing along on light airs towards the shipyard, Mairi reviewed the brief excursion. The little schooner had performed beyond her expectations, even with a crew as yet unfamiliar with each other and their ship. She still blamed herself for not having anticipated the shock of meeting the sea wind at the start of the day. However, she also reasoned that her shout had given everyone the instant they needed to clutch something to keep from sliding overboard. They had all performed well throughout the recovery, particularly Marley, whose skill at the wheel was impressive. Trogen's ducking had given her a measure of satisfaction, but she knew that he was still resentful.

When they had secured *Cygnet* to her buoy and come ashore at the shipyard wharf, Lindey was waiting. While the rest of the crew talked eagerly with the shipwrights, Mairi and Lindey started up the hill towards the mansion. They fell into step, their shoulders close.

"Mother, you must be exhausted. The attack, Father injured, the ship holed, a difficult passage home under jury rig, Father not able to oversee the preparations for *Cygnet*'s first voyage ..."

"Enough, Mairi. It's not as if you haven't been busy as well. You stood most of my watches when I was below with Astreya. Betel and you brought *Cygnus* home. So no false modesty, Mairi. You're the logical choice to command."

"... umm .... Thank you, Mother."

A few steps later, Lindey spoke carefully.

"Trogen won't be easily led."

"That I know, Mother," Mairi replied with the same calculated understatement.

Lindey nodded, and they walked on in thoughtful silence until wheels creaked behind them. They stepped off the road to let two huge horses clop past, pulling a lumber wagon loaded with the Cygnets. The driver made as if to stop to pick them up, but Lindey waved him on. When it had passed, and before they could start walking again, Lindey again fixed her level, blue-eyed stare on Mairi.

"Mairi, you didn't push your brother over the side, did you?"

"Mother! Of course not! Who told you he fell in? Marley?"

"Ah ... No. It was Cam." Lindey's tone changed. "Mairi, we haven't told you everything. Astreya knew about the attack on *Cygnus* before it happened. Marley warned us, but your father and I didn't take him seriously. Until then, we thought the stones would be safe aboard *Cygnus* and *Elusive*. But they're not. And neither are you and your crew. It's not just about the stones, it's about those who have the power to use them. Mirak needs a wielder he can control. Someone like..."

"Seren!"

"Or Trogen, or Ellie. Even Peter or Neil. They've got the talent; all they need is a stone with more power than their rings."

"Or me?"

"Not you, Mairi. You would never let him. And that's why you have *Cygnet*. You're the best person for the job, Mairi. Know that."

She patted Mairi's cheek and abruptly changed the subject.

"In case you hadn't noticed the wagonload of people that passed us a little while ago, Becky's prepared the Cygnets a farewell feast. I'm telling you ahead of time so that you can be suitably surprised and grateful."

11. In which Becky hosts a party for Cygnet's crew

After her quiet walk with Lindey, Mairi was overwhelmed by the crowd around the big table in Becky's kitchen. Lindey and Catriona flanked Astreya, who still clung to his stick. Mairi saw Walt's broad figure push Trogen and Drew against a wall to make way for Astreya to be the first to sit at the table, around which Seren's younger sisters were still setting places. The double doors to the adjoining room opened, admitting Seren and Marley, carrying chairs. At the far end of the kitchen where the wood stove radiated heat, Mairi could see Becky stirring one of many pots. Strawberry curls had escaped the knot at the back of her head and were clinging to her neck. Mairi took a step towards her, thinking to help, but was stopped by Cam.

"Don't 'cha dare, Skipper. Me an' Becky's got it all under control. You sit right here in the chair what Marley's brung yer. Now then, Master Dabih, would it please you to carve the roast what yer missus Becky has just pulled out of the oven. Peter! Neil! Where have you two got to? We need more wood for the stove. Hop to it, but don't get in Becky's way. When yer done, I want you sittin' next to me at the table where I can keep an eye on the both of yez. All you other folks, sit yerselves down. You, Marley, right here beside Mairi."

The room full of people resolved itself into two ranks down the sides of the big table, with Astreya in a chair at one end with Lindey and Catriona on either side of him. At the other end, Becky stood ready with pots of potatoes and vegetables. A mouth-watering aroma of roast beef floated around the room.

Mairi stood behind her chair and scanned the room. To her left, Marley was talking to Drew about schooner design. Seren stood next to Mairi, talking to Ellie. Though she was seventeen, Seren looked like a woman in her early twenties and behaved with the maturity earned from being the oldest sibling. Her hair, usually plaited tight to her head, framed her face in a halo of shiny, russet curls. At half her height, Ellie was fearless, outspoken and self-assured. Her small body and delicate features made most people instinctively want to protect her, none more fiercely than her sister Seren. Mairi noticed that as Dabih waited to carve the roast, his eyes were resting fondly on his two eldest daughters.

Across the table, Peter gazed steadily at Ellie. The gangly, red-haired sixteen-year-old from Teenmouth was about to make his first blue-water voyage. He was strong, capable and determined to show that he was the equal of any of the young men of Matris. He, too, was under Ellie's spell.

Neil glanced anxiously around the room from under black, unruly hair as if he expected someone to point at him and laugh. Across the table from Mairi, Cam made room to sit between the two boys. Trogen stepped around him and sat next to Walt, whose earlier officiousness seemed much subdued. They bent their heads together, talking quietly. Little Lena cannoned into Mairi's knee before being grabbed by her sister Seren, cautioned, and sent on her way. Mairi watched the interaction affectionately and smiled at Seren. A soft green dress set off the bright gold glints in her hair, giving her a grace usually concealed by the neutral sea-going clothes she wore aboard ship. Mairi wished she was not still in her shapeless shirt and breeks. Seren's clear blue eyes met hers.

"I'm glad to be a member of your crew," said Seren formally, then looked down and murmured, "though I wonder why I was chosen."

Mairi stared in surprise at her cousin's diffidence, which was at odds with her usual air of competence.

"You're a navigator, a healer, and an outstanding sailor."

"Outstanding, as in tall for a girl," said Seren.

"Don't say that, Seren. You did your time before the mast, same as we all did, and you did it well. You climbed the rank ladder faster than I did. You had your clasp at sixteen. You're a healer, and Cat says you're a good one."

"An apprentice. A helper. A second mate."

"So's Trogen. Until very recently, so was I. That's because there are only two big ships and the system's top-heavy with men and women more than twice our age."

"So how come more of them aren't aboard *Cygnet*?"

"We've got Cam and Marley."

Seren's blue eyes strayed from Mairi's to Marley, who was listening respectfully to Dabih.

"You needed two tall hands in your crew, then," said Seren, her eyes still on Marley.

Mairi patted Seren's arm and smiled up at her. "I like your dress, Seren. Suits you."

Seren blushed to the roots of her curls. They both sat down and soon became part of a chain of hands passing loaded plates. Mairi fumbled with the plate Seren was passing, then they looked up and grinned at each other, a minor disaster averted. Mairi turned to pass the plate to her left and found herself looking into Marley's dark eyes.

"Miz Mairi, my congratulations."

"Thank you," said Mairi.

He took the plate from her, passed it on to Drew. For a moment, she was looking at black ropes of hair, held by a leather strip at the back of his neck. They swung across his shoulders as he turned to her, his deep voice rumbling.

"May I also say, I'm happy to be under your command."

"I'm glad you're aboard, Marley."

His teeth flashed in a smile, but Mairi was once again occupied as more plates made their way along the table. When the last meal reached its destination, everyone began to eat. For a while, there was silence punctuated by murmurs of appreciation. Then as the edge of hunger was dulled and people began to talk, Mairi heard snatches of conversation.

Mairi saw Trogen still talking with Walt, and in a fleeting quiet moment heard a fragment of what her brother was saying.

"...but don't ask me why we have Neil and Peter aboard."

Mairi did not hear what Cam whispered to Peter and Neil, both of whom had heard Trogen's remark. Marley's fork paused in mid-air for an instant, and Mairi guessed that he, too, had heard. She turned her attention back to her plate, embarrassed for her brother's tactlessness. Then individual voices were lost in general conversation as once again plates were passed up and down the table, this time for second helpings. Eventually, as Seren and her sisters started to clear away, Lena, the next to youngest, looked curiously at Marley's hair.

"Does your hair grow in thick bits by itself?"

"Lena!" Seren admonished.

"Not exactly," said Marley. "It's just that it's much curlier than yours..."

"Curlier even more than Seren's?"

"Much more. Curly so it curls around itself and then locks up tight—like a rope."

"Does it have to be that way?"

"Well, I could shave it all off to fuzz, but then my head would be cold in the winter."

"Wow."

"Lena," said Mairi, but the little girl was gone. "Um ... Marley ... she didn't mean to ..."

"She's curious, that's all. I'm guessing that you don't have too many black folks around here."

"You're probably the only one within more than a week's sailing."

"I figured that might be so."

Across the table, Trogen scowled in their direction. Then the plate-passing chain began again, and the smell of cinnamon and apples wafted around the table. Talk came a distant second to eating.

Eventually, the table was cleared for the last time. Mairi was about to help with the washing up, but Becky's hands on her shoulders pushed her gently down.

"Not anymore, Skipper Mairi. Rank has its privileges."

Mairi sat back down and looked around the room. With the feasting over, the party had fragmented. The older generation moved to the adjoining room, except for Cam, who was directing the clearing and dishwashing. Where Astreya had been sitting, Mairi's crew were playing a game involving coloured stones that rattled and clicked when slapped onto the table. Noticing that Marley was watching with a puzzled expression, Mairi explained.

"It's called the Game of Stones. Or the Lying Pebbles, or the Bag o' Rocks, and sometimes Reef or Die, although properly speaking that's the way you challenge."

"New to me."

"It goes back to the Wandering—when the great ships stayed at sea for a century and more."

One of Marley's eyebrows rose.

"I've heard that story."

"Not a story. Once there were a dozen great ships. *Cygnus* and *Elusive* are all that's left."

Marley nodded, and tactfully changed the subject.

"About the game they're playing: are there teams, or what?"

"It's a tournament. Everyone plays at least one game, and the winners face each other until there's a champion. It looks as if Neil and Peter have already been eliminated."

Trogen and Seren were hunched over opposite sides of the table, a miniature wooden bucket between them. Neil, Peter, Ellie, and Lena peered over their shoulders as coloured stones rattled and thudded onto the table.

"How is it played?"

"There are twenty-four stones in six colours: red, orange, yellow, green, blue and purple. Just say 'Reef or you're going bare poles,' and you'll remember."

"The colours of the rainbow."

"Precisely. Purple stones have a value of one, blues are two, greens are three, and so on up to reds, which are worth six. The players take four stones each from the bucket and try to conceal what they've drawn. The first player puts down a stone or stones that he hopes will be more useful to his final count than they will be for his opponent. Then he takes a replacement stone or stones from the bucket. They take turns to lay down a stone or stones, or they can stand pat, or draw one or two more. They have to play or discard the same number as they draw. This goes on until one person declares what he hopes will be a winning score when what's in his hand joins what they've both played. Then the other either gives up or if he thinks it's a bluff, he calls. It there's a call, they both have to spread out the stones in their hands and count their scores."

"What's a win?"

"It depends on which game they're playing. Children just add up the stones by value. In the grown-up game, points are doubled for a run of three or more of the colours, which makes for a longer game and more guesswork about who has what."

Marley watched gravely while stones rattled and clicked and the onlookers commented. Trogen played with his right hand and held his stones at table height in his left fist, checking by peeking through his fingers. Seren drew and discarded with her left hand, with her stones on the table under her cupped right hand.

Trogen drew a stone, discarded, and grinned. "Orange, yellow, green, twice!"

"Lucky man," said Seren, as they slapped hands. "Now you face Ellie."

"The smallest member of our crew," observed Marley.

"And the youngest," said Mairi.

Ellie took her place opposite Trogen. She shook her long black hair so that it rippled down her back, widened her green eyes innocently, then raised her chin and peered at him through slitted lids.

"Reef or die, Trogen."

"That's the cut-throat game," Mairi whispered to Marley. "In Reef or Die, the discards are open—they don't go back into the pot, and they can be used to complete a run or make a run twice, which is then doubled again."

Trogen nodded and rattled the bucket. "Challenger draws."

They both drew, their faces expressionless. As in the previous game, Trogen held the stones in his left hand and slapped his discards onto the table with an open-handed crack. Ellie hid what she had drawn under one small hand laid flat on the table. When it came time for her to play, she flicked the stones across the board to strike the bucket just hard enough that they bounced back by a finger's width.

At his second draw, the muscles around Trogen's eyes relaxed slightly. But when Ellie's discards slid across the table, his eyebrows rose for an instant. At her third draw and discard, he rattled the stones in his hand. Ellie watched him through half-closed eyes.

"Looks like Trogen's got a good hand," whispered Marley. "He's not even trying to hide his confidence."

"Unless he's bluffing," said Mairi.

Ellie drew two and sent them back across the table to join the cluster around the bucket. Trogen drew two, grinned, stared at Ellie and laid down his stones, calling them as he set each of them down with a click.

"Red for *reef*, orange for *or*; yellow for *you're*; green for *going*; blue for *bare*; and purple for *poles*, the last two twice, so I double the whole run. Beat that, little Ellie!"

"Doubled at the low end," said Mairi. "Hard to beat."

Ellie's even little white teeth gleamed and her green eyes twinkled as she laid down the stones.

"Same to you, cousin Trogen, and doubled at the *high* end."

She laid out her stones precisely, her lips announcing each score, but nobody heard for shouting, clapping, and cheers.

"And now for my forfeit," said Ellie. She tapped her lips with one small finger, pretending to be thinking.

"It's a cool night. I could have Trogen run around the house a couple of times in his skivvies, but I think I'd rather he fetch six big pots of hot water up to the third floor, where I will have a nice last bath before we all sail off together."

Trogen policed up the stones into the bucket, his teeth clenched. Mairi heard Marley chuckle, but when she looked for him, he had joined the rest of the crew and was talking with Seren, their eyes almost level. They were smiling together at Ellie, who was pointing a demanding finger at Trogen.

The Cygnets, she thought. My crew.

Book Two

Venturing South

1. In which Cygnet sails into the wet

A northwest wind dragged ragged grey clouds low over the hills that protected Matris and its anchorage. It was three days since the party, and Lindey, Becky and her youngest daughters Lena and Maia, stood on the wharf saying goodbye. The shipbuilders took time off to watch *Cygnet* hoist sails and slip her lines to the shipyard wharf. In all the embraces and whispered farewells, nobody questioned Astreya's absence. Lindey offered an innocuous explanation that deceived no-one. Like most of those present, Mairi feared that all the activity of the past few days had set back his recovery.

Trogen had held himself apart from the hugs and handshakes, preferring to be the first aboard *Cygnet*, where he stayed below making unnecessary adjustments to the positioning of the shipstone in its gimbals above the chart table. He told himself that he was preparing to navigate through the first few days, while they were in waters where the compass swung uselessly and they had only the shipstone to guide them, but as he worked he remembered the tears in Becky's eyes as she hugged Ellie until she waved both arms in the air, pleading for mercy. He wished that his own mother had done more than pat him on the shoulder. When he heard Mairi give the order to hoist sail, he climbed quickly to the deck, pulling a glove onto his left hand where his scar had torn open when he had lost his grip and gone overboard. He shoved Neil out of the way and joined Seren on the main halyard, where he worked mechanically in silence.

As the little schooner gathered way and headed down the bay, *Cygnet* luffed up into the wind for a brief moment during which all the Cygnets lined the rail to wave goodbye. Mairi thought she saw Lindey raise an arm in farewell, but they were far enough away to make her doubt what she had seen.

Soon they were through the passage between the Two Feet. When *Cygnet* had the wind on her starboard quarter, Trogen distanced himself from the rest of the crew and stood on the foredeck looking past the curve of the jib at a narrow strip of watery blue sky to the southeast. A distant shaft of sunlight gleamed and was gone. As he watched, smoke-grey clouds closed over the horizon like a lid sliding over a bowl. Unconsciously, his hand felt for the clasp on his left arm as he anticipated three days of sailing during which their compass would be useless.

Trogen had a knack with the navigation stones that surpassed Seren's, Mairi's and his mother's; and in his own mind, perhaps even his father's. Astreya and his cousin Dabih had been taught by their grandfather Oron, the Grand Master of more than half a dozen great ships, all of which, save *Cygnus* and *Elusive*, were long gone, the victims of storms, wrecks, and in at least one case, a master's decision to abandon the endless wandering.

Astreya, Lindey, and Dabih had taught their children only the skills necessary for setting and maintaining a course when the compass spun in its binnacle. They also shared a simple messaging code that they used for distances within the horizon. Mairi and Seren were both confident from their years of apprenticeship but were silently aware that there was more that their parents could do, but did not teach.

From the beginning, Trogen had wanted more. He looked beyond what he had been taught and deviated from procedure whenever he could. After being admonished by both Lindey and Astreya for straying from the skills he had learned along with Mairi and Seren, he experimented secretly. When he was transferred to *Elusive*, Trogen found Dabih's abilities to be less than Astreya's, making it easier for him to investigate the power of the stones more thoroughly, without his father's oversight.

Except for Marley, everyone aboard *Cygnet* had a stone. Cam, Neil, and Peter had small stones in rings that they wore on their left hands. Cam was content with the limited powers of his little green stone, but the two lads were eager for the day when they would wear a navigator's clasp like those worn by Mairi, Seren, and Trogen, and to everyone's continuing amazement, Ellie.

When Ellie was only twelve, Astreya and Lindey had called her to be tested in the Forbidden Room aboard *Cygnus* and had asked Trogen and Mairi to witness the procedure. They had all stood around the dark pit of the navigating table where Astreya had placed two rings and the last remaining arm clasp. Ellie had been barely tall enough to see over the edge. Her green eyes lit by the eerie glow of *Cygnus'* shipstone, she stared intently at the unawakened arm clasp and rings. In their roles as grandmaster and navigator, Astreya and Lindey had intended to ask Ellie to slip one of the rings on her finger and try to make it glow. However, without waiting for anyone to speak, she stood on tip-toe, reached across the table, picked up the arm-clasp and clipped it onto her skinny little arm. They all gasped in unison as the green stone brightened, and kept on getting brighter until it rivalled the shipstone at the centre of the navigating table. When they looked up from the stone to Ellie's green-lit face, her teeth flashed in a triumphant grin.

"Ellie," said Astreya slowly, "you're going to be a powerful wielder. But first, I must tighten the clasp. None of us wants to see it slip from your arm."

"You won't take it away from me," she had said, her voice resolute, her chin raised.

"No, my dear," Lindey had answered. "We're going to help you learn to use it."

Ellie danced around the table and held her arm up to Astreya. Trogen stepped back, glad that the dim light hid his shock that his little cousin had a talent that might be superior his own.

Over the years, he had seen that Ellie had power perhaps beyond even the master wielder, his father. As he watched her skills grow, it was clear that he was no longer the only one capable of taking the lore of the stones beyond what they all had been taught. As they headed south, Trogen had to cope not only with serving under his sister's command, but also with the possibility that his abilities might be surpassed by the youngest girl aboard.

Resolutely ignoring his misgivings, Trogen went below to check that the spear of light in *Cygnet's* shipstone belowdecks was repeated into the binnacle where the steersman could see it. When he passed Ellie on his way back up on deck, he saw that her left eyebrow was somewhat higher than the right. When he looked again, it seemed to him that her eyes, as green as his father's, were evaluating him. Trogen was glad when cold rain began to slant out of the northwest across *Cygnet's* decks and into her sails so that he could pull the drawstring of his hood tight to block Ellie's stare.

With the coast invisible astern, *Cygnet's* crew struggled into their oiled-canvass foul weather gear, each of them aware that celebrations were over, and they were embarked on an ocean voyage. The weather closed in around them and the light wore down to a grey and early end to the day. Rain started to blow under hoods and hats, leak around collars, run up sleeves, and puddle in shoes. Watch change at a dark and invisible sunset sent wet people below, passing responsibility over to the next watch, still damp from their earlier trick.

When Trogen finished his last round of the deck, he heard Marley's laugh, and when Trogen climbed down into the cockpit, he saw Ellie sitting on the cabin top, swinging her feet. Green light from the binnacle lit her face, which was animated by whatever she had been saying to Marley. As she slid past Trogen to go below, her wide-eyed glance seemed devilishly mischievous. Moments later, Mairi appeared at the head of the companionway.

"Your watch below, Trogen," she said.

Trogen grunted acknowledgment as he passed her in the puddle of rainwater that slopped back and forth in the cockpit. Belowdecks, the darkened living space smelled of wet oilskins and wool, which did nothing to improve his mood. Peter was standing in the passageway at the galley, which occupied a scant two arms' length on the starboard side of the living space. It consisted of a sink, a drop-down table no bigger than a serving tray, a compact array of lockers and a tiny stove, all dimly lit by a small lantern.

"The water's hot, would'ja like a mug o' tea?"

"Get knotted, lubber," said Trogen

He pushed past Peter on his way to his bunk amidships. Ahead of him at eye height, blankets heaved in an upper berth, and Seren's head appeared, her curls tousled.

"That wasn't nice, Trogen. Peter's on his first blue-water voyage, and he's doing his best."

Biting back a resentful reply, Trogen clambered into his own berth. He rolled over so that he faced the ship's side, pulled his blanket over his head, and later, slept.

~∧~

On deck for the night watch, Mairi looked astern to where Cam was handing the wheel over to Marley.

"Here y' go, Marley. There ain't nothin' t' see but the green line in the binnacle. The wind's come around to the sou-sou-west, it's holdin' up nicely, so there ain't no problem keepin' her headin' in the right direction."

Cam lowered himself carefully into the cockpit beside Mairi. He stood with his shoulders raised, the dim green light gleaming on the hood of his oilskin.

"You all right, Cam?" she asked.

"Never better. Jus' a bit stiff from standin' in the wet."

"I passed Ellie as I was coming on deck. Where's Peter?"

"I sent him below a while ago. No point in gettin' any wetter when all it takes is two of us to take turns on the wheel."

"Makes sense. Tell Seren and Ellie to stay below for now. Maybe bring us a mug of something hot in a bit. Good night, Cam."

"'Night now."

Mairi climbed out of the cockpit onto the deck and made a circuit of *Cygnet,* checking that the sails were drawing in the steady, rain-filled wind. She reassured herself that no halyards were slack, no sheets tangled, no hatch covers loose, and that the little rowboat on the foredeck was securely lashed down. The schooner was on the starboard tack, a few points off close-hauled, moving easily on sea flattened by rain into steady, rolling swells. *Cygnet's* masts were slanted only a few degrees to port, nonetheless, Mairi moved carefully as she made her way astern on the wet deck, stepping around jib and staysail sheets, then ducking under the fore and main booms. Her inspection complete, she settled herself into the starboard quarter of the cockpit, her back to the wind, and prepared to endure the night watch.

After a time measured only by the rhythmic creak of wet rigging and the patter of rain onto the hood of her oilskins, she heard Marley's deep voice over the sounds of wind and water.

"That Ellie's a sharp one for her age, isn't she?"

Mairi nodded, forgetting that with the light of the binnacle between them, Marley could not see her.

"Beggin' your pardon, Skipper. I didn't mean no disrespect."

"Not a problem, Marley. Yes, she is. Ellie is ... well, she's always seemed more ... aware ... than you'd expect from someone her age. It was so when she was little more than a tiny baby. Now she's thirteen..."

"She's only thirteen? I mean, she looks young, so slim and all, but I thought..."

"You thought that one so young had no business being part of the crew. But she's already the veteran of a season aboard her father's ship."

"I wasn't meaning to criticize."

"Again, no offence taken, Marley. Our ways must seem strange to you, sending boys and girls to sea when they're still children.

We're used to being stared at and sometimes shunned by people in our ports of call. Our shore folk at Matris only accept us because we bring them things they never had before my father took command of the great ships. The farmers and the women in the Home can't understand the way the family lives and works."

"The masters and officers are all related?"

"It's complicated. Cam isn't related to us, nor is Damon, but they're closer to Trogen and me than if they were uncles. Our parents are Astreya and Lindey, as you know. Seren and Ellie are children of Dabih and Becky—she's originally from Teenmouth, on the far coast to the north of Matris. Dabih's mother is Catriona, the healer, the tiny, black-haired woman who's making Father get better. Dabih looks a bit like Father, probably because his father was Gar, who was cousin to Father's father, who was also named Astreya. Am I confusing you?"

"They all grew up at Matris?"

"Actually, none of them did. Astreya, that's Father, was born in the Village, at least two to three good days of sailing north of Matris. Nearly forty years ago Father's father, the first Astreya, blew ashore in a skimmer, close to death from exposure. When he got better, he married Alana, the only black-haired woman in the Village, and lived as a fisherman in the Village until he was lost at sea, before Astreya—Father—was born."

"The only people I've seen with black hair and green eyes are Grand Master Astreya and Ellie."

"Strange, isn't it? They're separated by degrees and generations, and yet they have the same colouring. What's more, Father is an absolute wizard with the stones, and it looks as if Ellie's going to be as well. Nobody has ever worn a clasp so young. Trogen and I didn't get beyond a finger ring until we were almost seventeen."

"What about young Peter? He's got a ring. Is he related to the family as well?"

"Not a bit. He's from Charton. But then, neither is Mother, and she can work the stones. Father taught her. Lit her clasp the year they met—the year before Trogen and I were born. Mother gave birth at sea, aboard *Cygnus*, where we grew up. She said that if she could work the stones, then so could anybody, and then along came Peter to prove it. If there had been another wielder's stone, Peter would be wearing it. He tested almost as well as Seren."

"How did that happen? Did he just volunteer?"

"Mother discovered his talent. She'd known his mother, so when Peter's father was lost at sea, Peter came aboard *Cygnus*. Mother spotted his ability almost by accident. She asked him to hold a ring stone, and it lit up in his hand."

"They're all natural sailors. At home with the sea."

"What makes you say that, Marley?"

"This afternoon when we lost sight of land, they all came up on deck, took a look around and then got on with whatever they were doing."

"Why shouldn't they?"

"First time I saw nothing but sea, it was like something inside of me screamed. Still gives me a turn, every time there's nothing solid to aim for. That's why I like bein' where I can see the compass. It points north, no matter what. Except that around about here, it doesn't."

"How do you feel about steering by the green light of the stone?"

"It'll do, I guess. I don't know how it works, but then I can't tell you what keeps the needle of a compass pointing north, either."

"You know nothing of navigation?"

"Enough to follow the bearing I'm given. Nobody ever told me anything more."

"Do you want to learn?"

"D'y' suppose I could?"

There was a gleam of lamplight on the companionway, and Seren appeared.

"Seren, take the wheel. Marley and I'll be below at the chart table. He wants to see how it's done. It's wet, but the wind's steady. Bang the deck over our heads if you need us. I'll send Ellie up with a mug of something hot. The two of you can handle her easily."

~∧~

Ellie stood in the cockpit with both hands cupped around her mug.

"She's needing a bit of helm," said Seren.

"I'll crank in the main. Tell me when she balances."

"Do you think we should? I mean, maybe we ought to ask Mairi first."

"Before hauling a few handspans of the sheet? Come on, Seren. Be brave. Think for yourself."

"After one voyage aboard *Elusive*, you can trim a schooner?"

"After one voyage I know when to sheet in the main."

A block squeaked as Ellie adjusted the mainsheet. The light of the binnacle gleamed on the wheel as Seren stepped back and allowed it to steady itself with the centre spoke amidships. Her voice came out of the darkness.

"She's holding. As long as Mairi doesn't adjust the shipstone..."

"She has no need to, Seren. Check your own clasp. We're heading due south, and have been since we lost sight of the Two Feet."

"Trogen's the navigator. He should..."

"For goodness sake, Seren, it's not difficult. Find north and head the other way. Cam could do it with his ring."

"Cam's not the navigator. Trogen is."

"Trogen's stupid-angry that he wasn't made skipper."

"Trogen is ..."

"Trogen's a silly man. He's got everything upside down in his head. He hasn't even noticed that your fondest wish is to crawl into his bunk."

"Ellie! That's not so!"

"T'is. You just won't admit it."

"Trogen's my cousin!"

"Of course he is. But calling someone cousin just means you're related. What matters is how close the relationship is. Everyone's related, somehow. I bet we're related to Marley in some way."

"Not possible. He's black."

"He's really good on the helm. And he's really good looking, too."

"I hadn't noticed."

"Liar."

"Anyway, we're certainly not related to him."

"I've got black hair."

"That's because you're family."

A wedge of light cut across the companionway and Mairi climbed back into the cockpit.

"You two arguing again?"

"Just keeping awake," said Seren. "The rain's letting up and the wind's veering. Ellie …. We hauled the main, but *Cygnet's* needing to be sheeted in again."

"Trim the main some more, Ellie, and the jib, too. Stay in the cockpit. I'll handle the fore and staysails."

After the wet, finger-numbing work was done, Mairi and Ellie stood side by side in the dark, listening to the steady sea sounds.

"Where's Marley?" Ellie asked.

"I told him to get his head down for a bit. He's been at the wheel for the best part of the day and night."

"Mairi," said Ellie, "why not shift to four-hour watches? Any two of us can handle *Cygnet* in light winds."

Seren, used to the formal deference to seniority that was habitual aboard the great ships, was shocked by Ellie's direct advice to the skipper.

"Ellie," Seren admonished. "We always..."

"It's *Cygnet's* first voyage," Ellie continued unabashed. "We haven't been at sea long enough to have an always. Six-hour watches are a silly enough tradition on the great ships where they are knee-deep in crew. We'd be stupid to do the same thing with only eight of us."

"Ellie! You don't tell a master what to do!"

There was a silence during which they all attended to *Cygnus'* new rhythm. The schooner eased gradually up the lee of the waves, hung momentarily on the crests long enough for all three of them to shift their weight from one leg to the other, and then the ship ran down the windward sides, spray hissing around her bow. The little schooner was picking up speed, her sails firm. When Mairi looked windward into the night, cold fog dampened her face and hair, but rain no longer stung her cheeks. She yawned, stretched, and folded her arms.

"Seren, Ellie's making sense. We'll finish the night as we are, and change in the morning. Now I'm going to take a turn at the wheel, and Ellie's going to make us a mug of ... of whatever she makes it with."

"It's wild cherry, sweetgrass, honey, and a bit of slippery elm. I made up the recipe after we ran out of cacao.'

"Just get it, Ellie. I don't want to know what's in it."

"On my way, skipper."

2. In which Mairi has night thoughts

The next day the wind slackened, but the rain returned, beating the waves into long grey swells. *Cygnet* rolled back and forth, her sails flapping from side to side like wet washing, her masthead arcing across low, murky skies. The motion was sickeningly irregular, making the Cygnets queasy and irritable. Belowdecks, the living space smelled of wet socks and the little stove kept going out. Towards noon, Cam kept the fire lit long enough to give everyone a mug of hot soup, but when the dull day slid towards evening and all that could be cooked for supper was lukewarm fish stew and ship's biscuit, tempers started to fray. The older members of the crew recognized the feeling and retreated into themselves lest they provoke or be provoked.

The two boys Neil and Peter were at odds, repelling each other like the poles of a magnet. As they raised the table to the cabin top and lowered their bunks for the night, Peter stumbled and fell across Trogen's berth.

"Clumsy little son of a crab-hauling fisherman," Trogen muttered as he shoved Peter aside and headed back on deck.

Cygnet's uneven motion combined with Trogen's push made Peter stagger to the forward end of the space and past the curtain that screened Ellie and Seren's bunks. He found himself only an arm's length from Seren, who was pulling her shirt over her head. Blushing furiously, he stepped back so quickly he sat down on the cabin sole. Moments later Seren, now fully clothed, twitched aside the curtain and strode past him.

"Put your nose in here again, and I'll punch it flat."

"I didn't ... I wasn't ... I didn't mean ... I'm sorry..."

He was still stammering as her tall figure disappeared up the companionway.

"Easy, lad," said Cam from the tiny galley. "Everyone's a bit tetchy."

"I'm not used to having girls ... er ... women aboard," said Peter. "Back when I was on me dad's boat, we was all boys ... er ... men."

"You got a sister, right?"

Peter nodded.

"Well, think o' the women as yer sisters or yer cousins. That's what they all do. We're crew together, young Pete. All shapes and sizes."

If Neil overheard Cam's timely advice to Peter, he did not take it to heart, because he was watching Seren's long legs disappearing up the companionway. Ever since he had held her feet when Trogen had gone overboard, Neil's attitude to Seren balanced uneasily between reverence and lust. He was usually careful that his infatuation was not apparent, but when he followed her up the companionway, he pressed against her as they climbed into the cockpit to start their watch. Seren glanced at him suspiciously. She had overheard Cam's calming words and had belatedly realized that Peter's incursion beyond the curtain had been an innocent accident. She stifled her first impulse to challenge Neil and instead set about her watch-keeping duties.

While Neil was watching Seren make the first sail-check of her watch, Cam skillfully tripped him.

"You did that on purpose!"

"Uh-huh. Just like you rammed into Seren just now. 'Cept I know what I'm doin'. An' you don't."

"I don't know what you're talking about."

"Let me put it to you this way, lad. Are you ready t' take charge of Dabih's ship?"

Neil looked puzzled.

"Command *Elusive*? 'Course not. I ain't ready for that."

"An' yer ain't ready for Seren, neither. So ease yer sheets an' bear off."

Neil's jaw clenched, and he went to work casting suspicious glances through the black hair that hung over his eyes.

That night, the wind freshened and *Cygnet's* sails filled. Heeling at a constant angle, she eased across the seas in a steady, predictable rhythm. Though it was her watch below, Mairi was unable to sleep. She stood on the windward coaming, one hand on the main shrouds, balancing easily as *Cygnet* swayed up a long, rolling wave and slid down the other side. Above, the masthead swung back and forth across the Milky Way; ahead, the sky was still cloudy, obscuring the southern stars that the ship had raised as she sailed into warmer waters. *Cygnet's* sails were beginning to catch the light of a rising gibbous moon. Spray hissed into the waves below her feet and the fingers of her right hand could feel the standing rigging vibrate as if the ship were a huge purring cat.

She swung inboard to stand on the narrow deck between the ship's side and the thigh-high cabin top, let go the shroud, and in a couple of long strides had a hand on the main halliards. Moving sure-footed in the dim light, she trailed her fingers along the main boom until she was standing in the rush of air that spilled off the jib, into the stay-sail, on to the foresail and then to the mainsail. Judging by eye, ear, and touch, she made her way aft, checking that the wind-filled slot between the sails was accelerating the flow of air along each sail, transforming the wind's energy into speed, delicately balanced to avoid the forward sails back-winding those astern to distort their optimum shape.

"I can do this," she muttered as she made her way aft. A moment later she recalled the adage, *An easy passage does not prove a master's worth.* The old sailors' saying took her to the moment when Astreya had announced her command of *Cygnet*, with Trogen as navigator. Had Astreya intended that Trogen should be poised to take over if she was deficient? Despite her parents' assurance that she was the right choice to command *Cygnet*, once again, she felt her brother watching for the moment when she would fail.

Mairi ducked under the main boom and walked the slanting deck back to the command position astern, where Marley was a tall, dark shape dimly lit by the soft light in the binnacle. Feet wide apart, his shoulders hunched over the wheel, his hands cupped the spokes like a dancer holding his partner. He and the ship were responsive to wind and waves, on course, sails full. Mairi nodded approval, and then realizing that she could not be seen, spoke instead.

"Nice night."

"'Tis that."

The exchange was brief in the extreme, but it carried a huge freight of approval that began with the weather and included the satisfaction of being on a well-designed ship.

"Seren?"

"Below. Fixing mug-up. Cam will be on deck soon."

"Good watch."

"T'was. Can't say that too often o' the graveyard shift."

"True."

As she came up the companionway steps, Seren was briefly silhouetted against the light in the galley. *Cygnet* yawed off course for a couple of heartbeats. Mairi saw Marley shake his head, and decided he must have nodded off. Moments later, Mairi was thanking Seren and cupping her hands around her mug. She did not see Seren hesitate as her fingers touched Marley's, nor how his eyes lingered on her dimly lit face. The galley light gleamed again, and Mairi looked up from her mug as Cam appeared.

"Well, I see didn't manage to drown us."

"We tried," said Marley solemnly, "but the weather wouldn't cooperate."

"Our turn."

Mairi ran through the ritual of watch change.

"We're back on the compass. The course is south-east-by-east, nothing's in sight. Sails are as they were at sunset: working jib, staysail, fore, and main all drawing nicely. We were making just over eight knots half an hour ago, but the wind's freshened a bit, and the high cloud to the south is clearing away."

Two more figures climbed the companionway and looked about them, adjusting their eyes to the darkness. Cam assumed responsibility casually before Trogen could become officious.

"Away you go then, you three; we got her. Trogen, would'ja make the first round, an' take Pete with you? I got the wheel. Ellie's doin' good work wi' hot drinks."

"Mug up!"

Ellie appeared a couple of steps below on the companionway, holding two mugs. Peter and Trogen both reached down for their drinks, but only Peter thanked her. Ellie was on her way back down for her own mug when Trogen's outburst made her tun around.

"Peter, you dreck-eating sculpin, you took my drink! I just drank from your filthy mug. And you've had your scum-sucking lips on mine, you slack lubber."

Peter held out Trogen's mug. "Honest, I only held it by the handle."

Ellie spoke up fearlessly.

"Get a grip, Trogen! The mugs got switched in the dark. It's not Peter's fault."

"You stay out of this, Ellie. Don't try to protect him. I've seen the way he looks at you."

"Steady, Trog," said Cam softly from behind the wheel.

"Mind your own business, Cam. I heard what happened with Seren. Watch this, you rotten little red-haired trouble-maker."

Trogen smashed Peter's mug on the cockpit coaming and flung the shards over the side.

"Enough!"

Mairi's command silenced everyone except Peter.

"That were me dad's mug. Me mum gave it to me for luck when she heard I was goin' on my first voyage."

"Then your luck's just run out, lubber."

"Ellie, go below. You too, Peter. Exactly what is happening here?"

"The little snot took my mug," said Trogen.

"It were all a mistake," Cam reported. "Ellie come up the companionway, one mug in each hand. Trog n' Pete took the mugs nearest them in the dark, an' they each got the other's. It weren't no biggie. That is, 'til Trogen started shoutin'."

Mairi spoke slowly and softly, but with determination.

"Trogen, you are way out of line. That is not how we deal with any crew member, least of all a young first-timer. And it is not worthy of the family."

"Do you want me to whisper gently like our father does when he gives me shit jobs to do, or when he beaches me ashore?"

Trogen was still belligerent, but his tone had gone from rage to bluster.

"I want you to go forward and think about what you've said. When you're calm, go to the chest in the trade goods locker, find a new mug, and give it to Peter."

For a moment, it seemed to Mairi that Trogen would challenge her. Cam coughed, cleared his throat, and spat eloquently to leeward. Trogen climbed out of the cockpit and headed forward in silence broken only by the sounds made by *Cygnet* as she rushed southwards through the night. Mairi took a breath and made another check of all the sails, starting forward along the lee side, and returning astern to windward, carefully avoiding her brother. Calmed by the process, she stood at the stern, an elbow hooked around the backstay, looking over Cam's shoulder.

"Cam, what do you think of *Cygnet*?"

Cam's attention was on the compass, the set of the sails and the feel of the wheel in his hands. He matched her conversational tone.

"Mairi? I thought you was below. So, what do I think of *Cygnet*? Well, she's a right nice little ship, that's for certain sure. But I imagine mebby yer thinkin' more about yer crew, an' our sailin' orders."

"I didn't expect to be heading straight to the Sunny Isles. Still less for Father—Astreya—to command me to sail by compass alone when we were away from our coastline."

"Well, I wouldn't know about that. I got me an itty-bitty-find-me-way-home ring stone, so what you do with a shipstone's beyond me. Now, if yer thinkin' about the crew, I'd say we're all whatcha might call in'erestin' picks.

"I didn't expect to be skipper."

"Yer a good skipper fer a small ship an' a young crew. You attend to what they're thinkin' an' feelin'."

Cam twitched the wheel, the jib flapped, and *Cygnet* yawed into a wave. Spray drenched the foredeck. Trogen's curse was carried astern by the wind. They both pretended not to notice.

"Ah ... Thank you, but..."

"Young Trogen's all wrapped up in hisself. Not a good turn of mind for a skipper, an' not even a mate." Cam's tone softened. "Maybe I shouldn'a said that, seein' as how he's yer brother."

Mairi shrugged, invisible in the darkness. "Cam, I've been thinking..."

"Thinkin'. Always a mistake. Just bleedin' get on wi' it. Like you just did, an' right fair it was, too. Young Trog deserved every word, and mebby more. Point is, you didn't lose your grip. Y'know, y'didn't start screamin' an' carryin' on. You straightened him out and sent him forrard where he just caught a capful of spray what he richly deserved, thanks to me. Yer doin' jus' fine, Mairi. Like you was when I stuck me head out fer a quick look around, and you an' Marley was busy bein' right pleased wi' yerselves, enjoyin' a nice night full o' wind an' stars wi' a good ship under yer feet."

After another pause, Mairi asked a question to lead away from talking about her family.

"Where did Marley come from?"

"'Streya found 'im in Glaston. 'E was lookin' fer a ship, 'cause his last—a scruffy little coasting ketch—dumped him when the owner wanted his favourite to be the leadin' hand. Leastways, so he says."

"I'm wondering whether it had anything to do with him..."

"Bein' black? It sure didn't make no difference to 'Streya, nor to the crew of *Cygnus*. We've all been south, seen lots of people what weren't all fish-belly white folks what sunburns to brick red. A sailor's a sailor. If he came in green, I'd work with him, so long as he knows his job."

"Well, you can't fault Marley for seamanship. The moment he took the wheel, anyone could see he has the touch. No, what I was wondering at first was how he'd take to me. He's obviously much older than we are."

"But not as old as me, in case you hadn't noticed; an' thank you very much for includin' me among you youngsters. Back aboard *Cygnus*, when Lindey took command after 'Streya got hurt, I asked Marley if he could take orders from a woman. D'y know what he said? 'If you knew me ma, you wouldn't need to ask.' So I think we can be fairly sure that you bein' skipper don't bother him. As fer you, you know yer job. You handle yer' crew jus' fine. You got the stone on yer arm. An' yer somethin' of a wonder for the way you can get a fix on a star an' turn it into a position on the chart."

"Trogen's better than I am with the stones."

"Don't you go worried on me. Trog's all tied up in a knot about provin' hisself. Bein' a worthy son. Makes him seem like he don't care, or ain't interested in what's goin' on wi' the people around him. That ain't your problem."

"How do you know so much, Cam?"

"'Cause I'm some smart. Here comes Trog now."

Mairi and Cam watched Trogen go below, listened to the sound of searching in a chest of trade goods under their feet, then heard a subdued exchange in the galley.

"Peter?"

"Yes ... sir."

"Replacement mug. Here you go."

"Ah ... thank you."

Cam and Mairi exchanged glances in the light from the binnacle.

"I wouldn't want to be tellin' the skipper what to do, but from where I stand, it looks like a good moment for you to grab some shut-eye in yer bunk."

Mairi nodded. She made her way below, grateful for the darkness. She had barely entered her quarters astern before sleep took her.

3. In which Trogen plots a fix

A couple of days later, Mairi shaded her eyes against close to midday sunlight on the open ocean. Matris was nearly a week astern. They sailed over blue-green waves flecked with white crests. Thin, feathery clouds trailed eastwards from high above the western horizon, streamed overhead in wide-spaced ranks, and then blew on into the east. The crew had breakfasted, the bilges had been pumped and found dry, the ship set to rights in daylight and fair weather, and the Cygnets were taking a well-earned respite from a steady upwind beat that had kept them tacking for the last three watches. Mairi had them hoist the topsails above the main and foremast gaffs, and then let them enjoy the morning, but now it was time for a task they had been unable to do for days.

"It's time for our first sun-sight. We have two sextants aboard, so we'll take turns one minute before and one after noon and split the differences. Trogen and Ellie will go first, Peter and I will follow."

Mairi stood amidships where she could see into the cabin where the ship's chronometer hung in gimbals. Trogen and Ellie stood side by side in the cockpit, a contrast in size and height. Sextants up to their eyes, their fingers adjusted scales and mirrors to measure the apparent height of the sun. They stood swaying to *Cygnet's* rhythm as the schooner rose and fell. Mairi counted out the seconds.

"Three and two and one and NOW."

Trogen and Ellie made final adjustments and then lowered their instruments to read the calibrations. Trogen thrust the sextant at Peter, swiftly resetting all the dials to make his task more difficult. Then he pulled a notebook from his pocket and scribbled down the numbers he had been muttering. Ellie carefully handed her sextant to Mairi and took her place to observe the chronometer.

"Three and two and one and NOW."

"Down we go, then," said Mairi. "We'll calculate and compare positions."

When both sextants were stowed in their slotted boxes, they lowered the cabin table from its nighttime position under the cabin roof, and sat on bunks on either side, consulting manuals, calculating, and checking their results.

"Finished? Good. Let's find out where we are."

Mairi led the way to the cabin astern of the companionway. They crowded together in the limited space that did duty as the master's cabin, the navigation centre, and storage for cargo unsuited to the main hold, forward of the cabin. Only Ellie was able to stand to her full height, Trogen and Peter stood with their heads lowered, side by side along the centreline, Mairi bent over the chart table, her shoulder against the ship's side. The rush of water around *Cygnet* and the bubbling wake under her stern were louder here, blending with the soft creak of the ropes in the steering gear that transferred the movements of the ship's wheel above them to the rudder below. Behind Mairi, the ship's sides curved inward towards the stern. Trogen stood possessively close to the bowl that hung at eye height in which was the shipstone, covered by a black cloth.

"Who wants to go first?" Mairi asked.

Peter took an awkward step forward, propelled by a covert shove from Trogen. He stammered out the latitude and longitude he had calculated, Mairi measured and plotted a tiny x. Her attention focused on the chart, she listened to Ellie's lighter, higher voice call out her numbers and marked a second x, close to the first.

"Trogen?"

When she heard no answer, Mairi entered her own x, making the third corner of a tight triangle.

"Trogen?"

Trogen edged Mairi out of his way and took possession of the chart table. He slid the parallel rulers across the chart, clicking them over the compass rose as if to show off his skill. He added his own x in the middle of the triangle that Mairi had plotted, and left the ruler lined up along the line of tiny crosses he had drawn by dead reckoning watch by watch, day by day since they left Matris. Trogen scowled at the chart until Mairi dismissed the two youngest. When he looked up, Peter and Mairi were on their way back on deck. Ellie turned, looked at him and rolled her green eyes before vanishing up the companionway. Trogen took his time before following the order. He nodded at Seren, who was at the wheel, and then noticed Ellie sitting on the cabin top staring at him, her eyes at the same level as his. He did his best to be condescending.

"So, Ellie, your observation and calculations got you a reasonable fix today."

Ellie wrinkled her nose.

"Not like yours." Her voice was pitched so that only he could hear.

"What do you mean?" Trogen replied in an irritated whisper.

She swung her legs back and forth.

"I saw how you moved the ruler. You knew where your mark was going to be, and then used the lat and long I'd already plotted. Your fix wasn't calculated from what you observed with the sextant."

"Of course it was."

Ellie shook her head.

"No, it wasn't. You did something tricky with the shipstone ahead of time. It was like what we do to make messages, except much faster."

"Nonsense. You can't use a shipstone to plot a fix."

"*You* can, Trogen. I've been watching you do it."

"Ellie..."

"Quietly, Trogen. Smile. Look like I've made you laugh. Or someone will ask what we're talking about."

Trogen clenched his teeth, deliberately smoothed his brow, forced a chuckle and spoke out of the side of his mouth.

"There's nobody I could be messaging."

"Exactly. That's what got me interested." Her voice rose. "Thanks, Trogen, that was really helpful. I'll remember for the next time we shoot the sun."

Trogen turned and saw Mairi appearing up the companionway.

"Um... glad to help," he muttered.

Mairi nodded approvingly at both of them.

The rest of the day *Cygnet* sailed on a broad reach. The sun shone and the west wind felt like a friend. Laid over at a comfortable angle, all sails set and drawing, the little schooner eased over the waves with a rocking rhythm, making good and comfortable speed. Whoever was at the wheel had little to do but cooperate with the slight back-and-forth movement of the rudder.

Mairi sat on the stern deck, enjoying the change in the weather while watching her crew. Cam brought up jackets and pullovers still damp from previous days of rain and hung them to flutter on an improvised clothes line between the main and foremast stays. Soon the space between the two masts was a demented scarecrow of jiggling, waving garments. Trogen was not happy with the homely display of flapping clothes. Mairi watched him as he obsessively adjusted the sails throughout the four hours of his watch as if he were sailing in a race. She prudently said nothing, having decided that Trogen was so wrapped up in his own concerns that if she confronted him, his attitude would probably grow worse, and affect the rest of the crew.

Neil swung down into the cockpit from the cabin top, bumping into Peter, and knocking a bundle of clothes out of his arms. Mairi saw Neil's lips shape a crude insult as he pushed past Peter on his way down the companionway, and saw Peter's one-word reply as he picked up the fallen garments. Neil's behaviour towards the red-haired youngest aboard was frequently disdainful. Plucked from *Elusive*, where he had been expecting a promotion, Neil was masking his resentment poorly.

Peter's red curls blew across his eyes as he carried his bundle of damp clothes towards the clothesline. He avoided Trogen, to whom he was a mere fisherman's son. Before she could start to worry about the friction between them, Mairi heard Seren and Ellie laughing together below decks as they prepared the evening meal. Then Marley's deep voice roused Mairi from her thoughts.

"Wind's backin' a bit, Skipper."

"Can we maintain our heading?"

"When she's trimmed."

"Then let's do it."

Mairi joined Neil on the mainsheet and then the topsail, while Trogen took charge of the foresail and its topsail, the staysail, and jib, shouting orders at Peter. Eventually, the wind sang a slightly different note in her rigging as the schooner settled into a new attitude. The two who had gone forward climbed back into the cockpit. Behind her at the wheel, Marley confirmed what she had been thinking.

"She's carryin' a course south so easy I could walk away from the wheel. Y'know, I never seen anythin' like it. Get her leanin' over like she is now, an' she just slides over the waves."

Mairi smiled for the first time in days. Whatever the strains among the crew, her little ship was a constant delight.

4. In which Cygnet makes landfall

"Land ho!"

Early the next morning, Mairi was roused by the words every sailor hears, awake or asleep. Although by the clock she could have had another hour in her bunk, she was soon on deck, along with the entire crew. As Seren put a steaming mug in her hand, she saw that Trogen was at the wheel with little to do. Late in the previous day, they had struck the topsails for the night. Now the ship was almost becalmed, her mast perpendicular, the sails limp. Sunlight spilled over a band of low, pinkish cloud on the horizon, lit *Cygnet's* sails, and dazzled along the water. Mairi bent to peer under the main boom, which was swaying gently above the centreline. Ahead and to starboard, the top of a dark, distant lump on the horizon was just catching the early morning light. The gloom in the southwestern sky faded, sunlight lanced across the sea, and the shape became a blue-green jewel of an island. At its northern end, a mountain fell steeply from peak to the sea: to the west, the land sloped down to what might be the white line of a reef. Behind it, the sky was still dark.

"Dat's de island o' the skinny women."

Heads turned toward Marley, who was grinning with the pleasure of a man returning to home waters. His voice had acquired a lilt that had always been beneath the surface of his careful speech.

"And why is that, Marley?"

"Well, Seren, it seems that long ago there was this bad, bad season when there weren't much to eat, an' since the men were in need o' the sustenance to keep 'em out in their boats, tryin' to catch fish, all o' the wives and daughters stinted themselves somethin' fierce, so's when people from the other islands came to help, they was all right amazed at how skinny they had become."

"The women are still skinny?"

"The most o' them is plump and happy now, Ellie, but the name stuck."

Peter piped up eagerly.

"Plump? Are we going there?"

Cam patted his shoulder.

"Down, lad. We've not come all this way to go island-hopping so's you can be lookin' for plump girls."

Ignoring the exchange as well as giggles from Ellie and Seren, Mairi sat on the cabin top, sipped her drink, stared ahead and to port, and then announced quietly, "We're raising Three Peak Island."

Heads turned and hands were raised to shield against the level sunlight, as the crew all stared southeastwards.

"And that's where we're going," she added. "Now if the wind would just perk up, we'll be at Port Claire before the day's out, trading tools, glass, and salt fish from Charton for coffee, sugar, cacao, and rum."

Peter turned to Cam.

"What I don't understand is why the folks down south here should want a box of salt cod when there's an ocean all around them full of fish for the taking."

"Well, Peter," said Cam, "that there's one o' the mysteries of tradin' by which we live. There's folk in them islands what is wantin' salt cod they ain't got. An' there's our people at home what likes coffee an' cocoa an' sugar what they ain't got, an' what these here islanders grow so much of they can't use it all. An' at the ports in between there's corn, an' cotton, an' glass, an' metalware, an' spars, an' rope, not to mention rum and whiskey that the folks what don't make nor grow just can't wait to get their hands on and their gullets full of. And all that thirstin' and wantin' is what we depend on when we arrive ready to start negotiatin' our hold-full of what they ain't got an' we're carryin'."

Mairi smiled at Cam's succinct explanation of trade, and in the same instant recognized what she should be doing.

"Trogen, Cam, we need to refresh our memories of the approaches from our rutters and the chart. Marley, if you would join us, you may have local knowledge that will be helpful."

They followed her below, Cam pausing to admonish the members of his watch.

"Ellie, you mind the wheel. Seren, you'n Neil are our eyes. Bang on the deck if y' see anythin'. An' you, Pete, keep your mind off plump girls, y' hear me?"

Mairi stood astern of the little chart table, facing Trogen, Marley, and Cam. Cam stood to his full height: Trogen stooped, his brown hair brushing the underside of the deck above, and Marley hunched over, the ropes of his black hair swinging beside his cheeks. A chart of the open sea lay in front of her, flattened by recent days of use. She pointed to the long, pencilled line from Matris to the Southern Islands, interspersed with tiny notations beside the crosses that represented their position day by day. At first, the marks were along a straight line southward, charting their positions over the first three days as estimated by dead reckoning. Then the line ran through crosses that if connected would have recorded the zig-zagging involved in tacking against headwinds.

"We've had a good passage. Trogen took us out of home waters and we're exactly where Astreya wanted us to go."

Mairi watched her brother frown and preen at the same time.

Mairi unrolled a more detailed chart of the islands and laid it on top of the open ocean chart, placing dividers and a pair of parallel rulers to keep the edges from curling.

"Now that we've raised the island, it looks like we've got a reasonable line to enter the harbour on the sou' western side."

Trogen picked up the leather-bound notebook, consulted a page marked by a slip of paper, and read out loud.

"'Three Peak Island, Port Claire. Good anchorage, deep water, negligible tides so far south. *Cygnus* and *Elusive* visit alternately every two to three years. Wind permitting, approach from the south.' That means we need to go most of the way past the island and then come back. 'Keep the tallest of the three peaks—that's the one that looks as if it smokes—bearing nor' nor' east. Then as you approach the gap in the reef, look for a large red building with a square tower, on the same bearing.' It's not a difficult approach. I did it aboard *Elusive,* and you've been there as well, Mairi, aboard *Cygnus.*"

"Same as me," said Cam. "But watchin' ain't the same as doin' it."

Mairi did not need his reminder that the moment-by-moment decisions were hers. Trogen continued to read from the rutter.

"'Anchor in three fathoms on the western side of the harbour. Firm sand bottom, room to swing.' That's where *Elusive* drops the pick. If we go to the east side of the harbour, there's not so much room, and it's a bit shallower, so we might have to lie between two anchors."

"What about goin' alongside the dock?" Cam asked.

"It'd be a whole lot easier. We draw less than half the great ships, and there's a fathom and more at the dock, so we can make fast and heave the cargo straight onto land."

Make the decision, now, Mairi told herself. "We'll enter, anchor to the west, and find out after we arrive if we're welcome alongside."

Mairi looked at the three men in turn, saw nods of agreement from Cam and Marley, and a shrug from Trogen.

All at once, parallel rulers slid across the chart; sheets creaked in their blocks, heels thumped over their heads, the ship shuddered as sails swung from starboard to port. They all staggered.

"On deck!" Mairi shouted.

All four of them started for the companionway simultaneously. "Go, Marley, Trogen, Cam!"

Marley went up the companionway steps doubled over to protect his head, Trogen and Cam close behind him, Mairi at their heels. Before she reached the deck, she heard Cam's voice.

"Ain't good, I c'n tell yer that, right easy."

A squall line raced towards them. Foam scudded across the long swells that they had been riding southwards. Above, a solid bar of blue-black cloud had rolled up from the southwestern horizon and was moving closer with terrifying speed. The sea was patched with black catspaws of down-drafted air. Under the lowering clouds, flashes of white spray flashed in what was left of the watery sunlight. The sea darkened to black. *Cygnet* dipped her lee rail deep, filling her port scuppers.

Mairi did not hesitate.

"Ellie, luff her up! All hands shorten sail! Peter, strike that jib before it blows out. Trogen, strike the foresail! Cam, Seren, Marley, double reef the main!"

Cygnet shuddered. Sails flapped as sudden, short gusts struck the schooner now from ahead, now broadside, now astern. Mairi pulled herself hand over hand past the binnacle to relieve Ellie and then shouted orders as she took charge of the wheel.

"Ellie, I've got her. Neil, help Trogen. We'll keep the staysail. Ellie, get the storm jib from below."

The schooner bucked and jerked in conflicting blasts of wind. One moment, Mairi was holding the ship from turning downwind, the next spinning the wheel to avoid being taken aback. Spray stung her bare arms, still in rolled up sleeves from the morning's warm weather. The ship lurched, the main boom shuddered above her head, its sail rippling as three pairs of hands clutched at the flailing reef-points and dragged them down to be belayed. Ellie, the lightest of the crew, appeared from below, both arms around a bundle of canvass. Mairi heard her own voice squeak as she shouted to be heard over the storm.

"Ellie! One hand for yourself!"

Mairi felt *Cygnet* yaw and refocussed her attention on sails, wind, compass, and her battle with the wheel. She looked ahead, past Neil and Trogen, who were wrestling the foresail into submission. The day darkened as if toward sunset. She hazarded a glance to the east. Three-mountain island was disturbingly close— too close to chance running before the wind around the northern end into the island's lee. She had gambled that under reduced sail they could weather the western side of the island until they could turn downwind into the harbour, but now the ship was lying head to wind, making more and more leeway as her crew reefed and re-balanced the schooner's sails.

They were losing ground with each wave. *Cygnet* wallowed as Mairi strove to keep her pointing into the wind's eye. With each glance astern she saw the lee shore clearer. Individual trees thrashed above curling breakers where moments ago she had seen only a green wall of forest behind the white line of a reef. She gritted her teeth, wondering whether she had made the right decision. There was no point in shouting at her crew to hurry: even if they could hear her, they all knew that their situation was dire, and were making every effort, regardless of bruises, grazes, stubbed fingers, and torn fingernails.

Agonizing moments passed as Mairi struggled with the wheel. Marley's long arms wrapped around the main boom, smothering the flapping canvass as they tied the last of the reef-points. He dropped down to the deck, landing in a crouch as a wave slapped the stern, jerked the rudder and spun the wheel out of Mairi's grasp. Without pausing to stand to his full height, Marley reached into the blur of twirling spokes. Together, they corrected a lurch that would have jibed them all standing.

Mairi left the wheel to Marley and peered through the spray. The storm jib rose jerkily, shivered, and flapped. Only just audible over the wind noise, she heard a shout.

"We're done!"

"Ready, Marley!"

"Takin' the strain!"

Shouts competed with wind and thrashing sails as the warning was repeated up the length of the ship. Marley swung the wheel. *Cygnet* heeled violently to port as first the storm jib, then the staysail caught the wind.

"She's sailing. Stay with her, Marley. South by west, if she'll do it."

At first, *Cygnet* made no headway. Then the double-reefed mainsail grabbed wind, the bowsprit punched into a wave, and water ran down the ship's length, smacking the side of the cabin and drenching them all. For an instant, Mairi feared a knock-down, the sails flat on the water, but the schooner recovered and surged forward. Knee-deep water rushed down scuppers that had seen only rain and spray throughout their voyage south. With her lee rail buried, *Cygnet* struggled to make way. Ahead, the bent figures of her crew worked the sheets and struggled to hang on.

Then steady, rhythmical plunging replaced the confused wallowing and pitching they had endured while shortening sail. No longer the victim of the sea, *Cygnet* stole power from the storm and sped forward.

Wind and water tore at the ship, making shouts inaudible. Mairi clutched the binnacle, looking along the windward side, counting heads. Seren clung to the high side of the cabin, her hair plastered to her scalp. Further forward, where the staysail quivered, a sea-soaked figure clambered to windward. She recognized Neil's black hair, and beyond him, Trogen's broad shoulders, one elbow hooked around the shrouds, the other hand pulling Peter to his feet.

Where were Cam and Ellie? She felt a qualm of dread that her hasty orders had mismatched the teams she had sent forward. Then, before she could move to see better, two heads appeared around the mainmast, and Cam held up a hand, thumb up.

She waved them all astern, anxiously counting as they worked their way aft through the spray, crouching low, clutching at anything solid lest they be swept overboard.

At last, they were all clustered in the cockpit, sheltering astern of the main cabin, leaning against the coaming, hanging on to keep their footing. Seren had one hand on the handle of the mainsheet winch, and Cam held the tail of the sheet, ready to haul or ease. Peter, Neil, and Ellie were wide-eyed and apprehensive, Trogen grimly determined. Mairi beckoned them closer until they huddled near the binnacle, where their heads were only an arm's length apart.

"Good work, everyone," she shouted. "But more to do. Ellie, jackets for everyone. Peter, check the bilges and pump out what we've shipped. Neil, I want you on the jib sheets. They're run aft, so stay safe in the cockpit. Cam and Seren, you keep the mainsheet. The staysail should take care of itself. Trogen, rig lifelines and then stand ready to back up the others as and when and where you're needed."

She kept her voice low enough that it did not crack or squeak. As the crew nodded and went about her orders, she turned towards Marley.

"How are we heading?"

"She's makin' south by west, an' maybe a bit better. But there's more weather coming."

Mairi nodded. As if to prove him right, the wind strengthened and *Cygnet* heeled further to port, recovered, and surged forward even more swiftly.

"She's stayin' on course. A long way from so's I can walk away from the wheel, but she's balanced."

Mairi crouched to peer at the island over the binnacle. She did not notice that Trogen was standing amidships until he spoke.

"The island's bearing a little north of east. We have a way to go before we can make our heading. Trouble is, the peak isn't sharp against the sky. Jibe her and get into the island's lee."

Trogen's advice was a challenge to Mairi, spoken as if he were giving an order.

"Beggin' yer attention," said Marley, "T'other side be foul wi' rocks, an' in a blow like this there'll be wicked eddies an' downdrafts off the mountain, as well."

Mairi crouched over the spray-splashed glass of the binnacle to take a bearing on the mountain, acutely conscious that Trogen was doubting her judgment. Her wet hair whipped across her eyes, and she almost misgave. She wiped the domed glass over the compass, and when she had blinked spray from her eyes she saw that they were still on course. Her mind made up, she tensed with sudden anger. She faced Trogen.

"Trogen, the lifelines, now."

He hunched his shoulders and went forward.

Buffeted by gusts, *Cygnet* continued to thrash her way southward. Mairi revisited her plan. To continue was dangerous, to run into the harbour before the storm riskier still, but the alternative of taking shelter behind the island was fraught with unknowns. Mairi glanced at her crew, clustered in what little protection the cabin top provided. Trogen was no longer close to her, which made decisions easier.

"When we've reached the bearing, we'll go about and then run in on a reach."

"It's for sure we don't want to jibe her 'round in this weather."

She appreciated Marley's approval but did not even glance at him as she continued to peer over the binnacle. The mountaintop now bore south-east, but leeway was taking them towards waves breaking along the ragged white line of a reef. The green, tree-clad island writhed, its forest tossing back and forth in the gusts. As she watched, the colours deepened and darkened still further.

"I can almost do sou' west," said Marley.

For a fanciful moment, she saw the island as a face with tumbled green hair, its mouth a line of cruel white teeth.

"We've lost clear sight of the mountain peak."

Trogen reappeared beside her, raindrops sliding down his face and blowing downwind off his beard. A quick look at the island told her he was exaggerating. Rain squalls patched the mountain, but although the peak trailed a line of cloud, it still stood clear. She resolutely ignored him.

Cygnet punched into steep, choppy waves, shuddering at each blow. Every second or third wave, the bow drove into solid water, dipping the foot of the jib and throwing spray down the length of the ship. The crew huddled together, wiping salt water from their eyes, waiting for orders. Whatever Marley was thinking, his concentration on the difficult task of steering made his face unreadable. Trogen moved to stand behind her shoulder, his tension palpable.

He wants me to crack and let him take over.

Had she said the words aloud? Nobody could hear, anyway.

Mairi bent over the binnacle once more, focussing one instant on the rim of the compass card, the next on the peak. *Cygnet* lurched and swayed. A capful of spray obscured the glass dome over the compass. She wiped away the runnels of water and looked again. The red arrowhead of northeast swung in line with the mountain, the thinner mark of north-north-east lined up momentarily, and then as the red triangle for north swayed into view, she knew she was right. Doubt and anger gone, her voice was strong as she gave her orders.

"Stand by, everyone, we're going about. Marley, on my count: three ... two ... one ... GOING ABOUT!"

Mairi watched as each person's world narrowed to his or her specific task. Trogen bent over the port jib sheet and the smooth curve of the sail became a wriggling, flapping flag blown out over the waves. Then as Marley swung the wheel and the rudder bit into the water, the jib fluttered over the centreline. *Cygnet* came level, her masts up and down, and then plunged her bowsprit into the heart of a wave. Spray blotted out the entire foredeck. Pitching, rolling and swaying, the ship headed into the wind's eye and hung there. Mairi stopped breathing. They were caught in irons. Sea, wind, sails, and rigging howled above the hunched figures of her crew. Nobody could hear her.

Trogen lurched forward, fell to one knee, both hands in front of him. For an instant, she was sure he was lost, but he regained his balance, braced, and hauled. The jib shook and filled, regaining its curved triangular shape on the opposite side. The bow buried itself in another wave. The staysail thumped over, and *Cygnet's* bow disappeared yet again. Mairi looked up, and saw the head of the mainsail tremble, then shudder all the way down. She ducked as the boom swung inboard, felt it pass over her head and heard the thud as Cam and Seren checked its momentum. They had come about and were on the opposite tack.

"Marley, nor' nor' east. Bring her on course," said Mairi.

The tall man nodded as he swung the wheel now one way, now the other, picking his way through cresting waves that could slap the bow awry before *Cygnet* gained enough speed to settle into her new course. They now depended on Cam's and Seren's control of the main as much as on Marley's skill at the wheel. Though mismatched in size, the two worked in harmony; Cam in control with Seren's strength to back him up, he nimbly shaped the sails full, but not too full; drawing, but not dipping into the sea; using the wind without being overcome by it. Neil and Peter echoed them, ensuring that the staysail did its job of balancing the ship's rig in the absence of the mizzen. Now that Trogen had the jib set, all they could do was hope that it would not blow out.

With the wind abaft, spray stayed on the foredeck. *Cygnet* surged forward, overtaking the waves. Exhilarated by the speed and no longer drenched by gouts of water blown off the crests, Ellie and Peter grinned at each other. The older members were not so quick to celebrate, knowing that running with the wind on the quarter was chancy for both steersman and sail-handlers. *Cygnet* rushed up the windward sides, foamed through the crests and slid down into the troughs. One moment the stern was chased by a following wave, now it was deep in a trough, then raised high above a crest with the rudder almost in the air. Cam, Seren, and Marley synchronized their movements in a complicated dance.

Sensing that their responses to the wind and sea needed no interference from her, Mairi looked along the centreline of the ship towards the mountain peak. For a moment she could see nothing but heaving water. Then Marley sung out the words she had been waiting for.

"On course! Nor'nor'east it is!"

Cygnet crested a wave, Mairi sighted a red building through the gap in reef's line of white water, dead ahead. She knew they were going to make it.

5. In which Mairi, Seren, and Ellie go swimming

Mairi came up the companionway to find the morning sun slanting across the deck and *Cygnet* no longer at anchor. A second look revealed Trogen, dangling his feet over the starboard side, looking into the water. She took a breath to speak to him, then let it all out, and said nothing. Her ship was safe alongside the wharf, even if it was no thanks to her. She could not fault what had been done, only that she had not ordered it, which meant she had failed in her responsibility. She went back below, and to drive out self-flagellation with constructive activity, brewed coffee and took two mugs back up on deck.

Cygnet dipped almost imperceptibly as Mairi sat down beside Trogen, a mug in each hand. He accepted the drink and grinned at her. For a moment they were brother and sister again, her annoyance and his resentment both forgotten. Side by side, they watched a school of tiny red-and-yellow fish turning and wheeling in and out of *Cygnet's* shadow on the sandy bottom, nearly two fathoms below. The deck steamed in the morning sun, the sky was clear, and the sea beyond the harbour mouth stretched turquoise blue and smooth to the horizon. Morning sunlight dazzled on a white line of waves breaking on the reef beyond the harbour mouth, but in the anchorage the water barely pulsed. The reef protecting the island's beaches had roared all night long, even after the wind had fallen away and the rainstorms moved on, but now it only murmured in the distance. From the shore came the scent of wet earth and growing things.

"It doesn't come much better than yesterday," said Trogen. "Wasn't it the most marvellous sailing you ever had? Did you see Cam, whooping it up with the rest of the crew? Marley was singing as he steered. I couldn't hear the words or the tune, but I could see his lips moving."

"He was concentrating. So was I."

"Somehow we all knew nothing could go wrong. And nothing did. Right through the harbour mouth, hard-a-port into the wind all standing, let go the anchor, lash, stow, mug up, and then crash in our bunks, as if someone was watching over us."

"Well, someone was. Me. Anchor watch. Until the wind fell at dawn. Belief is not enough."

"You sound like Mother."

"Thanks, I'll take that with pleasure. Now, would you explain why you're sitting here doing nothing? Where is your watch? In fact, where is my crew?"

Trogen's grin faded.

"Cam and Neil are making nice to the harbourmaster, explaining that the skipper is taking a well-deserved nap after yesterday's inconvenient weather."

Mairi replied evenly, ignoring his sarcasm.

"A nap that began after the storm had moved on."

"Duly noted. If I know him at all, Cam's finding out who will give us a good deal on the stuff we brought, and a better deal on the coffee, sugar, cocoa, and rum we'd like to take away. I sent Seren and Peter to stretch their legs ashore with Marley, who's going to arrange for water."

"Ellie?"

"Below. Relieved of duty. She got a finger caught in one of the winches as we started our downwind run. Nobody noticed. Not even her. We were all too excited. Now she's uncomfortable."

"Did you see the damage?"

"No. I noticed she wasn't pulling her weight when we warped *Cygnet* over to the wharf earlier this morning while you were still asleep."

"And you didn't examine her hand?"

"Seren told me not to worry."

"And you left it at that?"

"She's the ship's healer. It's her job."

"And I'm the ship's worrier. That's my job."

Trogen scowled into the water, and Mairi turned away. He had taken the cup of coffee she had offered as a prelude to talking like sister and brother rather than master and mate. But the moment of companionship was gone. She had rebuked him, and he knew it was justified. He had overstepped his position by giving the crew leave to go ashore. He should have been more concerned for Ellie. He should have been aware that Mairi was standing anchor watch throughout the night when any other master would have kicked him out of his bunk and made him do his share. He should not have moved *Cygnet* without consulting the skipper. And behind each 'should' was his resentment that he was not in command.

Mairi took what was left of her coffee below. She had barely started down the companionway when *Cygnet* bobbed as her crew jumped aboard, the younger ones talking together excitedly.

"There's going to be a party!"

"Belay that, Peter," said Cam. "Afore y' get yerself in a flourish, there's work t' be done. You'll not be goin' to chase after them plump girls until the skipper tells you yer off duty, an' not much after if I have anything t' do wi' it."

Mairi reached the last step of the companionway and met Cam's grin at eye level.

"Reportin' in, Skipper. We're welcome ashore, Marley's got water arrivin' right soon, along with folks who'll help us unload an' set up right here on the dock to sell our stuff. It turns out we arrived in time for market day, so we don't have to go lookin' fer our customers. An' the folks in the big house what run this here island will be expectin' you in the afternoon to pay your respects."

"Well done, Cam. Now, will you and Trogen divvy up the chores between your watches? Get the hatches off the holds, tidy up the ship, dry out what got wet yesterday. Then we'll take turns ashore for a wash in freshwater, starting with Seren, Ellie, and me. After that, we'll shift into our shore-going rig to visit the people in charge."

~^~

It was a tall step from *Cygnet's* deck to the edge of the wharf, so the three women tossed their bags of towels and clothes ahead of them. As she climbed ashore, Mairi heard Ellie asking Seren where they were going. Remembering her own first visit to the island, she smiled when Seren replied, "You'll see."

A short walk took them past a few shacks huddled under palm trees bent by the prevailing winds, along a cart track through a stand of banana plants, their long, dark leaves still dripping away the night's rain, then on along a narrowing, sandy path among man-high shards of fallen black rock. They followed a path through a cleft where a massive piece of the mountain had split from the rest of the island in some ancient catastrophe. They walked into deep shadow, a ragged slice of vivid blue sky above, a damp, cave-like smell around them, following the winding sand-floored passage out through a gap like a tall doorway into blinding sunlight on a beach.

Mairi paused to let Ellie walk ahead of her onto the curved strip of sand, her slim figure casting its thin shadow. At either end of the achingly bright white sand, house-sized shattered fragments of jet-black rock had fallen from the cliffs, enclosing a crescent of beach not much longer than a stone's throw. Gentle, steady waves hushed along the shoreline, lifting and dropping debris from the night's storm.

"Great! It hasn't changed!"

Seren's shout mingled with Ellie's whoop of delight. Mairi stared seaward, past the transparent, green shallows on to the azure of the open ocean that stretched to a horizon where dark blue sea merged with deep blue sky. She blinked and turned from the dazzle of light to where the cliff face cut the sky, high above her. Her head back, she looked up at a stream of water falling from a notch at the cliff-top. The cascade started from a single source, fell in a smooth curve down the cleft, shattered on the first of many rocky outcrops, multiplied into rivulets that showered bushes, plants, and ferns growing on either side, and then gathered into a single sheet of gleaming water for a last leap into a clear basin. Across the pool, a wandering runnel trickled into the sand to disappear into the beach before it could reach the saltwater of the bay.

Mairi joined them at the water's edge. They dropped their bundles of clothes and waded into the pool, peeling off their salt-stiffened sailing garments as they went, tossing them back onto the sand. Soon they were neck deep. A few strokes took them to shelving stones fallen from the cliff face, where they could stand and let the waterfall shower down on them, rinsing the salt from their hair. Seren shook out her braids and watched the droplets spray in the sunlight. Mairi stood under the falls, the water drumming her shoulders free of tension. Ellie bobbed underwater like a white seal and came back up with her hair a wet, black ribbon down her back.

None of them noticed that they were being watched.

～∧～

Later, wearing the blue skirts and white blouses they had brought with them, and carrying their sailing outfits in damp canvass bags, they started back the way they had come. Marley's deep voice boomed out of the sand-floored passage between the cliffs.

"Is them mermaids all swum away now that the handsome sailors is here?"

"You're too late, you lecherous lubbers!" Ellie shrilled back.

Marley, Neil, and Peter emerged from the split in the rocks, grinning.

"Trogen?" Mairi asked.

"He told us seawater was good enough for him, took a header into the harbour, and sent us on our way," said Neil.

"Cam's mindin' the store," said Peter. "He's wheelin' and dealin' wi' the island folks. Said he didn't need no help from us."

The three young women retraced their steps to the ship in silence, now serious again after enjoying the pool like children on holiday. For Mairi, the swim and change of clothes had been a welcome interlude when she could forget her responsibility for the ship and crew that kept her tense, even when asleep. Now that they were dressed in the long-sleeved blouses and calf-length skirts prescribed for going ashore in foreign ports, duty and responsibility closed around her.

Ashore, she felt more a shopkeeper than a skipper. A part of her wanted to be back in her sailor's clothes instead of the white blouse and blue skirt. However, in some of the ports they visited, where women were considered either protected as virgins, wives, and mothers, or available as whores, she and her crew required carefully neutral female attire as a necessary shield against being scorned or molested. This was when she envied Seren her height that gave an instinctive physical confidence of which she was blithely unaware.

The swishing of her skirt against her legs reminded Mairi that though she was the skipper of her ship, in the eyes of the landlubbers, she was a woman, defined and limited by her sex. She barely noticed the sparkle on the sea, the gently waving palm trees along the harbour beach, or the intense green of the tree-covered hills as she picked her way back towards her ship among the few puddles remaining from the night's rain.

6. In which Mairi talks with Lady Orinda

As Trogen climbed up the companionway, he saw Mairi's bare feet, then her ankles, then her blue and white shore-going outfit, then the parcel of books under her arm, finally her face framed with still-damp blonde hair.

"Better put your shoes on before you visit the big lady."

Mairi frowned. Was he simply reminding her, or finding fault? Should she thank him as a sister or remonstrate with him as a commanding officer? She returned his look with an assessment of his white shirt and blue breeks, then took a calming breath, and slid her feet into the shoes she had been holding. She spoke in a carefully neutral tone.

"Cam not coming?"

"Cam's minding the store, with Peter and Neil helping, and we hope, learning how it's done."

"Then if Seren and Ellie are ready, we'll be on our way."

Moments later, four Cygnets started across an open space of hard-packed red earth between the wharf and the little town. The ship's trade goods were neatly piled under awnings alongside, where a couple of men were examining picks and shovels while Cam bargained with a woman in twice his size, whose vividly flowered tent-like dress fluttered when she moved and bared her plump brown arms each time she held up some object to bargain. Beside the wharf on the harbour's beach, dark-skinned men wearing sun-bleached shorts were unloading fish, crabs, and spiny lobsters from brightly painted boats with upswept prows. Young women and girls flirted with the men while wives, mothers, and grandmothers examined the catch. Other women in colourful dresses evaluated fruit, vegetables, chickens and anonymous pieces of meat at shopkeepers' booths, and then carried baskets of fish, fruit, coconuts, plantains, and bananas to where people were setting up an outdoor kitchen. Voices rose and fell in cadences strange to Mairi's ears, the words indistinct, the lilt musical.

Mairi tried to look at Seren and Ellie with the same analytical eye with which she had looked at the islanders. Their blue skirts and white blouses proclaimed them Cygnets; the ease with which they walked together, despite their different heights, was the only clue that they were sisters. When she turned her attention to Trogen, a thought struck her as if she had spoken out loud. *He really does look good in his blue breeks and white shirt,* and at that moment she felt subtly diminished. She knew the confidence in Trogen's manner would make the islanders think he was *Cygnet's* master. She stiffened her spine and lengthened her stride.

Conversation stopped as buyers and sellers alike turned to watch the four uniformed strangers walk towards the jumble of little houses that formed a half-circle around the marketplace. Even the scantily dressed children stopped picking up boughs and branches that had blown down in the night and stared. Seren hesitated to admire the little boys and girls until Ellie plucked at her sleeve.

They chose the broadest of the narrow roads that led up through the little town towards the tree-clad slopes of the three peaks that gave the island its name. The narrowing road blocked the breeze that had cooled them in the harbour, and they had barely started up the first of many steep switchbacks before Mairi felt sweat trickling down her spine. She wished she had worn a hat against the sunlight that pressed down from above, reflected back from retaining walls on the high side of the road, and radiated up from the warm, red earth under their feet. As they climbed higher, they glimpsed the ocher roofs of whitewashed stone houses that were now below them. When they rounded a bend, she took her parcel in the other hand, grateful that Trogen slowed his pace. Three or four more turns and they were high enough to feel the wind again, fragrant with the smell of the bright scarlet and purple flowers that hung in long fronds down from terraces above the road.

They rounded another turn, and the road diminished to a lane. They paused for a moment in dappled shade between trees overhanging the beginning of a gravelled path. Ahead was an impressive residence, built so long ago that it had blended into its surroundings as if it had grown there, ages before. On either side of the house stood huge trees with grey trunks, bare to where their green canopies met above the roof. Six slender white pillars rose up from a wide porch to a second-floor balcony and continued on up to support the red-tiled roof, which was blotched with green moss.

"Is anyone as hot as me?" Seren asked, plucking her blouse away from her body.

As their feet crunched on the gravel, Mairi began to see into the shadow under the balcony, where the pillars framed open double doors and windows. The symmetry of the house would have seemed formal, were it not for a casual, disorderly collection of brilliant crimson, red, and purple flowers that grew in big, randomly placed pots up and down the shallow steps leading up to the entrance. It was as if the serious old house had broken into a wide smile, its authoritarian past softened by a more colourful and comfortable present.

A low-pitched female voice came from behind the array of flowers.

"Well then, you sailin' people, come on up and see the lady of the house. That's me. The big man, the important fellow, he havin' a little rest for now so's he be ready for the big party tonight. Come up! Come up! I bin waitin'."

They threaded their way among the flower pots and gratefully entered the shade. Trogen would have taken a step ahead of Mairi, but the tall woman rose gracefully from her chair and reached out both hands to Mairi. Her dark-brown shoulders were bare above a single multicoloured garment that fell in fluted columns from her shoulders over her generous figure and down to her feet. Her hair was a black cloud above and behind her, twice the size of her head. Her dark eyes smiled her thanks as she took the parcel Mairi offered.

"Girl, it's bin a long, long time since I first seen you. Seems I missed you when your daddy and mammy came visiting the last time or so. Where you bin all these years?"

"Lady Orinda..." Mairi began, feeling that she had shrunk to the size she had been when first they had met, six years earlier. She was about to explain, but she never got the chance.

"None o' that 'lady' stuff, now, Mairi; you all grown up and important, not a little girl no more. I've known your brother, too, since he was little. So, tell me, who are these two good-lookin' girls?"

"These are assistant navigators Seren and Ellie, daughters of Dabih, Master of *Elusive*."

"Welcome to you both. Unless I miss my guess, Seren, you is younger than you look, and Ellie, you is older than you appear, which means that I'm going to send you both inside to meet my daughter Corinne, who'll be right in the middle, age and size, both. 'Way you go now. Now, Mairi, you sit down by me an' tell me why it is your daddy isn't here in his great big ship, an' you all alone in that pretty little sailboat you is so ably commandin'?"

Her loose dress billowing, she sat and patted the seat of a chair next to her. Her long-fingered hand then gracefully indicated a stool for Trogen, who pressed his lips together and scowled.

"An' you sit yourself down, too, Trogen, you handsome boy. I see you got your mammy's eyes. But you, Mairi girl, you got the look o' that man Astreya, not that you're all tall, slim, and supple like him, mind. An' you, Mairi, you got your mammy's fearless blue eyes, too. Mama Orinda sees more than looks. I see the green jewels on your arms. I knows all four of you 'herited the magical powers."

Mairi heard Trogen's wicker stool squeak as he sat down. A tall figure came out the shadows inside the doorway. It was Marley, his hands expressing an apology to Mairi.

"Come on out here, Marley, you scamp. Take Trogen, go find your brother an' talk 'bout somethin' that you men find interestin'. Leave us women to talk 'bout important stuff. Mind you tell one of those lazy girls to bring Mairi and me cool drinks. Away you go now, boys."

Mairi could not repress a smile as Trogen and Marley were dismissed like children. And then she was once again fixed by dark, hypnotic eyes. The Lady Orinda smiled and lowered her voice into a conspiratorial whisper.

"Tell me now, Mairi, are these new books you brought me? And how 'bout the salt fish?"

~∧~

Hours later, when Mairi started back down to her ship, a basket of colourful fabric under her arm, the path was patched with shadows. Seren and Ellie had left early to show *Cygnet* to Corinne, Trogen was somewhere with Marley, and Mairi was not entirely sure what had happened after they had left.

She had expected to give a brief account of the attack on *Cygnus* and Astreya's injury, the commissioning of *Cygnet,* and the mission south. However, what she had said was not the sparing, factual statement she had prepared. Instead, she had talked more openly than even to her own mother about the sudden terror of the unprovoked strike on both *Cygnus* and Astreya, her fears for her father, the mingled elation and stress of commanding her own ship, the complexity of managing her crew, and the welcome support of the two older men, Marley and Cam. Trogen's resentful behaviour she left unsaid, but she was sure that Orinda had noticed.

Late in the long afternoon, a cloud shadowed the island, rain briefly cooled the air and then stopped before Mairi could begin to worry about her ship.

Mairi had been so comfortable speaking freely that she had not once asked herself whether she was being too candid about her fears for her father's life, too open about her consternation that Lindey and Astreya had not told her all she needed to know, too willing to talk about the tensions and relationships among her crew.

As she walked down the hills, Mairi recalled her surprise when Orinda casually told her that Marley was her son, the older of two. She had briefly tried to estimate Orinda's age, but those dark eyes had her talking again in moments, her curiosity forgotten.

She came out of the shaded roadway into afternoon sun dazzling on the beach and harbour. In the distance, where the sky met the sea in a blue-on-blue line, bulbous white clouds sailed above the western horizon, blooming upwards from flat black bottoms. In the distance, one of them hovered over a neighbouring island, its rain darkening the green-clad hills.

On the red earth between the houses and the wharf were lines of benches and tables. Heat shimmered above a fire pit from which came a mouth-watering smell of roasting meat. Nearby were tables where women and girls were preparing food. Beyond, where *Cygnet* lay alongside the wharf, she saw Cam standing in the cockpit. He began to talk before she arrived.

"So, Skipper, yer back. Trogen an' Marley told me you was gettin' along just fine wi' Lady Orinda, but I was beginnin' t' wonder if the old lady had decided to keep yer here f'rever."

"We were talking about ... about a lot of things."

"Well, now that you're back, you should know that business has been a long way from brisk. If it weren't for a run on tools— axes, pickaxes, shovels and just about all the nails and spikes we carry—we'd a' come across a lot of saltwater for very little in the way o' trade. We got sugar, cocoa, an' coffee, but I'd 'a liked it better if we'd gotten more, an' for less."

As Mairi climbed aboard, Cam glanced around and lowered his voice. "Did the old lady let fall what they want with the salt fish?"

"I think we will find out tonight, Cam. You don't have to worry about making supper, we're all invited to the feast. Now, where are Seren and Ellie? Lady Orinda has kindly presented me with island dresses, as she calls them, for the three of us. What you men wear is up to you."

As she went down the companionway into the cabin, Mairi heard Cam talking to himself in the voice of a man who hopes to be overheard.

"Trogen and Marley can wear them island skirt-things if they want, but there ain't no bleeding way anyone's gettin' me to wear anythin' but me standard shore-goin' rig."

Later, as afternoon sun backlit the procession of swelling clouds along the horizon, and a steady wind pushed low waves onto the shore, Mairi, Seren, and Ellie were below in the cabin, trying to find the best way to wear the big squares of colourful material they had been given. They were used to the comfortable loose white blouses and the practical breeks they wore on board that conformed to the great ships' standards for women living and working among men, and they had little enthusiasm for the severe, calf-length blue skirts they wore ashore at their ports of call. Now they were faced with a dilemma: politeness demanded that they honour Orinda's gifts, but they were unsure of how to go about wearing them. Orinda's daughter, Corinne, had shown Ellie and Seren several ways to twist, knot, loop, and fold, but each method seemed less secure and more revealing than the last. Ellie had the least difficulty because she had more than enough material to clothe her slim figure modestly. Her head on one side, she watched Mairi and Seren struggle with material unfamiliar in its strong colour, delicate texture and bewildering shapelessness.

"It's easy, Seren. Hold the material in front of you by the corners, walk into it, cross the ends at the back and then tie them in front. Or behind, Mairi, if you haven't got enough slack left over. Here, let me help."

Material puffed, flapped and strained. Seren frowned. Mairi stood awkwardly. Ellie giggled.

"Now, Seren, comb out your hair and look girly. You too, Skipper."

A little while later, they came up the companionway. The warm wind fluttered the fabric, pressing it against their bodies. They stood looking at each other, more embarrassed than if they had arrived on deck wearing nightgowns. Mairi tried to forget that a couple of knots were all that kept the entire garment from puddling around her feet. The breeze pushed the fine fabric close against Seren, outlining her body like a second, multicoloured skin. Loose material clung to her legs and fluttered behind her. She looked down at herself and frowned.

"I don't care what you two do, but I need a ... a something around me."

She undid a stopper cord from around the mainsail and tied it above her waist. The wind no longer billowed the garment behind her, but a pattern of white and red flowers now clung to her breasts.

"Ooo ... wow ... um ...."

Seren whirled around to face two heads looking over the top of the cabin. Neil was blinking at Seren, his knuckles to his lips. Peter's face turned scarlet, and he hurried towards the bow to busy himself coiling the forward lines to shore. Seren breathed deeply to stop the blush that flowed from below the material across her chest, up to her bare shoulders, neck, and on to her cheeks.

Cam folded his forearms on the cabin roof and looked at the three women in turn. Unlike Peter's embarrassed reaction, there was nothing in Cam's evaluation to make any of them abashed. Ellie twirled, and blue-green material flared. She grinned as it came to rest around her.

"In'erestin'," said Cam. "Good thing it'll be dark. Otherwise, you'd catch yerselves a serious case o' sunburn on the bits that don't usually show."

Cygnet bobbed as Trogen leaped aboard the stern deck, saw his sister and cousins, and had to grab the backstay to avoid going over the side. His mouth dropped open, but no words came out. Mairi glanced at Seren, expecting to see the return of her bashful blush. To her surprise, Seren stood and looked back at Trogen, who had still not found whatever he had intended to say. To distract his open-mouthed gaze, Mairi climbed onto the stern deck beside him. His eyes were wide under arched brows.

"Mairi, we have to talk. It's about ...

"Yes. We do. Let's go for a walk, Trogen. You go first and give me a hand up. This dress ... garment ... thing ... isn't made for jumping and climbing."

Trogen did as he was asked. When they were both on the wharf, he lowered his voice to an urgent whisper.

"Mairi, there's something going on here that isn't right."

Sunlight flared across the sea between the billowing, mountainous clouds as they walked along the wavering line where sea met shore. She matched his stride, her new dress slithering across her legs.

"Mairi, Marley is ..."

"Mama Orinda's son."

"You know. Right. He's home and he's in a swither, on account of his brother, who's planning something. He wanted to talk to me about it, but at the same time, he didn't."

"Explain, Trogen."

"His brother has been doing business with a trader."

"Who?"

"Dunno. He didn't say."

"I suppose that's fair. Nobody said we were the only ships on the sea. What do they carry that we don't?"

"Guns, Mairi. A shed out back of that big house has enough guns for, I don't know, maybe a dozen or more people."

Mairi turned her gasp into a question.

"Marley showed you that?"

"He didn't show me. He accidental-done-on-purpose let me see. I think Marley wanted me to know, because I know that he's been around, up and down the coast, seeing stuff we've been kept from knowing. I think he's grateful to us for bringing him south, so he wants to do us a favour."

"He wants us to have guns? And how is that a good turn?"

"Listen, Mairi, there are a lot more people out there like the ones who blew a hole in *Cygnus*. *Cygnus* wouldn't have been damaged if there had been guns aboard."

"Do you think whoever it was would have known if there had been?" Mairi stopped walking and faced him. "Trogen, if you think I'm about to..."

Instead of answering, he strode ahead, leading the way along the curving beach. His shadow on the sand stretched out ahead of him in the level light from the setting sun. He stopped, and as Mairi caught up with him, he turned away, exasperated.

Mairi's question was out of her mouth before she could stop herself. "Orinda doesn't know about the guns ... does she?"

"What do you think?"

"She didn't say anything..."

"Wake up, Mairi. Come out of that all-girls-together, let's talk about how nice it would be if only the boys would behave."

"It was not like that, Trogen."

"Well then, what did you two women talk about?"

"Orinda spoke kindly of Father. And Mother too. Over the years, Mother brought her books, and Orinda's been teaching the Island women. She wants to know more about how the women of Matris choose their men and decide when they will have children."

"I bet the men of the island all love that. Mama Orinda tells their wives and daughters about all the wonderful things the nice white people on the big ships do when they're at home."

"You ... misunderstand," said Mairi, swallowing the word 'deliberately'. "She respects our parents as teachers, counsellors."

"Wonderful. Our parents, the peaceful guides to brother and sisterhood. The seagoing couple from the north who foster consciousness improvement as they make their regular trading visits, bearing subversive books, and giving heartwarming talks. Thank you oh so much for having such wonderful parents, Mairi. Here, little white girl, let me give you some nice new dresses."

Mairi's patience snapped. She took a breath to use the voice of command that she had been trained to keep for emergencies at sea, but at that moment the fingers of her right hand reached for the clasp on her arm. In the gloom, she was aware that Trogen had mirrored her unconscious gesture.

"Did you?"

"No."

"Must be Seren or Ellie with the shipstone."

"Something could be amiss. I must get back to the ship while we still can see."

They were whispering because the wind had dropped, the sea hushed, and the trees were silent. Mairi looked westward, almost expecting to see *Cygnus* or *Elusive*. Instead, as they started back to their ship, she saw the sun distort into an oval, which as she looked, was sliced by the horizon first at its bottom, then at its middle, then at the upper third, until with a final flash, it was gone. She glanced eastward to where the shadow line climbed the three hills and saw the last light leaving their tops. Darkness surged out of the east, enveloping the island.

They both began to run, but their first few steps turned into a walk when they could no longer see where they were going. Then, at their feet where the sea met the land, the gentle pulse of the waves became a white, meandering line. Dimly at first, then brighter as the western sky went swiftly from purple to black, phosphorescence traced a path for them to follow along the meeting of land and water.

As they walked around the rocky point that was the harbour's edge, ahead of them was a bubble of yellow light. When they climbed up from the beach onto the market square, Mairi saw lamps on the tables and on head-high poles. As they came closer, she could distinguish the silhouettes of people already at their places. Children milled about, the younger ones staying close to their parents, the older attempting to avoid them. Women were standing ready with trays in their hands. Cam walked towards them.

"Skipper! Where y' been? Me and Marley an' the boys have been loadin' coffee, sugar, and rum. Ellie's been securin' the stones afore we leave the ship. The island folks is waitin' on us."

7. In which people eat, drink and dance

Cam herded Mairi and Trogen towards the tables where the Cygnets were already standing, looking around, feeling out of place. As Mairi's eyes adjusted to the flickering light of the lanterns on poles, she saw Lady Orinda standing tall beside a stooped man whose loose, dark clothes blended into the night. A puff of wind plucked at Orinda's robe so that shadows slid across its peacock colours, alternately dazzling and darkening. Torches gleamed in her wide-spaced eyes and shone on a silver chain wound in loops and coils to hold her hair piled high above her head. Her outstretched hands were welcoming, but the old man beside her was as still as a weathered rock.

"Skipper Mairi and Mate Trogen, meet my boy Chad's daddy. This is Maximilian, the big man o' the island."

Maximilian was large, old, heavy, and hunched over. His face was expressionless, the skin so black it absorbed light, except for a gleam along the edge of cheek, brow, and chin. His eyes were deep set, and apart from the occasional glint, invisible. His voice was sombre, deep, and resonant; his lips barely moved when he spoke.

"You, Skipper, must be 'Streya's son."

Trogen scowled. Before he could speak, Orinda murmured in Maximilian's ear, and he turned his attention to Mairi.

"Tell me, why does 'Streya send girl children to trade with us?"

Mairi took a breath to explain that her father and his ship had both been injured in an unprovoked attack, but she was ignored.

"Never mind. Come, little girl, and you, the big tall one with hair like polished copper, sit down beside o' me, an' let us be eatin' together."

Seren sat hesitantly on one side of Maximilian, Orinda on the other, beckoning Mairi to sit beside her.

A voice spoke close behind them.

"An' how is it that three girls wear stones like the skippers o' the big schooners?"

Piqued by the patronizing tone, Mairi stood and turned. Orinda reached up a calming hand to touch her arm.

"Now, Chad, you behave yourself. Show respect. This is Mairi, who is in command of that fine little boat."

A sleekly handsome young man stepped uncomfortably close and gazed boldly into Mairi's face. Remembering her mother's training, Mairi deliberately took a small step forward and stared back. He nodded, his head tilted slightly to one side, then stepped back, holding his hands in a parody of his mother's welcome. Torchlight shone on his heavily muscled forearms as he completed his gesture with an ironic bow. He turned and walked away out of the light.

Mairi sat, a pulse beating in her throat. She took a deep, calming breath and looked around her. Trogen half-stood when Chad confronted Mairi and then sat back down opposite Maximilian. Ill at ease, he scanned the people waiting at the edges of the torchlight, ready to bring food and drink. Neil sat near him, gazing raptly at a full-figured girl who was holding a tray of food below her ample bosom. One table away, Cam was deep in a nautical conversation with one of the island's boatmen, mostly conducted in gestures; Ellie was near him, having avoided the children of her own age. Most of her crew accounted for, Mairi was suddenly aware that Marley sat opposite her. She intuitively grasped that he was embarrassed by the way his father and brother were behaving.

"Bring on the fish!"

At Lady Orinda's command, the women and girls who had been waiting stepped forward to present everyone with a hand-sized leaf, on which was a small piece of dried salt fish. Mairi heard Maximilian grunt.

Orinda rose to her feet, and everyone fell silent.

"Long, long time, hundreds o' years ago, when our island was bigger and the sea had not swallowed the old town, white people kept our ancestors as slaves."

All the Cygnets looked down at the table.

Before Orinda could continue, Maximilian took over. Bracing both hands on the table, he heaved himself to his feet beside her. When he spoke, the sound was deep, resonant, and powerful, as if the island itself had found a voice.

"There was a time when we were afraid. Not now. Eat. Remember. Know that this was, is now, and will always be our island."

The islanders all picked up their small portions of fish, chewed and swallowed, not only the children making faces of distaste. Some eyes were on *Cygnet's* crew, who dutifully ate what they had been given. Maximilian nodded and sat down. Orinda stretched out both arms.

"Now let the real feastin' begin!"

At her command, more women appeared out of the shadows, pitchers in both hands, which were plucked from them, the contents poured into mugs and cups, which were soon raised to drink. Other women plunked platters piled with flatbread onto the tables along with fragrant, steaming bowls of spiced fish and rice. Then they unceremoniously shoved their men and children along the well-filled benches so they could all sit and eat together. The night was filled with many voices. Maximilian leaned closer to Seren and growled in her ear.

"What you think of our fish, Seren girl?"

"Excellent," said Seren. "Much better than what we brought. Why do you start with ..."

Maximilian patted her arm, then pointed an age-crooked finger at his second son.

"You there, Chad. 'Splain to this tall white girl what we just did with the fish we had that man 'Streya send to us."

At the end of the table, Chad nodded and stood up to talk, relishing the attention he was receiving from the islanders.

"Way-way back, when there was more island, white folks like ..."

He paused and let his eyes slide over Seren and Mairi. Orinda interrupted him.

"They were white, Chad, but they were *not* like the family of Lindey and Astreya."

Chad inclined his head.

"...when those *other* white folks ruled us as slaves. Every flat place on the island grew sugar, and the steep parts grew coffee, and we did all the work. The whites didn't let us have boats, lest we escape. They didn't let us grow our own food. They fed us the salt fish they got from the ships that came for the sugar and coffee and rum. Some say that after a long, long time things got better, but it was still them that made the money and us who did the work—damn near for nothing. But the sea climbed up over the beaches, drowned the old town and swallowed some of the neighbour islands. That was when the great sickness came an' the white folks died. But we didn't."

"Chad has the nub of it," said Marley quietly, "though maybe..."

"Chad knows the meanin'," Maximilian's voice rumbled. "An' if *you* did, Marley, you wouldn't have gone off to sea for all these years, 'stead o' doin' what you should'a been doin', helpin' your baby brother."

Marley turned his face away. Maximilian nudged Seren, who had allowed her hair to curtain her face, obscuring her pained expression.

"Are you beginnin' to be understandin', long tall Seren? Or has that waste o' space Marley got you under his thumb?"

Seren shook her hair back and answered his first question.

"Because the salt fish tastes so bad, it makes you remember how life was *Before*."

"What you call *Before*, big girl, is the time when the white folks thought we were deaf, dumb, blind, an' stupid."

More food and drink arrived. Mairi poked at her food, her appetite gone. Maximilian continued to focus on Seren, who was not enjoying his attention. Chad maintained a rapacious stare at Mairi, and Marley looked thoughtfully into his mug. Mairi turned to Orinda and whispered.

"Then why are *we* here? Why did you decide to trade with the great ships—with my father and mother?

"That's a long story, sweet girl, and one that some time I shall tell you. Let me just say that your mommy and your daddy are different. They understood us in a way we never thought would ever happen."

"Respect," said Marley. He raised his mug as if in a toast and drank.

Mairi drank, tasting rum behind the fruit juices. A young woman leaned over Trogen's shoulder to refill his mug. He turned towards her, and his face almost grazed her breasts. He looked up into her eyes and smiled. Mairi thought she saw her fingers touch the back of his neck as she left him. His gaze lingered on her as she walked away, her loose green dress clinging to her thighs.

Orinda followed Mairi's look.

"Your handsome brother looks like he's enjoyin' himself. That bold girl is one o' my nieces." When Mairi did not speak, Orinda shrugged. "There's times when there ain't much you can do 'bout your own fam'ly."

Women regularly brought still more food. Mairi dutifully ate shrimps fried in spiced batter, jerk pork with mango, bananas cooked in sugar and rum, and fruits she could not name both sweet and tart. Finally, strong, black coffee arrived and with it, sticky little balls of fried spiced dough dipped in honey. Across the table, Trogen avoided Mairi's eyes as the young woman in the green dress returned to re-fill his cup more often than was necessary. Mairi heard Maximilian's deep voice whisper something to Seren that made Orinda frown. Seren stiffened her spine to its full height, her hair gleaming in the torchlight, and the old man slapped the table with one hand, laughing hugely.

"Long tall Seren, you make me young again!"

Mairi saw disgust in Marley's face. Sitting a little straighter herself, Mairi looked around for the rest of her crew. She was relieved to glimpse Cam's shore-going white shirt. He had left the boatmen and was sitting beside Ellie at a table of teenagers, insulating her from a cluster of boys by his steady flow of banter and repartee. At the other end of the table, half a dozen girls whispered and giggled, pretending to ignore the newcomers even while shooting covert glances at them. Neil sat between the two groups, awestruck by a girl whose yellow dress strained across her chest each time she put more food on his plate.

Mairi made a second scan around the tables but failed to locate Peter. She was about to stand up to look again when fresh torches flared in the open space beyond the tables. Someone tapped a compelling rhythm on a metal drum. Another answered with a deeper note. A third layered a high, fast counter-beat and the throbbing, pulsing sound swelled, drowning all talk. A tuned drum wove a skipping melody in and out of the texture of sound. Light gleamed on black hair as people at the tables nodded in time.

Mairi felt her pulse quicken. In the torchlight near her, she saw that children could not sit still, and their older brothers and sisters were no longer content with glancing at boys and girls of their own age. Young men and women stood and made their way into the flickering light of the torches, their hands gesturing with the treble drums, their feet following the rhythm of the bass. Some pairs briefly appeared in the patches of light only to disappear into the dark. More and more people of all ages joined the bobbing, swaying dancers. Light gleamed on brown and black shoulders, arms and palms flashed. One moment, bright-coloured garments flared, obscuring the bodies they covered, the next they drew taught, accenting what was beneath. The sinewy arms of men rippled, the smooth shoulders of women shone. Mairi saw Trogen leave the table and follow the green-gowned woman, intent on her swaying thighs.

Maximilian's hand closed on Seren's arm. She stood to her full height, silhouetted by the torchlight, the material of her dress clinging to her body, then swayed and almost fell as the old man used her to pull himself up from his chair. Orinda laid one hand on his arm.

"Old man of mine, we have to stay here and watch, don't we, Max?" Her voice was outwardly pleasant but very determined.

Maximilian regretfully released Seren.

"Long tall Seren, like I said, you make me young again. But not quite young enough. Away you go. Dance, girl."

Maximilian patted her bottom and shoved her towards the dancing.

"Dance, Seren," said Orinda. "Take her with you, Marley."

Marley led her from the tables, Seren frowning and hesitant until Marley took both her hands and the rhythm flowed from him. Her awkwardness softened, and they mingled with the dancers, oblivious to Orinda and Mairi watching them. Maximilian looked after them briefly, then leaned both forearms on the table and stared into his drink. Orinda looked at Mairi and smiled.

"My boy Marley's found a girl tall as he. But that's not the way you dance in your home far, far away to the north, is it?"

Mairi shook her head, thinking of jigs and reels, squeaking fiddles and the staccato rattle of a different kind of drum. A pair of white arms flashed in the light, the fingers rigid.

"Your brother's feelin' the beat."

"My brother's been ashore in places where ..."

"... places where a sailor-woman like you don't go."

Mairi gave her a questioning look.

"Oh yes, Mairi. I bin off-island, seen places where women is fish to be caught whether they want it or no—special if they's different, foreign, strange."

"Mother told me how to go ashore in foreign ports that aren't as friendly as your island. She told me, 'Don't meet their eyes in a crowd or on the street. Unless you have to. Then don't look away. Your eyes should tell them that you won't hit *back*, you'll hit *first*—and much harder than they expect.'"

Orinda laughed.

"You can tell 'em that with just the looking of your blue eyes?"

"Well, Mother does."

"I think maybe you can too, Mairi girl. I seen how you stood up to Chad."

8. In which there are shots in the dark

A hand touched Mairi's thigh. Instantly, she was on her feet and stepping back. Someone had tunnelled under the table on hands and knees. A white face looked up at her.

"Skipper, s'me, Peter. There's a ship just outside the harbour mouth what's goin' to steal *Cygnet.*"

Mairi grasped his arm and pulled him to his feet. "Peter, how do you know this?"

"There was this man, keepin' to the shadows, but I could see him because he was pale, like us. That feller who talked rude to you was tellin' him about how we was here aboard *Cygnet* cause *Cygnus* had been holed. Skipper, he was that pleased about it, like he'd done it himself!"

Orinda bent to look in Peter's eyes.

"Who you talkin' 'bout, little feller?"

Peter glanced at Chad, then back to Mairi.

"The white man said he was goin' back to his ship to fetch his crew, an' then they would take *Cygnet.*"

Orinda turned on Chad.

"Chad, tell me right now what you know about this."

"Nothing. Never heard of it. The boy's lyin'." He took a long swallow from his mug and banged it down on the table. "But men like that is why we need protection."

"What do you mean, protection?"

Cygnet's ship's bell clanged in the night and went on ringing. The drumming faltered and paused.

"Cygnets! To the ship!" Mairi yelled as she ran past the dancers, Peter a pace behind her. Men with torches began to follow them, the light flickering on *Cygnet's* shiny woodwork. Trogen caught up with her, and Seren and Marley were close behind. As they ran the last few strides to their ship, a grotesquely huge man loomed out of the cockpit, holding a much smaller figure, who was flailing at his head with both fists. Beside them, a lean man climbed nimbly over the rail and disappeared. The colossus hunched and lowered his kicking captive over *Cygnet's* outboard side.

The Cygnets leaped aboard and threw themselves at the big man. Marley fastened onto a huge arm, Seren grabbed for the massive head, caught an ear with one hand and a handful of hair with the other. Mairi clutched at a wrist so thick she had to use both hands. Trogen darted down the companionway.

For a moment, surprise made the giant pause. Then, with the ponderous force of sheer weight, he turned and shook off his attackers as if they were house cats. Mairi hung from his wrist for an instant, then slid to the cockpit sole in a heap. Seren reeled backward from an open-palm slap, tripped, and nearly fell over the port side. A solid thump below the chest drove Marley into the port quarter, winded. The monster swung himself over the side, his hulking body slowly disappearing until only his prodigious hands clung to the rail. Peter hammered at the big fingers with his fists.

Trogen charged up the companionway and fell over invisible bodies in the dark cockpit. He almost sat on Mairi, staggered, righted himself, and stood, momentarily confused. Yelling incoherent oaths, he swung a sword in a wide arc, narrowly missing Peter's head. From over the side came a bellow, followed by a confusion of shouting and thumping as an unseen rowboat shoved off against *Cygnet's* hull. Rowlocks squeaked, oars splashed. A loud report deafened *Cygnet's* crew. Before they could react, it was followed by five more explosions, spaced less than a heartbeat apart.

Something zipped past Mairi's head and thudded into the other side of the ship.

"Stay down!" shouted Marley.

Mairi stood up, most of her body shadowed by the cockpit. To the landward side, she saw more men running towards her, their torches trailing flame and sparks. Fearful of them igniting her ship, she waved them to stop. By their flickering light, she saw Trogen vault onto the narrow deck beside the cockpit and run forward, waving his sword. He paused on the foredeck, swore when he saw what had been done to *Cygnet's* rowboat, took two steps backward, yelled, "I'm coming!" and flung himself over the side in a racing dive, his sword outstretched. The splash of his body hitting the water faded into the regular pulse of oars diminishing into the night.

Mairi counted her crew. Seren bent over, dishevelled, clutching at the dress Orinda had given her. Marley stooped, his hands on his knees, his back heaving as he tried to catch his breath. A torch came closer, with Neil under it.

"S'all right, Skipper, I won't set the ship alight."

Flickering red light lit the corners of the cockpit. Mairi saw Peter on his hands and knees over a body. She turned around, her voice shrilling.

"Ellie? Where's Ellie?"

She felt a hand on her foot. As Peter helped Cam raise his head, she saw a bloody gash across his face. She dropped to her knees beside the crumpled figure.

"Cam!"

"Mairi, they took Ellie," he whispered hoarsely.

"We have to go after them!" yelled Peter, dancing with frustration.

"Can't," said Cam. "No wind. And they smashed our boat on the foredeck."

"They've shot holes along the waterline," Marley gasped. "Even if we could get under way, we'd be leaking from half a dozen places."

Seren tried to speak around a split lip, stopped, spat blood over the side, and mumbled. "Something went past me. Whizzing. Like a big bee."

"Me, too," said Mairi.

She reached under the side deck where they stowed oars, boathooks, and spare spars. When she ran her fingers along the ship's side, one of them touched a hole.

"Found it. Or one of them, anyway. Almost the width of my thumb."

Cam's heels scrabbled for purchase on the cockpit sole.

"Seren, we'll need softwood tree-nails and oak wedges."

"Belay that, Cam," said Mairi. "You're in no shape to do repairs in the dark. Sit still and tell us what happened."

Seren stepped over them and disappeared below, muttering. Cam subsided on the cockpit sole and spoke more calmly as Mairi dabbed at the blood on his forehead.

"First thing I heard was footsteps on the foredeck. Giant steps, makin' *Cygnet* list to starboard like we was beatin' t'wind'ard. Then a big crash when he stove in our rowboat. Ellie'n me were below. Neither of us was havin' much fun at the party, so we decided to go back to the ship an' pack it in for the night. She was gettin' into proper seagoing rig, an' I was strikin' a light to look for me mug. Big feet thumped into the cockpit. I knew right off it wasn't one of us. When I went up, this bloody great monster picked me up, slapped me silly and dumped me—here, I guess. Next thing I knew I was bein' tripped over an' trod on."

"Trogen," said Mairi ruefully. "He walked on you when he was fetching that damned sword he burned his hands to make. And now he's swimming after the rowboat full of men who attacked us."

"No, he's not," said Neil. "He's ashore on the beach, walking back. Still got his pig-sticker, though."

"Careful with that bucket, Peter. What are you doing?"

"Washin' blood off the deck afore someone slips on it."

"That must have been from Trogen's knife-thing," said Seren.

"An' from me head," said Cam. "Dryin' up nicely now, though."

Trogen jumped from the wharf into the middle of the crowded cockpit, sword in hand.

"Careful with that," said Marley.

"It's my sword. And I'm going to use it on the bastards who boarded *Cygnet*."

"Put it down, Trogen," ordered Mairi. "You're drunk."

Trogen's sword wavered as he turned to reply.

"No more than Seren, cuddling up to that evil old man, and then writhing around with *him*."

He jerked his thumb at Marley as Seren came up the companionway carrying a bag of tools and wood. She let go of the bag, and as it thumped on the cockpit sole, she took a pace forward and hit Trogen's face with a solid, loud, open-handed smack. He staggered and let go of his sword, which dangled on a lanyard from his wrist. Everyone froze into silence.

"Here's the wood, Cam," said Seren in a matter-of-fact voice. "I'll be with you in a moment. I have to go below, get a light, and put on clothes I can work in."

Mairi looked up to see faces looking down from the wharf at *Cygnet* and her crew. She craned her neck, then climbed onto the stern deck, where her head was at the waist level of the people on the wharf. The torch-carriers held their flames at arm's length, their yellow light gleaming on curious faces. A few of them shuffled apart to make way for Lady Orinda, Maximilian, and, a few steps behind them, Chad. As if their appearance had caused it to happen, a full moon rose over the shoulder of the island. The torches seemed to dim. From across the still water of the harbour came the first breath of the night wind. Ignoring the new arrivals, Mairi climbed onto the stern deck and gave orders.

"Stoppers off, hoist sail. Single up to the stern spring. Shove off from the bow. Fenders inboard. She'll ghost until we're outside the harbour. Cam and Seren, find and stop those holes. I've got the main with Marley. Trogen, get rid of that foolish weapon and join the boys on the foresails."

She was about to jump back down into the cockpit when Orinda's voice stopped her.

"Mairi, where you goin'?"

"Someone has kidnapped Ellie. Probably trying to steal our ... our navigation equipment."

"You wearin' your magic stones. Can you chase them in the dark?"

Maximilian's voice rumbled. "What you goin' t' do when you catch up wi' them?"

Mairi did not answer. She had not thought beyond going after Ellie.

Marley's voice came from beside the mainmast.

"First, we get little Ellie back."

Chad's voice came out of the shadows, each word a taunt.

"Dey ain't yo' people, Marley. You runnin' 'way again?"

Marley's voice was harsh.

"I ain't been paid off, an' as long as she wants me aboard, I'll sail for Skipper Mairi."

"You hankerin' after the white girl?" Chad taunted.

Marley took a step away from the mast. His eyes flashed in the torchlight. Maximilian's voice rumbled again.

"Chad, enough. You, Marley, you think twice 'bout what you doin'."

"I done that."

"Then Marley, you had best go," said Orinda. "An' good luck to all o' you."

Maximilian's hand fell heavily on Chad's shoulder.

"You'n me got some talkin' to do 'bout the folk you bin dealin' with. An' by that, I mean you should ready yerself fer a whole lot o' listenin'."

Orinda spoke to the torch carrier next to her, then stepped to the edge of the wharf, her voluminous dress fluttering in the night wind.

"Mairi, by the time you cross the harbour, there'll be a light on the south side o' the gap."

A torch fluttered flame and trailed sparks as the man carrying it jumped off the wharf and ran along the beach.

"Thank you, Lady Orinda, for everything. Marley, we got the main, you take the wheel. Neil, hoist the jib, cast off the bow. Peter, stand ready to slip on my command. Right, Cygnets, let's get on with it!"

"Wait!" said Cam. "Where's Trogen got to?"

"Last seen heading below," said Seren. "Presumably to hide his pig-sticker."

"It's a sword," said Trogen as he came up the companionway. "Mairi, you can't take *Cygnet* anywhere. She's holed all along the starboard side. It was some kind of a handgun. I saw five, maybe six flashes."

"Join the boys on the foresail, staysail, and jib."

"But..." Trogen began.

"Now, Trogen."

Trogen hesitated, then moved to obey.

"Cam, how long until we can sail on the starboard tack?"

"Wi' a bit o' luck, we're good 'til the wind strengthens," said Cam. "Jus' try t' keep her on an even keel or maybe heelin' a bit to port. Seren and me have it in hand, Skipper. We'll be ready to start repairs, soon's I taper the end of these here cedar plugs t' fit the holes."

As *Cygnet's* sails caught the soft night wind, Mairi saw Orinda raise her fingertips to her lips and wave. A torch flared at the harbour mouth. The rising moon cast a glistening path of light across the long, slow, heave of the ocean all the way to the horizon. Inside the harbour, it shimmered on the tiny ripples made by the wind that lifted Mairi's hair from neck, reminding her that her shoulders were still bare. A match flared, and a pool of yellow lantern light filled the cockpit.

"Seren, did you by any chance...?"

"Your shirt's beside the binnacle." Seren's voice came from below Mairi's knee. "Don't fall over me."

As Mairi pulled her shirt over her head, Cam's voice came to her from over the starboard side. He was sitting in a bight of rope, his feet trailing in the water, a mallet in one hand and in the other, a finger-length cedar peg, tapered at one end.

"That you, Seren? I can see light coming out the holes. I'm going to plug the hole athwart the binnacle."

"I'm ready. Bang it in."

Cam fitted the tapered end of the peg into the hole by feel and thumped it in tight. Seren pushed a hardwood sliver into the slit Cam had made in the peg, and together they hammered both ends of the peg.

"Moving to the next one forward. Shine the light ... good, that's right."

They repeated the process, then Seren went to the cabin to locate two more holes. Ashore, the music started again, somewhat tentative at first, as if the musicians were unsure, then the full chorus of drums rolled across the harbour. Mairi summoned Peter to sit on the top step of the companionway and relay what Cam and Seren said. When he repeated Seren's first message, Mairi drew in a quick breath.

"Seren says the holes are where the bullets would have hit Marley and Cam if they'd been sleeping in their bunks."

The music was suddenly cut off, as if by order. They heard only the small liquid sounds of *Cygnet* making her way softly through the ripples.

"They aren't playing the drums anymore," Neil began. "Do you think..."

"We're getting near the harbour mouth," said Trogen.

"Quiet!" Mairi snapped.

The hole-plugging began again. Eventually, Cam's bag of tools thudded onto the deck, and moments later, he clambered aboard and made his way astern.

"Well, that were right some lucky. Whoever shot at us banged his last bullet through the planking to sink itself in one o' the ribs. It's doin' no harm. Sheer luck I found the hole, jus' by feelin' around in the dark. I plugged it, anyway, to be tidy. We should do 'til we get to port an' I can smooth an' seal the plugs wi' varnish. But they'll hold, right enough."

"Coming up on the headland, Skipper," said Marley.

"Keep her as she goes, Marley. Douse the lantern, Neil. Peter, call Seren on deck. Trogen, come aft. You too, Cam."

The *Cygnets* clustered in the cockpit. Ashore, the drums were still silent, and they could see only a couple of torches, dimmed by distance. The mountains were a black shape against a dark sky, moonlight whitened the beach. Only the brightest stars shone overhead.

Mairi stood in the cockpit and looked under the main boom towards the orange-yellow flare at the harbour mouth. Her confidence had evaporated, leaving her hollow with uncertainty. The garment that the Lady Orinda had given her fluttered against her legs.

"Breezin' up, Skipper."

Mairi did not need Marley's deep voice to remind her that they were almost at the harbour mouth, and she had no idea what course to set. She rolled back her sleeve and stared at the sliver of white light at the heart of the stone in her clasp. At her shoulder, first Seren and then Trogen copied her.

"Nothing," said Seren.

"Our shipstone is shielded. Ellie must have put it into its container when Mairi and I were on the beach," said Trogen.

Mairi swung around to confront him.

"I thought you were ... you mean it wasn't shielded before?"

In the dim light from the binnacle, she saw Trogen's shoulders twitch.

"Umm ... I was checking something the morning after the storm. There was a lot going on, and ..."

"We were ordered not to use the stones..." Mairi began.

All three of their clasps gleamed at the same moment. Cam shook his hand and stared at the ring on his finger.

"Direction! Quick!" said Mairi.

"North-west," said Seren, with a glance at the binnacle.

"North-north-west," said Trogen.

"I agree. Ready about: bring her around, Marley. Course to steer, nor' nor' west."

Cygnet turned slowly through the wind's eye, the yards swung over, the crew trimmed the sails and stood in the moonlight. The ship steadied on the port tack leaving the light on the harbour mouth astern.

"My stone's not telling me where she is," said Seren.

"Look again," said Trogen. "I'm picking up Ellie's stone. She's messaging."

"That's impossible," said Seren.

"She can and so can I. So shut up and let me concentrate..."

"Is she all right?" Seren's question was more like a prayer.

Trogen waved one hand for silence, then nodded.

"Are you sure?" Seren demanded.

"Do you think I'd make it up? She's alive, I tell you."

"We must ..." Seren began.

"We follow," said Mairi.

9. In which Ellie is held prisoner

Huge hands grabbed Ellie as she climbed into the cockpit. She kicked, yelled, and furiously hit at the head of the man who held her, but was silenced by a crushing hand on her mouth. Still struggling, she was swung over the side down to fresh hands aboard the skiff. Someone pulled a bag over her head, crossed her wrists, tied them together, and dumped her onto the bottom of the boat. She took a breath to scream in the evil-smelling sack, but an explosion above her head stunned her into silence. Five more shots slapped at her ears. Strangely muffled voices reached her as if from a hollow distance. The first was high-pitched, angry.

"Gimme back my gun!"

"'Ain't yours."

"Don't shout at me!"

"I ain't shouting."

"Y'are, Jake."

"What'cha say, Moke? I'm near to deaf!"

"You got no idea how to shoot."

"I put six into the hull."

"Luck. An' the fac' you was only an oar's length away."

Ellie squirmed. A man's deep voice spoke close to the bag over her head.

"Lie still, little squirt…"

She wriggled and was rewarded with a kick in the ribs.

"We told yer," said the shrill voice from the stern. "Lie still."

Ellie shut her eyes tight and tried to ignore the smelly bag. She began to hear normally again. Wood squeaked on leather. A soft splash and a man's grunt of effort. A whuff of breath close above her head. More splashes from quick, deep strokes ... two ... three ... four ... five ... at six the rower slowed and then settled into his rhythm. She felt the pulse of the boat's movement; heard soft trickling sounds along the hull. Then from astern, came a ragged, noisy splash.

"Whazzat?"

"Damnfool's swimmin' after us. Dig in, Jake. Leave 'im behind."

Ellie tried to sit up. Another kick, this time in the thigh.

"Did'ja check that the one we caught had one o' them bracelet things?"

The question was from the high-pitched voice in the stern. The reply came in deeper, slower words from the bow.

"'Course I did. I ain't stupid."

"Y' could fool me."

"Leave him alone." (Breathe, creak, splash.) "The kid's got a bracelet." (Breathe, creak, splash.) "You c'n see it." (Creak, splash.) "Glowin' through his shirt." (Breathe, creak, splash.) "C'n y' see the swimmer?" (Creak, splash.)

"Nah. Bugger must' a turned back. Or drowned."

Ellie became dispassionate, analytical. The three men had been sent to kidnap someone with a navigator's clasp. They had seen the gleam of green light of her clasp through her shirt. One was shrill, argumentative. Another, presumably the giant, was deep-voiced, slow-spoken, resentful of being thought stupid. The third, the rower, was more measured.

She took a breath, ignored her throbbing shin, the pain in her ribs when she breathed, the oppressive presence of three men. Her fear ebbed as she set her mind to what she thought of as "listening," even though what she did had nothing to do with sound.

She felt *Cygnet's* shipstone like a background buzz or a distant light. It was where she had placed it in its shielded container aboard

Cygnet, hours ago. She relaxed somewhat. The shipstone had not been stolen while she was struggling with the monster.

The regular sounds of rowing ceased, and the skiff bumped against its mother ship. Hard hands gripped Ellie under her armpits. She was hoisted upward, and another pair of hands caught her and dumped her down. Her feet thumped onto a deck.

"What'll I do wi' the kid?"

"Take him t' the stern cabin."

The voice belonged to the rower. The cord around her wrists cut the skin as she was half-shoved, half-carried down shallow steps. Ahead of her was a new voice: clear, unemotional, curious.

"Bring him in here. I want to find out how his stone works."

"An' if he ain't keen t' tell us?"

"Then we persuade him."

"I'm good at that." Again, the high, chilling giggle.

"An' in the meantime?"

"See if he cooperates. If not, Moke holds him down, and Cookie goes to work."

"Um... I dunno. He's jus' a little 'un. Ain't right to..."

"You'll do as you're told, Moke."

"Let's take a look at him."

Sailcloth scraped across Ellie's face as the bag was plucked off her head, taking her watch-cap with it and dragging her hair over her eyes. She stood before a table in a small stern cabin. A lantern cast light on a chart; everything else was in deep shadow. She could hear, feel, and smell two men behind her in the darkness. She could not see the face of the man who sat on the other side of the table. Despite herself, Ellie made a sound midway between a gasp and a sob. She straightened her back and shook her hair back from her face.

"It's a girl. Leastways, it's got hair like a girl."

The hand on the ropes around her wrists eased. She turned and looked up to see a craggy face, the eyes shadowed by bushy eyebrows, the jaw shadowed by a short black beard. The precise voice behind the lantern spoke again.

"Jake, did you get the big stone?"

"Nope."

"Three of you, one big as a house, and all you could get hold of was a child?"

"Moke didn't fit down into the cabin, an' me an Jake was ... well, we was busy wi' the gun."

"Pathetic. Did you make sure he—she—has a green stone?"

"Uh-huh."

"Show me."

Jake hesitated.

"Like—you want me to take her shirt off?"

A high voice laughed mirthlessly.

"Embarrassed, Jake? Just undo her hands."

A hand reached up to tip the lantern. The face that looked at Ellie was young, beardless, pale, and oddly expressionless. Blue eyes stared as if assessing an object rather than a person. Ellie frowned back.

"I'm not going to tell you anything."

"Determined, ain't she?"

"I like 'em young."

The high voice came from behind her. Against her will, Ellie flinched, took a step forward and grasped the edge of the table.

"Don't try anything, little girl. Roll up your sleeve. Hold your arm where I can see it."

The young man's directions were quiet but strangely reasonable. She saw her hand extend in front of her, despite herself. She saw curiosity in the gaze of the young man, wide-eyed wonder on Jake's weathered face, and heard a rapacious intake of breath from the man they called Cookie. She set her teeth, concentrated on her stone, and made the necessary mental *shove*. The white spear of light at the stone's heart flashed, blinding everyone except Ellie, whose eyes were closed. All three men stared, transfixed by green light. They twitched, stepped back, or shook their heads while for three or four heartbeats an afterimage followed them wherever they looked. Ellie staggered, suddenly giddy. The faint she had intended to be a sham became real. She clutched at consciousness and hung on, even as her knees buckled. She felt someone catch her before she could slump to the deck. Voices shouted.

"You killed the kid!"

"Whatcha goin' t' tell the old man now?"

With a glow of stubborn triumph, Ellie let herself slide into oblivion.

10. In which Cygnet follows Ellie's kidnappers

Marley spoke from behind the wheel.

"It'll be a stern chase. "Slow work catching up."

"We don't even know what we're following," said Seren.

"She's a ketch, 'bout our size, but a lot older," said Marley.

"Then it's likely she's got a foul bottom," said Seren. "We can catch up."

"Wait a bit," Trogen demanded. "How does Marley know? We don't even know why he's aboard."

"Astreya offered him a passage to his home in the Sunny Isles," said Seren.

"We know that. But why is he leaving his family?" Trogen's voice rose.

"Whose side is he on?"

"Marley volunteered to stay with us..." Seren began.

"Sure he did. But why? How come he knows about a ship none of the rest of us has laid eyes on?"

"Marley?" Mairi asked quietly.

"That's a fair question, Skipper."

"You're going to believe what he says?" Trogen demanded. "The words of a liar?"

"I have never lied to you or to anyone else aboard."

"I don't trust you, Marley," said Trogen.

"That's a pity, because your father did, enough to send me on my way with all of you."

"Explain, Marley," said Mairi.

"Here's my story, Skipper. Like many a sailor's tale, it begins in a pub. I was down on me luck in Glasstown, let go from a coasting tramp because the owner wanted his son to have my place as mate. I was drinkin' a bit. This old man came to me an' asked if I was lookin' for gainful employment. That's what he called it: 'gainful employment'. He had himself together and was a lot more sober than me. Maybe I shouldn't't'a, but I went with him to a ketch alongside a wharf nearby. No sooner we were aboard he asked me if I wanted a berth aboard or a job ashore. What I'd seen of his crew as I came aboard had sobered me up a bit. There were five, countin' the old man, an' they all bunked in a small cabin ahead. All o' them were white. One was a weasel-faced little low-life they called Cookie, another was a hard-lookin' man 'bout my size. There were two more, different as chalk from cheese. The one was all eyes with nothing behind them—just lookin'. The other was that monster that grabbed Ellie. I don't know which of them I liked less. I asked the old fellow what he had in mind."

"You told Fa ... Astreya ... this sailor's yarn?" said Trogen.

"Not at first. I just said what I was paid to say. But your father looked at me—much as you're doing right now—so I did."

"What you were paid to say?" asked Mairi.

"Here's what I memorized, an' told to your father. The old man made me repeat it twice, so's he knew I had it right. 'Tell him I'm coming for him. I want him to squirm before I take him down. I want him to be thinking about what I'll do to him and his family.'"

"Who was this person? What's his name?" Trogen demanded.

"Dunno. He didn't say. He seemed real sure your father would know who he was."

Cam's voice came from the darkness at the top of the companionway.

"He was old, right? Like grandfather age or more."

"Right. But he was sharp. Ordered everyone around and they did it."

"Mirak," said Cam. "For certain sure."

"Who?" Seren asked.

"Nasty piece of work what did his best to kill 'Streya back when they were both on *Cygnus* and she was under Oron's command."

Mairi heard invisible voices below on the companionway steps.

"Shut up you two, I'll explain later," said Cam.

"I must be stupid," said Seren. "I just realized that Astreya sent us south in *Cygnet* so that Mirak wouldn't steal the stones."

"You ain't stupid, Seren," said Cam. "You're right, but it's more than that. 'Streya, an' Lindey an' Dabih, too, they all wanted the bunch of you a long, long way away, so's Mirak couldn't grab you and make you run the stones for him, same as happened to Dabih, yer da, 'til 'Streya an' Lindey changed all that."

"So Grand Master Astreya shipped all of us south aboard *Cygnet*," said Trogen. "Nice work, Father. You sent us straight into Mirak's clutches."

"Well, up north in Matris, it seemed to the three of 'em that the Sunny Isles was the last place Mirak would look," said Cam.

"That was stupid. They were wrong, and now Mirak's got Ellie," said Trogen.

"So now we have to get her back," said Seren.

Marley's deep voice held a note of urgency.

"I don't think you're hearin' what I'm tryin' to tell you about him an' his crew."

"Afraid, are you?" Trogen mocked. "Like when you scuttled off instead of going back to Mirak?"

"Concerned. Like when I told your father everything I knew."

"You were Mirak's messenger. Why should we trust you? You may be just ..."

Mairi cut across Trogen. "Because Astreya trusted him. And I do, too."

"So what do you plan to do? Just sail away?"

"Trogen, Mairi gave the order to chase after them, which is what's happening while we're arguing," said Seren.

"Seven of us. Five o' them," said Cam.

"Scared, Cam?" Trogen asked.

Peter's voice came from behind Cam. "Well, I ain't!"

"Me neither!" Neil echoed.

For a long pause, there were only the sounds that came from wind urging *Cygnet* onward. Mairi took a deep breath.

"We follow. But we need to stay out of sight, just over the horizon, until we know exactly where they're going."

"I can do that," said Trogen.

"Right then. We catch up, but we don't close until we know where they're going. Three watches: Cam, you and the boys take the morning watch. Trogen and Seren, you have the graveyard. Marley and I'll take her until midnight. The rest of you, get your heads down. Grab some shuteye while you can."

Seven people all decided not to say what they were thinking, and then five dark shapes found their way down the companionway in silence. Mairi stood in the cockpit and looked over the cabin top, past the ghostly curves of the foresail and jib and on into the night, resolving not let herself imagine what could happen to Ellie. She wondered why she was so calm, even though she had no destination and no rescue plan. She had started a stern chase, and there was nothing to do but hope that a solution would present itself.

Something fluttered at her ankles. She looked down and realized it was the loose, flowing garment Orinda had given her. Exasperated, she went below to pull on the lower half of her seagoing clothes, muttering to herself. Once in her cramped stern cabin, she stood silent for a few moments to listen, but heard only *Cygnet* easing through the water and the sounds of people fumbling their way into their bunks. She changed and threw Orinda's gift on her bunk. Feeling a lot more comfortable, she climbed up into the moonlit night. After doing her rounds of the ship, she took over the wheel. A short while later, Marley handed her a steaming mug.

"Tea, but it's sweet," she said.

"What is it?"

"Molasses. Got me a jug while I was ashore."

"It's good."

"Thank 'ee."

There was a long silence between them filled only with the sounds of their ship responding to wind and water. Marley coughed and spoke diffidently.

"Skipper, would y' take it amiss if I asked what's up wi' Trogen?"

Mairi looked down at the compass, then ahead to the horizon where the moonlit sea merged into a black velvet sky. Marley's silence was irresistible.

"You have to understand that we're different, even though we're twins. People seem to expect us to have some kind of special knowledge of what the other's thinking. It's not like that. We're seaborn, we grew up afloat, we were in each other's company when we were little children, we learned about ships and the sea at the same time, but as I say, we're different. I don't know any more than you do about what's going on in Trogen's head."

"I 'magine your mother and father must'a had a hard time bein' even-handed 'tween a boy an' a girl."

"Oh, no. Father and Mother are the most fair and equal of all the parents I've ever known." She paused, realizing how defensive her words had been. "Of the many, many parents I have carefully observed over the course of my long life," she added solemnly.

Reassured by Marley's soft chuckle, she looked up at the sky for a little while.

"When we were around seven, Trogen found a pair of wooden balls and tied them together with an arm's length of string. *Cygnus* was at anchor—I forget which port. Trogen grinned at me, took hold of one of the two wooden balls, twirled the other around it and then let them both go. The balls flew whirling through the air, staying apart at the ends of the string until they wrapped themselves around the mainmast. Then he retrieved the device and threw it again, and then again. I lost interest and walked away. All of sudden: Swish! Clack! Thump! I was on the deck, my ankles bound together."

"Must have smarted."

"I was furious. When I got myself untangled, I stamped off, full of self-righteousness, and told our mother. Trogen appeared at Master's Court and had to apologize to me in front of the whole crew. For nearly two weeks, nobody aboard *Cygnus* spoke to him other than to order him to do unpleasant things like cleaning the heads and holystoning the deck."

"Sounds amazin'ly familiar."

"Eventually I asked him what had been said in the Master's Court. He told me that he had broken some incomprehensible law called the Projectile Rule."

"The Projectile Rule?" said Marley. "Can't say I've ever heard of that."

"Neither of us had. So we went to ask Mother. She always had reasonable answers.

"We found her in the great cabin. She sat us down at the big table where the master held his daily meeting with the navigator and mates, and where later each day mother-the-ship's-navigator turned into mother-the-schoolteacher and taught us—well, everything.

"I asked about the rule. Trogen kept saying 'It's not fair' over and over. Eventually, mother held up one finger, and we both were silent.

"'It's not logical,' she said, and then she took us through our history. How Astreya's family—our ancestors—stayed at sea for almost a century on *Cygnus*, *Elusive* and half a dozen other ships. We joined in the telling because we'd heard it all so often before, about how they escaped the chaos that happened as *Before* fell apart, and while *After* was a-building from the ruins. The Wandering was reasonable enough at first, but eventually, it turned into a sad business of blindly following useless rules and laws. I said, 'Father and you changed all that, didn't you?' And mother said, 'We were instrumental in the collapse of the old ways of the fleet and the beginning of a new approach to seagoing commerce.'"

"She said that?" Marley asked.

"When mother has the wind in her sails, she leaves a very straight wake behind her."

"I'll say."

"I asked her, 'What's the Projectile Rule? Is it from back during the Wandering?'"

"I wondered if you might come back to that," said Marley.

"We're getting there. Mother explained that when Zubin started the Wandering more than a century before, he believed that *Before* had failed because of plague and warfare. So he ended all contact with people ashore so that the Men of the Sea wouldn't catch diseases, and furthermore, he banned all weapons at sea. When we got to that part, I asked, 'What about knives and hammers and chisels and cleavers and clubs?' And Trogen said, 'I asked the same thing, but all they say is, that's different. But it isn't. It's just their way of saying, don't ask.'

"'You asked *me*,' Mother said, 'so I'm going to tell you. It's all in the way you name things. Every man and woman aboard this ship carries a knife, but it's a tool, not a weapon. Weapons are made for killing people, first and foremost.'

"'All right,' said Trogen, 'I understand, but it's fuzzy because knives can be used as weapons. What I don't understand is why everyone made such a fuss about my toy.'"

"I'm wonderin' that, too," said Marley.

"That's when I shouted, 'Weapon, not toy!' and I would have said a lot more, but Mother shushed me. This is what she said:

"'See what I mean about point of view, Trogen? To you, a toy. To Mairi, who was on the receiving end, a weapon. And to everyone aboard, the difference is not just a matter of a word, it's held as a truth that's what they were taught by their parents and have passed on to their children.'

"It isn't reasonable, Mother,' said Trogen. 'You said so yourself. It's not fair of father to punish me.'"

"He had to," Marley interrupted.

"Exactly. As Mother said, 'If Astreya had not punished Trogen, his son, he would not be accepted as the master.' He had to. But it seems to me that Trogen's resentment began that day."

"So ...there are no weapons aboard the fleet, 'cepting Trogen's sword o'course, which I now figure should prob'ly be judged contraband."

"That is correct," said Mairi.

"But that don't make weapons always a bad thing," said Marley.

Mairi looked into the night, thinking once again how her father and mother had used the stones to put an end to Mufrid. Marley spoke into a long silence.

"Skipper, you do know that following the ketch..."

Mairi completed his thought.

"...is most likely exactly what they want us to do."

The rest of the watch passed in silence.

11. In which Moke takes care of Ellie

Something disturbed the beautiful nothing where Ellie had been hiding. She tried to decide what it was, but her brain didn't seem to be working as it should, and that was even more terrifying than whatever might be outside her closed eyes, beyond her bruised body. If she could not think, if her mind wasn't functioning properly, then she was lost and sinking into the unfathomable depths of the ocean where strange fish would soon be swimming up her nose into her skull, drinking her blood, and chewing on her bones. Her heart thudded in her chest, her neck, her ears. She clamped her jaw shut and let herself sink into the bottomless depths.

She took a throat-rasping lung-full of air, and then another. Her body had ignored what she was thinking, feeling, fearing. *How clever of it to go on working without me*, Ellie thought. *Maybe I can lie here, wherever I am, and pretend to be unconscious. It'll be easier. Maybe that's because it's still true. But no. If I were unconscious, I wouldn't be uncomfortable. And I certainly wouldn't be pretending, because that's what I do when I don't want people to know what I'm really thinking. So there must be someone to deceive. But who? Eventually, I'll have to open my eyes and find out if this ugly dream will fade as they always do when I swing my legs out of bed, avoid hitting my head on the top bunk, stick my feet into my seaboots, and go on deck to stand my watch. Right. It's definitely time to get up.*

Ellie opened her eyes. Less than an arm's length away was a bushy nest of black hair containing two brown eyes and the pinkish end of a bulbous nose. Ellie froze. Moments earlier, when she was still hovering on the edge of sleep, she had almost dismissed the night's events as a nightmare, but now the dream was real.

"You all right, missy?"

The brown eyes blinked, she nodded, realizing as she did so that the talking hairy bush was the head of the giant who had captured her aboard *Cygnet*.

"I'm Moke," said the bush, none of its hairs moving. "They're all doin' stuff. I'm s'posed to make sure you're all right."

"Er... thank you, Moke. I'm Ellie. And I'd like to sit up now, but you're sort of in the way."

The hairy head retreated abruptly, its departure followed by a resounding thud, followed by a succession of smaller thumps as Moke lurched about the tiny cabin, unsuccessfully trying to stand without hitting his head. Ellie pushed back the smelly blanket that was over her and sat up on a settee that ran across the stern of the cabin. Light from scuttles to port and starboard revealed narrow bunks doubling as seats on either side of the chart table, which was now folded with its leaves hanging down to the deck. Moke leaned over it, completely blocking the door behind him. His big, shaggy head swung from side to side.

"You all right, Moke?" Ellie asked.

His head stopped moving and then tipped to one side. She saw one brown eye blink.

"Yeah. Banged me nut on the overhead. Be better in a moment. S'all right for a little person like you, but I'm a bit big for bein' back in here, 'stead of the main cabin."

His voice was so slow, deep, and sad that had he been closer, she would have patted his head as if he was a very big dog.

"It's kind of you to look after me."

"T'aint nothin'. I come in here t' see if there's somethin' I c'n do for yer."

"Could you get me a bucket?"

"Yer feelin' sick?"

"No, it's that..."

"Oh. That. Yeah. I'll get a bucket."

Ellie watched Moke bend almost to his knees, lower his head and back out of the door one shoulder at a time, steadied by a set of knuckles on the cabin sole. The ketch swayed under his weight. Moments later, a massive arm reached through the doorway, a bucket in its big fist. The arm withdrew and then returned with a large jug, which it put beside the bucket. The door closed. Moke's slow, deep voice came from outside.

"I'll be right here wi' me back to the door, Miz Ellie."

After she had used the bucket, she discovered that the jug contained fresh water. Her first sip told her she was thirstier than she had ever thought possible. She drank most of the water and was using the little she had left for a welcome face wash when she was interrupted by heavy knocking on the cabin door.

"You all right there, missie?"

She called a brief assurance, hurriedly completed her wash and opened the door. Moke's huge bulk blocked the view. When he turned around and reached in to recover the bucket, Ellie glimpsed a hillside studded with big, leafy trees, lit by mid-morning light. She took a breath to ask where they were and then paused.

"Thank you so much for the fresh water. That was thoughtful of you."

"'T'weren't nothin.'"

His big, shaggy head bent down to look at her. She moved a little to one side for a better look around his bulk but saw only his shirt, which looked as if it had been crudely stitched out of an old sail. *Distract him*, she thought and asked the first question that came into her mind.

"Do you have sisters?" she asked.

Moke's moustache puffed outwards as he heaved a sigh. "They died. Same's me ma and pa."

"I'm sorry."

"T'were a long time ago. None of 'em liked me much, 'cept for Rosie, my littlest sister. She called me her very own private giant."

The gleam of Moke's black eyes blinked slowly behind his mask of hair.

"You miss her."

"Don't much think of her. 'Cept when kids run away from me." His big head inclined to one side, and his tone changed to wonder. "Say, missy, how come *you're* not scared?"

"I suppose it's because I have a cousin who has a big beard. Like yours, only red. Some people say they can't tell if he's angry, but I always know."

Moke stared at her, cocking his head to one side. Ellie hazarded a question.

"Where are the rest of the crew?"

"Ashore. Lookin' to take over the great ship. They made me stay, 'cause they thought I'd scare you outer yer wits, an' that would make it easier for them to get you to do their biddin'."

His words rumbled into an apologetic silence.

"Well, they were wrong. Moke, so long as we're alone here, do you suppose I could have something to eat?"

"Fer sure, missy. But I'm going to have to keep you locked up in the cabin like they told me."

Ellie nodded and backed further into the cabin without looking away from him. Once inside and with the door closed against her, Ellie kneeled on a settee to look through the scuttle. Accumulated filth from oil lamps and tobacco smoke blurred the glass, so she scrubbed a peep-hole through which she saw a huddle of weathered wooden houses, sheds, and barns. They looked as if they had been built of timbers retrieved from demolished buildings or scavenged from shipwrecks, and were bare of paint save for the occasional faded patch of colour that survived from some previous use. The houses leaned and sagged against each other, no two alike. Random timbers propped up bulging walls, low-ridged roofs sagged above ragged eves. When she looked out of the scuttle on the other side of the cabin, she saw fishing boats tied up side by side at a crude wharf. While she watched, their masts swayed as men and boys climbed from one boat to the other, wicker baskets on their shoulders.

The sight was familiar to Ellie, who had often seen fishermen landing their catch at Matris and at Charton, Peter's village. However, here she saw unmistakable signs of poverty and need. None of the boats were painted, their hulls were tarred, their spars were worn to grey for lack of varnish. Wherever her captors had taken her, it was neither big nor prosperous enough to be one of the ports of call frequented by the great ships.

The ketch rocked and swayed under Moke's weight as he made his way to the stern cabin. Ellie clicked her tongue, irritated that she had been slow to realize that the ketch was at anchor. Her mind raced ahead to escaping ashore. She did not doubt that she could outwit Moke, and probably move faster than he, but getting ashore would be difficult. Swimming was a possibility, but only as a last resort. But what then? She hesitated, but not only because she did not know where she could go. To her consternation, Ellie realized that part of her did not want to get Moke into trouble.

A heavy fist on the door announced his return. He hunched over and entered cautiously, holding out a big wooden plate on which was half a loaf of bread and a chunk of cheese. His other hand held a pewter mug. Ellie took the mug and plate while he set up the table for her and then lowered himself gingerly until he was hunched almost double on the starboard settee. Ellie sat in what was clearly the captain's chair, surreptitiously sniffed mug and plate, discovered that she was ravenous, and immediately started eating.

"Yer hungry."

Ellie nodded, chewing vigorously, all caution banished. "Yer bracelet's glowin' again. That's got to be a good sign."

Ellie swallowed hurriedly. She shut her eyes to concentrate, but when she was unable to detect anything from her stone, she turned her attention back to Moke, revising her earlier opinion of his intelligence.

"Umm, Moke, what happened last night after I ... after I passed out?"

"Well, first off, when I stuck me head in, they was all o' them talkin' about how the light from your stone thing had all of a sudden flared an' then gone out. Fred blamed Jake, an' Jake said maybe I had done it, and Cookie was mutterin' to hisself like he was scared. Then Fred told Jake to put you in the stern. I found a blanket an' laid it over you."

"Did my stone light up again?"

"Nope. Not 'til now."

Ellie changed the subject.

"Did they say where they were going?"

"Nobody tells me nothin'. But I got ears. As they were headin' fer the shore, I heard Fred talkin' 'bout how he'd get you to start it up again after we do the big ship."

"*Elusive's* not here. This little bay isn't big enough."

What little Ellie could see of Moke's forehead puckered in a frown.

"How'd ya tell?"

"I looked out the scuttle. There's no room to anchor."

"This is Back Bay, where black folks live. Cott'nt'n's 'round the point, where the big schooner is."

"Cottontown?" Ellie scoffed. "That's more than a night's sail from the Sunny Isles."

"Right you are, missy. You bin' out of it for two nights an' a day in between."

Ellie's composure cracked. She had lost most of two days, and her kidnappers were planning to attack *Elusive*.

"Father's got a full crew, and that's a lot more than the four of you."

"Seven. There's me, an' Jake an' Cookie, an' Fred—he's the smart one. Then there's Will an' Ian, an' the Old Man what's ashore."

"Moke, what's going to happen?"

"Uh, I dunno, zactly. I s'pose Fred an' the fellers all meet up wi' the Old Man, an' he tells us."

"When does all this happen?"

"Soon. After I take care of you."

Ellie almost gagged on a mouthful of bread and cheese. Taking a big breath and letting it out again, she contrived to speak with a calm she did not feel.

"And just how are you going to *take care* of me, Moke?"

"Lock you in the cabin, Miz Ellie. Yer didn't think I'd do something bad to yer, did'ja? I had to stay in case you woke up. We wouldn't want you to wake up an' do somethin' foolish to yerself."

"Moke..." she began.

"Y' won't tell them we bin talking, will ya?"

"No, Moke, it'll be our secret."

"Well then, if there ain't nothin' else I can do for ye, I'd better be gettin' about it, 'cause it's nigh on time."

Ellie slid out of the chair and lunged for the door, but Moke was already in the way. She tried to push past him, but his huge hand pushed her back. Ellie desperately threw herself at the door as it was closing, but he was far too strong.

"I un'erstand why y' had to try, missie, but I can't let you go. We shouldn'a talked. I'm real sorry, but there it is."

Ellie pounded uselessly on the door with her fists. Then as a crossbar thumped into place, she sank to her knees. She stared into the dim corners of the cabin until she blinked. She stayed kneeling, tasting salt from the tears of frustration that slid down her cheeks. Ellie shook her head vigorously and clenched her teeth, willing the tears to stop and demanding her mind to think usefully. After a few moments of staring blindly at the deck, a curious pattern caught her eye: dark spots under the table that could not be from pegs or nails. She pushed up her sleeve, and the green stone in her bracelet glowed. By its light she crawled across the cabin sole, trying to ignore the accumulated filth. Under the table and below one leg of the captain's chair where the floorboards were less grimy than the rest, she saw that several planks each had a finger-sized hole. She pushed the chair aside and yanked at one of the boards. By the light from the stone on her arm, she saw the necks of many bottles sticking out of wooden frames filled with straw. Her first thought was that she had found a smuggler's hoard, but when she eased one of the bottles out of its nest and tipped it sideways she saw it was barely liquid. Whatever was inside was neither wine, whiskey nor rum. She pulled up the next board and the next. The third cavity was empty, save for a few fragments of burlap. Then she remembered stories of Walt's concoctions that spewed smoke and spread fire that could not be dowsed with water.

They're going to blow Elusive *up, just as they did to* Cygnus!

Shutting her eyes, she used her bracelet to search for the familiar signature of *Elusive's* shipstone, on which she had learned her wielding skills. She focussed her mind on making contact and sent a coded distress signal. She waited expectantly, counting her heartbeats. When she knew that a minute had passed, even allowing for her excitement, she re-sent her message. Again, nothing. She reasoned that because the ship was in port, *Elusive's* shipstone had been dimmed. She tried again, focusing on *Elusive's* only wielder, her father. She strove to contact him but felt no answer. He must be ashore, she reasoned. Or sleeping, or engaged with some duty aboard his ship.

"You there, in the ketch!"

The voice sounded familiar. Ellie stopped trying to send a message. She crawled out from under the table and pressed her face against the salt-stained glass, but the ketch had swung on her anchor, and all she could see was a pile of lobster pots on a rickety pier. She heard Moke's heavy tread and felt the boat sway under his weight.

"What's up?" Moke shouted. "Did they send you back fer me?"

"There's nobody here?"

"Sorta. There's jus' me. An'…"

"Then get ashore."

Ellie strained to hear as well as to see. "I got no boat. They took it when…"

"Heave me a line, and veer a couple o' fathoms on the anchor,."

"I don't think I oughter. I don't rightly know you, an' Fred tol' me he was leavin' me fer…"

"Belay that! Do as I say!"

Moke did as he was ordered, the ketch moved shoreward, and Ellie saw a broad, squat figure hauling on the rope he had been thrown. It was Walt. Her father had sent Walt to rescue her. Now she could warn the ship. Ellie pounded on the scuttle and screamed, but at that moment, the ketch scraped alongside the wharf. She almost fell off the settee when the boat bobbed as Moke jumped ashore. She screamed again as the ketch swung on her anchor back away from the wharf into the harbour. More and more water separated the ketch from the wharf. The boat tugged at her anchor and steadied in the tide. Helpless, she watched two ill-matched figures, one squat, one monstrously huge, walking towards the untidy houses.

For the first time since she had been captured, Ellie despaired.

12. In which Cygnet arrives too late

For the night and the day after leaving the Sunny Isles all Mairi could feel was stomach-clenching anxiety. She had decided to keep *Cygnet* out of sight of the ketch, and while she believed this was the only thing she could do, she was tortured by doubt. She split up the crew into three watches with herself on call at all times. She came on deck before each watch change and stayed to assure herself of how *Cygnet* was handling alterations in the wind and weather. She grabbed cat naps whenever she could, but never really slept.

Each watch tried to outdo the last in speed and distance and had to be held in check by Mairi's order to keep the ketch just over the horizon. Trogen had not challenged Mairi's decision, but she could tell that he chafed at the delay and wanted to catch up and confront their quarry at sea. Like him, the younger Cygnets wanted to crowd on sail and show the ketch and her crew that they had the better, faster ship. All wanted to rescue Ellie, none more than Mairi, who blamed herself for losing the youngest and most vulnerable member of her crew.

The weather was her constant concern. When the wind fell away and then shifted, Mairi knew she had to decide whether the ketch was changing her course for a new destination, or merely tacking. Less than an hour later, when they successfully shadowed the ketch as it tacked again, Mairi asked Seren and Trogen to independently predict where they were headed. When they met over the chart table and compared opinions, they were unanimous.

"Cottontown," said Trogen. "An average heading of nor' nor' west. It can't be anywhere else."

"Then we agree," said Mairi.

"We're almost in horizon range of Ellie's stone," said Seren, "but the strange thing is that I can feel a shipstone on that bearing. It's like when you sense a great ship even when there's nobody working the stones in the Forbidden Room. Can we go closer to find out? We could maybe team up with *Elusive* if she's close, and then we'd have enough people to attack."

Mairi saw Trogen frowning at Seren, but could not decide whether it was from surprise or vexation. She refrained from asking questions that would make him more irritable.

"It can't be *Elusive*," said Mairi. "She's supposed to be further north. Stick to the plan: keep them just over the horizon."

"I can do that," said Trogen, again.

"What about Ellie?" Seren asked. "Is that her trying to message us? Can either of you pick up anything from her stone?"

Trogen frowned and Mairi shook her head.

"I don't think that anyone can distinguish a person's stone at this distance," she said.

"*You* can't unless they're wielding a shipstone," said Trogen. "Which is good news. They haven't forced her to work for them."

"They haven't got a shipstone for her to wield," said Mairi.

"She never would." Seren's voice blended pride with anxiety. "Nobody's more stubborn than my little sister."

"Then we carry on as if for Cottontown," said Mairi as decisively as she could.

Seren and Trogen went back on deck in silence. Mairi pulled out the log that Astreya had given her and turned through the pages where she had recorded position, weather, the ship's behaviour under the sails she was carrying, and the occasional note on the crew day by day, watch by watch since they left Matris. She carefully noted the time, recorded her decision, and then paused to reread her earlier entry: "Ellie kidnapped. Made running repairs to gunshots in the hull, followed unnamed ketch NNW towards Cottontown." The facts were correct, as far as they went, but they did not even hint at the concern that permeated the ship. They all knew that they were on a stern chase after a ship manned by a crew of ruthless men with a history of violence and betrayal. Moreover, as Marley observed, if the people on the ketch knew they were following, then *Cygnet* was almost certainly sailing into a trap.

Mairi rested her head on her hands and listened to the sounds made by *Cygnet* as she sailed close-hauled on the port tack. Water hissed past the hull and gurgled astern in the wake. A sheet rattled against the cabin top in a brief tattoo, quickly silenced. In the galley, a spoon scraped a pot as Cam prepared one of his stews. Light, quick footsteps climbed the companionway, stopped halfway up, where they were joined by another pair. Peter spoke first.

"D'y think we can go up against them?"

"They got that monster," Neil replied. "What we goin' t' do against' somethin' that big?"

"We gotta get Ellie back. Maybe we could steal their gun somehow and shoot the bugger."

"Fat chance."

"We got Trog an' his pig-sticker..."

"Yeah. An' that's worked out real good so far, hasn't it?"

"Maybe he can do better next time. Me, I'm gonna sharpen up me clasp knife. Mebby stick it in his foot when he ain't lookin'."

"Lots o' luck wi' that."

"Neil, do you think she's still alive?"

"Gotta be. They need her to work the stone they stole."

"Yeah, but maybe ... I mean, she's little an' ..."

"Well, if that happens, maybe they'll save her stone. Then if we can get it back, they'll give it to me and then I'll be able to work a shipstone."

"I'm thinkin' the skipper's got a crafty plan what she ain't tellin' us 'til we get wherever we're goin'."

Two pairs of feet padded up the last few steps to the cockpit. Peter trusted her to have a plan and was preparing to stab the giant in the foot; Neil hoped he would inherit her stone. Distressed by Peter's naive determination, and appalled by Neil's selfishness, Mairi stared after them, unable to think clearly. Before she could shake off her indecision, she heard Cam banging a pan with a spoon. In his usual, competent way, he had prepared the midday meal. Gradually, she remembered what he had told her on the late-night watch as they sailed south. "Thinkin'. Always a mistake. Just bleedin' get on wi' it." Mairi took a long breath, put thought aside, composed her face and joined her crew in the cockpit.

～∧～

A few hours later Trogen climbed up from the cabin, followed by Seren. Mairi came on deck and went forward to the bow, rather than stand over them. Marley handed over the wheel; Seren and Trogen ran through the terse, efficient routine of watch change. They measured and recorded speed, wind direction, sail trim, and course, then went below to chart their position by dead reckoning. Then they went back on deck, where Trogen checked the stone on his arm, his body masking whatever he saw. Mairi went through the same motions, rolling back her sleeve to consult her bracelet. She stared at the sliver of white light at the centre of its green glow, trying to detect the ship ahead of them, but when after several tries, she had felt nothing, she became impatient with Trogen's apparent success. Piqued when he nodded, she could bear it no longer, came aft and confronted him.

"You might at least give me a clue as to how you're doing it."

"What?"

"I can't detect Ellie's stone anymore, and I don't know how you can."

"I can. That's all there is to it."

"So can I, when someone's close."

"You can't detect them when they're over the horizon. I can."

Rather than succumb to anger, Mairi turned on her heel and strode foreword. Behind her, she heard Seren voice the words she had been about to shout in Trogen's face.

"Nobody can do that."

"Except me."

"So you say," Seren snapped, and when Trogen shrugged elaborately, continued, "Which means nobody can verify what you say you're doing."

"Why don't you just accept that I'm better at it than you, Seren?. Or go along with it, like Mairi? She's angry, she doesn't really believe me, but she won't admit it in front of the crew."

"Ellie was right. You're a silly man, Trogen," said Seren.

"Whereas all you girls know exactly what you're doing."

"We're heading for Cottontown because that's where the ketch is going. It's been obvious from the moment we all three got a bearing on her before we lost contact with Ellie's stone. All you're doing is mystifying everything."

"You and Mairi agreed with me earlier, when I saw they were tacking."

"We tacked when we had to. They're coping with the same wind as us."

"Yes, but I know when they did it, and where they are right now."

"So you say."

Mairi stayed on the foredeck, listening to Seren and Trogen, and taking big breaths to calm herself. Above her, the wind continued its long sigh across the sails. She felt the ship pulse below her feet as the bow cut into the waves, and sympathized with Seren's irritation at Trogen's arrogant certainty. Standing under barely visible sails in moonlight that did nothing to reveal what lay ahead, Trogen's confidence made Mairi feel inadequate. She imposed on herself the discipline of navigating by the stones of power, shoved back her sleeve and again checked the green stone clasped to her arm, the way she had been taught to find her way when the compass twirled uselessly in the northern ocean. Green light patched her arm, and the white arrow at the heart of the stone swung northwards. Moments later, the jib-sheet at her feet squeaked in its fairleads. The ship sang a lower note as Trogen eased the main.

"We need to slow down," he said. "Seren, slacken the foresail and staysail so they're spilling wind. Same with the main."

"My clasp..." Seren began.

"They're inside the horizon," said Trogen. "We'll hold course, but drop back."

Mairi made her way aft, pretending she had not heard.

"Getting a bit too close?" said Mairi as calmly as she could. "A good thing it's still dark."

"You saw me easing the sheets," Trogen asked.

"That, and a gleam in the centre of my stone."

Swallowing the sour comfort that Trogen's claim had become more likely, Mairi went below to her bunk.

~^~

Mairi woke to voices on deck and the sound of people climbing the companionway. She had fallen asleep in her clothes, so she was starting up the steps as the last pair of feet disappeared ahead of her. Joining Neil, Seren, and Marley in the cockpit, she looked ahead and she saw Trogen on the foredeck, beside their ruined dinghy. Cam was at the wheel. They had the wind abeam on the port tack, under high cloud out of the north-east.

"Where's Peter?" she asked, sharper than she intended.

"Up here!"

She looked up past the belly of the mainsail, and Peter looked down at her. He was standing on the throat of the yard, one arm crooked around the mast, his face barely visible past his body and feet.

"Land's in sight, Skipper! A bit misty, but clear enough to be sure."

"What about the ketch?"

"Peter's been watchin' her masthead on the horizon since sunrise," said Cam. "I sent him up. Tell the truth, it was his idea, an' a good one, I thought."

"He swarmed up the mast, hand over hand by the halyards," said Seren.

"T'was nimbly done," said Marley.

"Where's the ketch now?" Mairi called upwards.

"Dunno, Skipper. Lost sight of her just after we raised the land. She prob'ly rounded the headland in the mornin' mist."

"Then she's in Cottontown harbour," said Trogen. "Where we've been heading all along," he added smugly.

Mairi ignored Trogen's self-congratulation.

"Right, Cygnets. We need everything cleared away and ready for arrival. Anchors on deck, ready to let go. Peter, we can see the headlands now, so you can come down for breakfast."

"Bergoo, again," Neil muttered.

"Yer talkin' about Marley's fine, hot brew of oatmeal topped wi' molasses from the Sunny Isles," said Cam. "So you better get up here an' take your trick at the wheel, young Neil, an' be sure to smile an' say thank you when he gives you yours, you ungrateful young pup."

That's not like Cam, Mairi thought. Her own anxiety had blinded her to the tension in all of her crew. She scanned their faces. A thin-lipped concentration replaced Cam's usual grin. Trogen looked disdainful, and Neil surly. Seren stared fixedly ahead. Marley met Mairi's look through half-lowered eyelids. He raised one eyebrow and nodded, the motion subtle. Moments later, as she was wondering what he might mean, Peter called from above, his voice shrill with excitement.

"Skipper! The fog's blown clear. Guess what? *Elusive's* there!"

A rounded headland appeared through the fog as if conjured from the misty sea. They looked down a narrow cliff-edged bay to where the unmistakeable three-masted schooner swung at anchor.

"Sheet her in," said Mairi. "Head up the harbour, please, Cam. The tide's full and at the turn."

As *Cygnet* began her run landward between the granite cliffs on either side of the harbour mouth, the wind faded. The little schooner slid towards the town at the head of the bay on calm water, her sails slack. *Elusive* lay to starboard of the main channel, with her bow pointing seaward, well clear of the smaller craft that clustered around the town's wharves and jetties.

"She's lying between bow and stern anchors," said Trogen. "We should..."

Mairi cut him off.

"Trogen, Marley, I want both anchors ready to let go. You've got the bow, Trogen. Let go on my word and then veer without checking our way. Cam, take us in a broad turn so that we end up in line with *Elusive,* heading for the sea. Marley, stand by to drop the stern anchor when we're further inshore."

"There are ships and boats three abreast along the wharf," said Seren.

"I see them," said Mairi. "That's why we're anchoring."

"It would be easier to go alongside _Elusive,_ then we could..." Trogen began.

"I did not ask for discussion," said Mairi, her voice crisp. "Stand by to dowse sail. Neil, you have the foresail, Peter, the jib. Seren, you have the main."

The rounded outlines of the shoreline were now distinct. Wind-stunted pines and spruce grew on rocky ledges above the sea's edge with wisps of fog still clinging to their boughs. Seaweed and flotsam swirled along the waterline. Cam swung the wheel as they passed the big schooner. Intent on the anchoring maneuver, Mairi only had time for a glance at the salt-stained black hull, before _Cygnet_ described a half circle and her bowsprit lined up with _Elusive's_ stern.

"Stand by to let go..."

Cygnet slid towards _Elusive,_ losing way. Peter's voice came from above.

"Skipper, there's summat amiss aboard _Elusive!_"

"Let go the bow anchor! Come on down, Peter. Marley, stand by with the other anchor. Peter, now! Seren, Neil, prepare to douse sails. I said NOW, Peter; get the foresail!"

Cygnet was barely moving. Peter slid down the mainsail, checking his descent hand-over-hand on the leech-line, which he let go in time to run inboard along the boom. His feet thumped onto the cabin top.

"Skipper, there's two strange men on _Elusive's_ quarterdeck. An' there's nothin' else goin' on! I never seen..."

"Pipe down, Peter, the skipper's busy," said Cam. "An' don'tcha dare slide down the sail ever again. Get the fores'l, right now."

"Last fathom of hawser on deck," Trogen shouted.

"Set the pick," Mairi ordered. "Peter, back the jib. Luff the foresail. Cam, bring her head around a bit more. Marley, let go. Trogen and Marley, haul the bow anchor. Seren, strike the main."

Helped by the start of the ebb tide, the little schooner gradually completed her circle. Pivoting on her bow anchor, *Cygnet* slowly turned to face the sea and hung motionless. Trogen and Marley hauled mightily. Mairi watched the shoreline as they pulled abeam of a tree she had chosen as her mark.

"Trogen, belay. Marley, walk your hawser aft. We'll shorten up and lie between them."

"Neatly done, Skipper," said Cam. "I ain't needed on the wheel no more, so I'll help furl."

Mairi nodded. "Send Peter aft, soon as you can, will you?"

The sun shone through light mist caught between the protective cliffs where the two schooners lay in smooth water. Mairi looked towards *Elusive's* stern, a stone's throw to seaward. Above the stern rail, the main boom rested in its crutch, the sail neatly furled, but because *Cygnet* had less than half *Elusive's* freeboard, Mairi could not see the bigger ship's deck.

Peter arrived at her elbow, breathless with excitement.

"Skipper, there's two men loungin' aside *'Lusive's* binnacle. An' I never seen them before."

Mairi realized what had been at the back of her mind while she concentrated on anchoring. No one had been on deck watching *Cygnet* arrive. Not Dabih, nor Walt, nor Damon, nor a single member of the crew. Were they all ashore? Where were the people who had cheered them when they were leaving Matris?

"An' another thing, Skipper. The ketch ain't here."

"Are you sure?"

"Forward mast taller, aft mast shorter, like a schooner, but backwards."

Mairi nodded. "Then where is she?"

"Back Bay," said Trogen. "Small-craft harbour. Too small and shallow for the great ships."

"Back Bay on the chart, maybe, but around here, it's called Black Bay."

Marley's deep voice made both of them turn. He knotted off the last stopper on the mainsail and leaned on the boom.

"Trogen's right, o'course, but there's more to it. Black folks ain't welcome in Cottontown, leastways not unless they're doin' something that the white folks ain't keen about doin' for themselves. An' there's another thing about Black Bay..."

"Smuggling," said Cam.

"Fishing by day," said Marley, "But you're not wrong about the night."

"Then that's where they've taken Ellie," said Seren, her voice rising. "We have to get ashore right away and ..."

"In what?" demanded Trogen. "Our dinghy's smashed, remember? I said we should moor alongside *Elusive*, but now..."

"We got company," said Marley.

A fresh voice came from over the port side.

"Hey there in the schooner. You need water? Vittles? Rowin' ashore?"

Mairi looked over the landward side at an elderly man in sea-stained clothes, resting on his oars in a large, battered dory. He looked back up at her. Broken teeth flashed in an ingratiating grin above a scruffy black beard.

"I wonder what she's going to do now," Neil muttered.

"If he rows us ashore, we can get to Back Bay by foot," said Seren.

"Can't say we was doin' a fine job o' lookout," muttered Cam.

Mairi sensed her crew fragmenting around her, and in that instant knew what had to be done.

"How much to take a couple of us to the other schooner?" Mairi asked.

"Yer don't want t' do that, missus. The two they left at anchor watch ain't friendly. Pointed a gun at me, they did."

"Summat's wrong," said Peter. "Like I said, there's…"

Mairi cut him off with a gesture.

"*Elusive's* been captured. We have to secure her shipstone."

Heads turned, hearing authority in Mairi's whisper.

"Then we can use it to know exactly where Ellie is!" said Seren. "But how do we get aboard?"

"I can swim around to her bobstay and ..." Trogen began.

"An' get yerself shot," said Cam.

"We could drift down on the falling tide on the stern anchor 'til we're alongside," said Marley.

"Pipe down, all of you," said Mairi. "We're going to board *Elusive*, and this is how we'll do it. Neil, fetch the storm jib. Cam, ask the boatman to come alongside and negotiate a price. Peter, rig fenders."

Book Three

Stern Chase Northward

1. In which men meet in a tavern

Keef's Tavern lurked beside the road that linked the port of Cottontown to the village of Black Bay. Any daytime traveller and certain nighttime visitors could find refreshment at the crest of the road. A wealthy man had built the original house many years *Before* so that he could enjoy the view of both Cottontown harbour and Black Bay. During the troubled century that followed, it was rebuilt as a fort that changed hands so often and violently that it was reduced from a mansion to the ramshackle hovel where Keef was born. It was also where he grew up and rebuilt most of the structure to his own taste and needs. It was there that he established a business based on being in between. The tavern was a tiny, neutral domain outside the town limits and beyond the boundaries of the village. Keef's Tavern was a place where men and women with flexible standards of conduct could do private business in an atmosphere of rigorously maintained calm.

Keef's dogs barked him awake a little after sunrise after the daily procession of people had trailed up from Black Bay past the pub on their way to start work in Cottontown. Since Keef was not constrained by the business hours inflicted upon tavern owners by the upright elders of Cottontown, he pulled on a pair of breeks and took a look through the peephole in his front door. Two steel-grey eyes looked back from a weathered, lean face with a short, white, beard. Keef ordered his dogs to be still, pulled back the deadlock and opened the door to a man wearing an officer's dark blue jacket with a watch-keeper's telescope under one arm.

"'Mornin', Mister Mirak. What can I get for you?"

"A comfortable chair out here in the morning sunshine, Keef. And if you have it, a cup of coffee."

"Always ready to help."

As he brewed and delivered Mirak's coffee, Keef exercised his most valuable business asset, which was the habit of keeping his mouth shut. Mirak nodded his thanks, crossed his booted feet on the table, and undid the top two brass buttons at the neck of his jacket to reveal a spotless white shirt. He opened his telescope, settled his elbows on the arms of the chair and looked first at Cottontown Harbour, and then at Black Bay. He nodded and composed himself to wait. About an hour later, a short, squat figure stumped up the hill from Cottontown.

"Mirak."

"Walt."

"Coffee or beer?" asked Keef from the doorway.

"Beer."

"There's fog in the approaches," said Mirak. "Before it closed in, I saw *Elusive's* longboats being swung out. Your doing?"

"Ready when you are. It's on for today, then?"

"The crew from the ketch will be here any time soon."

Walt had barely halved the level in his mug before Fred, Jake, and Cookie came up the hill from Black Bay. As they topped the rise, they paused and looked down into the main harbour.

"Can't see nothin' fer fog," said Cookie squeaked.

Mirak's voice from the tavern's courtyard surprised them.

"*Elusive* made port last night."

"*Elusive*?" asked Fred. "You sure?"

"How many three-masted schooners do you know, besides the one you blew a hole in?"

As he spoke, Mirak raised a hand and beckoned. They silently obeyed. He did not ask them to sit.

"Fred. Report."

Fred stood with most of his weight on one leg as if preparing for a hurried departure. Fixed by Mirak's unwavering stare, he spoke well at first.

"You were right, Mirak. The little schooner did go to the Sunny Isles, just like you said it would. We were there three days ahead of her. I did some trade with the head man's son: fifty guns, a hundredweight of ammunition, and a promise to buy more the next time we go there. We landed the weapons on a beach away from the harbour..."

Fred paused. His eyes swivelled between his two listeners. Walt regarded him disdainfully. Mirak did not even blink. Fred's words began to tumble out of his mouth faster and faster.

"... because Chad didn't want everyone to know what he'd bought, which was a good thing, because that afternoon there was a bit of a blow, well, really, quite a storm. There were black squalls and rain and gusts that were enough for a knock-down, but we rode it out just fine in a little cove, and later, we saw that the little schooner had made it to the harbour in one piece. We saw the crew after she arrived, in fact, I watched ..."

"Did you secure the shipstone?"

Mirak's incisive question stopped the flow. Fred blinked, swallowed, and took a deep breath and lowered his head between hunched shoulders.

"Ah, no. Not really. But we holed the little schooner in six places."

Mirak shook his head and sighed. Fred, who had been expecting an outburst, straightened up a little.

"Where's your fourth man?" Mirak asked, almost as if he had not heard.

"Moke? He's aboard the ketch."

Mirak raised an eyebrow, and Fred again began to gabble.

"He and Jake—and Cookie, too—were the ones that boarded the schooner. They ..."

"Stop rattling on and listen. In somewhat less than an hour, be at your workshop to meet a work party from *Elusive*. Sell them the ... ah ... instruments and glassware they ordered. Return here when you're finished. You do have things ready, don't you?"

Fred nodded.

"Right. You two, go to the tavern on the waterfront called the Binnacle, where I will have the other men you need to take *Elusive*. On your way, all of you."

Walt's chair crashed back onto the paving stones.

"I'll fetch the big fellow an' be right behind the pair of you, so don't get no ideas that this is a drinkin' party where we all play silly buggers in the pub."

With a speed surprising in so short and stocky a figure, he started down towards Black Bay.

Fred opened his mouth to speak and then closed it again. He nodded to Mirak and started down the road to Cottontown. A cunning little smile twisted his lips.

An hour or so later, fog swirled up the road towards the tavern. Mirak moved to the taproom. He did not see two contrasting figures, one short and square the other hulking and huge, as they passed Keef's tavern on their way to Cottontown harbour.

2. In which Mairi and Seren board Elusive

Neil climbed the companionway to the cockpit, waving his hands for attention and pointing astern and below. First Peter, and then Trogen, Marley, and Cam stopped what they were doing and listened. With *Cygnet* at anchor in calm water, they could hear Mairi's and Seren's voices in the skipper's cabin.

"How in blazes did Ellie tie this thing so it won't fall off?"

"Mairi, we don't have time for this. We have to get Ellie ..."

"Seren, this is how we're going to get her back. When we have *Elusive's* shipstone, we can find exactly where she is."

"Do we really have to wear Lady Orinda's dresses?"

"Only way I can think of to get invited aboard."

The expressions on the men's and boys' faces ranged from the boys' bemused puzzlement, through Marley's dawning comprehension, to Cam's nod of approval. He was about to begin negotiations with the boatman when they heard Seren's voice again.

"Right. I've found a lanyard for up top, but I can't climb a ladder with all this material flapping around my ankles."

"True. But our seagoing breeks aren't going to fill them with uncontrollable lust."

"So let's shorten them."

"Right."

"Cut about here?"

"No, higher."

"Tie the rest like this, do you think?"

"Right. But higher up below, and lower down above. Tie the coloured stuff and tuck any extra material into the top of the breeks."

The boatman's seamed and weathered face crinkled as he, too, listened. He was a grizzled old man with hands permanently clenched, whether he held an oar or not. His mouth opened in a gap-toothed chuckle.

"Heh. Won't be the first time I rowed girls to a ship. Heh, heh."

Trogen's face reddened.

"Mairi, cease and desist!" he hissed down the companionway. "You can't do this. I forbid it."

Marley raised one eyebrow at Cam.

"Now it's goin' t' happen, for certain sure," said Cam softly, before continuing in a normal voice. "Neil, you got that jib? Hand it down to George, here, our boatman. Pete, can you climb the mast if it's a bare pole?"

"Watch me!"

"Not just yet. Wait 'til the officers ... ah ... women ... ah ... boarding party ... come up from ... here they are."

There was an audible intake of breath from all five males as Mairi's head, bare shoulders, green and scarlet top, abbreviated breeks, bare legs and finally, her bare feet appeared in the cockpit, immediately followed by Seren, who was furiously trying not to blush.

"This is ... this is simply not ... not acceptable," Trogen spluttered.

"I don't recall asking you," said Mairi.

"Y'look great," said Cam. "Don't she, Marley?"

Marley nodded gravely, resolutely keeping his eyes on Seren's face.

"Oh ... wow," said Neil.

Seren's copper curls gleamed. No longer tightly plaited to her head, her hair was a glimmering nimbus that almost deflected the males' gaze from the rest of her.

"She can't go like that," said Trogen "She's ..."

"She has legs, Trogen. But you won't be staring at them, because you'll be hiding under the jib as we approach. Seren and I will distract them, giving you time to climb up to the deck. Since we can't conceal weapons in these clothes, you should bring..."

"Un'erstood," said Cam. "Over you go, Marley, Trog. I'll just be a moment."

He ducked down into the cabin. When he reappeared with his leather satchel, Trogen and Marley were already in the rowboat, and the boatman was offering help to Mairi and Seren, which they ignored. Cam jumped nimbly aboard and became a third lump under the jib. The boatman shoved off from *Cygnet,* with Mairi and Seren sitting on the centre thwart. From under the canvass by Mairi's knee, a hand emerged, holding a bottle of rum.

"Here. Just in case they ain't in'erested in women," said Cam.

The boatman shipped one oar into the groove in his boat's transom and sculled over the stern with practiced ease. With the falling tide helping them along, they slid towards *Elusive.* He rested on his oar to offer advice to Mairi and Seren in a creaky whisper.

"When I hail 'em, miss, you wi' the blonde hair, you stan' up an' wave. An' you wi' the long legs, kind'a stretch yerself out so's they can see whatcha got. Heh. The rum, I mean, o'course. Heh. Heh. Heh."

Indistinct sounds of suppressed fury came from below the canvass, abruptly stifled when the boat bumped against the schooner. The boatman grabbed a rope ladder that hung on *Elusive's* black, salt-stained side and hailed.

"Right. 'Ere yer go. Ahoy there, 'board the schooner!"

A head and shoulders appeared above them. Mairi waved extravagantly at the bearded face that peered over the rail.

"Hey, sailor! Feelin' lonely?"

"Come on down!" Seren chimed in. "Let's have some fun!"

A second, younger head appeared, staring open-mouthed.

"We can't leave the ship."

Seren held up the bottle and stretched out her legs. The two heads bowed together, conferring.

"C'mon up!"

Seren stood up, balancing easily as she reached for the ladder.

"Act girly, Seren," Mairi whispered.

Seren obediently staggered, caught herself by one hand on the wooden rung of the ladder, swung around with a high-pitched little scream, passed the bottle to Mairi, and scrambled up awkwardly. Behind her, Mairi climbed one-handed, clutching the bottle. Halfway, she saw Seren's feet stop, hesitate, and then disappear over the rail. Two voices made blatant evaluations and debated ownership. Mairi continued climbing. An open-mouthed face looked down at her. She waved the bottle and ignored the reaching hand. Then she was half-over the rail, trying to pull her face into a smile at the man waiting for her. He was coarse, scruffy, unkempt, unwashed, and rank. She tried to focus on his leering face, but she had seen a dark stain on the right arm of his shirt. She looked down at the deck past a drying puddle of blood to where the other man had his arm around Seren's waist and was pulling her towards the wheelhouse.

Mairi swung into action.

~∧~

Peter swarmed up the mast, put one arm over the truck at the top, and hooked a foot around the topsail halyards. He reached down and hauled up some slack, hitched a bight over the mainstay and stood in the foot-rope he had improvised. Neil's voice came up to him from the deck.

"What do you see?"

"The skipper's comin' over the rail, wi' a bottle in one hand, an' there's this big bastard goin' to grab her. She's dropped the bottle. He's got her ... no, he hasn't! She nailed him under the chin wi' her head when he looked down! Nice move, Skipper! He's staggerin' back, but she's got him by an arm, an' she ain't lettin' go. She's turned around, an' she's bearin' down hard on his wrist, an' will y' look at that! She's dumped him on the deck, an' she's holdin' him there wi' her foot on his neck."

"Is that who's yelling?"

"Nah. That's the other feller shoutin' at Seren. He's haulin' her over to the wheelhouse, but she ain't makin' it easy for him. Here come the others: Cam's goin' t' help the skipper, Marley's tryin' t' get aboard, but Trog's gettin' in his way. Silly bastard near took Marley's head off with that pig-sticker o' his. They're gettin' themselves unsnarled, an' ... what's the matter wi' Trog? He's runnin' for the companionway! But Marley's headed for the wheelhouse, all right."

A sharp clap echoed across the water.

"Pete, what was that?"

"Oh yeah. That was some right smart. Seren stood tall, held her arms out like she wanted t' hug him, an' then whacked both his ears at the same time. Slapped him silly. Better an' better: she's kneed him in his rocks! He's all curled up on the deck, moanin'. An' he's a big one, too!"

"Where's Cam? What about Marley an' Trog?"

"Trog's run off forrard. Marley's wavin' a hammer at the bugger what Seren decked like he was lookin' to crack his head open. Now he's throwin' somethin'—it's a gun!—over the side. Seren's gotten a line around one of his wrists and she's tyin' the other end to his ankle. Marley's helpin' now. They've got the bastard in a knot, right hand over left shoulder tied to right foot up his own back, neat as neat! Now, where d'ye suppose she found a length of line that quick... Oh. She just stood up. Yeah. I see....”

“What?”

“Well, a lot more'n usual.”

“What are you talking about?”

“You ‘member how back at the island Seren ran one of the mainsail's tie-downs around her ... under her ... like, to secure the top of her dress?”

“Yeah, but what's that ....”

“Well, she just took it off an’ tied the bastard up wi’ it. So he's knotted, an’ she ain't got it around her no more, an’ ... an’ ...”

“What?”

“Well, I can tell yer old Marley's havin’ trouble takin’ his eyes off’n her front.”

“You mean, she's bare?”

“Not anymore. She's fixed up the top of her dress-thing.”

“Wow.”

“Y’ could say. Right now Marley an’ she's draggin’ the bastard over to where Cam n’ the skipper are. Wish I could hear what they're sayin’.”

A yell of pain came across the water.

“What's happening?”

“I'm guessin’ they're encouragin’ the one what the skipper decked to tell ‘em where *Elusive's* crew's got to. An’ he's doin’ just that, but now he's talkin’ real fast an’ quiet.”

“Now what?”

"The skipper, Seren an' Marley's is all headin' to the companionway. Cam's puttin' the finishin' touches on tyin' the two of 'em to the rail."

"What was that?"

"One of 'em shoutin'. Or maybe screamin'. But he ain't goin' t' do that again, 'cause Cam's shoved somethin' into 'is mouth. Now Cam's left 'em both tied up and gone after the others. I can't see nothin'. I'm comin' down."

3. In which the Cygnets make a horrid discovery

Mairi ran down *Elusive's* companionway steps, Seren at her heels. After the misty sunlight above, the 'tween decks were darkly shadowed. They could not see where they were going, but because both had served aboard the big schooner they did not hesitate. Mairi slipped and would have fallen had not she braced herself on the sides of the passageway. A quick drawn-in breath brought her the coppery smell of blood. Ahead, green light spilled from the half-open door of the Forbidden Room, silhouetting a figure crouched on the floor.

"Trogen?"

"Mairi, don't let Seren..."

Mairi almost fell a second time as Seren pushed past her. Her lean, tall body momentarily blocked the light that gleamed from *Elusive's* shipstone in its round navigation table. Then as Seren knelt, Mairi heard something between a gasp and a moan. Guessing the worst, Mairi took the last few steps into the Forbidden Room as if wading through deep water. Trogen stood up to meet her, and they faced each other across the navigation table, their faces ghastly in the green light.

"Dabih's dead. They cut him open, Mairi. Damon ..."

"Damon's in here too?"

"He's been wounded, and he's bled a lot, but his heart's beating, and..."

Cam pushed past Mairi, stepped around Seren, who was bent over her father's body, shouldered Trogen out of his way, and kneeled beside Damon, who was slumped in a corner.

"Out o' the way, Trog. I got me kit wi' me. An' if'n you could get some real light down low, so's I c'n see what I'm doin', it'd be right useful."

While Trogen lit a lantern, Mairi stood with her hands gripping the edge of the navigation table, staring fixedly at the shipstone to keep herself from succumbing to emotion. Her heartbeat speeded and her breath came short. As the green stone in front of her flickered, she grasped the implications of what had happened around her and knew what had to be done.

"Seren, just as soon as Cam says he can be moved, help us get Damon to his cabin. Trogen, there must be some of *Elusive's* crew still aboard. Find and release them. Hoist the recall signal for any that may be ashore."

Trogen nodded, his face expressionless, and headed for the door. Seren stood up and took his place at the navigation table opposite Mairi, whose hair glinted in the green light. They looked into each other's eyes and silently agreed that grief would have to come later.

"Ellie's echo stone," said Mairi.

She pulled a black square of cloth from under the table, carefully picked up a small green stone from a rack on the bulkhead behind her, and placed it on the navigation table, where it glowed with its own green light.

Seren's voice was flat, without feeling.

"Ellie's at Black Bay."

"Her stone is clear and plain," Mairi agreed. "But I'm getting two ring stones ashore, as well."

"I have to..." Seren muttered, wincing as she stepped over the blood pooled around her father's body.

Mairi leaned over the table, concentrating. Cam's face appeared in the green light.

"Right, Skipper, an' you too, Seren. We can move him now he ain't leakin'. I got his head."

Mairi and Seren bent over and worked their forearms under Damon's body, then exchanged glances with Cam, who nodded. Together they lifted, turned and shuffled down the starboard passageway to Cam's cabin and got him into his bunk. They were rewarded with a soft groan. When Cam lit a light, Mairi lost the numbed efficiency of dealing with Damon as a body to be moved and looked at the face of the man she had known all her life. Whether from pain or the drug Cam had given him to ease it, Damon was oddly expressionless. His mouth was slightly open, robbing his face of its usual intensity. As Mairi looked, his eyelids fluttered and he looked up.

"Thanks, Cam," he whispered. He coughed, then took a breath shortened by pain. Ignoring Cam's cautionary finger, he continued in a softer version of his normal voice. "When I got to Dabih, they were cutting at him, yelling for him to open the door. I marked a couple of them and got to where I could fight alongside him. They pulled back. Then they rushed us, and one got past me. Came in low, stabbed Dabih in the stomach, slashed the back of my leg, took me down. Dabih palmed the door open, pulled me in and slammed it shut. Then he fell and bled all over me. I held him ... and he ... he said your name, Seren. And Ellie, and Lena, and Becky, too. And then he ... he died. After that, I must have passed out."

As Mairi murmured words she knew to be inadequate, she heard Seren choke a single, throat-clenched sob. Damon's eyes closed. When they stayed shut, Mairi bent over him, so that her face was close enough to feel his breath as he whispered to her alone.

"You're in command now, Mairi. You're mistress of both ships."

Mairi blinked as if she had been slapped. As skipper of *Cygnet*, she had taken responsibility to do what had to be done next, in the way she had been trained to do, but some part of her mind had always been expecting that any moment the Grand Master would take over and either confirm or amend her orders. She had been making decisions as if at any moment she might have to justify herself to the four who had given her command of her own ship.

As Damon's breathing slowed and deepened into sleep, Mairi stood in the tiny, dimly lit cabin, lost in the implications of his whispered words. Damon had stripped away the last vestiges of her habitual desire to measure up to her parents' expectations. She no longer had to test her decisions by whether or not they would meet with approval. It only mattered that they would work.

When she looked up, Seren was gone.

Mairi checked Damon's breathing, left the cabin, and climbed the companionway to the quarterdeck. She looked astern and saw a rowboat heading for the wharves of Cottontown, the boatman a humped shape at the oars, an indistinct figure in the bow. Seren was in the stern, pulling a white blouse over her head. Mairi saw her shake her curls free, drag her multi-coloured top out from under, and toss it onto the thwart beside her. Then she half-stood to pull a shore-going skirt over her shortened breeks.

"Seren!"

As Mairi yelled she knew that her shout was useless: the boat was already barely visible through the wisps of fog that were moving up the bay. She scanned the deck for her brother.

"Trogen! Marley!"

"Bad news, Skipper," said Cam at her elbow. "Trog's taken off for shore in one of the skimmers, an' Marley scarpered along wi' Seren."

Mairi slapped her open hand on the stern rail, swung around and marched back towards the companionway, her bare heels stamping on the deck. Cam's voice followed her.

"I got the crew below freed, an' the first of the shore party are back."

Amidships, some of _Elusive's_ crew were climbing aboard. As they reached the deck, they were taken aback by what they saw and milled about, unsure of what to do next.

"Cam, tell them what's happened and have a couple of them wash the blood off. I'll be back on deck shortly."

Mairi's voice was firm, but she went down the companionway steps with her knees shaking. Grief and anger were confusing her mind, magnifying even small decisions. She chose one of the two first mates' chairs that flanked the master's, which was not quite aligned with the table. Mairi glanced at the door as if Dabih was about to return, sit beside her, and they would talk together and solve the problems that beset her. The dream-like wish faded. She stood up, rearranged the master's chair, and sat in it. She had never been so alone, but at the same moment, she felt that she had been set free.

4. In which Fred is condemned and reprieved

When Fred, Moke, Jake, and Cookie returned to the tavern, it was late in the day. The shadowy taproom stank of beer, tobacco, and forgotten meals. They sat down around a table in the darkest corner and began drinking with the determination of men who need to forget. When the front door opened, all three squinted at the figure silhouetted against the evening light.

Mirak scanned the room, kicked the door closed behind him, strode to an empty chair, hooked it back from the table, sat, leaned back and raised one hand to summon the taverner. He surveyed the men at the table one by one. Moke hunched his big shoulders and stared into his beer mug. Jake shaded his face with a tattooed hand. Pale-faced Cookie fidgeted with his clasp-knife, clicking it open and shut. Fred sat glassy-eyed, staring at nothing. Mirak sipped his drink thoughtfully. He spoke into the silence in a calm, uninflected voice that was more chilling than a shouted tirade.

"Fred, I told you to meet the crew from *Elusive* at your warehouse. Instead, you decided to secure the shipstone yourself. You failed."

Fred's blank stare persisted.

"Where are the men I arranged for you to meet?"

Fred's voice was almost a whisper.

"Things got out of control. Two still guard the ship."

"Where are *Elusive's* crew?"

"Most are ashore somewhere."

"I know about them. What about those aboard?"

"Three or four dead. And also one of the ... the hired help. Moke tossed several over the side. Maybe a few made it to shore. Some are locked between-decks, staying quiet because of the guards."

"What were you trying to do, Fred?"

"I wanted to get the shipstone. I thought..."

"You weren't ordered to think."

"I saw a chance to ..."

"You failed. Again. Last time, too many explosives. This time, when blowing things up might have been useful, you had none with you. Where is the shipstone now?"

Fred's voice rose as he sputtered his excuse.

"*Elusive's* stone is below in its special room along with the skipper and an officer, barricaded behind a steel door. They're probably wounded. I left the guards so I ... we ... can return and ..."

"Blow the door?"

"No. Persuade the youngster with the bracelet to open it for me."

Mirak's grey-haired head tilted to one side. His right hand lowered his mug onto the table and then drifted upward to stroke his short white beard.

"So you did grab one of them. Why didn't you tell me?"

"I tried. But you told me to…"

"Never mind. Who did you get?"

"The youngest."

"Mistake. The boys only have ring stones."

"But the skinny little girl with long black hair and green eyes has a bracelet like the ones used by skippers and navigators."

Mirak's white-flecked eyebrows rose. His fingers brushed one side of his short, grey-white beard.

"And she will open the door of the Forbidden Room for you?"

"Cookie says he can be very convincing."

The door of the tavern slammed open, and a squat, powerful figure stumped towards the table, growling as he came.

"You stupid, stupid, stupid goonie-bird. Miserable arse-munching sculpin, you boarded *Elusive,* and you got it all wrong. All you had to do was meet me at your workshop. You weren't there. You scuppered our plan, Fred, and my shipmates' blood is all over *Elusive's* decks. So let me tell you about *my* plan, which is to take my knife and make a hole two fingers wide above your belly-button, haul out a fathom or so of your tripes, wind them around your throat and hang you from a yard-arm where everyone can see what a stupid, gutless..."

"Easy, Walt."

"Don't give me 'easy,' Mirak. Your plan was to cripple *Elusive* just enough to keep her here in Cottontown, 'stead of crawlin' back to Matris like *Cygnus* did when Fred got it wrong the first time. We could'a come out of this with a ship and a shipstone. 'Stead of that, we got less than nothin', an' I can't go back to my ship."

Walt yanked a chair from the neighbouring table and thumped himself into it. Mirak's voice remained calm.

"I think you can, Walt. Fred's boarding party will have to stay out of sight, I agree, but you're clear. You were ashore, doing your best to find Fred at his workshop."

"An' searchin' for him when I saw he weren't there. Right. I get it. It's even true: I went lookin' everywhere, tryin' to find out what he did and how to make sense out of the mess he's made."

"No fault on your part, Walt. But you, Fred, you're a whole different kettle of rotting fish. I'm almost inclined to let Walt string you up by your innards, if it wasn't for the fact that though you're a nuisance, you're a confoundedly lucky nuisance, because you brought me another ship all the way from the Sunny Isles: a nice little schooner, crewed by Astreya's and Dabih's children."

"I did?"

The question was out of Fred's mouth before he thought. Realizing his mistake as four pairs of eyes focused on him, he repeated himself as firmly as he could.

"I did. I did. They must have guessed where we were going, repaired their ship really quickly, and had luck with the wind."

"They didn't have to guess, Fred, you claw-footed ullage," said Walt. "They followed the stone on the girl you kidnapped."

"They couldn't have! Her stone flashed once and went dark, and then she passed out."

"Until this morning."

Moke's slow voice surprised them all.

"I been tryin' to tell yez. 'Tain't like the night afore last when Fred figgered she was dead. Me too, 'till I picked her up. Poor little thing, she was just tuckered out. An' when I looked at her stone out of the lamplight, I could see it was glowin'. Not much, but sure 'nough lit in the middle. An' when she woke up this mornin', the stone on her arm was green as seaweed, wi' a line down the middle."

"She's still aboard the ketch?" Mirak demanded. "Fred, you imbecile, when were you going to tell me?"

"He's a wonder," said Walt. "That big brain of his what makes him so superior to us common sailors who don't have his book-learning, an' experimentin', and experience at blowin' things up, all o' that doesn't stop him from makin' a great big mess wherever he goes. I'm stuffed if I know why you keep him around, Mirak."

No longer in fear for his life, Fred found new confidence.

"I can still get the stone from *Elusive*. No problem."

"Big problem, Fred," said Jake, his voice slurred. "When Walt's work party gets back aboard, they'll find out what's happened, and then the two guards will be swimming — more likely, sinking. The crew will be ready and waiting like they weren't when we boarded 'em."

Walt shook his left hand as if he had been burnt; Mirak stared at one of his fingers. They frowned at each other.

"Yer ring, too?" Walt grunted.

Mirak nodded.

"Which one of them did that?" Walt asked.

"More than one," said Mirak. "I'd say that now they know where we all are." He stood and stared deliberately at the men who sat, open-mouthed around the table. "Walt, get back to your ship. The rest of you, to the ketch. Now."

5. In which rescues fail

Seren ran from the Forbidden Room, completely overwhelmed. Her father was dead, and her sister taken. A few almost blind steps took her to what had been her cabin when she served aboard *Elusive*. It was almost as she had left it. She pulled her sea chest out from under her bunk, rummaged among some spare shore-going gear that she had not taken with her to *Cygnet,* and hurriedly chose a blue skirt and a white shirt. Stepping into a pair of watch-keeping shoes, she ran up the companionway, across the quarterdeck and to the waist of the ship, where she saw the boatman preparing to row back to shore. She was over the side and climbing down the ladder in an instant, barely noticing Marley behind her.

Seren sat in the stern of the rowboat trying to ignore the boatman's lascivious stare as she pulled her shirt over her head and then extricated Lady Orinda's gift from under it. Irritation at the old man ripened into an unfocused fury that mercifully dimmed the image of her father's lifeless face. She stoked her anger, counting the regular splash of oars as the rowboat made its way toward the head of the harbour, trying not to recall what she could not forget.

When they arrived at the wharf, the tide had fallen, exposing weedy pilings. She ignored the boatman's upturned, grinning face and climbed a green-slimed ladder to the wharf's deck. Marley followed. She turned and confronted him, her voice stiff and formal.

"I didn't ask you to accompany me, Marley. I do not need your help to find Ellie."

"Yes, you do."

"I can look after myself."

"You sure can fight."

"What did you expect? That I'd wave my tiny hands in the air and scream like a little girl?"

"I was concerned for you and Skipper Mairi. I expected that..."

"You wondered if we could defend our so-called honour until you men could rescue us."

"I'd seen Mairi stand up to my brother, but I didn't expect either of you to take down your man that fast."

"I was angry. I still am. Now get out of my way. I have to find Ellie."

"You don't know how to get to Black Bay. I do."

Seren stared into his dark eyes, looked for any sign of condescension, saw none, and reconsidered.

"Very well. Let's get on with it."

As Seren turned to go, she almost ran into two men.

"Young lady, is this nigga causin' you any distress that my friend and I can speedily, and may I say, forcibly alleviate?"

Seren suppressed the impulse to push them both out of her way. Instead, she stood her ground and looked the landsmen up and down. Only a little older than she, they were both stylishly dressed, sporting elaborately curled moustaches above high-collar tailored white shirts, grey waistcoats, and matching jackets, all of which told her that they were traders or perhaps ship-owners' sons.

"Thank you, gentlemen," she replied evenly. "I have the situation well in hand. Now, if you will permit, I have an appointment to keep. Come, Marley."

She was almost a head taller than they were, and she used her height to advantage as she strode towards them. They separated to let her pass. Hoping that Marley was behind her, she kept her head high and her steps even along the length of the wharf until she felt a stone walkway under her feet. Her confidence was a hollow pretence: she had no idea where to go until Marley's whisper came from about a pace behind her.

"Take the first turn on your right, follow the road until it splits. Then go left."

The encounter on the dock had reminded her that Cottontown custom and law forbade Marley from walking beside her, so she kept her chin up, and avoided eye contact with people they passed, most of whom were intent on their own business anyway. At the second turn of the road, she stepped aside to avoid a substantial matron wearing a fur-trimmed jacket above a purple dress festooned with ribbons and flounces. Beside her walked a white-haired gentleman in a dove-grey suit, carrying a black, silver-chased cane. She overheard the woman ask her companion who was the tall, hatless girl, to which he replied with two disdainful words: "Northern traders." Seren gritted her teeth, despising them and their town.

They waked up a narrow, cobbled street that zig-zagged uphill. The brick and stone facades of two and three-story buildings stood close to the roadway edge with only a couple of stone steps to their doors. Seren read signs above lintels: "Gordon and Sons, Ship Chandlers," "Smith: Fine Cutlery," "Blair & Co: Wines & Spirits." The white-on-black lettering on the signs grew increasingly ornate as they ascended, until the last, "Colbert & Colbert, Law Office," was both raised and picked out in gold. From time to time, she had to walk close to the wall while a cart clattered past on pavement that was making her painfully aware that she was wearing soft-soled deck shoes.

The close-set buildings that shaded the road gave way to high walls pierced by wrought-iron gates, through which Seren glimpsed impressive mansions set back at a distance from the road. She did not slow her resolute pace even though the sun had burned through the mists, and she could feel perspiration on her forehead. They passed the last mansion, and the road climbed even more steeply, diminishing to little more than a battered strip of grass between two tracks. When she was sure that nobody was in front or behind them, she slowed until they were walking side by side. Eventually, they reached a saddle between rocky ridges, where a lone building stood at the crest of the road. They paused before starting down towards the huddle of houses, barns, and sheds that curled around the shore of Black Bay.

"I'll get you through Black Bay," said Marley.

"I don't need..." Seren began.

"Same way as you got me past the white folks back there, only t'other way round."

Seren bit her lip, nodded, and let him set the pace. As she matched him stride for stride, his rhythm steadied her breathing and soon her emotions. A strangely detached calm replaced her rage with steely determination. Her mind cleared, she glanced at Marley and blurted out the first question that occurred to her.

"Why are you doing this, Marley?"

Instantly, she regretted her brittle tone of voice. His reply was equally crisp.

"To rescue Ellie. Is there some reason I shouldn't?"

She shook her head vigorously.

"Not as far as I'm concerned. But I wondered why, after you'd finally got home to your island, you decided to stay aboard *Cygnet*."

"Nothing for me to do there except work for Chad, who's the next big man on the island."

"You're older than Chad. Why wouldn't you...?"

"Be next in line? Because Max is Chad's father, not mine."

"That's..."

"That's the way it works. It's also why I left."

Seren wanted to know more, but her impetuous question had been out of place and time. It was right that Marley was curt and dismissive. She walked on in silence, feeling disloyal for letting herself be deflected from searching for Ellie.

At first, the foot-track wound its way past knobbed outcrops of grey rock like the backbone of a huge half-buried skeleton. The path was joined by tributary tracks that came from single-story wooden cottages crouching in the lee of scrubby pine and cedar windbreaks. Soon they were walking down a slope of smooth granite, past weathered wooden houses, built wherever there was a flat space in the grey bedrock that separated them. Washing waved on clotheslines strung between poles wedged at crazy angles in cracks and fissures.

Eventually, they were among the close-packed houses, sheds, huts, and outbuildings that clustered around the waterfront. Uneven wharves perched on poles rammed between boulders. A few dories rose and fell on the little waves that had found their way up the bay from the sea. Buoys bobbed on dazzling, sunlit water, waiting for their boats to return.

Seren ran around Marley and out onto the longest of the wharves that pointed down the narrow bay towards the sea. It creaked and swayed under her feet as she reached its end. In the distance, where the sun-dazzled water merged towards the blue-grey horizon, was a white triangle of sail. Seren shaded her eyes with one hand and squinted, but could only discern the boat's hull because she knew it had to be there. Marley appeared beside her. He took a small spyglass from his satchel and aimed it down the bay.

"Someone's on their way out to sea, but I can't be sure what they're sailing," said Marley.

Seren steadied herself on one of the wharf's pilings, raised her left arm and pulled back her sleeve, exposed her stone and swung her arm from side to side.

"Ellie, I know you're there," she muttered.

Marley handed her the glass, she raised it to her eye, then glanced down at her stone, stamped her foot on the wooden dock and yelled.

"Ellie, respond!"

She looked through the glass again, and as the boat turned to port, saw the distinctive two-masted silhouette of the ketch.

"NO! We've missed them! We're too late! We have to get back to the ship ... tell ... Mairi ... follow."

Marley heard the dismay in her voice as he held out a hand for the spyglass. Their fingers touched. She pulled away, and the glass would have fallen into the sea had he not caught it. When he looked up, Seren's fists were clenched, her jaw set.

"Seren," he began.

"Ellie's gone. Don't you try to calm me down, Marley. My father is dead, my sister is kidnapped, and I am very, very angry."

Marley stepped back, his hands expressing apology. Seren looked past her toes into deep, clear water where seaweed swung back and forth. She blinked away unwanted tears.

"You 'bout to go swimmin' wi' the white girl, bro'?"

Seren and Marley swung around to face two men and one woman. All three were black, dressed in shabby work clothes, and wore shapeless hats that shaded their eyes.

"Spies!" the woman hissed. She held a long-bladed knife at waist height, her thumb pointing along the blade. "Ben, you an' Andy take the man. I got the white bitch."

Seren's heels left the boards of the dock, her knees bent slightly, her hands drifted outwards from her body, ready.

"Steady," Marley murmured.

The man called Ben held out his right hand, palm down, cautioning his companions.

"Neither of you was aboard the ketch this morning," he said. "What brings you here?"

"Those were the bastards who kidnapped my sister," said Seren.

"I didn't see no woman when we were..." the woman began.

The man's hand gestured 'hush' again as Seren continued.

"She's a little girl, black hair, they could have been holding her below, where you couldn't see. We have to get back to our ship so we can chase after them. Listen, please listen. We're not from Cottontown. We're ... we're northerners."

"You maybe. He don't come from anywheres north."

"I'm from the Sunny Isles," said Marley. "Where they stole the girl from us. We followed them, but 'cause of the fog we didn't see them make the turn for the Bay. We thought they'd gone to the main harbour."

"You arrived at a bad time, friend."

The man's voice lost its edge; Marley matched his tone.

"Seems to me something's going down that has nothing to do with us. So why don't you just let us go back to our ship and you folks can get on with ... whatever."

While he was talking, people appeared from doors between buildings and sheds and began to cluster in the road that had brought Seren and Marley to the waterfront.

The woman pointed her knife at Seren.

"And let the white bitch warn the watchmen? No way."

"We're merchants. We don't get involved," said Seren.

"That's what *they* said when they were leaving. You say you're not with them. They sold guns to us, did you sell them to the town?"

"We don't sell guns to anybody," said Seren.

"More fool you, then," said a deep voice.

Seren's saw a tall black man walking confidently towards them. The three who had confronted Seren and Marley turned towards him, and the men conferred. The woman's knife did not waver, but Seren saw her head tip to one side to hear what the men were saying. Their voices were low and fast and their words indistinct, but it was clear that Ben and Andy were reporting to their leader. When he took a quick, evaluative glance at them, Seren sensed his authority.

"Bring them," he said, and without waiting to see if he was obeyed, he turned back to the larger group of men and women.

"You heard," said Ben.

His right thumb twitched his loose jacket and the metal of a handgun gleamed in the afternoon sun. Seren glanced at Marley, who nodded. They walked together along the shaky dock towards the three who had confronted them. When they reached the stony waterfront road, Ben and Andy closed in on either side. The woman followed a pace behind.

"I still got me knife," she whispered.

Seren looked at Marley, who shrugged. They walked side by side, surrounded by silent men and women who were too intent on their purpose to give them more than a quick look.

6. In which Trogen chances on Walt

Trogen stood outside Damon's cabin in the shadowy passage, reliving the moment in the Forbidden Room when he knelt beside Dabih's body. His uncle's blood pooled on the deck; shiny, liquid, and black in the green light of the shipstone. It was on his hands, his breeks, on Dabih's dead face. When he tried to stand up, his feet slipped, when he tried to brace himself, his hands slid against the bulkhead, and when he finally stood, his fingers stuck to the navigation table.

Trogen had no idea of what he was going to do. He stood for a moment in the passageway, closed his eyes and tried to think, but instantly, he was again reliving the moment when he opened the door of the Forbidden Room and saw the crumpled body of the man who until recently had been his skipper, and as far back as he could remember, his uncle.

Trogen shook his head, stared up the companionway, shuddered, and ran towards the light. He pounded up the steps to the quarterdeck, saw Seren climbing into the boatman's dory, and Marley on his way down the ladder to join her. Trogen turned his back on both of them. His feet took him amidships, to the skimmer he used to race when Dabih was still his skipper. He chose an oar from below the skiff's cradle, removed the mast, boom, and sail, unshipped the tiller, rudder, and centreboard, and clipped the lowering gear to the stern and bow. He swung the derricks outboard, took hold of the falls, stepped aboard and lowered the skiff hand over hand, balancing with the skill of long practice. Once his feet were at the schooner's waterline, he pulled the quick-release line and the skimmer splashed onto the water. He knelt, then lay flat in the little craft and plunged his arms into the sea again and again until blood no longer trailed into the water.

Trogen stood and paddled standing up, the better to see his way along the shoreline through skeins of drifting fog that deadened all sounds except for the swish and plop of his oar. Reaching the northern end of the bay where a stream joined the saltwater, he headed for a hard beach where the falling tide had left several boats heeled over, drying after high water. Among rowboats and fishing smacks, he saw *Elusive's* two longboats, hauled out above the tideline.

As the skiff's bow touched the packed sand, Trogen stepped into knee-deep water, wading ashore to wash the blood off his feet and breeks. When he bent over the bow to haul the little craft towards *Elusive's* longboats, a hand plucked at his sleeve.

"I wouldn'a get too close to them big rowboats, mister. Them Men o' the Sea what beached them there paid me to shoo off anyone that might swipe an oar or summat like that."

Trogen straightened his back and looked down on the grubby face of a boy of perhaps a dozen years. His eyes had the calculating look of someone three times his age, who had seen much and remembered the worst of it. He shrewdly stepped back out of Trogen's reach.

"I'm from the same ship as they," said Trogen.

"Then how's about you pay me, too?"

Trogen fished in a pocket and extracted four small coins.

"One now, and three when I return."

"Make it six and I'll wait all night."

"Listen, my lad, when I get back, my boat better be where and how I left her or I will hunt you down and larmer the living daylights out of you. Got it?"

"You won't need to be doing that, Skipper."

Trogen tossed him two of the coins and set off across the beach toward the docks and wharves, sand crunching under his wet feet. He scrambled up the tumbled boulders that protected the pilings and vaulted onto the first of a succession of piers that thrust out into the harbour. He had landed at the fishermen's end of the wharf: nets and lines dried on poles, lobster pots were piled along the shore, their colour-coded buoys beside them. Complicated smells of tar and cordage competed with the odour of fish—fresh, dried, and rotting. Trogen's heels first drummed on uneven boards, leaving wet footprints. Then he walked along a wooden wharf past shacks and sheds, flanked by dories stacked three and four high, some festooned with sails and nets hung to dry. Soon his footsteps were quietened by the substantial deck of the town's main wharf. On his right were two-story prosperous warehouses with their owners' names on signboards over their double doors. On his left, sturdy coast-hugging little schooners and sloops were tied up alongside, their masts gently swaying. Even numbed by unexpressed grief, Trogen noticed that none had *Cygnet's* fine lines and gleaming woodwork. As he made his way further, he saw larger vessels, their crews loading and unloading bales, boxes, sacks, chests and barrels. Automatically, he identified goods and their origins, as he had done in many ports to report back to Dabih.

He stepped around men laden with coils of rope, ducked between two at the ends of a fresh-varnished spar, and avoided a line of people shoving wheelbarrows to and from the stores and shops that lay up the narrow roadways into the town. He glimpsed well-dressed men making their way to the ships, followed by servants equipped with bags, packs or satchels to carry whatever their employers might purchase. As Trogen had been to Cottontown before, he saw but did not take much note that although most of the sailors and all of the elegant traders were white, those who followed them to carry were black, as were most of the men and boys wheelbarrowing goods up and down the steep roadways. Everywhere he looked, the workers were intent on what they were doing, and the bosses insulated from their surroundings by prestige and hauteur.

Trogen made his way through the thickening crowd. He muttered to himself, drawing occasional sidelong glances from people he passed. Pursued by the horrible scene in the Forbidden Room, he wanted to punish someone for all that had gone wrong since leaving the Sunny Isles, but at the same time, he harboured a sneaking feeling that it was he who was to blame. He had ignored the order to navigate conventionally and instead used the shipstone. He had gotten drunk and not only failed to rescue Ellie, but also made a fool of himself. He resented that Mairi and Seren had overcome both thugs before he could rush in to protect them. He wanted to be the one to get Ellie back but did not know where she was. He also had a confused notion that he might find Seren so that they could rescue Ellie together, but he did not know what route she had taken. He discretely consulted his stone as he walked. As he expected, it was blocked by the ridge between Cottontown and Black Bay. He began to regret his impulsive flight from the ship.

Trogen was so wrapped up in his own misery that he had walked to the most prosperous end of the waterfront before he realized that he did not know where he was going. He paused, and anxiety overcame him. He stood with people hurrying by on each side, looking vaguely for someone to ask the way to Black Bay, and becoming swiftly aware that this would not be a good idea. A dapper stranger cursed him as an obstacle to be pushed aside. Alone and rudderless, Trogen craved a ship and the people he had known all his life. His heart pounded and his half-open mouth was dry.

"Trogen!"

Trogen stared at the backs of people ahead of him, swung around to look at those behind him and on either side, then decided he must be mistaken. The deep voice spoke again.

"Trog, what in blazes are you doing here?"

He looked down at a familiar squat figure.

"Walt! *Elusive's* been attacked! I—we—the Cygnets boarded her and took her back again, but before we got there, Dabih was knifed. He's dead, Walt, dead. And Damon's cut really badly. I have to find…"

"Not here, Trog. Fill me in where we can talk. Pub 'round the corner."

Walt's big hand gripped him above one elbow. Trogen let himself be led, guided and insulated from the press of strangers shoving, shouting, pushing, talking, ordering, and swearing all around them. The bandy-legged man was no more than two thirds the height of the shortest men on the dock, but his girth and presence cleared the way through the crowd and up the nearest street. Trogen had no clear understanding of what was happening until he found himself in a tavern booth with a mug of beer in front of him.

Trogen stared across the table at Walt. Shrewd dark eyes looked back at him from under thick eyebrows in a face topped by curly black hair. When Walt's lips parted to reveal his big, uneven teeth in a wolffish grin, Trogen was once again a little boy talking with the one uncle to whom he really was related, albeit complicatedly. Overcome with gratitude, Trogen spilled out how they had boarded *Elusive* and despatched the two thugs guarding her. Walt looked away when he knuckled tears from the corners of his eyes as he spoke of Dabih, seeing again the bloody face, vacant eyes, and slack mouth. He responded to Walt's questions about the voyage south, what had happened at the Sunny Isles, and how *Cygnet* had come to be in Cottontown harbour. Trogen supposed that his account was coherent enough because Walt nodded sympathetically throughout.

At length, he stammered into silence, "Ellie. I have to find Ellie... have to ... have to ..."

"Calm, Trog. Take a round turn and make fast. You need to hear what I'm saying. The ketch is gone, and Ellie with her."

"We have to follow, get her back, and her stone with her..."

"Right. Her stone. Do you know if it and she are still alive?"

Trogen nodded.

"I felt her trying to message Dabih as we boarded *Elusive*. Maybe Mairi and Seren felt it too, but there was a lot going on, Walt. I tried to reply, but I don't think I reached her."

"I'll believe yer, though I'm damned if I know how you do it. So she'll keep for a bit, at least until I fill you in about what's been happening at my end of the ship. More beer?"

Trogen shook his head.

"Right. Today started out with me leading a detail ashore to head up to Frederickson's warehouse for a load of fine glass and instruments what had to be carried by hand on account of the fact that Fred's shop is way the blazes up a rough road, far out of town where folk won't be disturbed by the smells and explosions from his workshop."

"Glass? Explosions? What has this to do...? Who's Fred?"

"The same smart-arse egg-head what cooked up the clever coating on the stone that's on your arm so's it can't be drowned if you take a ducking in the salt-chuck. Fred's bright, so bright he's near to blind about what's going on around him. Prob'ly don't recall he made the boatload of explosives that near sunk *Cygnus*. Got his head so far up in the clouds—or more likely up his own hawsehole—that he doesn't remember deals and appointments, like the one he made with me that had me pounding on his door a few hours ago, when from what you say I should 'a been back aboard *Elusive*, tossing thieving, murdering bastards into the harbour, after I'd made a few knife-shaped holes in their shirts and weskits. Anyway, there I was, and there he wasn't, so 'stead of goin' back to the ship, I hunted for the miserable sculpin all along the waterfront, up and down the roads and streets, in and out of the pubs and eateries, and finally all the way to where I could look down on Black Bay, where I seen him board a ketch what must be the one you've been chasin'. They was making ready to cast off when I saw them, but I was so far away that by the time I'd have run to the shore, all I could'a done was wave. And like you know, I'm not much of a man for runnin'."

Trogen nodded again. Keeping track of Walt's words was holding him from spiralling back into horror and confusion.

"Now listen real close, Trog. I think Fred was after the shipstones for hisself. He'd held 'em in his hands, played with 'em, but couldn't figure them out, which ain't no surprise, 'cause they're nothin' more than water-worn pebbles, 'less someone like you lights 'em up. Maybe he wants to figure out how they work so he can use them for somethin', somehow. For all I know, he wants to make false teeth out of them. But I'm sure that ever since 'Streya an' me got him to make that waterproof coating, he's been lusting after them. Today he made his move, but as usual, he outsmarted hisself and it all ended with blood on the deck an' the death of a good man."

"Dabih. He was family, Walt. Much more than just my skipper."

"So he was, Trog. So he was. An' now you have to respect his memory by carryin' on. You'n me have to get back to *Elusive*, where you can use her shipstone to work the magic like he did."

"Rescue Ellie!"

"That, too. First of all, take command. Sail north, cut him off from where I don't doubt he's heading."

"Where's that, Walt? How do you know where he's going?"

"Well, y' see, Trog, I think your da said more than he should have to Fred about where the stones come from an' how few of them are left. So now that Fred's gotten himself a boat an' a wielder..."

"Ellie!"

"...he is plannin' to make her find the mother lode where he can have all the stones he wants."

"We have to cut him off, stop him... Hold on, Walt. There aren't any more stones."

"No, Trog. It's just that you don't know where they came from. 'Streya never told ya, did he? Well, Trog, they came from the Village where he was born. His da, the first 'Streya, found them and 'Streya, your da, inherited them."

"Why didn't he go get more?"

"Dunno. Beats me."

"So, how does Fred know where they are? Father ... Astreya ... wouldn't tell a stranger what he wouldn't share with ..."

"With his son? With you? Well, Trog, I can't say, 'cause I just don't know. Anyway, what's important is to stop Fred from getting hold of them, right?"

Trogen nodded.

"And rescuing Ellie."

"That, too."

"So we have to get after that ketch just as soon as we can. Little *Cygnet's* not going to take down four or five men, one of them a giant, but *Elusive's* got the speed, the size, an' the crew."

"And you, Trog, me lad, you can find them."

"Yes, I can."

Trogen's words came out slowly, but with a conviction, unlike anything since he joined *Cygnet*. Walt nodded with satisfaction that had been absent from his day so far.

"Now you get back to the ship in your skimmer, and once I've rounded up my crew, I'll be right behind you."

7. In which Mairi takes charge

Mairi set about restoring order. She began by raiding the ship's stores and changing into officer's blue-and-white, for the first time in her life grateful that the same uniforms were worn by men and women. She came on deck to find Cam and the returning crew liberating those who had been barricaded below.

The first test of her authority was when *Elusive's* crew appeared from belowdecks. A group of six or eight saw the two who had been their guards, tied and gagged by the port rail. Before muttered threats and curses could mature into action, she stepped between them and their quarry, Cam a step behind her.

"They prob'ly can swim after a fashion," Cam told her quietly. "And anyway the tide's setting in along the near shore."

Mairi nodded and stood firm.

"I want these two off the ship. Untie them and pitch them over the side."

"You're not just going to let them go?" asked a voice.

"You heard the skipper," said Cam.

"She ain't our skipper."

"She's the one what took down these two while you lot were below."

"Thank you, Cam. They heard me."

Mairi stood still, facing the group. They hesitated for a heartbeat, and at that moment her confidence triggered their training. She walked to the quarterdeck and stood looking into the middle distance while Cam cut the two men loose. Neither he nor *Elusive's* sailors were gentle, but there were no screams or moans. She heard two splashes, and then Cam was reporting at her side.

"They're wet, but they ain't drowned. Now what?"

"Cam, the moment Seren and Marley return, send them directly to me. If Walt and the rest of *Elusive's* crew show up first, immediately assemble the entire crew and call me. I want everyone to have the same story of what's happened, and also to know what going to happen. While we're waiting, would you have *Cygnet* alongside to starboard, and make sure both ships are watered?"

Cam gave her a quick approving look and nodded.

"And Cam, find the bosun and send him to the Forbidden Room, along with a cleaning detail."

"I'm on it."

~^~

Alone in the stern cabin, surrounded by Dabih's books, charts, and instruments, Mairi almost lost the objectivity that she had worn like armour ever since the bloody horror in the Forbidden Room. She heard voices on deck giving orders and the hurrying footfalls of those who carried them out. She imagined the evolution that was about to take place, starting with floating a rope from *Elusive* to *Cygnet* on the rising tide. She wondered whether Peter and Neil would be able to cope. When she heard Cam shouting to the boys that a towrope was on its way, Mairi almost stood to go on deck and supervise. She checked herself and sat back in the skipper's chair. She knew that Peter and Neil were both capable and intelligent and that when they had secured the tow and raised the anchors, the rest was straightforward hauling by experienced sailors who would soon have the little schooner alongside. She sighed and turned her attention to command decisions of a different order than practical seamanship.

Steeling herself against emotion, Mairi went back to the Forbidden Room, where a man and a woman waited to begin the cleanup. She palmed the door open and gave the sailors permission to enter. By the light of a lantern strong enough to overcome the green glow from the shipstone, the room lacked its usual uncanny aura. The bosun positioned a roll of sailcloth and his sail-mending kit beside Dabih's body, which Cam had composed, eyes closed, hands crossed at the wrists. Mairi intervened before the bosun could begin wrapping the body for burial at sea. He stood respectfully with his face turned aside as she knelt, unclipped the bracelet from his arm, and then gently touched Dabih's cheek in farewell. When she stood and looked down at the man she had known her entire life, it seemed to her that his body was now somehow irrelevant. Her vision blurred with unshed tears.

She turned away, rubbed dried blood from Dabih's clasp and placed it near the shipstone, then covered the round table with its black cloth, before leaving the Forbidden Room with a muttered "Carry on," to the bosun and his mate. Then she and returned to the stern cabin, where she reviewed her limited options.

Later, she heard boats coming alongside, orders being shouted, the rattle of oars being tossed and stowed, the measured tread of men hauling in unison, the squeak of blocks, and the thump as the longboats nested in their cradles. She was bent over the table, poring over a chart of the passage to Matris, when Cam put his head in the cabin door.

"They're all here in a bunch."

"Send them in."

Cam's feet thudded back up the companionway. Mairi looked at the skipper's chair for an instant and was taking the seat beside it when she heard a second, softer knock at the door. It slid open, a hand gripping its edge at eye-height. Damon stepped into the cabin, took two hesitant steps, caught the back of a chair to steady himself, and sat down with a sigh. When he looked up at Mairi, his face was pale under his weathered tan, and his eyes were sunken into his head.

"Damon, what are you doing out of bed?"

"Reporting for duty."

"Your first duty is to get yourself better," said Mairi. "You're in no shape to stand your watch."

"Yes, well, standing *has* become something of a challenge," said Damon.

He brushed the corners of his moustache with the knuckle of his index finger and sat carefully opposite her. For as long as she could remember, she had enjoyed the gesture that signalled his self-deprecating humour. For the first time that day, Mairi smiled.

"Then for goodness sake, why are you here?"

"I don't want to miss the transfer of command."

The door slid open again behind him and Trogen appeared, talking as he entered.

"There's a riot ashore. Mutiny. Boats trying to get away. I heard shots. It looks like a raid on the warehouses. We got here as quick as we could. People are fighting on the waterfront. Walt charged through them, headed for the two longboats. The shore detail was waiting, and my skimmer was still there. Walt was aboard the second boat and about to pull away when Seren and Marley came running. They made it just in time. What are you doing out of bed, Damon?"

"Making sure I don't miss anything," said Damon. His voice was weak, but he smiled at Trogen and again preened his moustache.

Trogen took the chair beside Damon, and the two looked at each other. Damon, silent; Trogen animated. Mairi knew how their affection had to be masked by rank when they were both aboard *Elusive,* so she was surprised to see Trogen's hand reach for Damon's shoulder. As they muttered formal words of condolence to each other, Mairi detected a change in Trogen. He carried his head higher, he was looking at Damon directly, and there were none of the furtive glances that had become his habit. Before she could wonder why and how resentment and anger had slipped from his shoulders, Seren came through the door, her voice interrupting Mairi's thoughts.

"She's gone. They've taken her. The ketch is ..."

"I know, Seren. "

"...we must..."

"We shall, Seren," said Mairi. "But first we must organize. So sit, everyone. Here is the situation. The ketch is headed northward. They need Ellie to navigate where the compass is unreliable, so she's safe for the present. Ellie knows we can track her clasp, but she's not using it to try to make contact..."

"Because they're watching her!" exclaimed Seren.

Mairi nodded.

"Probably. And I guess she's pretending to have a whole lot less skill than she actually has. We should therefore make no attempt that might lead to their guessing the extent of her talent. We will monitor her stone, standing ready should she get the chance to message us about their course and objective."

"It's Matris," said Seren.

"Where Mirak wants to humiliate Astreya," said Damon.

"Nah," said Walt. "It's the shipstones that Fred's after. He's been lustin' after 'em ever since he waterproofed the few we got. He's the one that snatched Ellie, not the old geezer. Mirak's prob'ly dead by now."

"Betel said he recognized Mirak by his voice..." Trogen began.

"Silly old bugger's blind in one eye an' can't see out of the other, an' he sees a whole lot better than he hears."

Mairi brought her hands together, claiming attention with a soft clap.

"For the present, their motives are as unclear as their destination. We must follow, and defer any decision until we have more information. Meanwhile, it is my opinion that an open-sea rescue is out of the question."

Trogen gave her a quick glance and then a slow nod.

"Now as to the compliment of our two ships. With Dabih's death, *Elusive* lacks navigational capability."

She pursed her lips and glanced around the table. Eyes fell, as each of them supplied their own content to her emotionless formula.

"She has also lost men from her crew, and although Damon has risen from his bed unasked in order to attend this meeting, for the present he's in no shape to fulfill his duties as mate of the starboard watch. So, here is what I propose. Walt will undertake the rank and responsibilities of sailing master, and in consultation with Damon, will promote two senior leading seamen to the rank of acting mates. Trogen, as the ranking navigation officer, will become *Elusive's* provisional master, pending confirmation at a formal meeting of the masters and navigators."

Heads came up, glances were exchanged, mouths opened to speak, but Mairi continued.

"By himself, Trogen cannot continuously monitor Ellie's stone, and neither can I aboard *Cygnet*."

"There isn't another clasp or anyone who can ..." Walt began.

"Yes, there is. Dabih's clasp is not completely extinguished. I have placed it on the navigation table close to the shipstone, where we will see if either Neil or Peter can revive it, which is what we must do next. Cam, would you please summon them from *Cygnet* to meet with Trogen, Seren and me in the Forbidden Room?"

As Cam left the cabin, there was a general stirring over which Mairi prevailed by continuing in the same firm and reasonable voice.

"Assuming for a moment that Neil is successful, *Cygnet* will need a replacement. With your approval, Trogen, Walt, and Damon, I'd like to second Drew's son Alan to my ship."

The three men looked at each other. Trogen nodded, as did Damon. Walt shrugged.

"Then we are in agreement. Trogen, would you lead the way to the Forbidden Room?"

As all three left the cabin, Mairi saw Damon give her a slow, approving wink.

8. In which Ellie and Mirak match wits

Ellie sat in a corner of the stern settee, her knees drawn up to her chin. The steady rocking motion of the ship that had lulled her past despair almost into a coma now changed its rhythm. She felt her spine press against the ship's side as it heeled to starboard. The wake no longer bubbled softly astern the transom but instead churned and hissed as the ship picked up speed.

For a glorious instant, Ellie had been certain that Seren, Mairi, and Trogen knew where she was and would soon be on their way to rescue her. But the men had returned, the ketch had sailed. Ellie shivered, pulled the blanket up around her, sniffed it, grimaced, and pushed it away. Then as the cabin door banged open, she drew it back up to her chin, stopping herself from pulling it over her head only at the last moment. Two men blocked most of the level light through the doorway. Ellie saw a silhouetted figure clutch at the doorframe before lurching across the cabin to dump himself down in the skipper's chair. The black-clad man who followed him moved with the instinctive grace of someone to whom the motion of a ship is second nature. He stood, deftly swaying, looking down with disdain at the seated man, who looked up, flinched, scrambled out of the chair, and stood, his pale face screwed into a frown. The man in black took an agile stride, slid into the skipper's chair, and turned to face Ellie.

She saw that he was old; more than twice the age of the clumsy landsman who sat opposite him. She felt the authority that had silently compelled Fred to obey. Narrowing her green eyes, Ellie reasoned that the old man must think there was something she could do for him. Recognizing that as yet unknown need gave her a sliver of hope. She stared back, motionless.

"You're very young to be a wielder."

He knows the right word, Ellie said to herself. She was apprehensive, but she did not blink.

"You must be unusually valuable to be given the last clasp."

How does he know that? Ellie asked herself, barely maintaining her mask.

"And since I respect Astreya's amazing luck as much as I despise him, I shall also respect you."

Ellie continued to hold his stare. *Now he's trying flattery.*

".... for the present," he added.

"Oh, for goodness sake, Mirak. I'll get Cookie in here and he'll have her dancing to your tune in no time."

Ellie blinked, despite herself. *Point made,* she silently admitted.

Disconcertingly, Seren's agonized message tingled on her arm, testing her ability to keep her face expressionless. Then family history merged with fragments of overheard conversations, and she recognized her adversary.

Mirak! Oron's executioner! Cygnus' *treacherous mate!*

"Hold your tongue, Frederick, or I'll have Cookie cut it out. You'll still be useful if you can't talk, and much less annoying."

"You don't scare me, Mirak. You need me. Face it."

Fred's words were bold, but he could not keep his voice from whining.

"Not at present. Leave us," said Mirak, without looking to see that he was obeyed. "Now let us discuss your situation, young lady. You must be Eliana, second-to-youngest of Dabih's children. I regret to say that I have bad news for you. Thanks to the colossal stupidity of the man who just left us, your father is dead."

Mirak's words paralyzed Ellie. She could neither move nor think. But she could not stop listening as Mirak's words continued to crush her.

"So you see, Eliana, *Elusive* is now a semi-permanent fixture in Cottontown harbour, as is the little schooner in which Astreya hoped to protect you and the other three young wielders. His usual luck has deserted him. The situation of his last two ships is precarious. Their crews are either stuck aboard at anchor or wandering around ashore, where they have happened into the middle of an armed revolt. The long-suffering black folk of Back Bay are at war with the prosperous white people of Cottontown. And thanks to my little ketch's recent cargo, not only the whites have guns. The black people know their enemies are white. The white people know their enemies are black. Both are desperate. Because of Astreya's rules, all his ships are unarmed, which means that they are very likely to be despised by both sides. This is not a good time to be neutral."

Neutral. Desperate. The words penetrated Ellie's numbed consciousness. Slowly at first, she reasoned her way to the conclusion that Mirak's choice of words was probably appropriate. *But they don't apply to me. I'm not neutral. And I won't despair.* The ghost of a possible plan prowled the back of Ellie's mind, taking more form and substance the longer she refused to be struck down by Mirak's verbal assault. She evaluated him as an opponent in a game of stones.

He's good at this. He talks people down until they've nothing left except to obey. It's a trick that's worked for him in the past. He's confident, so he's sugar-coating his poison because I'm smaller, I'm younger, and I'm a woman. This isn't about truth, or fact, or what happened or didn't. He expects to win because he always has. It's about power. His power over everyone. Everyone ... except for Astreya. The one who got away, who isn't the same as all the men and women he betrayed and murdered. Death is for people who get in his way. Luckily, I'm not an obstacle. I'm a strategic asset. He doesn't want me dead, or that's what I'd be, long ago.

Slowly Ellie relaxed. She shut her eyes, lowered her head, unclenched her hands, let the blanket slip from her knees. She felt tears slide down her cheeks, but she smiled inwardly because she knew they came from staring at Mirak, not from the defeat that they must be signalling to an old man fixated on bending her to his will.

"This must all be so difficult for you, Eliana. Nobody wants to feel used. Especially the way Astreya used your father, your brothers and sisters, indeed everyone he's ever encountered. Oh, I know he and the woman he picked up on his travels have their own version of what happened, but did you ever think about the wreckage they left behind them? A priceless library burned. The end of a way of life maintained over more than a century. A sad fate for Oron, the hereditary Grand Master, and his sister Meissa, as well as her great ship the *Silver Swan*. Her shipstone, that Astreya stole, is even now in the little schooner. I saw them, you know. Oron and Meissa, brother and sister, both dead, in *Cygnus'* Forbidden Room. He wrenched from their arms the clasps they had worn their entire lives, and he left them to die. Then he went on to the killing we all witnessed when he and that woman murdered Mufrid. All members of his own family. Unhappily for you, they are your ancestors as well, my dear. That must be hard for you to bear when you are entirely innocent. However, Astreya isn't your father, he isn't really even your uncle. He's only the man who gave clasps to you and your sister and taught you just enough to navigate. He is using you, as he uses everyone. And it will go on. When he retires in comfort, you and your sister will be under the whim and will of his son, Trogen."

Ellie looked at Mirak, her green eyes wide with wonder at his distortion of the truth. Putting aside the desire to shout down his lies, she dissembled.

"But I thought..."

"I know, my dear. Older and wiser people than you have been deceived. For a while, I was as well. To my everlasting shame, I showed Astreya the ropes aboard *Cygnus*. Oron's ship—my ship. I taught him to sail the longboats and skimmers. I protected him from the same crew he tricked into serving him after he'd set me adrift at sea, near the wretched little northern Village where he was born."

Ellie regarded him fixedly, her eyes glistening. _Go on lying, Mirak._ She thought. _I'm listening. I will remember what you said._

"No gratitude. No acknowledgment. No thanks. Totally selfish, just like his father before him. And lucky. Lucky to be descended from Zubin and Oron, even though he was one of the bad seeds. His father, the first Astreya, mutinied, you know, along with his cousin, Gianfar. A pair of spoilt brats if ever there were. They should have been deep-sixed for their sins. Oh, no. They were family, so they were given a skimmer within sight of that flat and fortunate land where you were born. Lucky they were, for a while. Not like yours truly, set adrift way up in the north where the sea freezes onto the cliffs and even the whales head south in the winter. There was little chance of me finding my way safely ashore so far north, and I had no desire to drown where Astreya's father was lost at sea, soon after he sired that ever-lucky, never-deserving second Astreya who put that jewel on your arm. So I used my skill to sail that skimmer far enough for me to begin again."

Ellie pushed back her left sleeve, revealing her bracelet.

That's what he wants to see. A suggestible, pliant, obedient little girl.

Mirak's eyes fixed on the green stone, and his thin lips twisted into an unkind smile.

"Luck, good or bad, doesn't last. Things even out. Gianfar burned to death. It was in a fire set by Astreya, did you know that? Not what either of them expected, was it? Same way, nobody thought that my fair and upstanding business that happens to include supplying firearms to people in need of protection would take my ship to the Sunny Isles where Astreya had sent his little schooner-full of children he'd equipped with stones of power so that they'd be a long, long way from the people who blew a hole in his great ship. Like I say, things even out."

Nothing bad is ever your fault, is it, Mirak?

Ellie shook her head at Mirak's self-serving manipulation of the truth. Mirak took her gesture for agreement and nodded.

"So you see how it is, Ellie. There are wrongs to be righted, ashore and afloat. High and mighty Astreya sails the great ships from port to port with no consideration for the lives of people to whom he sells his rum, whiskey, and coffee which he buys cheap and sells dear. I've been doing my coast-hugging best to give people the tools they need to prosper and defend themselves. Not like Astreya's ever-so-virtuous neutrality that only helps those on top hold everyone else down. Think what could be done, Eliana, if the great ships were a force for good, bringing the equality that comes from being able to fight oppression. Imagine an objective, fair-minded, righteous fleet carrying the means of self-respect and upright living to those who are downtrodden."

Does he think I'm a public meeting? Am I expected to clap? I'm trying not to roll my eyes!

She blinked and shook her head again.

"So here's what's going to happen, Eliana. We're heading north to Matris, where I'm going to take back *Cygnus*. I've been there before, I know the approaches, but there's the few days of sailing between where the compass stops working and landfall. That's the little bit where I may need you to keep us headed in the right direction, should the weather cloud over. It won't be too difficult. You can find north with your clasp, can't you?"

Ellie nodded, hoping that she looked puzzled.

I can do a whole lot more than that, old man, but I'm certainly not about to tell you.

"That's all we'll need for now. Later, we'll see what you can do when you've got a stone of power at your disposal. How would you like to be *Cygnus'* navigator, Eliana? Do you think you could do that?"

Ellie blinked so fiercely her vision blurred.

How about I fry your head the way 'Streya did to evil old Mufrid?

"Meanwhile, this will be our secret, Eliana. Especially from young Fred. He's useful, but he's... well ... erratic. I have to keep my eye on him or he has one of his notions and rushes off to do something that later everyone regrets."

He may be unstable, but you're deranged.

"So, Eliana, it's my watch on deck. You're probably hungry and thirsty. I'll have Cookie bring you some ..."

Despite herself, Eliana flinched.

"Not Cookie?" Mirak's voice exuded gentle concern. "I understand completely. Moke's big and slow, but he does as he's told. I'll send him. Eliana, you'll be safe here. The others all bunk forward, and you know I have nothing but respect for you."

The cabin door closed. Ellie let out the breath she had been holding. The battle of wits was over, and even though she had not won, she had held her own. She huddled in the corner, making herself small. After he locked her in the cabin, Ellie could still glimpse the distant shoreline through the dirty scuttles. She repeatedly tried to make contact with *Cygnet* or her father on *Elusive,* but all her efforts were unsuccessful. She could neither tell anyone where she was, nor expose Walt as a traitor, but only hope that Trogen or Seren and Mairi would be able to follow her stone. In the meanwhile, she formulated a provisional strategy.

I don't want to help them get to Matris. But if they put Cookie to work, I could end up doing anything and everything they ask. Better I show them north as and when they need it. Then we'll see.

9. In which three ships sail northward

1. Aboard *Cygnet*

"The sun's down, and with it, our last glimpse of the shoreline," said Seren as she entered *Cygnet's* stern cabin. "There's no sign of the ketch, but just before I came to report, I think I saw a light astern that might be *Cygnus*."

The two women looked at each other. Since *Cygnet* slipped her lines to *Cygnus*, they had been resolutely formal, but they both knew how much unexpressed emotion they were holding in check.

"Mug o' sump'n hot in there?"

Cam's voice startled both women. Mairi looked a question at Seren, who looked down, deferring to Mairi's rank.

"Thank you, Cam. Two mugs. Seren, you need to sit down. It's been a difficult day, and there's a lot I need to know about what happened to you after you ... went ashore."

"After Marley and I mutinously jumped ship."

"Recorded in my log as a reasonable decision in a crisis situation requiring independent judgment. And I added a note of commendation."

"You sound like your mother."

"I'll take that as a compliment."

A fist holding two mugs appeared between them, followed by Cam's head.

"'Ere's yer mug-up. Listen, you two: would you belay this 'umble-navigator-reportin'-to-her-ever-so-savvy-skipper   act   yer both doin'. Yer fam'ly. You both bin through a lot. You, Seren, for sure. Now I'm goin' to me bunk; Alan's mor'n capable at the wheel, Marley's got the watch, an' it's past time the two o' you let yer hair down an' gave each other a good old weepy hug."

The fist slid the mugs onto the chart table and withdrew.

Mairi stood, stepped around the table and embraced Seren, who hesitated only a heartbeat before wrapping both arms around her cousin. Drawing ragged breaths to control sobs, they stood, swaying gently to *Cygnet's* rocking motion, both whispering at the same time.

"I should have... not your fault... but we didn't say... he knew... how could they...? ...Don't think about it... I still keep seeing... So do I... We were too late... If I'd only... If they hadn't left... Even if they were ... I still can't... We owe... We have to..."

Some indeterminate time later, when sniffs punctuated tears and the words going back and forth no longer carried the poignancy with which they had begun, Mairi guided Seren to the settee, and they sat. Side by side, mugs in hand, they both went through the small gestures that repair not only hair and eyes and the set of clothes, but which also restore calm.

"Seren, how did you make it to the boats?"

"It was Marley. He grabbed my hand and towed me down an alleyway. We were right behind the front line of the Black Bay army as they charged down the roads to the waterfront. They'd turned into a mob, and weren't thinking anymore. I felt it, Mairi. If it hadn't been for Marley, I'd have been screaming and howling with the best of them. But he stayed rational, and we got to the quayside ahead of most of them, while the white people were taking cover aboard ships, in warehouses, and in shops. Some of them had pistols and swords and were using them against anyone with a black face. But it wasn't working for them, because there were too many longshoremen, all of them black, and they were already there. They didn't have guns, but ... oh, Mairi ... what they were doing with knives and hooks was awful. The dock was slippery with blood, and there were fights everywhere. We had to leap over bodies ... some of them alive but bleeding, some nearly dead but still reaching ... grabbing... Marley kept going, dodging around the action. When we jumped down onto the beach, I thought we were too late. I could see the first longboat pulling away, and the other half-launched. The bow men already had oars in the water. When they saw Marley, they must have thought he was part of the mob, and they nearly left without us, but I screamed and yelled and waved at them and they must have seen I was white, so when we waded out and I saw Walt, he convinced them to take Marley as well me and then... and then .... And then you know the rest, Mairi. We were too late. What we did was a complete waste of time. They'd sailed, taking Ellie with them."

"You're here, you're safe aboard *Cygnet*, and we're going after her."

"But she may be..."

"Most likely not, Seren. They need her skills to take them where the compass fails, so they probably won't ... mess with her."

"Probably."

"It's all that we've got, Seren. That and Trogen aboard *Elusive* bearing down on them with enough crew to handle even that monster we fought back there in the Sunny Isles."

Seren stretched, yawned, shook herself and almost flopped forward onto the cabin sole like a puppet whose strings have been cut. She stared at Mairi, blank-faced.

"I have to crash. I feel guilty. You're doing everything, Mairi."

"Go to your bunk, Seren. That's an order. And Seren…"

"Yes?"

"I'm proud of you."

Mairi sat for a few moments, listening to Seren's progress into the darkened cabin. When everyone below-decks was still, she climbed the companionway to the cockpit where Cam was standing close to Alan at the wheel, their faces lit by the green light from the binnacle. She heard whispers, and then both men chuckled.

"Good to have a happy crew," she observed to the night at large.

"We was rememberin' a time back at the 'cadamy," said Cam.

"Cam's hero academy? When were you in CHAOS, Alan?"

"He was a few winters astern o' you, skipper," said Cam. "But you knew that, didn't you?"

"A reason I picked him, Cam. That, and because when we named *Cygnet*, I saw him near to drooling because he wanted so much to be aboard the schooner his dad designed and built."

Mairi looked at Alan, and his fist caught the light on its way to his throat. She heard the time-honoured phrase.

"At your command."

"You're welcome aboard, Alan. I only regret it has to be under such sorry circumstances."

"But the Cygnets beat 'em, skipper, ashore and afloat," said Alan eagerly.

"We cut and ran, Alan, leaving an unholy mess behind us."

"'Trade fairly, avoid entanglements,'" said Cam.

"Correct, Cam. That's the standing order. But I wonder..."

"Beggin' yer pardon, Skipper," said Cam with uncharacteristic decorum, "but later for that, dontcha think?"

"You're right, Cam. As usual. And it's my watch below. Good night."

2. Aboard *Elusive*

Trogen sat looking across the big chart table at the door he had just closed. A rush of emotions swept over him. He was on his own, seated in his master's chair, looking forward, in command of the great ship *Elusive*. He had often imagined being a master, but he had not understood until that moment how much was involved.

Trogen closed his eyes to visualize the ship … his ship. He heard the constant hush of water along the hull, felt the gentle sway as she eased through a wave, imagined the crew … his crew … keeping watch on deck where a sailor had just hauled a sheet through a squeaky block. It would soon be time for the noon sighting: Trogen's first at sea as skipper. In the meanwhile, he reviewed the events of the previous evening.

Elusive had set sail a little after dawn, fully eight hours behind *Cygnet*, which had caught the previous evening's falling tide, and was now nearly half a day ahead, only a few hours astern of the ketch. Trogen recalled Mairi giving him both thumbs up as she stood at the stern of the little schooner. He had waved back as *Cygnet's* sails filled and she slid gracefully down the harbour bay and out to sea.

Only an hour before that parting moment, they had been standing side by side in *Elusive*'s Forbidden Room, looking down on the circular plotting table with the shipstone glowing green at its centre. The clasp that had been Dabih's also lay on the black fabric, its silver bracelet dull, its stone a green pebble. Mairi had told him how before the bosun had taken away Dabih's body, she had removed the clasp from the master's arm, polished it clean of blood and placed it on the plotting table. Her voice was husked with barely controlled emotion. Trogen winced as she spoke, recalling his own headlong flight from the blood-drenched Forbidden Room. They looked at each other, both thinking of Dabih's brutally stabbed and cut body, now sewn into a weighted canvass parcel, lying in the skipper's cabin awaiting burial at sea.

A soft knock at the door had interrupted their silent grief. Mairi palmed it open and Neil stepped in eagerly, followed hesitantly by Peter, and reluctantly by Seren. The two boys stood facing Trogen and Mairi across the circular table. All five faces were lit with green light from below, intensifying the boys' expectant looks, Seren's anguished expression, and Trogen's and Mairi's reticence about the responsibility they were undertaking.

Neil stepped close to the table, pushed up his left sleeve, thrust out his right hand and held it over the clasp as if he expected it to spring into his palm. The stone in the bracelet remained stubbornly dark. Neil closed his fingers around the hoop of patterned silver and clamped it onto his left arm above his elbow, and took his right hand away. Five people leaned forward, their attention fixed on the green stone, which remained persistently dull. Above it, Neil's face went from anticipation to anxiety to dismay.

Mairi pointed at the table, and Neil replaced the clasp and stood, incredulous, as slowly, almost hesitantly, Peter stretched out his right hand into the pool of green light. The ends of his fingers were still a hand's breadth from the silver clasp when its stone started to glow. He picked it up, and a spear of white light at the stone's centre gleamed as if a bright eye had opened. Mairi pushed up Peter's sleeve for him, and with a look of wonder, he closed the clasp around his arm. While Trogen congratulated Peter, Neil slunk back aboard *Cygnet,* and Seren left the Forbidden Room to call in Alan so that Mairi could present him with the ring that Peter no longer needed.

A knock brought Trogen back to the present. It was Damon, somewhat less weak than before, but still slow-moving. He stood, looking across the table. Trogen stared back at him for a couple of heartbeats, before realizing that Damon was respectfully waiting for the master's permission to sit.

"Sit, mister mate," said Trogen.

"Master," Damon acknowledged as he lowered himself into his customary chair.

The formal moment completed, Trogen was relieved to see a warm smile crease Damon's pale face.

Before either of them could speak, the door slid open, Walt strode in and thumped himself into a chair with the peculiar little backward hop necessitated by his short legs.

Damon frowned as Walt spoke without ceremony or deference.

"Hey, Damon. Good to see you up. Mind ye don't overdo it. Trog, you got a fix on that damn ketch yet?"

"We are on course. The ketch is well over the horizon, probably picking up more wind than we've got at the present."

"Right. An' so prob'ly this is a good time for us to deep-six the old skipper."

He slid off his chair and thumped out the door in his usual, rolling gait. Trogen, still feeling grateful to Walt for their meeting ashore, saw Damon's disapproving stare and spoke quietly.

"It's his way with everyone. It doesn't bother me."

Damon raised one eyebrow, levered himself upright on the arms of his chair and looked at a spot two handspans over Trogen's head.

"With your permission, while you decide on what you are going to say to the crew, I'll go climb the companionway. Somewhat more slowly than is my habit."

Trogen watched him go, wondering at the aversion between Damon and Walt that he had not observed when he served with them aboard _Elusive_. He spoke to Damon's back as he went through the door.

"Damon, will you do the ... tell the crew what they need to know?"

Damon spoke softly, without turning around.

"Your crew expects you to give voice to their sorrow at Dabih's death."

"The crew will follow my orders ... and so should you."

Trogen heard his words leave his lips and immediately wanted to disown them. Damon turned and looked into his eyes, and he flinched.

"Dabih died defending the shipstone, his ship, and his crew," said Damon, his voice hard. "As acting master, it is your job to conduct his burial at sea. Shirk this responsibility and you may give orders to the crew, but you will never command a scintilla of the respect and loyalty they gave Dabih."

Damon turned and slowly climbed the companionway. Trogen followed him, several steps behind. As he reached the quarterdeck, Walt was shouting orders to heave to. With her jib backed and the rudder hard over, *Elusive* no longer rode across the waves, but instead lay head-to-wind in a rising sea. One moment her bowsprit almost dipped into the water, the next it reared skywards. Trogen nearly lost his balance on the pitching deck, and as he did so saw that he was not the only unsteady one. The entire crew was shuffling, swaying and clutching at anything handy to keep their balance as the ship pitched and shuddered. Two men stood on either side of plank on which a canvass-covered shape waited by a gap in the starboard rail.

Walt plucked at Trogen's sleeve. "Over to you, Trog."

Trogen pressed his lips together, suppressing sudden irritation at Walt's familiarity. He raised his voice to compete with the sounds made by flapping sails, whistling rigging and rushing water, and as he did so, he intuitively reached for the formal tradition he had so often heard when Dabih and Astreya addressed their crews.

"Men and women of *Elusive,* landborn and seaborn. Some of you served with Master Dabih when he was navigator. Most of us joined the ship years after he took command. For more than twenty years, Dabih was *Elusive*. While he lived, he cared for the safety of the ship and the welfare of his crew. He died defending *Elusive*. In our grief over his loss, let us remember the excellence of his life and do our best to follow his example."

Trogen nodded to the men at the rail. They tipped up the plank, and the canvass shape disappeared into the side of a wave.

Damon took an unsteady step forward.

"Men and women of *Elusive*, let us affirm Trogen, son of Astreya, as master."

He swung his right fist up to his throat. Less than a heartbeat behind him, two dozen arms copied him, and the ship's company spoke in unison.

"At your command."

Trogen blinked. Damon's rebuke was still fresh in Trogen's mind. But it was Damon, not Walt, who had led the crew. The contradiction made him profoundly aware that his command was provisional, temporary, and required confirmation. Trogen looked at the crew with fresh eyes.

"I will try to live up to Master Dabih's memory and your expectations." He paused, and then lurched quickly on, speaking without plan. "There's a ketch a few hours ahead of us. They kidnapped Dabih's daughter Eliana. They are the same people who blew a hole in *Cygnus,* wounded Astreya, and organized the raid on *Elusive* in which Master Dabih was murdered. I plan to get Ellie back and end their evil plans."

"Then let's get on wi' it," said Walt. "Man the sheets for when she takes the strain. Helm down, let fly the jib!"

Elusive pitched and wallowed, then as the sails drew, she leaned into her port tack, and all aboard again moved confidently to a familiar rhythm.

"Well then," said Walt. "After that little pep talk, I'll crack on the tops'ls an' we'll have the bastards in sight before watch change, and catch 'em afore the day's done."

"Steady, Walt," said Damon. "They have Ellie as a hostage."

"So? We've got more'n enough men to take 'em."

Trogen gave voice to the image that was keeping him irresolute.

"When *Elusive* shows over the horizon, they'll lash Ellie to the shrouds, and by the time we catch up with them, we'll see a man standing behind her with a knife. If we make a move, we'll have to watch them kill her."

"She's no good to them dead," said Walt.

"Exactly," said Damon. "They need her to navigate beyond where the compass works. So it's safe for us to follow until we know where they're going, which appears to be Matris."

"Unless they think Ellie can lead them to the mother lode. The place where all the stones came from. Which Astreya never looked for. Inexplicably."

"'Streya's an' Cam's Village," said Walt.

"Maybe," said Damon. "We don't know where Astreya's father found them."

Walt's eyes narrowed shrewdly.

"An' nobody's talkin'. Right then. Belay the tops'ls. You go check on our target. We'll keep '*Lusive* goin' as she is, just as long as you keep us pointin' in the right direction. An' then we'll see what you got up yer sleeve."

"With your permission, I'd like to lie down," said Damon. "Master, I'd be grateful if you'd watch me as I go below."

They took the companionway steps one at a time, Damon clutching the handrail.

"You spoke well," said Damon as they reached the bottom step. "Until you rattled on to Walt about a mother lode. What possessed you to do that?"

"Another reprimand, Damon?"

"I have no memory of any such behaviour, which would be entirely inappropriate from mate to master, Master Trogen."

Damon's back disappeared down the passage and into his quarters. Alone in the stern cabin, Trogen again pondered the complexities of being in command. Damon, the mate he had always thought of as a friend, had taken him to task, then led the crew's acknowledgment of his command, and then had both rebuked him a second time, and then denied his criticism. Walt, the man who had protected him ashore, had stopped just short of challenging his authority.

Conflicting thoughts made him rise and pace the cabin, unconsciously following a line worn on the cabin sole by more than a century of masters' heels.

3. Aboard the ketch

"Here y'are, missie."

Ellie roused herself from a waking dream of Mairi and Seren climbing aboard the ketch, which had mysteriously shed all of her crew save for Moke, who was welcoming them, a bucket in one hand. The dream ebbed into reality as she looked past a huge shoulder at waves rising and falling. Barely visible around Moke's bulk, she saw Mirak's black-clad figure standing with his legs well apart, scanning the horizon ahead, then pivoting slowly until his telescope pointed astern.

"Moke, is there a ship following us?" Ellie asked the arm as she took a jug and the bucket from Moke's big fist.

"Couldn't say, missie. I just been sent to look after yer. Back in a jiffy wi' some food an' drink."

Ellie closed the door for privacy, noticing that they had decided that there was no need to keep her locked in when they were at sea. When she had washed her face and hands, finger-combed her hair and set herself as much to rights as she could, Moke reappeared with rock-hard bread and cheese, along with a steaming mug of something Ellie guessed might have been coffee many hours earlier. When he left the door open a second time, she ventured into the cockpit. She saw Fred at the wheel, one hand resting negligently on a spoke. The corners of his thin lips curled, but his pale eyes were as unreadable as they had been when she had first seen them.

"You're up. Old Mirak was snoring and farting all night, so I told Moke to leave the door open. I thought you'd like a breath of fresh air."

"I'll get my mug of ... of whatever it is."

She ducked back into the cabin, and when she came back out, mug in hand, she shook her hair loose in the wind.

Careful, Ellie, she thought. *Don't be deceived by mere politeness. This one's cold and cunning.*

"Mirak's in the forward cabin, terrifying the crew," said Fred.

"Terrifying?"

"Only way to keep them doing what he says. The compass started to spin last night, and we had to steer by the stars. Gave them all the willies. Especially when it clouded over towards dawn. All three of them arguing about whether the wind had shifted. Then the sun came up and they settled down. That, and Mirak giving them his ancient and fish-like stare."

"But you weren't afraid."

Fred shook his head.

"Not while you and your stone are aboard. Tell me, what made it flare when I was questioning you?"

"That wasn't me," Ellie improvised. "My ... the people aboard *Cygnet* were trying to ... to blow my stone out. To keep you from using it."

"But it lit up again. Whatever they tried didn't work."

"Too far away," Ellie nodded.

"So the big stones can project power. How is it done?"

Ellie sipped at her drink and looked over the rim of the mug at Fred.

"I don't know. Nobody's told me yet. I got my stone less than a year ago."

"What can you do?"

Ellie looked up at him, widening her eyes with feigned candour.

"Find north. And when I'm close to the shipstone in the Forbidden Room, I can help plot a course for the steersman. Such as following a heading on a compass. But I need help to sustain it. The shipstone keeps swinging around to north."

"By itself?"

Ellie nodded, her green eyes steady as she embroidered her deception.

"It's scary. Fierce. First time I tried to control the big stone, mine flared. Like it did when they tried to blow up my stone. Only worse. Then, I was out of commission for a week. They didn't care. Said they all went through it when they were learning."

A jib-sheet rattled along the deck, and overhead, the mainsail flapped. Fred turned his attention to steering, and the sails filled again.

"What's going on?" Mirak's voice came from the forward cabin.

"Puff of wind. We're all right now."

The wind's veering, Ellie thought. *There's cloud building astern. We're in for a storm. Mirak's below and even if Fred knows the signs, he hasn't noticed them.*

Fred began to mumble.

"Assume ring stones like Mirak's are a power of one ... means that the stone on her arm is a whole order of magnitude greater. So shipstones must be ... factorial ... capable of much more than navigation. It could involve communication ... extended mental powers? Maybe focus ... sunlight? ... Manipulate gravity? ... Raise ships off the water so they skim like pebbles? ... Maybe detonate explosives ... fuse metal ..."

As Fred's imaginings wavered from fact to possibility to fantasy Ellie's eyes widened again, this time involuntarily. Was he delusional? Or did he intuit a power in the stones greater than anyone had imagined? She reasoned that the covetous yearning she had heard in Fred's musings could motivate him to act rashly. Worse, if he had a shipstone, he might be able to transform it into a perilous menace.

Mirak's voice cut across Ellie's thoughts.

"Fred, what are you doing? Why did you let her out of the cabin?"

"She's not going to swim for shore, is she, Mirak? She's not stupid."

"No, but you are. Look astern. That's ugly weather bearing down on us, and we're not prepared. Jake! Moke! Get up here. Reef, or..."

"...or we're going bare poles," Ellie muttered.

"What's that? You still here? Get aft, Eliana. Now."

Mug still in hand, Ellie went back to the cabin.

Now that there are two of them who want to control me, perhaps I can drive a wedge between them.

10. In which three ships contend with a hurricane

1. Aboard *Elusive*

The storm caught up with *Elusive* close to midnight. Trogen heard the first boom of thunder while he was below in the Forbidden Room. When he climbed the companionway onto the quarterdeck, confused sounds of wind and water buffeted his ears. He could see nothing. Rain lashed his face as he followed a safety line across the water-slick deck to the wheelhouse, where greenish light from the shipstone coloured the steersman's face as he leaned into the wheel, straining to hold the ship on course. A flash of lightning lit *Elusive's* sails for a brief ghostly moment, long enough for Trogen to glimpse the leech of the foresail trembling. In the darkness that followed, he heard an ominous deep thrumming among the barrage of storm noises, which he identified as coming from the over-strained mainsail. For an instant he recalled Dabih's standing order and looked for someone to wake the master; then in a grief-stricken moment during the clap of thunder, he knew that the decision was his.

"Where's Walt?"

"Right here, behind you. That's lightnin', an' it's gettin' nearer. An' the wind's strengthenin' an' veerin'. Keeps this up, an' ...."

Although Walt was shouting over the noise of wind and water, Trogen heard the anxiety in his voice.

"We'll ease her. Douse the upper staysails. Reef the main, replace the jib and the staysails on the mizzen and foremasts with storm canvass. Rig more lifelines."

Walt did not answer.

"Walt? Did you hear?"

"Right. Reef the main. Douse the upper staysails. Hoist the storm jib and staysails. It's goin' to take a while, Skipper."

A new voice came out of the darkness of the wind-swept deck.

"It's watch change, Walt. We've twice the number of people out of bed and in their breeks. Use them to get it done faster."

"Damon! Should you be here?"

"No worries, Master. But I'll let you do the shouting, Walt."

"You got it."

Trogen and Damon stood side by side, looking over the steersman's shoulder. Trogen wondered what had changed. Walt was taking charge with confidence that he seemed to lack only moments before. And yet, the decision had been clear, the orders obvious. Did a man twice Trogen's age need reassurance from a younger man he still called 'Trog'? The contradiction triggered another incongruity in Trogen's mind. Why was Damon calling him 'master' after treating him like a misbehaving cadet only hours ago? The mates seemed to be changing character. He decided to study everything they said and did.

"I'll make the rounds," said Trogen. "You stay in the dry, Damon."

As he left the shelter of the wheelhouse, a flash of lightning gleamed on the wet deck. The dazzling white light froze the figures of the crew, bent over, heads lowered, hauling on sheets, halyards, and canvass. Wishing he had worn his oilskin jacket, Trogen started along the starboard side, making his way mostly by feel and by the memory of countless such circuits over his years as sailor, cadet, and eventually as mate and navigator. After *Cygnet's* quicker rhythms, *Elusive* felt solid under his feet. The waves hissed and crested as they had in the storm that had blown them into Three Mountain Island, but when *Elusive's* bowsprit creased the top of a wave, the spray stayed on the foredeck. Trogen wondered how the Cygnets would handle a storm such as this was promising to be. Before he could speculate further, he felt the wind strengthen and the seas rise.

As Trogen moved from handhold to handhold on his way forward, flashes of lightning momentarily froze spray in the air. He was at the mainmast when a gust pressed at the mainsail like a huge hand on his back. His fingers slipped, his feet slid, and an instant later his ribs met the fife-rail. Above all the rushing, splashing, howling noise he heard himself grunt. His wet hands clenched on a halyard and as he struggled to his feet, jagged lightning gleamed again, this time reflecting on the underside of roiling, dark clouds. The flashing continued while thunder pummelled at his ears. The halyard trembled like the string on a huge violin.

A big hand closed on his shoulder. Another flash and Walt's eyes were a handspan away, his hair blown sideways across his face.

"What now?" he shouted.

In all the confusion of light and dark, sound and action, knowledge kept Trogen calm.

"Double reef the main, strike the mizzen staysail. I don't see the lifelines."

"I'm on it."

For a long, wet hour, Trogen watched his orders being carried out. Eventually, Walt reappeared at his side.

"It's your watch below, Walt."

"Damon can't…"

"I've got it, Walt. Get some sleep."

Walt disappeared down the companionway. Eventually, as the watch huddled in the lee of whatever protection they could find, Trogen hauled his way aft along a lifeline until he reached the wheelhouse.

"Could be a long night, Damon. You should be…"

"Happier here than banged about in my bunk."

"Good, then. I'll be back soon as I've checked the plot."

Below, the storm seemed worse. He walked to the Forbidden Room, his right shoulder bumping along the starboard side of the passageway, even though his feet tracked down the middle. To stand erect in the green-lit room, he had to clutch the circular plotting table. Water dripped slantwise from his hands, his head, and his clothes. He had hoped to get a fix on *Cygnet* and the ketch, but poising the shipstone was clearly impossible. He was about to go back on deck and use his clasp to maintain their course when concern replaced caution. Using the power of the shipstone, he sent a message out into the night.

Elusive headed north

Strong east wind backing Reducing sail

He was halfway back along the passage when he felt a reply.

Ketch headed north

Following gale-force wind and seas

"Ellie!" he exclaimed. "But that can't be. She must be wrong. Unless…"

By the time he reached the wheelhouse, Trogen understood.

"Time to reduce sail again, Damon. This is no storm. We're in a hurricane."

"And Ellie is on the wrong side of it," he added inaudibly as *Elusive* rushed into the night.

2. Aboard *Cygnet*

"Alan, haul the jib! Marley, wheel hard over!"

The wind blew Mairi's shout to leeward so that her words barely reached across the cockpit. Alan bent over, hauling hand over hand until the jib backed. Close to him, Marley cranked the wheel hard over and secured it in position with a strop. It was the last moment of more than half an hour's dangerous, demanding struggle to strip the ship of all but the storm jib and a small patch of canvass on the double-reefed mainsail. There had been moments when the length of the ship was white with spray, and Mairi feared that Seren, Cam, and Alan might be swept overboard as they struggled to strike the same sails that earlier they had toiled to reef. Now they were hove-to, drifting downwind, losing distance they had gained before the full might of the storm was upon them.

Cygnet surged up and into the crest of a wave more than half her masts high. The storm jib took the wind aback, pushing *Cygnet's* bow as if to tack. The much-reduced main kept her heading towards the wind. The rudder bit into the water to turn her the other way, and she almost stalled. Instead of punching into wind and sea, stabbing her bow deep into each trough, she was wind-rode, still sailing, but sliding backward, wallowing in the troughs, her bow pointing into the leaden sky. She was at the mercy of the storm, but no longer in danger of careening, scuppers deep in water, pressed down by her canvass.

Mairi gestured, and five heads bent together in the cockpit. Though they were close enough for their shoulders to bump when *Cygnet* pitched, she still had to shout above the keening of the rigging, the slash of rain and spray on the decks, and the wail of the wind.

"We've done all we can. The light's going. Nobody leaves the cockpit until we can make sail again. Seren, Alan, go below. Cam, see how Neil's doing."

Three crouching figures in wet oilskins clambered over the washboards protecting the companionway and disappeared below.

"What happened to Neil?" Marley shouted.

"The mizzen gaff caught him on the shoulder, Seren helped him astern, Cam got him below and into his bunk."

Mairi was about to say that Cam was probably giving Neil something for pain, but at that moment her clasp tingled. She doubled up, almost kneeling, trying to concentrate on the message from Trogen. He was sending his position, course, and situation in a succession of pinch-like twinges from her clasp. Spray stung her skin, making her task almost impossible. She shook her head, trying to make sense of incomplete or garbled code, then when she was about to reply, she looked up to see Marley's puzzled expression. Faint and distant, another message began.

"Ellie!" she exclaimed.

The indistinct pulses ceased. Calling on the power of the shipstone in the cabin below her, Mairi sent and resent an acknowledgment, and then the code for 'hove-to'. She waited for a reply, but none came.

"Ellie's alive, but on the wrong side of the storm," said Mairi.

Seeing a question in Marley's eyes, she strove to explain.

"Hurricane. Cyclone. Circular storm. One side of its centre, the wind backs. That's our side. Other side the wind veers. The ketch has the wind astern."

"Blowin' like this, that can't be good."

Mairi nodded. There was nothing more to say. *Cygnet* pitched and wallowed into the night.

3. Aboard the ketch

Ellie went obediently into the cabin, but neither Fred nor Mirak saw the look of determination in her green eyes. She left the door partly open and stood out of sight behind it, watching and listening.

"Good wind, this," said Fred. "It's taking us right where we want to go, quickly, and without all that pounding, swaying, and leaning. I could begin to enjoy sailing if it was all like this."

Unseen in the cabin, Ellie rolled her eyes. She did not have to glance at the stone in her bracelet to know that the ketch had been driven eastward on an increasingly broad starboard reach. She had seen first Cookie and then Fred progressively slack off the sheets, sailing by the wind without a compass. The ketch was now almost by the lee. Mirak or Jake or even Moke would have long since realized the looming peril of a standing jibe, and at least rigged a preventer, but Fred was fecklessly unaware of what he was doing, and the men who should be responding to the situation were inexplicably below, unaware that the wind was veering under a sky that threatened severe weather.

Ellie felt the jibe start a heartbeat before it began. The storm that had been creeping over the horizon astern was now bearing down towards them in earnest. Fred steered to accommodate a sudden gust, then grimaced when the main boom kicked upwards and the jib flapped. He glanced astern and saw ragged clouds torn by the wind that was blowing a line of crested waves towards the ketch. For an instant, the ship balanced like a dancer, then reeled crazily. The wheel spun under Fred's hands, cracking his knuckles. The ship staggered sickeningly. The rest of the crew boiled up out of the forward cabin into the cockpit, Jake and Moke arriving in a tangle of arms and legs, getting in each other's way as they tried to shoulder Fred from the wheel. Mirak shoved past both of them and took over, shouting orders that had them desperately hauling the slack sheets hand over hand. They were too late. The ketch mounted a long wave, yawed on its white-flecked crest, and as half the rudder came clear out of the water, the leech of the mizzen sail trembled, fluttered, flapped, filled, and flew across the centre line, its boom cocked skyward. Almost immediately, the mainsail repeated the same abandoned dance.

Ellie saw the starboard stays sag loose as the mainmast bent out of true. Anticipating the inevitable impact of the jibe, she grabbed the doorframe in time, fell to her knees and watched the entire debacle. The rest of the crew was not so fortunate. The main boom swung above Moke's big head as the ship rolled drunkenly. Jake was yanked off his feet, his hands rope-burned by his effort to control the mizzen. Then the mizzen, main, and jib all crossed the centre line again, slamming to the limit of the sheets that were still slack, for all their efforts.

All four men lost their balance and slid into a thrashing pile of limbs. As the knot untwined, Mirak regained his position at the wheel. Moke crawled up out of the cockpit onto the forward cabin top, where he let fly the halyards, then stood with his arms around the mast and tugged the sail down in great handfuls. Ellie heard thuds and thumps on the cabin top above her head as Jake wrestled with the mizzen.

Fred's face appeared above her in the doorway. "Get out here, girl, and tell us where north is!"

Ellie rolled up her sleeve, looked at her clasp, and was shocked. In the frantic striking of sails, the ketch had turned completely around and was being blown backward. Clinging onto the doorpost as the ketch rose up a steep hill of water, she saw the setting sun gleam through a gap in the overcast and then vanish into a long black line of cloud at the horizon. Waves crested on both sides of the ship, as they slid down into a trough in a welter of spray, then plowed headlong into the next wave, taking water aboard almost to the centre line. The ketch shuddered as if about to plunge into the depths. Sheets of spray enveloped the foredeck as the ship wallowed, barely recovering.

All the men yelled at the same time, but Ellie could not make out a single word over the cacophony of wind and water. Spray and spindrift flew thick in a grey torrent. Then as the ship started up another mountainous wave, she saw Jake's lean figure at the wheel. Moke's bulk was wedged in one cockpit corner, one hand on the scruff of Fred's neck, holding him from going over the side. Then she was bowled off her feet back into the cabin, where she slid across the floor, rolling onto one shoulder just in time to avoid hitting the table. The door slammed, muting the screaming wind.

When she looked up, Mirak stood above her, water dripping from his hair onto her face.

"We're hove to, battened down, and still shipping it green. We'll be pumping all night. Eliana, can you point north again?"

Ellie stayed on the cabin sole and pointed. Mirak nodded.

"Not that it makes much difference. We're going where the weather takes us. Roughly north-east, I'd say."

Ellie nodded, but he did not notice.

"Stay here, girl. Keep as dry as you can."

Ellie watched as he opened the door, admitting a plume of spray into which he disappeared as he slammed it shut again. She retreated to her corner of the aft settee and wrapped herself in what she was beginning to think of as her blanket, despite its damp, musty smell. The ketch jolted her back and forth, one moment pressing her against the ship's side, the next threatening to toss her to the cabin sole, but she wedged herself with her knees up and her arms wrapped around them. The last light faded from the glass in the scuttles in a succession of increasingly dim gleams between the waves that rose over them. Ellie was in a small, dark space, able only to guess at what the ketch was doing. What she heard was not heartening. The ship groaned as it plunged into waves that broke over the cabin tops. It wallowed under the weight of water, then juddered as waves rushed off the decks and down the scuppers. Each time the ketch rose to a crest, the wind screamed in her bare poles. From time to time, the hull boomed as it was struck by a crossing wave top.

At first, Ellie held her breath at each new assault. She wondered how long she could breathe the air in the cabin before it was crushed out of her in a final plunge below the surface. Somehow drowning within the ship seemed worse than flailing about on the surface, even though death was equally inevitable.

After a while, she began to sense a rhythm in the ship's fight to stay afloat and death seemed less imminent. Eventually, she slid into a tense half-sleep made painful by repetitive jolts and bumps.

At some indeterminate time during the night, Ellie woke when spray-laden air rushed into the cabin, along with Mirak, carrying a dim light. His usual agility was not enough to keep him from staggering across the little cabin, narrowly avoiding the table. He stripped off his wet oilskin coat, hung a small lantern from a fitting above his head and sat on the settee opposite her. She stared at the yellow light, amazed that it still burned despite the welter of water she knew was outside the cabin door.

"Here," said Mirak, offering her a small metal flask.

She sniffed a sharp tang of strong spirit, recognizing poteen, a powerful whiskey with hallucinatory side effects.

"A sip won't hurt you."

Ignoring remembered warnings, she gingerly took a little less than she could cup in her tongue, swallowed, coughed, and passed the flask back to Mirak. He nodded, swigged, and replaced the stopper. At first, the liquor burned her throat, then warmth started at her middle and ran through her body, tingling in fingers and toes that had been numbed for hours. The metal flask gleamed as he slid it into a jacket pocket. It seemed to her that the lantern's light had doubled because she could see the lines on Mirak's forehead and down his cheeks. She stared at him for several cycles of the ship's repetitive groans, thumps, and rolls before she realized that he was talking. Mirak's voice gradually became louder, as the poteen sharpened Ellie's hearing.

"... and so Oron ordered up a puncheon of Peg's finest for the men and took himself and 'Dramin below. Astreya, the poor fish, didn't know he should 'a gone with them. Instead, he joined in the fun on deck and was heading for his second gill of the stuff when I stopped him. Don't rightly know why I did. Could have let him dance and skylark in the rigging with the crew until he either fell onto the deck, into the sea or ended up someone's toy for the night. The thing is, I liked him. Then. He was swift to learn. Smart. Stubborn. Dauntless."

Mirak's right hand slid into his jacket, closed around the flask, drew it out and held it below his chin. He looked down, grimaced, and thrust it back into his pocket. He saw Ellie watching him and grinned mirthlessly.

"Why do you hate him so much?"

The words were out of her mouth before she could stop herself.

"Because he threw it all away, and me with it. With Oron dead, and me to run the crew for him as I did for Oron, all he had to do was navigate, and once he'd given the order to arm the ships, he could have the upper hand ashore. But no. He did the soft thing. He babied the men, traded among the lubbers for a pittance when he could have owned the coast and everything they make and do— ports, islands, towns, the lot."

Again, Ellie spoke without forethought or plan.

"His way works. He's fair, and so is the way we trade."

"The way Astreya trades is stupid. He persuades and cajoles, but never joins, never takes sides. Astreya doesn't even defend his business. Coastal ships are making decent profits at low risk while he ships thin-margin goods over long, dangerous routes. I made more with this ketch in a few months than his two great ships have in years. The headmen of two islands and four towns know that if they don't do as I say, I'll set their neighbours on them. They know how it works because I sold them the guns they needed to get where they are."

"Black Bay against Cottontown."

"Object lesson for both of them. That's what happens if they try to outsmart me."

"You started a war that will destroy people on both sides."

"Neat, isn't it? By the time I come back, they'll need me to bail them out and get them back up and running—and paying me to keep them safe. And all those other ports and harbours from the Sunny Isles to Charton and back will watch and learn."

"You'll do this with only your gang of four?"

"I have more. I own all of them. I choose my men wisely and direct them according to their deficiencies. Cookie is a useful tool because he has an emptiness he can fill only by causing pain. Jake is competent but needs me to make up his mind what to do next. Moke is ugly strong, and only has enough brain to obey simple instructions."

"Fred has ambitions," said Ellie.

Mirak lifted his head and stared down his nose at her.

"You're observant. Can you adapt to a different way of doing things?"

Ellie ignored his question.

"He wants the stones of power," she continued.

"Three ships, three shipstones. I have one aboard *Elusive* in Cottontown. There's one aboard the little schooner, if it's still afloat tomorrow. The last one's aboard *Cygnus* with Astreya in Matris, where you'll take me. That is, if you want to steer clear of Cookie."

"I won't help you kill Astreya."

"Kill Astreya? Whatever gave you that idea? I only want his ship—and giving him the taste of losing all he's gained. Kill him, and he only suffers for an instant. I want him to endure years of humiliation."

Ellie tried not to wrinkle her nose in disgust.

"Eliana, if we survive the night, you're signed on for life. How long you live is up to you."

Ellie gritted her teeth, fought a traitorous desire to capitulate, and took refuge in ambiguity.

"I ... I understand."

"Good. You'll keep your clasp. And maybe your favourite sister as well? So long as you both cooperate, that is."

"Like Fred."

"I've Fred well in hand. He can have whatever's left. He can play with the ring stones and any spare clasps to his heart's content provided he gives me what I want. I have better things to do than to sail where the compass spins. When the last great ship is mine, there will be nothing in the northern seas but coasters and crab-hauling fishermen who aren't worth my time."

Mirak stared as if carved of weathered wood. She could not argue against him, so she played for time as in the hope of distracting him into revealing more. Hesitantly, she revealed a secret he might not know.

"What about the mother lode where the stones of power come from?"

"Nonsense."

"Fred wouldn't agree with you. He waterproofed the ring stones and clasps for Astreya. He's a cunning man: he's guessed where they come from. He knows how we use them, but can't do it himself ... yet. He's got some wild ideas about what he can do, and that includes finding more."

"He told you this?"

"I ... I overheard him thinking out loud."

"Yes. Yes. He does that," Mirak considered, muttering. "But the secret of where the stones came from died with Oron—maybe even with Zubin. And they're all lost except for the three shipstones, plus Astreya's clasp, his woman's, Dabih's, and three he gave to the children."

"And mine."

Ellie let go of the blanket she was hugging and tapped the clasp on her arm. It glowed softly through the fabric of her shirt.

"That stone came from the Forbidden Room aboard *Elusive* or *Cygnus,*" Mirak scoffed.

Ellie shook her head and set the hook.

"There were five clasp stones in the bag Astreya took to Fred. He ruined one experimenting. The other four are Seren's, Mairi's, Trogen's and mine. Cam carried them in his pocket through all their adventures, more than twenty years ago. I remember what he said: 'I was right some lucky not to drop them in the salt-chuck. 'Streya's dad found 'em back at the Village, and left 'em for his son, our 'Streya.'"

Mirak stared at her, his eyes narrowed into slits.

Ellie kept her face as open and honest as if she were bluffing the last pebble in the stone game. Mirak began muttering again, so low that had it not been for her strangely enhanced hearing, Ellie would not have heard.

"If that sculpin thinks he can do without me ... take the ship and all ... Well, that's not going to happen."

As his voice became a mumble, Ellie realized Mirak was repeating himself, echoing the self-justifying tirade he had aimed at her. Ellie kept her eyes shut, waiting for more revelations, but Mirak's mumbling became inaudible among the sounds of the storm-struck ship. Eventually, sleep took her into disturbing dreams where Mirak and his crew took turns throwing her back and forth around the tiny cabin.

11. In which three ships are storm-struck

1. Aboard the ketch

Ellie woke as she fell from the settee onto the cabin sole. She looked around the cabin, fragments of a dream still swirling in her mind. The lantern swung above her head. She stared at it for several heartbeats before noticing that it had burned out in the night and daylight was coming through the port scuttle. The ship cut through waves that no longer threatened to shatter spars or crush the hull. Water rushed past the starboard scuttle, drops forming along its brass rim and trickling onto the settee where she had been lying. She untangled herself from the blanket and tossed it over the skipper's chair, where the sodden half dripped into a crack in the planking. She wrapped her arms around herself and shuddered.

A heavy thump shook the cabin door, which opened a moment later to admit the top half of Moke, who knelt in the doorway holding a bucket in one hand and a jug in the other.

"Skipper wants you on deck soon as you can."

"Is everything all right?"

"We made it through the night, Missie, but t'were a near thing. Don't care if I never see another storm like that."

Ellie shut the door and tried not to think of hot water and clean clothes. When she came out of the cabin, wind tugged at the blanket she held with her hands crossed on her chest, and the wet hem flapped around her ankles. Fred was at the wheel, his back to her. Mirak stood with his chin tucked below the upturned collar of his black jacket. His legs apart, he leaned against the starboard quarter of the cockpit, looking ahead. She followed his gaze and saw white spray tossed onto the foredeck as the bow punched into a wave. She waited for it to subside so that she could look beyond the bowsprit, but even when the spray had run into the scuppers, all she could see was the next wave rolling out of the grey-white fog. When Ellie looked up, she could not see the truck on the masthead; when she looked to port and starboard, the waves were an indistinct blur until they met the ship's sides. The ketch sailed close-hauled in a cocoon of white. Sound was eerily muffled.

The blanket blew off her shoulders onto the deck as Ellie rubbed at her eyes. As she knelt to rescue it, Mirak's voice startled her.

"Show me north."

Ellie slid back her left sleeve to expose the bracelet on her arm.

"There," said Ellie. "We're heading north-east. Maybe north-east by east."

"But there's nothing there!" exclaimed Fred.

"Therefore nothing for us to run into," said Mirak. "And that to my mind is a whole lot better than charging through dense fog towards a rocky coastline we won't be able to see until it's too late. So pull yourself together, bang on the hatch and tell whoever's awake to make us something to drink that's hot, sweet, and quick."

Soon Ellie was accepting a mug from Moke's huge hand and acknowledging the smile she knew was there even though she could not see his mouth for hair. She stood sipping cocoa, while the ship sailed in a grey watery world in which nothing changed.

Cold green fire lit Ellie's left sleeve. Her arm twitched. Her left hand opened and the mug fell to the deck. She swayed on her feet, galvanized by her clasp. Seeing Fred staring, she waved a hand ambiguously, blew out her cheeks and headed for the lee rail where the vomiting she was going to pretend suddenly became real. Suddenly as the sickness had taken her, it disappeared, leaving her mind clear as to what she had to do.

Ellie willed her clasp to call out as she had done the night she was kidnapped. She saw the green flash as she sank to her knees. Dimly she heard shouting, and then felt hands under her armpits lifting her up, then carrying her to the cabin. The settee was once more under her back as she lay at the edge of consciousness.

Someone was covering her with a blanket—a dry blanket. She opened her eyes to see Mirak's hard face staring down at her, one eyebrow raised.

"That was quite a surprise, Eliana. The last time I saw anything like that, I was aboard *Wetfoot* watching Markab take the call from Oron. It was two hours before he could speak. But he knew what he'd heard. What did you hear, Eliana?"

Ellie shook rolled her head back and forth, trying to re-establish control of her body, which felt as limp as if it had been poured onto the settee, but her mind was clear, and dominated by a single thought.

He must not know what I heard and my response. He must not.

"Trogen is ... Trogen is ... gone," she murmured.

"Dead?"

She nodded. *Not a good bluff, Ellie,* she said to herself. *What if he asks me how? Or who told me?*

"Pity," Mirak grimaced as he spoke. "I wanted him alive."

Ellie heard neither pity nor concern in his voice. She pretended to be still confused.

"Who is *Wetfoot*?" she whispered. To her relief, the ploy worked.

"That's what we called *Tidewalker*. Last of the great ships to be lost. No, the last was Meissa's *Silver Swan*. We brought Meissa on board along with two boatloads of crew. There should have been four or five. All drowned. Just a few hours later, she was dead, along with her brother Oron. I don't know how he did it."

"Who?"

"Astreya, of course. I went along with him, faked it, smoothed the transition with the crew. Had to. He was the only one aboard who could work the stones. So off we went to that scummy village.

That was where Astreya and that woman killed Mufrid and set me adrift, hoping I'd drown. But I didn't, did I? And now I'm back to haunt him."

Mirak's voice changed as he rehearsed his obsession that everything wrong in his life had been caused by Astreya, stoking his wrath, almost spitting the words in her face.

She shut her eyes.

"Don't you conk out on me, Eliana. I need you."

Ellie kept her eyes shut.

He needs me to get to Astreya. To navigate him to Matris. Which is why he promised to keep me alive. But there's no chance of that. He'll kill me, or get Cookie to do the job, and he'll do it where Astreya can see. I'll be the first. Then he'll do the same with Seren and Mairi and Trogen. He just wants us for the pain he can inflict on Astreya ... and Lindey, who he hates so much he can't even say her name.

As the door closed behind Mirak, Ellie shuddered. She inspected what she had concluded and found it reasonable. Cookie's voice came back to her: "I like 'em young," and an intense, paralyzing fear gnawed at her hard-won composure. Her imagination conjured a succession of tortures staged to cause maximum pain not only to her but to those she loved. She wondered how long she could will herself not to whimper, scream, or plead. Eventually, she wearied of going around and around the same circle of doubt and apprehension and fell into a numbness something like sleep.

She opened her eyes at the sound of someone moving in the cabin. Fred looked down at her. He wore a loose brown raincoat that flapped around his knees, and he held a sextant in one hand.

"Hey, you. What happened? Did *you* make your stone flare?"

Ellie unwound herself from the knee-clutching ball into which her thoughts had driven her, and shook her head.

"You're going to get a fix?" she asked.

"Going to try."

"Can I help?"

She saw him hesitate and then shrug.

"Why not? Mirak's sacked out, the rest of them are too stupid. You've done this before, right?"

Ellie nodded.

"Then come on. It's nearly noon."

Ellie followed him into the cockpit, where Moke loomed over the wheel. They were sailing through patchy fog, the sails barely full of wet wind. The sun was a soft white blob of light overhead, strengthening and dimming as the ketch slid through featureless waves that appeared out of the fog to windward and disappeared less than a stone's throw to lee.

"You're going to have to guess at the horizon."

"I thought of that back on shore when I was teaching myself how to do it. I added a level, see?"

"Clever," said Ellie, and meant it.

He reached into the pocket of his coat and handed her a notebook, pencil and the smallest clock she had ever seen.

"Don't drop it. It's from *Before*. It doesn't even need winding. I have no idea how it works, but it's the only one, so I'm not in a hurry to take it apart."

Ellie gave him a countdown to noon and noted the settings he read off his sextant. Then they went back into the little cabin, where Fred raised the sides of the table to accommodate a chart. Together, they consulted a book of logarithms bound in some shiny material that Ellie guessed must have defeated more than a century of time, weather, and use. Eventually, Fred pencilled a little cross. They both stared at the distance between the mark and the coastline.

"Here's where Mirak wants to go. But you know that."

Ellie nodded.

"Listen, can you show me how to work that stone on your arm?"

His eyes were intent, his expression avaricious, the opposite of the blank stare he had fixed on her after she had been kidnapped. Ellie saw an opportunity.

"I think so. There's a fifty-fifty chance you have the knack, the power, the whatever it is that's necessary to be a wielder—that's what we call someone who can work the shipstones. Before you ask, I can't give you my clasp because then I would die, and then you'd have nobody to teach you." She paused, and then once again, set the hook. "The trouble is there aren't any more stones left, for you or anyone else."

"There has to be. They may be rare, or lost, or undiscovered, but there has to be more of them. Astreya had a bag of them his father left him. I overcooked one while I was working out how to waterproof them. It was just a water-worn greenish pebble until it blew into a million shards. Burned holes all over my shop. I'd gone out for a moment … luckiest pee-break I ever took. Anyway, Walt told me where Astreya came from, up north somewhere. That's where there has to be more, just waiting for someone to find them, mine them, pick them up somehow."

Ellie started to reel him in.

"I can take you there."

"How?

"This chart is pretty much the same as I worked on aboard *Elusive*. Except that ours had the lat and long inked in for our ports of call. Plus one more, where we don't go, north of Charton. Astreya's village."

"You remember the coordinates?"

Ellie nodded, wondering if he would believe her. Apparently, he saw nothing strange in someone able to remember strings of numbers.

"So plot it in for me... No. Don't. Just put your finger where it is and tell me the numbers."

Ellie obliged, silently approving Fred's decision to keep what they were doing from Mirak.

"West and a bit north from where we are," Fred mused. "Can you aim your stone? Point it at where you want to go and have it stay pointing?"

Ellie nodded.

"Then when Mirak asks you to point north, you could tell him what he wants to hear, but in such a way as to head us straight for Astreya's village."

Ellie looked into his eyes and nodded again.

"So do it, and ... and I'll keep you alive."

He rolled up the chart and replaced the books and the sextant, muttering to himself.

"Don't do that," said Ellie said to Fred's back as he went out the door. "Don't talk to yourself. He'll hear."

Fred turned, nodded and winked.

As the door shut, Ellie sent Trogen the coordinates she had helped establish.

2. Aboard *Cygnet*

When Trogen's blast from *Elusive's* shipstone reached *Cygnet*, Mairi was in the stern cabin with Seren. Less than an arm's length from their heads, *Cygnet's* shipstone flared bright green in its gimbal, dazing both women. They leaned onto the chart table and stared at each other, their faces a handspan apart.

Mairi was first to recover.

"Bearing, Seren. Where did it come from? Where's *Elusive*?"

"Southwest ... no southwest-by-south."

"I agree. Trogen's still trailing us. No way to know by how much."

"Wait, he's sending his position."

Mairi's pencil scribbled numbers in the margin of the chart, then moved parallel rulers and marked a tiny x.

"We can't be sure until we shoot the sun, but if we're about here, then..."

Mairi raised one hand to forestall the answer about to come from Seren's lips. They both closed their eyes to concentrate, and a moment later opened them at the same time. Their eyes locked, and they spoke simultaneously.

"Ellie!"

"North-east!"

"Perhaps east-by-north?" said Mairi.

She slid the ruler across the chart to indicate a bearing from their estimated position. Seren nodded. The shipstone flared once more and they both froze.

"Trogen again," Mairi muttered, her pencil poised. "North-by-east. That's his bearing on Ellie. Seren, now we can triangulate!"

"And with two of us and the shipstone, we can reach them!"

Mairi looked into Seren's blue eyes and they shared unexpected confidence. She reached for a second ruler and laid it at the correct angle from *Elusive's* position, touched her pencil at the spot where the two rulers crossed, and then drew a circle around it.

"Now I have to send our bearing to Trogen so that he can ..."

"Know where she is!" Seren exclaimed.

"A fair distance away," said Mairi. "While we were close hauled and then hove to, being punched by northerlies, the ketch must have had south winds and been taken along by the storm as it curved north-eastwards."

"Chances are they'll soon be facing the westerlies that are getting *Elusive* and us towards Matris," said Seren. "They'll have a long upwind beat." She paused, and when she continued, her eyes were bright with excitement. "We can get there first and rescue Ellie!"

Mairi nodded slowly, wishing she knew how.

3. Aboard *Elusive*

Trogen carefully made three new crosses on the chart and regarded his work with satisfaction. He had sent the latitude and longitude for Mairi on *Cygnet*, and Ellie on the ketch. To his surprise, both had replied with their positions, even though they were well over the horizon range that they all had been taught was the limit of messaging with the stones.

Walt lumbered into the cabin, talking as he came. He thumped towards the big table and got into a chair with his usual backward hop, and sat swinging his legs.

"Two sights today, Trog? Wasn't the one before dawn good enough for you?"

"It told me where we were, Walt, but I knew that. I wanted to know if *Cygnet* and the ketch made it through the storm."

"And?"

"*Cygnet* made it through, and Ellie's alive. There's Mairi's position, and roughly here is the ketch."

A soft knock made them both look up to see Damon in the open door, one hand on the doorframe.

"Did I hear you say they're all alive? I thought ..."

Trogen waved Damon to his chair.

"You thought we couldn't message over long distances. Well, I can. I sent our coordinates at dawn, and now I know their positions."

"Wait a bit," said Walt, looking at the chart. "Mairi and Seren ain't that far ahead of us, but Ellie don't have a shipstone. Maybe you can reach her, but there's no way she answers from that far away."

"I thought so, too," said Trogen. "I hoped my sending would reach her and maybe cheer her up. But she got back to me. A bit faint, but recognizable."

"I presume Mairi and Seren sent you their noon fix," said Damon. "But how does Ellie know where she is?"

"Maybe they got a noon position, and she saw," said Trogen.

"Fred," said Walt. "He's a real smart bugger."

Damon glanced at Walt, then looked back at the chart. "You've drawn both ships' probable course."

"I guessed the general area where Ellie was from her first reply," said Trogen. "Then later when I knew her position, it was easy. They're heading for Matris, but we'll get there first. They've got an upwind beat, whereas we'll reach for it, wind abeam."

"Same as *Cygnet*," said Damon.

"As long as the wind holds," said Walt. "Then what?"

"The problem is," Trogen began, paused, and hearing his own voice sounding considered and thoughtful, he pressed on, deliberately repeating himself. "When *Elusive* shows over the horizon, they'll lash Ellie to the shrouds, and by the time we catch up with them, we'll see a man standing behind her with a knife. If we make a move, we'll have to watch them kill her."

Damon dropped his eyes, frowning. Walt showed a double row of teeth in a cheerful grin and slid off his chair with a thump.

"Well, what do y'know, I think I got that sorted. C'mon up on deck when I call. I got somethin' to show ya."

Trogen looked a question at Damon, who shrugged.

12. In which ships converge

1. Aboard *Cygnet*

Another day and a night passed. The Cygnets fell into a regular pattern of watch-keeping, with its almost hypnotic repetition of tasks. Moment to moment, they coped with all the minor constraints of life at sea, automatically maintaining their balance as they took their turns steering, sail-tending, cooking, eating, and keeping the ship tidy, most of the time working quietly so as not to disturb those who were taking well-earned rest in their bunks. The more they worked smoothly together, the less they interacted. Conversations became increasingly rare as they all sank into their own thoughts.

Watch after watch, Mairi attempted to speak to each member of her crew, but all too often, the exchange was only a reassurance that nothing was wrong. Though they all wondered what would happen when *Cygnet* caught up with the ketch, they no longer speculated out loud. Neil, deeply humiliated by his failure to win a clasp, wore a resentful frown night and day. Unless she was actively performing some task, Seren stared distractedly toward the north-east horizon. Marley covertly watched her, his dark eyes soft with sympathy. Even Cam's optimistic attitude was failing as he went stolidly about his part in maintaining the ship and her crew.

Mairi still had no plan for rescuing Ellie. Twice daily, Seren helped her fix their position and then plot their progress in relation to *Elusive* and the ketch. Their brief enthusiasm at knowing that Ellie had survived the storm gave way to a gnawing fear that she might be abused. Neither of them spoke, since to do so would shatter the mask of composure they both wore in order to cope.

On the morning of the fourth day, *Cygnet* was loping along close-hauled on the port tack under the clearest skies since the storm. The air was cool enough that the crew wore jackets over knitted pullovers whenever they were on deck. Mairi and Seren were at work with sextants, Cam was at the wheel. Marley came up the companionway, looked around, and shivered.

Seren gave her sextant to Alan and disappeared below. She reappeared moments later, thrust a blue-grey garment at Marley, retrieved the sextant and busied herself with its knobs and slides. When Marley only looked at what she had given him, she spoke more crisply than she intended.

"Well, put it on!"

"A bit more chill in the air now," said Alan companionably.

"I'm guessing he feels it more'n us," said Neil.

Marley gave him an expressionless look, took off his jacket, put on the wooden pullover and murmured thanks to Seren as he tugged it down over his shirt.

"Marley, weren't you property kitted out aboard *Cygnus*?" Mairi asked.

"None the right size, I'll bet," said Cam.

"The first one they offered had room for two of me, only sideways, and second stopped at my elbows," said Marley.

"This one ain't too tight across the chest, anyway," said Neil.

Seren blushed, Cam scowled, and Marley's eyes narrowed, Neil tried to look unconcerned. Mairi decided that selective deafness was her best option.

"Comin' up on noon," said Cam.

Mairi and Seren pointed and adjusted their sextants, and were comparing their results when they both stiffened and spoke simultaneously.

"Ellie!"

They glanced at each other, nodded, pushed up their sleeves, and looked at their clasps at the same time.

"Calculate the fix later, Seren. Below, now! And you, Cam."

Mairi led the way, followed by Cam. Seren hesitated, then pulled at Marley's sleeve.

"You, too, Marley."

They crowded into the tiny stern cabin where only Cam and Mairi were able to stand without stooping. Mairi spread out the chart, conferred with Seren, shuffled parallel rulers, and pointed with a pencil.

"We were here yesterday. We should be here today. When we first felt Ellie's signal, Seren and I thought the ketch would head for Matris, but now it's much more likely that they're going towards..."

"The Village!" exclaimed Cam.

"Where Astreya and Cam were born," Seren whispered to Marley.

"We could arrive about the same time," said Mairi. "I can't tell who will get there first until we see them, when..."

"...it'll be too late," said Cam.

"...and we'll have lost our only advantage," Mairi continued, "which is..."

"Surprise," said Marley.

Mairi nodded, pulled a sheet of paper from under the chart and positioned it where the two ships' courses converged.

"This is Astreya's drawing of the Village, as copied by Trogen. Cam, can you tell us a bit more?"

"Y' see how the whole inlet looks a bit like a hand, wi' the way to the sea at the wrist, an' the Village at the end of the thumb, here? So there's a couple dozen, mebby thirty homes stepped back from the water in layers, goin' upwards. Here, close to where the stream runs out, there's a wharf. That's where the fleet ties up ... six, mebby seven boats. This time o' the year, they'll likely be goin' to the fishin' grounds south a ways, or perhaps north to the High

Islands. 'Close in, near the Village, the water's right some deep, so we go to where there's shoals an' banks, an' the fishin's better."

"That would be like the reefs around my island," said Marley.

"So that means the men are probably away," said Mairi.

"An' most boys over sixteen," said Cam. "Like 'Streya an' me was when all our adventures got started."

"I don't understand why Mirak wants to go there, so far north," said Marley.

"It's where Astreya came from," said Mairi. "So if Mirak wants to hurt him, he goes there first ... um ... wreaks havoc, then tells Astreya what he's done."

"Or makes us tell," said Seren. "Unless we get him, first."

"There's that," said Cam, "but Fred's aboard the ketch with Mirak, an' Fred just maybe got told or worked out on his own that the Village is where the stones came from, what 'Streya's da found, an' I carried around, an' 'Streya lit up, an' Fred put the waterproofin' on."

Marley looked puzzled by Cam's condensed history.

"If they're successful, it's win-win for the two of them," said Mairi.

"But they don't know where to look," said Seren. "The people in the Village don't know, either, do they?"

Cam shook his head.

"I don't know fer sure meself, Seren. But me hunch is 'Streya's da fished them out of the Village's stream. He'd have done whatever it is you folks do to make 'em glow green," said Cam.

"Which means Mirak and Fred need..." Marley began.

"Ellie!" said Seren. "They need her safe, so she can look for them..."

"Probably at night," Mairi added. "When she can see the dim glow that they make if a really strong wielder is close."

"Which she surely is," said Seren. "What if we sailed into one of the finger bays, and waited until night? Then when we saw them going to the stream, we could grab Ellie from them and..."

"We ain't got no rowboat," said Cam, "an' though fine seafarin' men and women we all are to be sure, I don't know how we can sneak *Cygnet* out one bay into the main one, right up to the stream, at night, when it's most likely flat calm, an' do all of it without the folks on the ketch catchin' on to what we're up to."

They returned to staring at the chart. Mairi broke the silence.

"Part of your plan might work, Seren, if we could get some of us ashore, somehow."

"There's a way to do that," said Cam. "See this little bay here, south of the channel? That's where 'Streya saved our sorry skins. There were six, seven of us, all chasin' after 'Streya to see him fight with Yan, the biggest of us all. An' the thickest. Here, on this black beach at low water, we caught up, an' Yan did his stupid best to kill 'Streya 'cause the ninny thought 'Streya fancied his girl. Well, they tussled, and then we all got into it, and right when it looked real bad for 'Streya, it looked even worse for all of us, 'cause the tide had come in and we was cut off by cliffs an' water. So then 'Streya, all cool like nothin' was amiss, says 'Take off yer belts an' join 'em all up.' An' we did that, 'cause we was all stonkered out of the smallest clue about how to save our silly selves from drownin' in the rips or bein' bashed to death 'gainst the cliffs what we couldn't climb on account of the fact that they was all green and slippery with weed, way higher than we could reach. So what does 'Streya do? He gets three o'the lads to kinda lean against the cliff, and tells me to climb on their shoulders, an' then he climbs up them an' me to where he can get ahold of dry rock an' scramble to where he can lower the rope of belts an' haul us up, one by one to where we could climb to the top of the cliff."

"And this is good news for us right now, because?" Marley asked.

Cam looked eagerly at each of them in turn, his eyes gleaming.

"'Cause I know the way, an' you an' Seren together is tall enough. We got lots of spare rope, an' at slack tide we can get *Cygnet* close so's we can jump ashore. Or leastways near enough."

"So then Alan, Neil, and I take *Cygnet* out of sight until..." Mairi began.

"'Till the three of us get up to the headland, here, where we can see most everything in all directions, and Seren can message you about where the ketch is, or if it isn't there yet, while you stooge about waitin', like you said, out o' sight, 'til you hear from us tellin' you we've got Ellie, and then you can come back to pick us up."

"There's so much we don't know..." said Seren, and fell silent, ashamed of doubting.

They stood listening to the steady, rhythmic sounds of *Cygnet* making her way over the water.

"See what we can accomplish when we work together," said Mairi, her voice studiedly neutral. They had a plan, to which she had contributed little, which she thought was largely wishful thinking, but which she recognized could give them all hope.

2. Aboard the ketch

"Wakey, wakey! Up you get, Eliana. I need you to find the Village."

Ellie blinked the sleep from her eyes, swung her feet over the edge of the settee, combed her hair back from her face with her fingers, and glared up at Mirak.

"Water, the bucket, and privacy."

Her voice sounded confident, even to her own ears. To her surprise, her assertiveness worked. Mirak turned and left the cabin. Ellie heard his voice giving orders, and moments later, Moke's big fist knocked on the door. Around the half-open door came a bucket, a jug, and Moke's hairy face.

"Here y' are, missie. Go easy on the water, would'ja? We're near to dry, an' we need it bad fer drinkin'."

Ellie certainly did not feel pampered, but she recognized that in the eyes of the crew, she was receiving special privileges. She drank, poured a little water on her shirt-tail and scrubbed at her face. Then, summoning confidence she did not feel, Ellie stepped out of the cabin into the cockpit.

The ketch was sailing in a light mist. She shivered despite the blanket she had wrapped around her shoulders. Gradually she noticed that she could see more than at first. When she looked up, the sun was a fuzzy white orb, which turned red as she stared. She shut her eyes until the afterimage faded. When she opened them, it was as if a doorway had opened ahead.

Above, the sky was a rich blue, brushed by thin tendrils of high, wispy white clouds. On either side, the backs of smooth waves glinted in the sun. Ahead, the sea dazzled into the west until it blended into a soft blue haze where the sky met a solid wall of cliffs.

"We can't be going there," said Jake. "That's mountains."

"Cliffs," said Ellie. "There's a gap leading into a salt-water lake where the Village is."

"If you say so," said Jake and thumped on the cabin top. "Land ho!"

Cookie climbed into the cockpit. Ellie moved as far as she could to windward, away from his furtive looks and the rancid smell of his unwashed body. Fred and Mirak consulted a chart spread out on the cabin top. The hatch of the forward cabin slid open, revealing Moke's head and massive shoulders.

"Mug up, missie?"

Ellie accepted the drink, resisting the impulse to pat his shaggy head before he slid the hatch closed. Mirak turned to her.

"Heading?" he demanded. "Point us to that little Village, Ellie. The one where Astreya's father found the stones."

Ellie risked a glance at Fred, who gave her a conspiratorial wink.

"Quite a story Mirak told me last night. Not the same as you were told by your family, I'm sure."

Ellie nodded slowly, mentally congratulating Fred on his powers of persuasion. She concentrated and pointed a few degrees to port.

"You're sure?" Mirak asked. Ellie nodded.

"We're off course," said Fred. "Head where she's pointing, Jake."

"Oh, for goodness sake," said Mirak wearily. "When will you learn, Fred? You can't sail into the wind's eye."

Ellie frowned at the chart then looked at her clasp. Fred's intelligence was keen where computation and abstract thought were concerned, but he was completely lacking the seamanship sense that came intuitively to Mirak, who scorned him as a lubber. She guessed how Fred had manipulated Mirak.

I pretend to believe Fred, Fred pretends to believe me, and Mirak's convinced because of his disdain for both of us.

Ellie's green eyes narrowed.

"If we're a bit north of our destination, it's all for the better. We can coast southwards, watching for the inlet. It's not obvious."

"How do you know all this?" Fred asked.

"I saw a drawing in a rutter aboard *Cygnet*. The gap is between a deep notch in the cliffs to the north and a big pointy rock that fell off the cliff to the south. It looks like a ship's bow, only sticking straight up."

Mirak nodded, recognizing her description from his own memories.

"Good. With those marks to go on, I can do the rest." He banged on the cabin hatch, slid it open and gave orders. "Send up the barrel. The big one. Fred, you need to practice with your weapon so I can be sure you'll do what I want. No mistakes this time."

Rumbling and thumping noises came from below, and a barrel appeared, followed by Moke, who was holding it over his head as easily as if it were a big pillow. He eased it onto the deck, produced a jimmy from his belt and popped off the head. Ellie stood on tiptoes, but could only see packing straw, which Fred pulled out and tossed over the side. He followed his first, careful handful with a quick second, then he scrabbled faster and faster, the straw blown astern by the wind. Fred's face screwed into a look of disbelief. Mirak took a step closer and peered into the barrel.

"Clocks? A sextant? Where's the gun, Fred?"

"It's got to be here. I packed it myself. I marked one barrel with an 'I' for instruments and the other with my initial. I don't understand."

"I understand perfectly, you lummox. You buggered it up. Again."

Ellie heard the barely controlled fury in Mirak's voice, but her eyes were on the chalk marks. She stepped closer and rubbed a corner of the 'F' with her thumb.

"It's been changed. There's a different colour underneath that's been rubbed out and re-written. It's an "I" that someone's altered to an 'F'."

"Walt," said Fred. "Walt must have done it. He was at my workshop."

"So he's got the gun aboard *Elusive* in Cottontown," said Mirak, his voice now back in control. "Not helpful, Fred. Not helpful."

"Could be not so good for him, too. It's a bit tricky to use."

"How so?"

"Well, because I employed the principle of gyroscopic stability ..."

"The point, Fred," Mirak interrupted.

"The point is that it stays on target, which is especially good for firing from a ship, but..."

"But what, Fred?"

"But I don't think he knows about the distance activation device."

"The what?"

"Well, actually, it's a piece of string tied to the trigger. It's a really good idea, because although the guns are a beautiful example of the gunmaker's art, the ammunition is about a hundred and fifty years old, and the first one I test-fired blew up. Fortunately, the string was long enough to reach behind the wall where I was, and..."

"So if Walt decides to fire it..." Mirak began.

"I made improvements after the first two exploded. The last one got off three shots before it blew. It's not my fault if Walt has an accident. He shouldn't have stolen it."

"Well, we'll just have to do the Village the old-fashioned way with knives and clubs."

Ellie's eyes widened, but neither of them noticed. She shivered. Mirak glanced at her and called down into the cabin for his boat cloak. When Cookie appeared with the black garment, Mirak wrapped it around Ellie and patted her shoulder. She tried not to cringe at the solicitude that was so much at odds with his icy heartlessness. Ellie kept herself from panicking by silently choosing words to describe her situation.

I'm an asset. I'm valuable to him, so he's looking after me, the same way he's putting up with Fred's mistakes. But the moment I'm no longer useful, I'm disposable. So is Fred. But they don't know that Elusive *is on her way north.*

3. Aboard *Elusive*

Trogen sat in the master's chair. The chart and his father's sketch of the northern fjord were in front of him, but he stared past both. It was a day since he had revised *Elusive's* destination, but he had yet to tell anyone. When he had realized that Ellie was navigating the ketch towards the Village, he had gone to the Forbidden Room and made a series of minor changes to the green line that kept the steersman on course. He had told no-one, and if Peter had noticed, he had not said anything.

Trogen was as ready as he could be for a landfall near the Village. Hours of meticulous copying had imprinted every word and line on his mind so that there was nothing more that Astreya's notes and sketches could tell him. However, a bewildering array of possibilities had him in a state of mind wherein even simple decisions seemed beyond him. One moment, his instinct was to take advice, the next he was unable to decide to whom he should turn. If he had a plan, then he could address the task of preparing his officers and crew. He was not getting any closer to a decision, because his mind kept on going over and over what Walt had revealed the previous day.

Walt had unpacked and assembled the gun by the time Trogen arrived on deck. It gleamed dully as the afternoon sun slid along its thin barrel, which was as long as Walt was tall. The gun was secured to a heavy tripod, in the middle of which was a swiftly spinning disk. As Walt swung the gun around to point over the stern, the barrel tipped up and down in time to the roll of the ship. Trogen had been about to say that the gun would be difficult to aim when he realized that it was the ship that dipped and swayed: the gun kept pointing where Walt had aimed it.

"Smart bugger that he is to put all this together, Fred never saw me swap the labels. Look astern. I flung a keg over the side while you were coming up on deck. Now, young Trog, you watch what I can do."

Trogen had to shade his eyes and squint to see the black shape bobbing in the wake. Walt crouched, the gun flared a short-lived flame. Trogen felt as if both his ears had been slapped. He blinked, thinking nothing more would happen. The keg leaped into the air and exploded. A curved barrel-stave spun lazily skyward, then joined the rest of the wooden shards showering into the sea.

"Bet you never thought that bein' short, square, and ugly would be useful, did'ja? But it takes a man like me to hold this thing down when it kicks back."

Walt grinned with the fierce savagery of someone tasting power he had long coveted. A hesitant footfall at the head of the companionway made them both turn. Damon looked at them dispassionately. He touched his moustache before speaking.

"Who are you planning to kill, Walt?"

When Walt looked up, Trogen and Damon saw his feral, bare-toothed expression. He shrugged, and his mouth softened into an aggressively cheerful grin.

"Oh, it's just for teaching 'em a lesson. Somethin' to get 'em into a cooperative frame of mind."

"Just a threat," said Trogen.

Damon looked at him.

Never threaten anything you are not ready to do.

Had Damon spoken? Or were the words from Trogen's memory of something Damon had said years before? Trogen could not meet his eyes. Damon turned away and walked carefully forward.

A day later, Trogen was still not sure what had happened. Walt had not simply used a gun, he had imposed his will half a horizon away. For a moment, Trogen had shared Walt's elation at the flash, the clap of sound, the invisible bringing of sudden destruction. At that moment, Trogen had lusted for the gun and its curiously impersonal power. However, Damon's words still rankled, taking Trogen back to the resentment he had expressed at his father's judgment so long ago.

All I wanted was to see what would happen if I threw a couple of wooden balls linked by a rope at Mairi, because I could, and I did, and it felt good until the balls were in the air and there was an instant when I misgave, but by then it was too late, and it wasn't my fault that Mairi was hurt, because I didn't know...

Except of course he *had* known, and Astreya had known that he knew and had punished him for knowing better and doing worse anyway.

"Land ho!'

A shout from the deck dismissed Trogen's reverie. He had decisions to make, and he had to be where everyone could see him make them, starting with explaining why the land in sight was not Matris.

13. In which three ships approach the Village

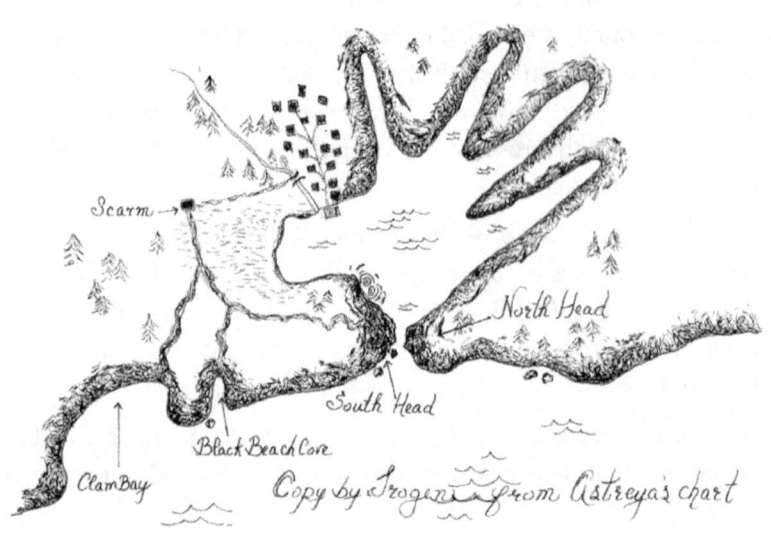

Scarm→

North Head

South Head

Black Beach Cove

Clam Bay

Copy by Trogen from Astreya's chart

1. Aboard *Cygnet*

Late in the afternoon, Mairi sighted the black pinnacle that marked the approaches to the Village. Assured by Cam that there were no outlying reefs and rocks such as she had seen when they first approached the coast, *Cygnet* sailed near the shoreline under a light northwest wind. The cliffs fell into the sea almost sheer from several times the height of *Cygnet's* masts to a ragged line of white where the waves broke and then reverberated back as confused choppy water.

All of the Cygnets were on deck, staring upward in dismay at the grey rock face that dwarfed their ship. Only Cam was unaffected.

"See up there at the top? Near the edge, them little trees ain't much taller than me, but they're real old—some of 'em more'n a hundred year. An' hard! You could break an axe tryin' to cut one down. Not that you'd want to, 'cause they're all bent over from the wind what keeps 'em from growin' upwards, like normal. When I was a nipper, they made me 'magine I was a giant, walkin' among 'em, lookin' down on their tops."

"You've not been way up there," Neil scoffed.

"Too right I have. Picking cloudberries fer me ma. She made the most won'erful pies you ever tasted. Back before she died, that is."

"You were raised by your father, then," said Marley.

"Nah. He was lost at sea afore I could walk. It were Scarm what kept an eye on me, but mostly I did fer meself, wi' the occasional meal or a new-to-me pair o' breeks from one o' the mums."

"You must have been lonely," said Mairi.

"Not really. Yer never alone in the Village. Trippin' over folks, more like. It were 'Streya what were the lonely one, cause he was diff'rent. Black hair. Tall. Lean. And some slippery-fast, let me tell you. Not one o' the lads could best him at wrestlin', even them what were two, three years older."

"What was he like, back then, when you were growing up together?" Mairi asked.

"He was ... he was ... I'll tell you sometime when we're not coming up on where we're goin'. See that bay? We ain't goin' to land there. Real bad approach. Rocks like great big teeth, just waitin' t' chew the bottom out of yer boat. Good clammin' at low tide, though. Right, now see that black rock-face fine on the port bow? Watch carefully, an' you'll see it's two sep'rate points wi' a black shingle beach in between ... leastways so long as it ain't at high water an' drownin' time if you hadn't got 'Streya to show you how to climb out."

"In there?" asked Allan dubiously, as *Cygnet* sailed past and they all stared into the little bay.

"Piece of cake," said Cam. "Now on we go, swinging wide of that rock that's awash at high water. That's the South Rock. Then there's the Gap Rock, just off to port as you come into the main bay. Then there's the Inner Rock right next to the whirlpools. Leave 'em all well clear to port. Then you're in. Four long narrow reaches like fingers on a hand, wi' the thumb to port, where the Village is. Stretch out yer right hand, and you'll get the idea."

"Is it much further?" Mairi began, and then paused as *Cygnet* sailed out of the shadow of the cliffs, and late afternoon sunlight lit the water of a passage through what until that moment had seemed an impenetrable wall.

"Look! It's like it just appeared. You'd never know it was ..." Seren began, then clutched the clasp on her left arm and whispered. "Mairi, did you feel that? It's not Ellie, and *Elusive's* still over the horizon to the south of us."

Mairi nodded, frowning. The stones on their arms tingled meaninglessly.

The looked at each other, puzzled, while the crew wondered at the size of the bay that opened up beyond the narrow passage. The evening light shimmered on water flat as a lake on whose far shore they glimpsed pine forest rising from the waterline up high, steep slopes. Then *Cygnet's* sails darkened as she sailed into the shadow from the north headland, and it was as if the gap had closed behind them, and the glimpse into a gentler world behind the forbidding grey cliffs had been an illusion. Seren and Mairi's clasps returned to normal.

Cam looked at their amazed faces, his grin widening.

"Neat, ain't it, the way it's there waitin'; an' then, hot damn, it's gone again. Special at this time of day. If yer wonderin', I can tell you that the fleet's not comin' home tonight. Red Ian likes to lead 'em in on a rising tide when he can ride the wave that happens when sea spills into the bay, an' that was more'n two hours ago."

"More water under the keel too, I'd guess," said Marley.

"That ain't a worry. The gap is deep, real deep, an' so's the bay. There's a bit of a ridge under the water what breaks up the incoming waves. It's the fingers what shallow up at the inland ends."

As Mairi listened to Cam's spate of information, she scanned the horizon, What started as no more than keeping a lookout turned abruptly into an immediate concern.

"How are the Village boats rigged, Cam?" Mairi asked, the urgency in her voice breaking the spell that kept the *Cygnets* amazed by what they had seen.

"Gaff rigged main, an' jib on a bowsprit."

Mairi deliberately lowered the pitch of her voice without reducing its determination.

"There's a sail catching the light to the northwest. It could be the ketch. Mirak was here before, so he won't be surprised to see Village boats. We can't hide or get far enough away to be out of sight, but if we strike the main and staysail, then the mizzen and working jib could look, at a distance, like..."

"... a Village boat!" said Cam. "Good one, Skipper. Re-rigged, like, *Cygnet* can stooge about like she was trollin' fishin' lines, an' you can drop us off at the cove. The weather looks like it's settled for a bit, you got the land and sea breezes all night, so there's small chance of yer bein' shoved onto a lee shore. You'll be right handy to pick us up when Seren messages you that we've got Ellie, and then we'll be away."

Neil burst into scornful speech.

"So when the ketch gets to the Village, you're just going to say, 'Pretty please, Mr. Mirak, can we have the skipper's cousin back?' And then Ellie tells him a polite goodbye, and you take her hand, and we all meet together for hugs and kisses at a beach that's only a beach at low water. Like my dad used to say, 'Give me strength!' This ain't going to work, Skipper."

"Neil, that's no way to ..." Seren began.

"We'll work with what we've got," said Mairi firmly. "And right now, we've got to be ready before the ketch knows we're here. Strike the main. Alan, bring her about, and we'll try to look as if we're fishing."

The light was fading and *Cygnet* was in the shadows of the cliffs, but Mairi could not stop thinking about the many ways in which their plan could go wrong. She took the wheel, partly to ensure that her crew was all actively engaged with no time for discussion, mainly to discover how the schooner would handle under such an unconventional sail pattern. With the wind on her port quarter filling only the jib and foresail, *Cygnet* behaved almost as if she were being towed. Lacking the driving power of the mainsail, the ship was unbalanced and difficult to steer.

"Stay well clear of the North Head, unless you're goin' in. That's when you should hug it close," said Cam. "Right now, we'll keep away from the two big rocks you can see off the starboard bow, just breaking the surface. I'm goin' below to pack a bag of spare clothes, in case we have to wade ashore. Tell Marley and Seren, so's they can get ready."

Mairi nodded approval, Cam moved aft, and then paused in the cockpit to speak softly to her before going down the companionway.

"I got an idea or two up me sleeve. Them buggers is sure to be goin' through the gap and then landin' at the Village. When they do, they'll have to take Ellie with them, an' that's our chance, 'cause I can find help if'n I get there first. An' if they leave her on board, it's even easier. Don't worry. We can do this."

2. Aboard the ketch

Ellie felt *Cygnet's* shipstone's nearness as if someone were wordlessly whispering in her ear. Ever since the storm, she had been aware of *Cygnet* and *Elusive* at the back of her mind. It was not just the wish that they would come for her, but an actual physical sensation, not unlike an itch just out of reach. When she consulted the stone on her arm, she had to drag it back from pointing first at *Cygnet*, then less strongly, at *Elusive*. This was not a new experience for her: the spear of light at the heart of her stone always tended to point at the nearest great ship. One of the first skills she had learned was to take control of her own stone before she could use it to wield a shipstone. Each of them had its own feel for her, a signature plain as that of each of her fellow wielders, particularly if Trogen or she was using a shipstone to navigate or to extend the range of messaging.

Ellie was standing in the crowded cockpit of the ketch, feeling grateful that Cookie was below in the cabin. On the port side, Fred kept trying to check a chart that would not stay flat on the cabin top. Mirak's attention was focussed on the looming cliffs ahead. Moke's head was a hairy lump above the cabin hatch. Jake stood to starboard, one hand on the wheel with his head tipped back, steering by the wind, keeping the ketch close-hauled.

The cliffs grew up from the sea a little higher every time Ellie looked ahead. She began to see lighter and darker patches below the ragged line of the cliff tops against the sky. Waves reflected from the rock wall ahead of them slapped the ship's bow, confusing the steady rhythm of the open ocean. The haze lifted. Then as they sailed into the late afternoon shadow of the cliffs, the sails darkened, and the sky above was suddenly a deeper blue. What she first saw as dark scars in the grey cliffs were now precipitous, black clefts. The shoreline was menacingly close. The wind fluctuated as it coiled and curled down and along the cliffs. Flashes of white showed where rocks broke the surface.

Seren what can you see

The Village

Most of the four fingers

No boats

Ellie winced. The messages came to her so clearly, it seemed impossible that the men standing an arm's length from her could not hear them. She closed her eyes, concentrated, and sent her own message.

It's me Ellie

Bound for the Village

Can't talk

She grabbed the cockpit coaming and held on, her head swimming from the effort.

"What's wrong?" Fred asked. "Mirak, she's fainting or something."

Ellie shook her head, trying to clear it of a rushing, hissing presence like that of a shipstone, but diffuse, enveloping, meaningless.

"We need to ..." she began.

"Got it," exclaimed Mirak. "North marker. Jibe her round, Jake."

"The girl's not well, Mirak," said Fred.

"I'm all right. Just a bit..."

"Missie needs food," Moke rumbled. "Poor little mite ain't had a bite since wakin'."

Jake spun the wheel, and Ellie shrank back into the stern quarter of the cockpit as it filled with a confusion of men. Fred hauled the jib, Mirak tended the main, and Cookie emerged from below to handle the mizzen. In the midst of it all, Moke waded through his shipmates, one huge hand offering Ellie a little loaf of twice-baked bread stuffed with a hunk of cheese, and a mug of what proved to be sweet, watery hot chocolate. When all four men had sorted themselves out, Ellie risked a quick look at where, despite the insistent interference, her stone told her *Cygnet* must be. She could not spot the distinctive silhouette of a schooner as seen from abeam, and she could not keep looking for fear that one of the men might follow her gaze.

"Whazzat way up ahead?"

Cookie's high voice froze Ellie's handful of bread and cheese on its way to her mouth. Her mug trembled in the other hand, slopping brown liquid onto the cockpit sole. Then voices spoke at the same time.

"... wave breaking on a rock..."

"... fishing smack on the way home..."

"... the light's going, an' I can't be sure, but ain't that a gap?"

"Yes, it is. Hard a-starboard. We're going in while we still can see our way."

"Are you goin' t' be all right, missie?"

Ellie tried to make herself small as Mirak gave orders.

"Cookie, go lookout on the foredeck. Moke, harden in the main. We need all the speed we can get because there's flukey wind inside. Jake, keep well to starboard as we go in."

"Rock, fine on the starboard bow!" Cookie screamed.

The ketch yawed, her sails a-shake, as Jake steered clear. Ellie heard Mirak murmur, "I forgot about that one." She opened her mouth to give advice, looked up at a precipice to starboard, a stone's throw away, and then shut it again. They were in the gap, cliffs on either side and then they were through into the hidden fjord.

"No boats at the wharf," said Fred.

"That's where we'll go. Not yet, you lummox! Hold your course! We have to get clear of the whirlpools."

The ketch left the narrow, cliff-girt gap astern and swung to port in a long, slowing curve. Random puffs of wind flapped her sails on one side and then the other, shoving her closer to the northern shore than Mirak intended.

"Weed at the surface," shrilled Cookie.

"Luff! Luff! Strike sail. We'll anchor. Get to it, Moke."

The ketch swayed as Moke casually tossed the anchor that Cookie had not been able to lift, and the ketch swung gently back and forth in calm water ruffled by puffs of wind from different directions, as cool night air spilled down the four finger-bays.

"Get your explosives, Fred," Mirak ordered. "Enough to blow a few cottages. Save some for the wharf … and a few of the boats when they return."

"That's not what we agreed," said Fred. "Our deal was that I get to look for the green stones. Then I help you do the Village."

"Stop whimpering and do as you're told."

"All right. But I look for stones first. I'll need her. And Moke to scare off anyone from interfering."

"Oh, very well. Go get your precious stones, if Eliana can find them. While she's fishing for pebbles, you set your charges. Start with the shacks by the wharf. Fire them the same way you did for *Cygnus*, only this time you'll do it as and when I say. Moke, lower the boat. Fred, this time, get it right."

Fred nodded and disappeared into the stern cabin. Ellie heard the squawk of a board being lifted from above the hole where she had discovered the case of bottles.

Ellie looked past Mirak at the row of bait-and-tackle sheds, on up a shadowy path that wound around grey rocks to the first tier of cottages, then zig-zagged on up to a second, a third and possibly a fourth level, each more obscured by trees and bushes than the last. She wondered why nobody had appeared. Surely the villagers must be wondering who had penetrated their almost invisible sea-lake, when none of their boats, and presumably most of the men, were at sea. Was nobody even curious?

Ellie watched the light fade, and with it her hope of being rescued. Moke launched the skiff from the foredeck, climbed in, and brought it alongside the waist, where he held it in position with a huge hand on the cockpit coaming. Fred fetched a small wooden case of straw-wrapped bottles from the stern cabin and passed it down to Moke, urging him to take care. Fred then took a canvass pouch from his pocket, removed six tubes the size of Ellie's index finger, and passed the bundle to Mirak.

"Here, you keep the rest of the igniters."

A desperate plan formed in Ellie's mind. She cupped her hand over her stone, tried to ignore the strange interference that filled the whole secret bay, and messaged as strongly as she could. Green light flashed between her fingers, but no one noticed.

We're at anchor close to the Village

Unless I stop them they're going to blow it up the way they did Cygnus

Her message sent, Ellie clung to the cockpit rail, breathing as if she had just run a race.

"What's wrong?" Mirak demanded.

"I don't know," she gasped. "I never felt this before. It's something here, in the bay."

"It's the source, the mother lode. It has to be," said Fred.

"Well then, Eliana," said Mirak, his voice condescending, "assuming Fred's right and there are more stones there, I want you to collect me some small ones that I can set in rings and sell. Big enough to point north and be really painful if someone pulls them off. Not the shipstones. Get Fred a few arm-sized to experiment with, but nothing big enough for him to blow himself up. I want him around for quite a while yet. And you too, of course."

Ellie shivered.

"Here, take my cloak," said Mirak.

Moke stood up in the dory, reached over the cockpit coaming, and with surprisingly gentle care lowered Ellie onto the stern thwart of the dory, Mirak's cloak hanging loose around her. Fred climbed unsteadily aboard and sat beside her. She composed herself, wrapped a handful of Mirak's cloak around her arm, and sent a final message.

Stay away

3. Ashore

Seren sat at the top of South Head, regularly scanning the bay, the gap between the headlands, and the offing to the east. The water in the bay was black in the shadow of the surrounding, steep-sided hills. Points of yellow light were appearing in the cottage windows of the villagers, even though above the line of the hills the sky was still bright. The water shimmered in the gap far below her feet, roiled by the incoming tide, but the water of the sea lake was a mirror smudged here and there by down-drafted puffs of wind. In the distance, the deep purple of oncoming night crept up from the eastern horizon.

The water into which they had jumped from *Cygnet's* foredeck had been icy cold. Expecting to get wet, Seren had worn the breeks she had cut short for the fight aboard *Elusive,* which proved to be a good idea as they waded ashore, shin-deep in water and rattling pebbles. Cam wanted her to wear shore-going rig in case she met with villagers, but she waited to put her skirt on until they climbed out of the black beach. He had prepared them for an awkward climb, but he had not mentioned the slippery seaweed that clung to the rocks, the barnacles that cut her finger-ends, or the sharp-edged outcropping stones under her bare knees as they scrambled to the clifftop. Half an hour later, when they reached the South Head, a cool wind blew off the distant highlands, and she wished she had worn her seagoing clothes. She tucked the blue skirt around her legs, folded her arms and shivered.

Seren watched shadows climb up the headlands until the sun disappeared behind the western hills, and the sea-lake below darkened to black. She reached for the packsack Cam had left with her before he and Marley started down the steep path to the Village. She rummaged around, felt a thick roll of material around something that glugged and sloshed, and then a soft package that she guessed must be food. She unwrapped carefully, her fingers detecting the buttons of her watch-keeping jacket, which was protecting a deliciously warm stoneware bottle. Moments later, her shivering stilled by another layer of clothing, she was sipping Marley's hot chocolate.

Seren let herself revisit what had happened at the top of the path to the headland. Cam had handed her the packsack he had been carrying, grinned, and started down the trail to the Village. She saw Marley hesitate, his weight on one leg. His face was in shadow, but the angle of his head was an unexpressed question. Letting go of the packsack, she put her hands on his cheeks, drew his face towards her and kissed him. For an instant, he did not react. She dropped her hands. Then she felt him kiss her in return. They stood, leaning forward, only their lips touching.

"You comin', Marley?"

Cam's voice split them apart. Seren stooped for the packsack, and when she stood to her full height, Marley was disappearing among the rocks on either side of the shadowy path.

Warmed by more than the hot drink and her jacket, and with a blush cooled by consternation and the night wind, Seren scanned the darkening sea, her mind a confusion of contradictory thoughts and feelings about her unplanned, unchecked, impulsive action. Still enwrapped in her emotions, she replied to Mairi's question about what she could see with a bleak negative, only to realize a moment later that it was no longer true.

Far below her, the last light of the sun lit the ketch as it sailed through the gap. At the same moment, Ellie's message came to Seren as if shouted in her ear. She went as close as she dared to the edge of the little grassy patch at the top of the headland, and peered downwards.

Seren saw the ketch in a bird's eye view, her sails three slivers of white. The crew were foreshortened shapes, the size of a fingernail seen at arm's length. She held her breath as the white sails flickered in the fading light. The ketch seemed to pause in the narrowest part of the gap, then all her sails bloomed into curved triangles again, and the ship emerged into the bay, where they once again lost their shape and hung slack. The ketch slowly turned in a lazy arc, heading for the Village. Gradually, it entered the shadow of the steep-sided shores, where the sails shivered and sank out of sight. Eventually, Seren could see the hull only because she knew where it had to be.

... at anchor ... Village. ...going to blow ... like Cygnus

Seren winced as she felt Ellie's message, and then relayed what she understood as strongly as she could.

Ellie in ketch at anchor close to Village

They're going to blow it up like Cygnus

Her message incomplete

I can't reach her

I'm going to find the others

She grabbed the packsack and was taking the first strides down the track when Mairi's reply stopped her. In an agony of indecision, she climbed back to the crest of the headland. She was barely at the top when two more words from Ellie reached her:

Stay away

Her mouth dry and her breathing short, Seren repeated Ellie's last message.

4. Aboard *Elusive*

Trogen knew he could procrastinate no longer. He had shirked discussion lest he display his indecision to his officers. By now, they would be doubting him, and his ship would be awash with rumours. Walt's demonstration of the gun had only increased the doubts that had possessed his mind since the storm—throughout which he had remained awake. His felt strangely distant from everything around him; his eyes prickled, and his mouth tasted rotten.

A soft knock roused him from staring at the tabletop. Quickly opening his captain's log, he poised an empty pen before saying "Come," with as much authority as he could muster. Peter's face peered around the half-opened door, his red hair tousled.

"Begging your pardon, Tro ... Skip ... Master, but I've just had a message from Ellie."

"Ellie! You can't have. I felt nothing."

"I was real close to the shipstone. It was like there was fog in the way or a whole lot of noise from many shipstones at once. Here, I wrote down what I could."

Trogen read the note Peter passed to him, amazed that so new a member of those with clasps had detected what he had missed.

Mairi: Seren, what can you see?

Seren: The Village. Most of the four fingers. No boats.

Ellie: It's me, Ellie bound for the Village. Don't talk.

"How did you do this?"

"Um... I can't really say. I've been watching you, of course, but since I got me own clasp, so much just seems ... like ... natural. When you do something with the stones, I just ... get it."

Trogen strove to keep his face expressionless.

"Another thing, Skipper. We're approaching a good vector to make the Village on the starboard tack, and..."

"You've plotted the course?"

Peter nodded. "I thought you wouldn't mind, it being good practice and all. Of course I didn't alter the heading you set at watch change, but I kinda wondered if you'd want to see what I..."

"Show me."

Trogen, stood, slid the chart in front of him, and beckoned Peter to stand on his left. As they bent over the chart, Trogen entered a dream-like moment in which it was he who was seeking approval from a master who was Dabih, then Astreya and then Dabih again. Trogen leaned both fists on the table and repeated the words "Show me," as he had heard them so many times before.

"Dead reckoning since the noon fix places us here." Peter slid parallel rulers into position. "Now if I lay in this course for the Village, and walk the rulers to the compass rose, I come up with almost precisely nor-nor-west."

Trogen breathed in, held it, and spoke slowly, formally, as if conducting a class in navigation.

"What led you to make these assumptions?"

"Well, um, you were busy, and it was my watch, and I wanted to see if I could anticipate what you might be going to do. And because everyone knows that we're going to get Ellie back, and because we're nearly three days further north than Matris, I just assumed we are headed for the Village, because it's the only place on the chart so far north, and it's the only spot where you've written in the lat and long, and..."

"Very good," said Trogen still using the measured tone that had emerged from his memory to rescue him from being flabbergasted by Peter's unexpected performance.

"And another thing, Master. I think you should know that the crew are right behind you on this."

"This?"

"Rescuing Ellie, sir. Real serious, too, because it'll be revenge for what them buggers did to Master Dabih. And the women, even more so. With them, it's like Ellie's the daughter they always wanted, and if they get a hold of anyone who's been messing with her... Well, I won't be volunteering for the cleanup crew when they're finished, if you get what I mean."

"Ah, yes, thank you," said Trogen. "Tell me, how did the crew learn about ..." he tailed off, hoping to sound casual.

"You know how news travels aboard ship, sir. And I've been asked quite a few questions about the Cygnets, specially Ellie, and her sister Seren, and Skipper Mairi, and ..."

Trogen could not keep himself from interrupting. "What about the ... new arrangements?"

"Well, sir, you're the new skipper, and naturally everyone wants to know as much as possible about ..."

"They already do. I served under Dabih for more than ten years. Sailor, leading hand, mate, until..."

"*Cygnet*," Peter continued eagerly. "Most of them expected you'd be master ... not that they have anything against Skipper Mairi. It's that you used to be a '*Lusive*, sir, a shipmate, one of them. And now that Astreya has made you a master, well, it's like you've come home."

"My father hasn't ..."

"...made it official yet. They all know that, too."

Trogen swallowed, took a deep breath and nodded. There was an uncomfortable silence.

"There's just one more thing, sir, and it's a bit awkward. I don't want you to think I'm taking sides against an officer, but I think you should know that among the crew there's quite a lot of ... *feelings*, sir ... about Mate Walt's gun, sir. Something about a pro... a prod... a proscriptive rule, sir."

Peter flinched as Trogen's frown narrowed his eyes.

"The projectile rule. I ... ah ... I know it well."

"That's it. I'm sorry, but it was new to me. Seeing as how I'm the son of a crab-hauling fisherman, sir."

Peter looked at his toes. Trogen frowned at the echo of his own insult. He pressed his lips together and stared in silence. When Peter looked up, Trogen heard his own voice sounding disconcertingly like his father's.

"That's either cheek or grovelling, and neither is appropriate. You are *Elusive's* assistant navigator. You wear a clasp that you have earned."

"Yes, sir."

"Now we will go into the Forbidden Room, where I shall watch you make the necessary adjustments to the shipstone."

"Yes, sir."

~^~

Under Trogen's watchful eye, Peter worked the shipstone, and as dusk turned into night, *Elusive* changed course and headed landward.

"Well done. Now we go on deck to see if ..."

The shipstone flickered. Trogen and Peter both cupped their right hands over their clasps. Trogen bent over the shipstone, concentrating.

"What? Who?" Peter asked.

"It's Ellie. But the signal is so faint I can hardly...

Village ... blow ... Cygnus

I can't make the rest of it out, sir."

The shipstone pulsed again.

"That's Seren sending," said Trogen. "She's repeating."

Ellie in ketch at anchor close to Village

They're going to blow it like Cygnus

That's all she sent

Her message incomplete

I can't reach her. I'm going to find the others

"What's happening? Why is Seren...?"

"Mairi must have landed her."

"Why isn't Skipper Mairi ...

"Quiet. Now it's Mairi, loud and clear."

Stay where you are Seren

I need you to repeat if Ellie messages again

Trogen glared at the shipstone, estimating how long it would take to reach the headland.

"Uh… Moonrise is in two hours."

Peter's diffident suggestion supplied the information Trogen needed and at the same moment, Seren repeated the end of Ellie's message.

Stay away

"Not a chance, Ellie." said Trogen. "We're coming to get you. On deck, Peter, right now."

14. In which nothing goes according to plan

1. Ashore

Climbing up from the black beach was strenuous, but Marley had little trouble following Cam, right up to the moment when they parted. Cam passed the packsack to Seren, said a brief goodbye, and started down from the headland to the Village. Marley was about to echo him, when, totally unexpectedly, Seren kissed him.

A few amazed moments later, Marley followed Cam as best he could in the fading light. Cam anticipated each switchback from memories of his childhood more than two decades earlier, but for Marley, the descent went much too quickly. He had no idea where his feet were taking him in the gloaming, and he dearly wanted to stop and think about what had just happened, when, totally unexpectedly, Seren kissed him.

Years ago, he left home as a young man without a destination or plan. For more than a decade, he had been guided by chance. Mastering the skills of seamanship earned him respect when his abilities were needed, and between those times a grudging acceptance. Women had wanted him either because or despite he was black. None had shown that they appreciated him as a person. He had been isolated, ostracized, and derided until he accepted loneliness and let himself become flotsam on the seas of chance. His survival strategy when threatened was to disengage and move on. He justified his behaviour by calling it flexible.

In explaining himself to the Cygnets, he had realized that Mirak thought him a man ready to compromise his self-respect, and he had even let himself acquiesce. However, Astreya had reawakened who he truly wanted to be, and as a result, he had told the green-eyed Grand Master much more than Mirak intended. Astreya had trusted him on his ship, in his home and with his children. Everything that followed made him commit to *Cygnet* and all aboard her. He had smiled to himself at being one of the Cygnets almost as if he were playing a game, but when Ellie was taken, he had turned his back on his island a second time.

Every step Marley stumbled down the path reminded him that he was part of a course of action that was being made up as they went along. He had silently acquiesced with each increasingly risky decision, from his own quixotic choice to stay aboard *Cygnet* and rescue Ellie, through the conflict in Cottontown that at any other time might have had him fighting alongside the men and women of Black Bay. When they sailed north with no clear plan, he supported Mairi without a qualm. Ignoring Neil's prediction that the rescue was doomed, he followed Cam ashore. As he waded ashore and climbed the steep path, all the misgivings he had been ignoring crept out of the back of his mind, and he was suddenly, catastrophically unsure.

That was when Seren kissed him. The last vestiges of his long-held cynicism disappeared, and he was her devoted warrior.

Marley descended the path in a haze of incoherent emotion. Somehow his feet found their way down the steep switchbacks until he caught up with Cam as the path levelled off into a track through salt-marsh grass. A gibbous moon was rising over the headlands behind him, by whose light he saw the gloom of scrubby trees rising up the hill to his left, and a brightness to his right that he guessed was a low sand dune at the head of the bay, only a stone's throw away. Cam paused to watch the moon draw a lengthening path of glimmering light across the water.

"I saw," said Cam. "Now what are you going to do?"

"Rescue Ellie," said Marley.

"An' then?"

"That's up to Seren."

"Yes, it is. But if you break her heart, I will cut your chest open with a dull, rusty knife, float your body out to sea on a falling tide, bait a lobster trap with your bloody heart, and then eat the lobsters. Clear?"

"Clear as the ketch at anchor in the bay."

Cam clapped Marley on the shoulder, hard enough to be a reminder of his threat, soft enough to be an encouragement to hurry. They ran between waving grasses, grey in the moonlight, guided by Cam's memory and the occasional faint glimpse of the path ahead of them.

A dark shape loomed to their left. Marley guessed it was a rocky outcrop until the path kinked and rose towards it when he saw the outline of a roof. As Cam led him closer, Marley glimpsed yellow-gold light outlining stones around a deep-set window and realized that the cottage had been set on a little hill, and rocks piled shoulder-high around it. They stopped, and Cam knocked on a door that Marley could not see.

"Scarm, it's me, Cam."

Marley heard a gasp, blinked at a widening vee of light, and saw the silhouette of a short, dumpy woman in a long dress.

"Cam! I feared you was dead."

"Only the good die young, Mollie. Glad t' see yer. Is Scarm all of a piece?"

A voice came from the inside the cottage.

"I'm right good, considerin' the alternative."

Marley followed Cam into the cottage.

"Scarm, Mollie, meet Marley, the best steersman I ever seen. Now let us in so's we can all decide what's to be done about the evil bastards in the ketch what just dropped her pick only a little ways from the Village wharf."

The grey-haired woman looked up wide-eyed and waved Marley to a chair. She cast wondering glances in Marley's direction as Cam told her that there was no time for food, drink or the questions she craved to ask.

Marley sat in a corner, silently watching and listening as Cam talked to the old man who was reclining in a bed set close enough to the fireplace for his face to be lit by the flames. Marley could see that Scarm's eyes were milky white, and his hands frail. However, the old fisherman had no difficulty in grasping the situation. He listened intently, and when he spoke Marley recognized the voice of a man who would never be doubted.

Scarm despatched Mollie to the nearest cottage to spread the word that there was danger at the waterfront and that all the women and children should stay in their cottages until given the all-clear. Mollie nodded, tucked the blankets more tightly around Scarm and bustled out the door, lantern in hand.

"When I get to Susan's house, we'll put a light in the kitchen window," she said as she left.

Marley wondered how this would warn the entire Village until Scarm loosened the blankets, chuckled, turned his blind gaze directly at Marley and explained as if he had read his thoughts.

"Each woman's kitchen window looks out on at least two others in easy talkin' distance. They'll all know before the first one has put a cup of tea in Mollie's hand."

"That's a bit like the island where I grew up."

"Foine 'ting. More about that, an' you, when it's all been sorted. There's another lantern what opens and closes here by me bed, me lead line's back o' the door, an' there's a couple stout sticks on yer way out. Come back soon's yer done an' tell me everythin'."

Cam hesitated.

"Yer ... yer lookin' good, Scarm."

"Yer still an awful liar, Cam, get away wi' ye."

As they went out the door, Cam took a deep breath. Marley recognized the sound of a man resolutely overcoming an uncharacteristic display of emotion. The moonlit path towards the Village was easy to follow at first, but after a short while it was shadowed first by shrubs and then bushes and finally it tunnelled in darkness under the intermingled branches of great pines whose resinous scent perfumed the air. Cam stopped to light Scarm's lantern, which he closed on three sides so that it only kept them from tripping over the tree-roots of the silent trees. Perhaps a hundred dark strides later, Marley heard the rushing sound of a stream, and they came out from under the trees onto a log bridge. Cam stopped, closed the lantern, and they looked down on the swiftly moving water. Moonlight glimmered on shallow rapids flowing in a rush towards the dark waters of the bay over and around the trunks of fallen trees. Marley could barely hear Cam's voice for the constant sound.

"Must 'a been a some fierce winter for snow, an' then a fast thaw to bring down so many trees an' rocks. We're lucky it didn't take out the bridge."

Silvered by moonlight, a rowing boat was approaching the stony outfall. An outsize figure sculled the boat until its bow grounded on the beach. The hulking shape of a huge man separated from the curved shape of the boat. Two more people stood up in the boat: a silhouette holding a lantern, and another smaller figure.

"Ellie!" Marley whispered.

"An' the monster," Cam whispered back, as he shrugged out of the coil of finger-width light rope he had carried over one shoulder. "I ain't as good as Scarm used to be, but I reckon if I can get a bit closer, I might be able to sling the lead around his legs so's he'll fall over, an' then you can get close enough to ..."

"Whack him," supplied Marley.

"You got it. Now, if we can stay in the shadows along the starboard bank, we might get close enough fer me to take a shot. We're going down to the beach. Come on."

He swung himself over the low handrail onto a huge boulder that anchored the end of the bridge. Marley followed him, picking his way first on unsteady, head-sized rocks then over successively smaller stones down to the stream, steadying himself with one of Scarm's club-like sticks. When another step would have put him in shin-deep water, he looked up past the log bridge, now higher than he could reach above his head. Upstream, between the trees on either side, a few bright stars prickled a slice of sky; downstream, beyond the moon-dazzle on the ripples, the stream fanned out onto a pebbly delta.

Marley and Cam saw the giant unfold himself, step out of the boat, hold it steady for a slim cloaked figure, and then take two strides to the bow. The third person stepped ashore, froze, and screamed, "No! Don't pick it up!" as the giant began to haul up the boat. All three silhouettes began to run, coalescing into a single shape.

A fireball rose above both stream and beach. The explosion punched Marley and Cam with sound so intense they felt it in their chests. They fell back against the black boulder, clutching at the rock to keep their balance. They both shouted, but could not hear their own voices. Destruction ripped past them, trees flailed overhead, shards of wood spattered on the rocks and splashed into the bay. A section of the boat's side howled past them and shattered against the bridge. At the water's edge, red fire plumed upward, shot through with airborne missiles. Where the boat and its occupants had been was a spreading pool of flame.

2. Aboard *Cygnet*

Mairi glimpsed *Elusive's* moon-lit sails on the horizon as she and Alan rehoisted the sails that they had struck to have *Cygnet* masquerade as a fishing boat. Working together, the three of them clawed *Cygnet* upwind and away from the black-beach cove where the other half of the crew had landed. Astern, Neil steered one-handed, his arm in a sling from the encounter with the mizzen gaff. Raising the main had taken all Mairi and Allan could do, even with the help of a winch. When they had the schooner sailing in good order and were back in the cockpit.

"Good work. We did it," said Mairi.

She patted first Alan and then Neil on the shoulder, pleased to see the satisfaction on both their expressions.

Knowing how difficult it was to detect the gap between the headlands, Mairi sent:

Elusive home on Cygnet

Monitor Seren

She then explained what she had done to the two lads. Gratified to be included them in her plans, they worked enthusiastically to tack *Cygnet* back and forth as close to the gap as she dared. Together, they watched the great ship bearing down towards them under a line of clouds blowing landwards from the east.

Like all schooners, when *Cygnet* tacked under full sail in a steady wind, only the jib needed tending, but as Mairi put her about for the eighth time, she knew that her ship was carrying too much canvass for a lee shore and a rising sea. Her much reduced, young crew had worked well to hoist the sails they had struck to disguise *Cygnet*, and they were enthusiastically keeping her sailing, but they would not be able to reef or strike sail safely when the wind piped up.

Resolutely refusing the trap of re-examining decisions she had taken, Mairi persisted with her plan to patrol the gap, wait for Seren's messages, and be a beacon for *Elusive*. As she completed the southward leg of her zigzag sentry-go, *Cygnet* dug her lee rail into waves that now splashed the cockpit coaming. Over her right shoulder, Mairi glimpsed *Elusive* emerge from cloud shadow, running downwind goose-winged, her staysails swelling on either side, back-lit by the rising moon. To her left, the south head loomed higher than *Cygnet's* masts. Breaking waves growled at the cliffs, breakers threw up white spray at the feet of the black headlands, the water in the gap shone silvery grey where it heaved up the waves that were forcing their way into the bay.

A red flash outlined the gap in the cliffs. Mairi blinked, and the wan moonlight returned. Out of the sea-lake came a drum-roll of sound, louder than the surf, the wind and *Cygnet's* rush through waves. Almost immediately, her arm prickled with Seren's message.

Explosion on shore

Ketch still afloat

I can't reach Ellie

Mairi did not hesitate.

"Ease the sheets! We're going in."

She sent her message as she swung the wheel.

Seren we're coming

Trogen if you follow keep to starboard

3. Aboard *Elusive*

Elusive charged landward, a rising wind filling every sail she could carry, with the westering sun blinding the lookouts to anything more than the outline of the rugged coast ahead. Trogen prowled the quarterdeck from side to side, now looking ahead to the thickening shoreline, now giving orders to trim *Elusive's* sails, now having Peter check the plot and shipstone, now glaring at his crew as if they were not attentive enough for him.

He had begun the headlong rush towards the Village with a peremptory demand to get the gun off his quarterdeck. His order took Walt by surprise, as did Trogen's refusal to discuss the matter after the gun had disappeared. Walt completed his watch in brooding silence and went below. Damon took over, looking frail but sounding confident. Late in the afternoon watch of a long, intense day, he tried to open a conversation with Trogen but received only a frowning stare. With a shrug, Damon left him alone. As the sun sank towards the line of the cliff-tops and the sea darkened, Peter appeared on deck to report their heading, progress, and speed. Trogen merely nodded. Emboldened, Peter voiced a thought shared by everyone aboard the big schooner.

"Sure hope the lat and long on the chart is accurate, or..."

Trogen did not let him finish.

"Do you think Grand Master Astreya made up a few likely numbers and scribbled them on the chart just to confuse us into wrecking the ship?"

"Um... No, sir. I meant no disrespect, sir."

Trogen bit back more sarcasm.

"Do you have a bearing on _Cygnet_?"

"Pretty much bang on the same as the lat and long, sir."

"And what do you deduce from that?"

"It's what Skipper Mairi sent, sir. Telling us to home on _Cygnet's_ shipstone, sir."

"And that's what we're doing."

"Right, sir. Sorry I spoke out of turn."

Trogen spoke as if the conversation had been exclusively for Peter's benefit, but he knew it was overheard. Inwardly strengthened by having voiced his intentions, Trogen watched the light fade into gloaming above the continuous wall of cliffs. He still could see nothing to corroborate their heading save the evidence of

Cygnet's shipstone and the coordinates Astreya had written on a chart twenty years earlier.

A brief red glow outlined the gap in the cliffs ahead. Seren's desperate message tingled on his arm. Whatever the cause, Trogen had confirmation.

"Leading seaman of the watch! Rouse all hands and the cook."

As footfalls thudded on deck and below, the moon rose out of the clouds that had been pursuing *Elusive* since before sunset. Ahead, the cliffs turned a ghostly grey against a starry, western sky.

"Sail, dead ahead!"

The lookout shouted from the foredeck. Mairi's signal tingled on Trogen's arm, and beside him, Peter twitched as he, too, grasped her intention to enter the bay.

"Steersman, keep us heading towards that sail," Trogen ordered, and then as *Cygnet* disappeared beyond the gap and the steersman looked at him anxiously, "Just hold your course."

Trogen continued in what he hoped was a calm voice, "Damon, Walt, we'll keep her goosewinged going through. Come out the other side on the starboard tack. There'll be wind fluctuations as we go by the headlands. I control the main; Damon, the mizzen stays'ls; Walt, the fore. Walt? Where's Walt?"

"Foredeck, I believe," said Damon.

"Then pass the word. Steersman, keep to the starboard side of the channel. Right. Here we go."

The cliffs were ominous black shapes in the gloaming as *Elusive* sped towards them with frightening speed, heading for the notch of pale sky that marked the channel. One moment the ship was in water confused by waves reflected off the cliffs; the next, as the headlands loomed on either side, her bow was lifted by a swell higher than the waves under her stern. She climbed the wave made of water compressed between the two headlands and rode it through the gap, where it spilled into the bay, falling away under her. Trogen felt the stern touch bottom in a brief, barely perceptible thump.

"We're through!" yelled Peter, dancing with excitement.

"Starboard tack!" Trogen roared, and then quietly to the steersman in the calm near-silence of the fjord, "Bring her round, easy now."

Her sails slack, *Elusive* silently described a wide arc around the middle of the protected water of the bay until she was headed to where it looked as if someone had left a bonfire to die on its embers. Framed by the black shapes of the surrounding hills, the still water of the bay mirrored the last light from the sky as the moon silvered the western end of the bay.

"Ready with the forward anchor, stand by with the stern kedge," Trogen ordered.

"There's *Cygnet* heading for what looks like a wharf," said Peter. "And isn't that the ketch, ahead?"

"We'll anchor. *Elusive* draws more than twice the depth *Cygnet* needs.... Stand by the forward anchor, let go aft.... Wait for it.... Set the stern kedge.... Now pay out the slack as we go .... Let go forward.... Take the strain astern and haul .... Set the pick ahead... Belay. Strike all sail."

Her way already lessened for lack of wind, *Elusive* eased to a standstill, her moonlit decks alive with activity. A sharp crack echoed and re-echoed off the steep, dark hills. Trogen was still concentrating on the maneuver he had executed, although a recent memory nagged at the back of his mind.

"What was that?" Peter asked. "Did we break a spar?"

Red fire bloomed upwards from the ketch, reflected in the water below, momentarily colouring *Elusive's* half-furled sails, which shook, flapped against masts, spars, and stays and tugged halyards from crew's hands as the shock wave struck. Hard on the heels of the blast came a roar that renewed and renewed itself as it ricocheted around the steep-sided bay with a sound like huge empty barrels rolling down a steep, rocky road.

Where the ketch had been, burning fragments fell hissing into the water.

Ellie

Trogen, Mairi, Seren, and Peter simultaneously sent out an agonized cry from their clasps. The tingling on their arms continued as all tried to ask questions at the same time. When they realized what they were doing, they all stopped. It was then that they realized only the four of them had reacted. None of them had felt anything from Ellie.

4. Ashore

Wind from the sea plucked at Seren's jacket, but her skirt hung in still air, protected by the waist-high, rocky parapet of her lookout. She paced the little grassy area at the top of the headland from which she had stared almost directly down on first *Cygnet* and then *Elusive* as they ran the gap, their sails ghostly in the rising moon. Then, as the two ships slowly moved across the still, black waters of the bay, she became increasingly impatient, feeling useless and forgotten.

The first explosion took her by surprise, plunging her into indecision. Her instinct was to run down towards whatever might have happened, but her orders from Mairi held her irresolute. When the second explosion lit the bay, Seren cringed as the echoes boomed around the bowl of steep-sided hills. Wrapping her hand around her clasp, she joined the anxious chorus and then shared the terrible recognition that Ellie had not answered. Seren stood appalled for a heartbeat while her stone tingled meaninglessly on her arm. She snatched up the packsack and threw herself down the steep path.

Her feet found the way through the first few shadowy strides but blinded by tears, she missed the first switchback turn and would have plunged off the cliff had she not stumbled onto knees already cut and bruised by the climb out of the black cove. She regained the path, her heart pounding in her throat. Realizing that she had barely avoided a screaming plunge onto the rocks below, she chose her way more carefully. Her clasp prickled her arm meaninglessly, and she cursed it for being useless now she needed it most. When she had climbed the headland, hours earlier, she had concentrated on keeping up with Cam and Marley; going down she had nothing to guide her. She hurried as fast as she dared, but the narrow trail was visible only in moonlit patches between the black shadows of rocks around which it zigged and zagged downwards.

After what seemed an interminable descent, the path levelled off. Her legs no longer ached with each downward step, although she winced whenever her skirt swept across the cuts on her knees. Seren almost welcomed the physical pain that distracted her from the hollow-hearted agony of losing Ellie.

The moon silvered the flat, marshy land at the foot of the headland, shone on the grasses and silhouetted the hills against a deep purple sky, wanly lit by the rising moon. She saw the track she followed widen and recognized the path they had taken from the bay where they had landed. She turned north, where to her right, she saw fire on the water. Seren saw it had to be the ketch, adrift, her moorings burned by the flames that still flickered up her masts. In glimpses when she could take her attention from following the path through knee-high grasses, she watched the burning vessel swing slowly past the Village into the outfall of the stream, which shoved the doomed ship towards the whirlpools at the base of the headland that Seren had just descended. What remained of the ketch twirled slowly as it burned to the waterline.

"Hey! Watch where you're goin'!"

Seren checked her stride and looked down on blond hair bleached almost white by the pale moonlight. A child looked up at her, his lantern casting light on small, booted feet, shin-high breeks, and the surrounding high grasses.

"Who're you?"

"I'm Seren."

"Sern. Foine. S'what he said. I'm Jack, an' I'm t'show yer the way."

"Who said?"

"Feller I never seed before, name o' Cam. Me Ma knew who he was, though. Welcomed him in't th' house like he was fam'ly."

"Jack, did he say anything about Ellie?"

"Who's she?"

"My sister."

"Don't know nothin' 'bout her. There was just the two of 'em what came to our door. Old Mollie brung 'em. Me ma an' me brother Al and her all went off together, headin' for the stream, where I'm t'take you. There was them, an' Cam, an' a real tall feller what must 'a got hisself burned black on 'is face 'n hands."

"Marley. He's not burned, it's ... Jack, can we get moving? I really need to talk to them."

"You got it, Sern. Jus' follow me lantern."

5. Aboard *Cygnet*

Mairi felt *Cygnet* subside under her feet. Running the gap had been exhilarating: the southeast wind had piped up, the waves tumbled the entrance to the gap into a chaotic chop until they collected into the huge roller that carried *Cygnet* into the bay. Dying firelight gave her a clue to her destination, and she could guess the location of the wharf because Astreya's sketch had told her where to look. *Cygnet* steadily lost way, her sails barely ghosting her in the fluky winds that ruffled the bay almost randomly.

"It's *Elusive!*" Neil yelled.

Mairi looked astern, confirmed what he saw, glanced to starboard, and saw the ketch at anchor, then stared ahead to gauge the distance to the wharf.

"Neil, can you take the wheel?"

"Sure can."

His good hand replaced hers on the centre spoke.

"See the wharf?"

"Maybe. I think so. Yes."

"Steady as she goes, then swing her around gently to line up, and then hard a-port to bring the stern alongside. Alan, ready the fenders and the lines to shore, please. You have the bow, I've got the stern. We'll strike sail at the wharf."

As *Cygnet* completed her oblique approach, moonlight gleamed on mooring posts along the wharf.

"I can see it now, for sure."

"Good work, Neil. Now, hard a-port. Alan, let fly the sheets!"

Neil spun the wheel, and *Cygnet* slid sideways into the wharf. Alan slung a fender over the starboard bow, took hold of the bow line and prepared to leap. A heartbeat later, as Mairi was securing the stern fender, she was rammed against the coaming by the shockwave from the explosion on the ketch. *Cygnet's* slack sails filled with the sudden gust. The ship heeled towards the wharf, lit by a red glow. The main boom swung out over the wharf in a murderous arc. Deafening sound caught up with the shock-wave, momentarily stunning all three of them. Alan scrambled to his feet first, found he was still holding the bow line, but hesitated when he saw that *Cygnet's* bow had surged beyond the wharf.

Astern, Neil was thrown against the wheel, his good arm caught between two spokes. By the red light of the burning ketch, he saw Mairi, doubled over the cockpit coaming. When she did not move, he snatched the stern mooring line from under her body and threw himself over the side at the wharf. He landed awkwardly, slammed his wounded shoulder against a bollard, and fell to his knees. Yelling with a mixture of pain and triumph, he slung a turn of the mooring line around the stump of wood, and hung on as the rope bit into the wooden post, checking *Cygnet's* forward momentum. Neil got to his feet, threw another turn around the bollard, leaned on it and looked around. He saw fire leaping out of the ketch, reaching higher than the mastheads. Debris from decks and cabins still rose into the night and splashed down into the water. The mainmast sagged, its stays on fire. The ruined ship drifted aimlessly. There was no sign of her crew.

6. Aboard *Elusive*

Elusive shivered from bow to stern, her canvass a-shake. On the quarterdeck, Trogen saw the ketch explode just before he was blown off his feet. When he got to his feet, winded and bruised but otherwise unhurt, he almost fell over Damon, who had also been struck down. Trogen knelt beside him.

"Damon! Are you all right?"

Damon's lips moved, Trogen heard nothing, so he shouted again, louder.

"Don't shout, Skipper. I'm all of a piece. How's the ship?"

"At first glance, she'll do. But the ketch is on fire, what's left of her."

"Trogen, just before the explosion I heard..."

"Walt's gun."

"Trogen, nobody could survive that blast. Walt's killed Ellie. Now he wants your ship."

Trogen ran forward, dodging the men and women who were picking themselves up and striking sail. He leaped onto the main cabin top, ran its length, grabbed the halyards and swung around the mainmast, repeated his breakneck dash toward the bow over the fore-cabin, around mizzen and foremast, and leaped onto the foredeck. Ahead of the anchor windlass, between the half-bundled jib and foresail was Walt, reloading the gun. He looked up at Trogen.

"Walt! You killed Ellie."

"Hold on, Trog," said Walt, his voice almost normal. "'Course I didn't. She was dead already. In the boat what Mirak sent ashore for shipstones. S'obvious. It's why they're here, isn't it?" Seeing Trogen's mounting fury, his tone changed to wheedling. "Yer upset about yer little cousin, ain't 'cha? An' it's making you foolish."

Peter shouted from the fore cabin top.

"He killed Ellie to stop her telling us what really happened in Cottontown."

"Shut your mouth," Walt snarled.

"You were in it with Mirak all along, weren't you, Walt?" said Trogen. "You knew about the attack on *Elusive*, didn't you? You never wanted to rescue Ellie, because..."

Walt swung the gun to point towards Trogen, crouched behind it, one eye screwed shut, his uneven teeth bared. Trogen froze.

"She was family, Walt."

"Family?" Walt yelled, his voice breaking. "My father, Mufrid, was family. He was Master of *Elusive,* what I should be, not you, Trog, you little snot. Don't you talk to me about family. Your da 'Streya killed my da. Then 'cause we is family, he gave me a diddly little ring, an' the job of lookin' after all of the buyin' an' sellin' an' dealin' he's too important t'do fer hisself. Fer twenty years I worked for 'Streya, an' then he gave Ellie the last clasp. She's nowhere as close to Oron as me, but she gets a clasp and training as a wielder like I wasn't twice more family than her. An' then he gives yer sister the little schooner, 'cause she's family. An' you got '*Lusive*, 'cause you're family." His voice went from a growl to an eerie scream. "Family! Family what never gave me nothin'. So now I'm gettin' even. Startin' with this ship. Me da's ship. My ship!"

Trogen stared at the gun, frozen, waiting for death to leap out of the muzzle.

Peter dived from the cabin top, his shoulder striking Trogen's thigh. They both saw the gun flash as they fell, rolling over and over in a tangle of legs and arms across the foredeck on into the loose folds of the jib. They strove to get free, even though to do so was to make themselves into targets.

Trogen struggled to his knees. As his head came clear of the canvass, he glimpsed tangled hair. Expecting a second shot at any moment, he put a hand on Peter's head and pushed him back down. Another gunshot slapped at their ears, followed by an agonized scream, cut short. Something whined through the air close above them, but all Trogen could see was a grey cloud blossoming up from the deck, coiling around the masts where it turned red in the light from the burning ketch.

"Walt!" Trogen yelled into the smoke. Nobody answered.

Trogen and Peter emerged unsteadily from the folds of the jib. Someone came forward with a lantern. They saw Damon, standing by the foremast, one hand holding a halyard.

"The gun blew up. A piece of it went into his eye." Damon's voice was flat, unemotional. "Walt's dead."

15. In which many people arrive at the Village

"Skipper Mairi? You all right?"

Mairi waved her hands and nodded. Gradually, her breathing steadied, she pushed herself to a standing position and took inventory of her crew and ship. Neil was on the wharf, one-handedly belaying the lines to shore. Alan, reassured now that Mairi was upright and looking around, was lowering the mainsail by the light of the burning ketch, which as she watched, drifted away from its mooring, born on the currents of the bay towards *Cygnet*.

"Get the sails off her, quickly," she whispered hoarsely to Alan as she clambered onto the cabin top. "And stand by to fend off!"

They cast off the main halyards and let fall the gaff, bringing the canvass down in an untidy rush, moved on to the foremast, repeated the process, and then hauled down the staysail and jib, glancing over their shoulders at the fireship drifting towards them. The sails roughly bundled, Mairi and Alan grabbed the ruined dory's oars and prepared to fend off the burning ketch, even though they feared their efforts would be futile. Seeing them with oars in hand, ready to defend *Cygnet*, Neil climbed back aboard, found a boathook and poised it on the port gunwale as best he could with one hand. The three of them stood watching the ketch as fire consumed the cabins, roared out the hatches, crackled up the masts and dripped blazing tar from the mainstay. The burning threat slowly turned broadside. They felt its heat on their faces, and they saw into what had been the cockpit. Oily black smoke rose from something that was not a part of the ship.

"Gimme strength," Neil gasped. "That's someone burning. Shouldn't we..."

"Too late," said Alan.

As the smoke billowed towards *Cygnet*, all three of them recoiled at the smell of burning flesh. Neil retched. The ketch slowly rotated until the stern faced them. Flames spurted from broken scuttles; the remains of the mizzen sail hung over the side, smouldering. As they watched, the shrouds burned through, the mainmast sagged, the ship lurched towards them, and the spar fell hissing into the water, so close that Alan reflexively poked with his oar, even though it was out of reach. All three were now convinced that the ketch would set fire to *Cygnet*, but at the last moment, the burning hulk gradually changed course, drifted past them, was caught by the outfall from the village stream and retreated towards the eastern shore of the bay.

Mairi reacted slowly. Gradually, it dawned on her that luck, fate, or circumstances had cooperated to save them. Now the threat was averted, she knew that she should have abandoned ship to save her crew when it became obvious that *Cygnet* was about to be set afire. With that realization came painful reminders of how she had been tossed into the cockpit coaming. Her chest ached every time she took a deep breath. Her throat still dry with anxiety and the hot air they all had been breathing, she spoke in a hoarse whisper.

"Alan, Neil ... are you all right?"

"A wee bit toasted," said Alan. "There's been some blistering to the paint and varnish..."

"Neil?"

"That was ... close. I thought we were cooked."

"You came back aboard..."

"We couldn't let her burn," said Neil, stating the obvious.

"Thank you."

"*Cygnet!* Mairi! Are you all right?"

Mairi swung around to see *Elusive's* longboat silhouetted against the moon. A lantern between the rowers lit Trogen, who was standing in the stern, yelling her name. Mairi tried to shout, but could only manage a croak, followed by a spasm of coughing.

"Skipper Mairi is safe aboard," Alan shouted.

While Mairi was still getting her breath back, the longboat drew alongside *Cygnet*. Trogen vaulted aboard the stern, rushed past Neil to the foredeck, where he grabbed Mairi and hugged her.

"Mairi ... Ellie's gone. Walt shot the ketch. His gun blew up. He's dead. So's Mirak, and ... and ... I thought you were too..."

"I lost her, Trogen. We were too late. I should have..."

"Mairi, it's not your fault. If I had only ..."

They clung to each other for a few heartbeats, and then recollecting their duty as masters, drew apart.

"Begging your pardon, Masters," said Alan, "but there's folks coming this way."

Mairi saw lights flicker down the path through the trees as people made their way down from the cottages further up the hillside. Four figures, two tall and two short, came onto the open area beside the wharf.

"*Cygnet!* Mairi! Are you all right? S'me, Cam."

Mairi climbed ashore and ran to meet them, Trogen only a pace behind.

Cam raised his lantern and grinned at her.

"Lass, when that ketch bore down on you, blazin' like a bonfire, I thought you was a goner."

"We're all right, Cam," said Mairi. Then her throat tightened and her voice rose. "But Ellie..."

A slim shape rushed into Mairi's arms, a black cloak billowing behind her. For a few moments, Mairi and Ellie clung together, wordless. Then Ellie pushed at Mairi's shoulders until she could stand on her own.

"Assistant Navigator Eliana reporting for duty, Mistress Mairi."

For the first time in days, Mairi laughed in a sudden explosion of air that was almost a sob, then hugged Ellie again, her eyes wet with tears.

"Ouch! Easy! Under this cloak, I'm a bit bruised."

"Did those bastards hurt you, Ellie?" Trogen demanded.

"They were scary, but no. One of them saved my life ... our lives. But it's so sad, Mairi. He saved me and Fred, and ... he's gone."

"Who?"

"Moke. The giant."

"The monster we all fought with?"

"He only did as he was told, and we were in the way. He's ... he was gentle. Like a great big friendly dog. But he was a lot bigger and stronger than he was bright, and Mirak took advantage of him. Mairi, did anyone survive the explosion on the ketch?"

"Ah ... I'm sure at least one didn't," said Mairi.

"There's one, maybe two bodies floating in the bay," said Trogen. "Our oars fouled one, but we were in a rush to get here, so we didn't..."

"Ellie, what are you wearing?"

"Mirak's cloak. He loaned it to me. It protected me from the fire after the explosion. Underneath, I'm wearing Village clothes Mollie found for me after I had the best hot water wash ever."

"Start from the beginning, Ellie. What happened?

"Mirak sent me and Fred and Moke ashore. I was supposed to look for stones, Fred was told to blow up the wharf and boathouses, and Moke was along to row and stand guard. On our way, Fred and I agreed ... well, I told him he'd better not blow anything up, or I'd explode his head like Astreya did to Mufrid ... and then he agreed. Just to make sure, I stole the ignitors out of his pocket. When we got to where the river reaches the bay, Fred and I climbed out of the rowboat, and I must have dropped one or two of them. Fred said ... well, never mind what he said. What happened was that before he could rescue the ignitor, Moke picked up the bow of the boat, and the igniters rolled down to the explosives, and set them off. We could hear them fizzling about in the stern, so we tried to run away, but we couldn't. And I fell, and Fred fell, and Moke threw himself on top of us so we'd be all right. And we were. But he wasn't. Mairi, he knew. At the last moment, he threw his big arms around us, and he saved us."

"She's right," said Cam. "Marley an' me seen it happen. We were the ones what hauled the big feller off'n her and Fred. He protected 'em from the biggest damn 'splosion I ever saw ... until the ketch went up, an' that was twice as big, an' more."

"Mairi," said Seren. "When I saw the boat blow up, I was sure Ellie was gone, and then when there was another explosion, I thought maybe you were too, and ..."

"Seren..." Mairi gasped as she was again hugged tight.

"Well, I wasn't," said Ellie firmly. "And neither was your skipper, who you are embracing in a decidedly unseamanlike fashion."

Seren abruptly disengaged.

"What about you, Marley, Are you all right?" Mairi asked.

"Ah ... never better, Skipper," said Marley.

Seren took his hand, and blushed. Mairi looked at them, puzzled.

"We got comp'ny," said Cam. "Looks like I'm about to be introducin' you to Red Ian, who's what we'd call the Grand Master of the Village fleet."

Mairi turned to see a shaft of dazzling light cut across the water as the rising sun pierced between the headlands. First one, then two, then a succession of sails appeared with the light behind them as they ran the gap into the bay.

"We're taking space at their wharf," said Mairi.

"I'm on it, Skipper," said Cam. "C'mon, Seren, Marley. We need to move her out of the way. Alan an' Neil, you too. Not you, Ellie. You still got more to tell the skippers."

"Ellie, what does Cam mean? What more do you need to tell us?"

There was a disturbance under the cloak that enveloped Ellie from her shoulders to the ground, and her hands appeared. One held many small green pebbles, the other three or four stones bigger than her thumb.

"Here, hold these," said Ellie, pouring the stones into Trogen's hands. "Now, look at this."

Her hands disappeared into the cloak, then returned with two stones the size and shape of big eggs. They glowed softly in her palms, lighting her slim fingers. Mairi's eyes widened.

"Shipstones!" Trogen gasped.

"There's more in all my pockets," said Ellie. "And over there is where I found them. Cam and Marley hauled Moke off me, and while they were finding out that he was dead and Fred's leg was broken, I looked down. We were standing on a glowing green river of stones."

From one of the paths leading to the wharf came a child's voice. "Here they come!"

Mairi saw children in homespun clothes appearing in the approaches to the wharf. Behind them, anxious-looking mothers talked in whispers, their youngest clinging to their skirts. The knot of mothers and children parted, and a very old man walked slowly towards them, supported on one side by a short, dumpy woman with white hair and on the other by a tow-haired youngster. Mairi and

Trogen glanced at each other, wondering what the villagers thought about the three ships that had appeared with such sound and fury into their harbour, so long a secret from the outside world.

"That's Scarm," said Cam, from aboard *Cygnet*. "He sailed south with 'Streya, an' he knew 'Streya's da."

"He's nice," said Ellie. "He asked me a whole lot of questions, but I liked it because he really listened to what I said. And I think he knows about the stones, too."

As the newcomers approached, Ellie performed introductions.

"Scarm, these are my cousins, Mairi, skipper of the little schooner, *Cygnet*, and Trogen, her brother, who's skipper of *Elusive* ... the big one. Their parents are Astreya and Lindey."

Mairi took the hand Scarm held out. Realizing that he was sightless, she murmured her name and a respectful greeting, marvelling at how his clouded eyes seemed to look into hers. Trogen followed her example. The old man took a moment to consider, but when he spoke his voice was clear and steady.

"It's been a right long time since I saw your father, an' I've missed him. But later for all that. About today: there's been lives lost, just as happened when 'Streya went south. It looks like the men who kidnapped Ellie and threatened the Village have all perished an' from what I've heard from Cam, Seren, Marley, and Ellie, it seems that most all of them that's gone invited their own deaths. By good fortune, none of you young people were hurt."

He paused, leaving room for interruptions, but when silence approved his summary of events, he continued.

"I'd like to tell you you're welcome here in the Village, but mine is not the only voice that needs to be heard. So now, if some kind person will find me something to sit on, we'll wait until Red Ian and the other skippers arrive, an' then we can sort the whole thing out."

16. Epilogue: In which Mairi and Trogen talk, three days later

"Trogen, let's walk to where Seren stood lookout. You and I need to talk."

"After three days, haven't you had enough talk?"

"More than enough. But it could have been worse. We were lucky that Scarm remembered Cam, and that the Villagers understand about complicated family relationships, or we'd still be trying to explain how Walt was and wasn't our uncle. That's over. Now you and I have to decide what and how we're going to tell Astreya, Lindey, and Cat."

"Start with Ellie alive, and the stones safe," said Trogen.

"Then we'll tell them about Dabih, and how Walt was involved, and that he's dead and his gun is at the bottom of the bay."

"Along with Mirak and his crew," said Trogen. "That's not going to be a short or easy story to tell."

"You're right," said Mairi. "And there's a lot of grieving that they'll have to go through. You and I have a head start, but we're not done yet."

"I know," said Trogen. "Every time I go into the stern cabin, I expect to see Dabih, and if I believed in ghosts, I'd say *Elusive's* foredeck will be forever haunted by Walt."

Matching strides, they followed the path past Scarm's cottage toward the South Head, their thoughts focused on Dabih's death and Walt's treachery.

"I was too late to save Dabih," said Mairi, "and I never noticed that Walt was so ... so embittered."

"It's not your fault Dabih's dead, Mairi. Dabih died because Walt turned traitor," said Trogen. "Mirak was using him, but Walt chose to do what he did, all the while believing that he was using

Mirak. Walt used me, too, and he planned to go on using me after
Mirak killed Father. Worse, when he realized Ellie could expose
him, he tried to kill her. Luckily, she wasn't aboard the ketch, and
he killed Mirak instead."

As they climbed up the switchbacked path to the lookout, Mairi
thought about how many more people might have been killed, both
in the Village and at Matris, had Mirak's revenge and Walt's
resentment played out. When they reached the top, she looked down
on the Village and the still water of the landlocked bays where the
second day of trading was drawing to a close.

"Isn't that Cam and Red Ian still making lists of what the
villagers are taking?"

Trogen nodded.

"They're cleaning us out of metalwork, glass, and cotton, but
they're not too sure about food and drink."

"The skippers aren't having too much difficulty getting used to
rum," said Mairi. "Trogen, do you think we should..."

"Stop them? Limit them? Tell them we don't approve after you
and I poured them all a toast to our agreement? Come on now,
Mairi. They make their own whiskey. They're adults. They can
decide for themselves. You know the rule: 'Deal fairly, don't get
involved.'"

"We're already involved. What I'm concerned about is the
'fair' part."

"We've got that covered," said Trogen. "I take Scarm, Mollie,
and Red Ian aboard _Elusive_, along with that seriously dangerous
fellow Fred, who but for Ellie I would happily shove over the side
with shackles on his ankles and rocks in his socks. Anyway, the
three senior Village people, are going to work out the details for the
future with the Grand Master, the Navigator, and the Chief Healer ...
plus you and me ... at Matris. We're to be part of the negotiation to
make sure the Village doesn't get greedy."

"Greedy? Trogen, we almost had to twist their arms to get them to exchange the ring stones, clasp stones, and shipstones that Ellie found for their pick of our trade goods."

"Until they saw what it is that we carry. We've dumped a lot of valuable cargo into their laps with nothing in return except a pocketful of stones. After this, we trade the stones in fair exchange of value on both sides"

"What's fair, Trogen?"

"What Scarm, Mollie, and Red Ian negotiate with Astreya, Lindey, Cat, and you and me. We're in command of ships bearing shipstones."

"What is the real value of the stones, Trogen?"

"Who knows? When we thought there were only three shipstones, six clasps and a handful of ring stones, they were priceless. Then Ellie found her river of stones running through the Village, and all of a sudden they have worth as items of trade. And as for value, don't forget that some of Villagers wanted to give them away."

"And then I told them that if they put a shipstone here on the South Head, and gave ring stones to all the skippers, they'd find their way home whatever the wind or weather," said Mairi.

"Assuming there's a wielder or two among them, and provided the great and wonderful Grand Master Astreya doesn't undermine everything that's happened..."

"He won't if he sees that the Village elders understand what the stones can do. Independent decision-making by those who have to live with the consequences. Same way as you and I decided Peter should have Dabih's clasp."

"Well, actually, Mairi, you just gave him the chance to try. He could, and he did, and he's a wielder, same as us. It happened. The same way it happened that Ellie and I can send over the horizon, and once you believed it was possible, so could you and Seren."

As they reached the top of the steep path up to the South Head, they both stopped and stared at the three-masted schooner approaching the gap.

"*Cygnus!*" Trogen exclaimed.

Mairi immediately started a message.

Elusive and Cygnet safe at Village

Before she could continue, a strong message from *Cygnus* made both her and Trogen wince.

We know following you since storm

What of Ellie

Mairi and Trogen replied at the same moment.

Ellie safe

"We have to warn them about running the gap," said Trogen. "*Elusive* touched bottom when I took her through."

"Too late. They're on their way," said Mairi.

They looked down at *Cygnus* as she sailed between the headlands. Seen from above, her masts were foreshortened, and her sails distorted. Mairi thought she saw the top of Lindey's blonde head, but she could not be sure.

"Come on, Trogen, we should be at the wharf when they arrive."

They were late. When they came out of the tree-shadowed path, Astreya and Lindey were ashore, surrounded by people from all three ships and the Village. Mairi and Trogen were beginning to apologize their way through the crowd, when Red Ian, who was talking to Astreya, saw them.

"An' here they are," he boomed. "Yer some right smart daughter and son."

The crowd parted. Mairi began to speak, but Lindey stepped towards her and hugged the breath out of her.

"We know about Dabih. And Mirak. Damon told us. So did Cam, and Seren and..."

"Mother, I was too late, Dabih's dead and...."

Lindey put her fingers on Mairi's lips.

"Not your fault. You did well, Mairi. We're proud of you. Of you both."

Astreya reached out and took Trogen's hand, smiling, his green eyes bright.

"Well done, Master Trogen," said Astreya.

"Master ... You mean ... I keep *Elusive*?"

Astreya nodded.

Then so many people spoke at once that Mairi could only stand beside Trogen, amused by his attempt to maintain the serious expression befitting a master when she knew he wanted to dance and shout. Some time later, the crowd thinned, and Mairi and Trogen were alone with their parents.

"How did you get here?" Trogen blurted.

"Drew cracked the secret of making woad," said Astreya. "After that, fixing *Cygnus* was straightforward."

"Easy, perhaps, but incredibly stinky," said Lindey.

"Only for the first couple of days, then it cured. Drew thinks it's just as strong as before."

"He had a new bowsprit and dolphin striker shipped within a week after *Cygnet* sailed," said Lindey.

"Then they set about replacing the standing rigging."

"That was when your father ignored both Cat and me and took a longboat outside the Two Feet," said Lindey.

"She came too. When we were out of the encircling hills, we both heard Ellie..."

"That must have been her sending after she was kidnapped. I was amazed by her power. I never thought..." said Trogen.

"...you thought you were the only one who could send and receive past the horizon, didn't you, Trogen?" said Astreya, a small smile curling his lips.

Mairi saw Trogen scowl, and quickly intervened,

"And now we all can," said Mairi. "What Trogen and Ellie did showed Seren and me what could be done, and then we did it."

Trogen's frown faded, but he still looked quizzically at his father.

"So why didn't you send to us?" he asked.

"We didn't have a shipstone aboard the longboat. By the time we got the crew back aboard *Cygnus*..."

"Along with Cat..." said Cam, as he appeared at Astreya's elbow.

"...we heard your exchange of status, positions, courses, and we realized that Ellie had to keep her abilities secret," said Astreya. "So we listened but didn't complicate the situation, knowing we'd arrive too late to do anything useful."

"But we were in time to be invited to a Village event, happening this evening," said Lindey cheerfully.

"Celebration," said Astreya. "For the two of you."

"An' Ellie," said Cam. "An' not a little for you too, 'Streya. They're still takin' it aboard that the boy what left them twenty years and more ago is now the Grand Master of two great ships an' a right smart little schooner. Come along, now, the bunch of yez.

Yer goin' to what yer might call a movable feast. You're supposed to visit everyone, so don't drink too much of the Village whiskey at any one cottage."

Lindey put her arm through Astreya's, and they followed Cam obediently.

"Mairi, look!" Trogen whispered. "Father isn't even limping. Cat's healed him!"

Mairi and Trogen stood and watched their parents start up the path from the wharf.

"Trogen," said Mairi suddenly. "How did I miss that Seren and Marley were falling in love?"

Trogen laughed.

"It happened, Mairi. You can't monitor everything, little sister."

"Big sister. Three minutes, remember?"

And they joined in the Village feasting.

About the Author

Seymour was born during an air-raid on London in 1941. After the war, his family moved to Mauritius, where his father taught him to swim and sail a dinghy. After three years, they moved to Canada. Some time later in the 70s a good friend let him sail aboard and even briefly take command of a 50 foot Nova Scotia schooner.

Notwithstanding these character forming events, Seymour acquired three degrees in English Literature and taught at universities on Canada's east and west coasts, and in Ontario. He also wrote and edited a great deal of very dull material for government and industry as a civil servant, and as a free-lance communication consultant.

Early in the 1990s, he and his wife Katherine moved to Chelsea, Quebec. On retiring, he re-started his life as the writer he had always wanted to be. A voyage from Nova Scotia to the south coast of Newfoundland aboard *Hakada* was the genesis of *The Astreya Trilogy*, published in in 2011, and it was to this imaginative world he returned in *River of Stones*.

There are more stories yet to be told about Astreya and his descendants.

More from Old Salt Press

Chris Durbin

Perilous Shore

The sixth Carlisle and Holbrook naval adventure. It is the latest of a series of books that follows Carlisle and Holbrooke through the Seven Years War and into the 1760s when relations between Britain and her restless American Colonies are tested to breaking point. Look out for the seventh in the Carlisle Holbrooke series, coming soon.

Rick Spilman

Evening Gray Morning Red

A young American sailor must escape his past and the clutches of the Royal Navy, in the turbulent years just before the American Revolutionary War. In the spring of 1768, Thom Larkin, a 17-year-old sailor, is caught by a Royal Navy press gang. He runs afoul of the cruel and corrupt Lieutenant Dudingston. Years later, after escaping, Thom again crosses paths with his old foe in Narragansett Bay. Thom Larkin must face the guns of the Royal Navy, with only his wits, an unarmed packet boat, and a sandbar.

Joan Druett

The Discovery of Tahiti

Romance and the islands have gone hand-in-hand since the bare-breasted young women of Tahiti gave a rousing welcome to the 18th century European adventurers who discovered the island. But it was not just a tropical port of call that Captain Wallis and his men found, for their tales of golden girls and a majestic island queen became a foundation stone of the Romantic Movement, an enduring inspiration for writers, artists, filmmakers ... and mutineers."

Linda Collison

Water Ghosts

"I see things other people don't see; I hear things other people don't hear." Fifteen-year-old James McCafferty is an unwilling sailor aboard a traditional Chinese Junk operated as adventure-therapy for troubled teens. Once at sea, James believes the ship is being taken over by the spirits of courtiers who fled the Imperial palace during the Ming Dynasty, more than 600 years earlier, and sailing to its doom.

Alaric Bond

Hellfire Corner

Alaric Bond's latest nautical adventure departs the Age of Fighting Sail where his other 13 novels are set, and instead goes aboard Motor Torpedo Boats and Motor Gun Boats of the Coastal Forces in the English Channel during WWII.

Antoine Vanner

Britannia's Innocent

This is the eighth volume of the Dawlish Chronicles historical naval fiction series. A prequel to the existing seven "Britannia's...." novels, the action take place in 1864, when the young Nicholas Dawlish is still an innocent. He finds himself plunged into the horrors of a siege, involving shore-bombardment, raiding and battle in the cold North Sea. He will need to learn fast.

V E Ulett

Blackwell's Paradise: Blackwell's Adventures, Book 2

The repercussions of a court martial and the ill will of powerful men at the Admiralty pursue Royal Navy captain James Blackwell into the Pacific, where danger lurks around every coral reef. Even if Captain Blackwell and Mercedes survive the venture into the world of early 19th-century exploration, can they emerge unchanged, with their love intact? The mission to the Great South Sea will test their loyalties and strength and define the characters of Captain Blackwell and his lady in Blackwell's Paradise.

www.ingramcontent.com/pod-product-compliance
Lightning Source LLC
Chambersburg PA
CBHW072012110726
47910CB00005B/1735